Edward Rae

The White Sea Peninsula

A Journey in Russian Lapland and Karelia

Edward Rae

The White Sea Peninsula
A Journey in Russian Lapland and Karelia

ISBN/EAN: 9783337127749

Printed in Europe, USA, Canada, Australia, Japan

Cover: Foto ©Andreas Hilbeck / pixelio.de

More available books at **www.hansebooks.com**

THE
WHITE SEA PENINSULA,

A Journey in Russian Lapland
and Karelia.

BY EDWARD RAE, F.R.G.S.

Author of The Land of the North Wind,
and The Country of the Moors.

MAP AND ILLUSTRATIONS.

LONDON:
JOHN MURRAY, ALBEMARLE STREET.
1881.

TO THE READER.

DEAR READER—If you are willing to embark on
this expedition to *The White Sea Peninsula*, I must
ask you to regard the account of our journey simply
as a sketch—as accurate as, under many difficulties,
I have been able to make it.   There appear to be
two ways of writing: one, to seek after somebody
else's style—the other to write as you talk yourself.
The latter is all that lies within my capabilities,
and it must be the excuse which you will require to
make for many things in the following pages.   An
indifferent Russian scholar, I found it fatiguing to
extort information word by word from the natives
with whom we associated : and the result by no
means represents the labour undergone.

I have taken certain details and statistics, chiefly
of the fisheries, from *En Sommer i Finmarken og
Nord Karelen*, by the modest and talented Norwegian Professor Friis, who skirted the region

which I am about to describe. For the map I am indebted to the courtesy of the Royal Geographical Society. Originally a Russian chart, amended by Middendorf, reduced by poor Dr. Petermann of Gotha for Stiehler's Atlas, revised by Professor Friis, and rendered into English by Lieutenant Temple, F.R.G.S.—I have made various additions and corrections based on observation : and I do not hesitate to say it is a good map.

Some of the woodcuts are from *En Sommer i Finmarken :* the others from the Expedition's photographs, transferred to wood by Mr. Arthur E. Smith's interesting and valuable process, *Cryptotype.* Of the etchings, with one exception, I can say little : they were experiments, made in haste, perhaps to be repented of at leisure.

My first acknowledgments must be to my friends Mr. Murray and Mr. John Murray, whose unvarying kindly consideration has helped to transform a labour into a pleasure. For friendly assistance in Natural History, I have to thank Messrs. Higgins, Moore, Rye, and Fraser.

Reader, I do not know if we shall meet again. I had contemplated one more journey for the past summer, to the lonely White Sea. My old companion ' the Doctor,' whose unshaken courage and monumental patience survived many a trial, seemed at last to feel that his taste for Arctic hardships had expired : and I have to express to my good friend Mr. Archibald Williamson my regret that the journey, which he readily agreed to share in the Doctor's stead, could not be carried out.

I am happy to think there are many humble acquaintances in the far North who would be glad to see us once more. The more languages we learn, the more races and classes of human beings we see, the more we feel that their distinctions are skin deep. We have but to identify ourselves with our fellow-creatures, to find warm hearts, virtues, and refinement among the very outcasts of mankind. Friendliness and courtesy will go farther than money, and a joke is a better weapon than a revolver.

And so the Doctor and I resign to others the regions through which, in more than one instance, we have been the pioneers : only cautioning our successors that such journeys call for more thought, nerve, and endurance than might be imagined. Apart from incessant impediments and frequent risks, the journey to *The White Sea Peninsula* was a hard one : and details which you, gentle reader,

will find wearisome, may, perhaps, serve as footprints to a future wanderer in one of the least
known countries in the world, when the good
Doctor and I shall have been long forgotten.—
Believe me, yours faithfully,

EDWARD RAE.

REDCOURT, BIRKENHEAD,
   Christmas 1881.

CONTENTS.

CHAPTER I.

CHAPTER II.

CHAPTER III.

CHAPTER IV.

CHAPTER V.

CHAPTER VI.

CHAPTER VII.

CHAPTER VIII.

CHAPTER IX.

CHAPTER X.

CHAPTER XI.

CHAPTER XII.

CHAPTER XIII.

CHAPTER XIV.

CHAPTER XV.

CHAPTER XVI.

CHAPTER XVII.

CHAPTER XVIII.

CHAPTER XIX.

CHAPTER XX.

CHAPTER XXI.

CHAPTER XXII.

CHAPTER XXIII.

APPENDIX.

LIST OF ILLUSTRATIONS.

THE WHITE SEA PENINSULA.

CHAPTER I.

WE left the Tyne on the 31st of May, passed Aberdeen
on Whitsunday 1st of June, lost the Shetlands on Monday,
and came out into the Atlantic, with a fresh northerly
wind and a moderate sea. For four long days and nights
the *Aurora* pitched steadily, the wind gradually increasing.

An African horned sheep was one of our enter-
tainments on board: an eccentric creature, who liked
human companionship, and enjoyed rope ends, small pieces
of coal, wood, or canvas, and especially relished wet paint.
A poor tired little snow-bunting, blown from the coast,
visited us on the third day: that night, as we were near
the polar circle, the sun did not set. We saw numerous
whales, and passed the circle on the fourth day. On the
forenoon of the 5th of June we coasted past the Lofodens,
the wind still dead ahead and increasing to a gale.

They proceeded to sea, and Master Chancellor held

B

on his course towards that vnknowne part of the world :
and sayled so farre, that hee came at last to the place
where hee found no night at all, but a continuall light
and brightnesse of the sunne shining cleerly vpon the
huge and mightie sea.   Note, that there is between the
Rost Is. and Lowfoot, a whirlepoole called Malestrand,
which from halfe ebbe vntill halfe floud maketh such a
terrible noyse that it shaketh the rings in the doores of
the inhabitants' houses of the said ilands ten miles off.
Also if there cometh any whale into the current of the
same, they make a pitifull cry.   *Purchas' Pilgrims.*

On the sixth afternoon we passed Tromsö and Ham-
merfest.   On the seventh morning the *Aurora* was
steaming at the top of the world under the North Cape,
the solid old cliff rising a thousand feet from the cold
Arctic Sea.   Snow covered more than one-half of the
purple mountains of Finmarken, the Arctic waves glittered
in a crystal atmosphere and in cloudless sunlight.   Midsummer and midwinter were face to face.   Whales were
peacefully spouting on the horizon, and the keen frosty
breeze blew in our faces.   We were in the latitude of
Jan Mayen.   We expected.to reach Vardö at some inconvenient hour after midnight.

We made more comprehensive arrangements for this
than for any previous journey.   To travel with a vast
quantity of baggage has the advantage that you are never
tempted to touch a package yourself.   I give for the guid-
ance of that eccentric and misguided human being—the
future traveller to Russian Lapland—an inventory of the
few bare requisites of life which our boxes contained :—

48 lbs. tinned beef and mutton : the most neglected of our stores as it proved.

36 tins of potted meat and game, of which we grew thoroughly tired.

72 tins of consolidated German army soups.

6 tins of sardines : given away.

2 tins of pâté de foie gras.

12 tins of Johnston's fluid beef : useful.

12 tins of ham and chicken.

24 packets of custard powder : given away.

40 lbs. captain's biscuits : very welcome.

4 tins of Swiss milk : unnecessary.

24 tins of jam : indispensable.

1 tin of cocoa : given away.

3 lbs. of chocolate : should have been 30 lbs.

4 lbs. Stilton cheese : given away.

1 box of muscatel raisins : given away.

1 box of figs : given away.

12 lbs. sugar : less would have done.

10 lbs. tea and coffee : less tea would have done.

A quantity of lemons : not necessary.

1 bottle of brandy, with a lock cork.

We hoped with these, and with salmon and other fish, game, wild-fowl, reindeer, eggs, cream, and bread of the country, to keep the wolf from the door.

We further took several gallons of spirits of wine, in tin canisters, for the service of our cooking apparatus : but as we never lacked wood or turf fuel, we often wished we had taken several gallons of curaçoa instead. We had three watertight wooden boxes, measuring two feet by one foot,—numerous handles being attached to each, for convenience of carrying or lashing. Two japanned tin boxes, also supplied with rings, and waterproofed : two japanned tin portmanteaus : two seamen's canvas bags—one waterproofed, for carrying quilts, pillows, coats, rugs, etc.

The tent case enclosed the Expedition's umbrellas and the camera tripod. Then came two mattresses specially made, and covered with American cloth. These we exchanged for two more portable Russian quilts. We had pillows, and air-cushions, a waterproof sheet, and a sheet of canvas to use in roofing boats, etc. Then we had brass eyelets, and a punch and die wherewith to insert them as required in the canvas sheet, or in the edges of the Doctor's pilot jacket, to make him fast to sledges or horses.

We took a good saw, gimlet, file, axe, a hundred or two of spare nails, an auger for sledge and raft building, or for constructing cabins on our boats. Our tent was similar to that we used on other journeys, but stouter and larger : its ground-plan measured nine feet by five feet, and its weight, including galvanised iron tent pins, was twenty pounds. It folded into a case measuring about four feet by nine inches. We carried our old Arctic ensign, some hundreds of yards of spare rope, cord, and twine : needles, thread, compass, aneroid barometer, revolver, boxes of matches in metal cases, swimming collars, a case of medicines : Griffith's cooking apparatus, table-napkins and towels, Indiarubber bath, a sleeping bag which had served a good-natured friend in the frosty Caucasus : a hundred and fifty cartridges, including some with buckshot and ball for wolves, reindeer, or brown bears. We had each a pair of rubber boots reaching to the hips, for fording rivers and swamps, or for open boats at sea. We took a photographic apparatus: eight dozen plates stowed in cedar-wood boxes—pine having in heat or damp a tendency to fog the plates: and a small developing tent, folding into the space of a waterproof coat.

Finally, we had the gun-case, and a leather portmanteau—the whole weighing a quarter of a ton: and we looked forward with some apprehension to the difficulties likely to encompass its transport.

We hoped to get at Vardö some one who could speak Lappish, do carpenter's work, pack and unpack our baggage, cook, take an oar in a boat, harness a reindeer, assist us in botany and minerals, light a fire, catch a fish, and do other small trifles, such as going first into a river or swamp to try the depth. I had written to Vardö on the subject. The Vice-Consul suggested a student, but I feared a student might have feelings, and expect to share our jam, and the tent which was constructed strictly to hold two persons. Among other money we carried a thousand roubles in Russian notes, a hundred and fifty roubles in small Russian silver, and a hundred marks in small Finnish coin, for use in the event of travelling home through Finland.

We took several dozens of pocket-knives and pairs of scissors, for the Lapland and Karelian ladies: and half-a-dozen musical boxes, to bestow upon children at crises when it should seem hard to reach their parents' hearts.

Our mosquito preparations were as follows. A flapper

made of wood and leather : coffee-coloured net veils, of circular cage form, passed over the hat and tucked in under the coat collar, having two hoops of whalebone to keep the nets from the features or neck.   Canadian veils, for which we were indebted to the kindness of some benevolent ladies —and which covered all but the mouth, eyes, and nose.

A preparation of tar and oil in equal parts, for anointing the features unprotected by the veil.   Carbolic acid and sweet oil, in the proportions of one to five, to neutralise the stings.   A second dilution of alum with aromatic vinegar and glycerine, in the relative proportions of four, two, and one ; lastly, strong aromatic vinegar and oil, this latter taken in the faint hope that, by being disagreeable to the mosquito, we might be spared the last resource of tar.   We had gauntlets reaching to our elbows, stiffened with whalebone—so stout that they would turn a sword cut, and so huge that they stood out from our fingers farther than mosquito's proboscis could ever reach.

I bought a steam lifeboat for the journey ; but the difficulty and risk of transport, scarcity of fuel, and chances of breakdown with the engines, decided us to leave her at home.   Besides, a steamer, however small, might have given the Russians the idea that we were in comfortable circumstances and able to pay liberally.   After this I bought a collapsible punt, for crossing rivers or lakes on an emergency : but after consideration—fearing to add to the weight of our baggage—the collapser was left behind with the lifeboat.

Finally, we arranged to sail from the Tyne in the Dundee steamer *Aurora,* bound for Archangel: Messrs.

Mudie, her owners, kindly agreeing to land us at Vardö, or, if the weather should be unfavourable, at some spot on the adjacent coast. I have occupied some time in detailing our preparations. Whether they may prove useful to any future traveller, or whether there ever will be a future traveller, I do not know : but I may say that had we had any source from which to inform ourselves, we should have saved much time and trouble.

A fair north-west wind sprang up in the afternoon, and before 10 P.M. the *Aurora* was in sight of Vardö. We sounded our whistle loudly : and after steaming patiently down the channel, in sight of the old fort, a Norseman put off in his boat, and we took leave of Captain Sangster and the worthy Scotch officers of the *Aurora*. Though late at night, there was a large assemblage on the wooden quay : our steam whistle had excited high expectations. The little town lies about a short and narrow neck of land, connecting two long strips of rock and forming the H-shaped island. The gray mossy rocks are lined, and in many places hidden, by racks of drying fish. The little wooden warehouses reek with fish, the boats are steeped in the smell of fish, and the air is full of it. Vardö lives upon fish and fishing. There are no old men there, it is said : few of the poor fishermen end their days in bed.

We sought, with our baggage, *Hansen's Hotel og Billard*, where we made ourselves comfortable for some days. We retired at 1 A.M. in brilliant daylight, and slept profoundly in two small box-beds measuring five feet seven inches

long enough only for the Doctor, who has the advantage
of me by five inches.   We were smothered in eiderdown
quilts ; and if, as the hostess had threatened, the stove
had been lighted with birch faggots, we should have dis-
solved and been seen no more.

We were awakened by a clock which struck XIII., a
mistake we attributed to the constant daylight.   It was
Sunday, and we strolled up on to the rocks overlooking
the Sound and the snowy coast of Finmarken.   Then to
the clear white wooden church, where we heard a sweet-
voiced Lutheran pastor preach, and afterwards baptize two
infants.   The ceremony over, the parents and god-parents
marched round behind the altar, reappearing on the other
side.   In passing, each placed on the altar a coin or note,
and what seemed to be a visiting card at the gate of the
chancel.   In two instances I saw the donors help themselves to change out of the money lying on the altar.
The Vice-Consul dined with us at our Hotel og Billard,
and we had a good meal of fish, reindeer-venison, Norwegian pancakes, and a fruit dish drenched in cream.

In the afternoon we sallied out with a Norwegian
doctor, who took an interest in our journey, and had
called upon us.   He had been in the Red Crescent service
at Erzeroum when Ghazi Mukhtar so ably rallied his
forces after the severe defeat on the Aladja Dagh.   He
saw the poor Turkish soldiers die by the hundred in the
hospitals, of wounds and fever—patiently and nobly.

We went to the old castle of Vardöhuus—the most
northerly fort in the world, once the bulwark of Northern

Scandinavia, and the terror, now the jest, of the Mus-
covites.   After wandering half round the ramparts of this
superannuated battery, we were dislodged by an indig-
nant sentry.   Once, many years ago, when an heir was born
to the throne, the fort of Vardö was directed to fire a
salute of one hundred guns, or as many as were practicable
before sunset, and to recommence at daybreak.   Fifty shots
were fired, and that was the last day of autumn.   The sun
set for the winter, and ere it reappeared the royal baby
had died, to the terrible perplexity of the commandant,
who did not know whether to complete the salute.

We spent our days in endeavouring to extort information from Mûrmansk mariners, and from one or two natives
of Kola.   One man told us we should find wooden roads
throughout the Kola peninsula : but he proved to be an
enthusiast—that is, a person who believes about four times
as much as he can prove.   We had heard of a linguist
and interpreter who seemed to realise in his single person
all we had ever hoped for, and we determined to go in
search of him to Vadsö.

We first chartered a small Norwegian steamer for the
voyage to Kola, at a cost of £24—about half the value
of the vessel.   The Vice-Consul wrote a special *visé* to our
passports—describing us as inoffensive wanderers, uncon-
nected with any mercantile business, and in search of
pleasure and information.   Russian traders and others are
apt to be suspicious of travellers when they profess to
travel for pleasure to such countries as the White Sea Peninsula.   Geologists and naturalists they look upon as half-

crazed and harmless, but otherwise the erratic Englishman must be travelling for commercial or political objects. The Doctor generally passed for a naturalist, and I for a geologist or antiquary—whichever word happened to be understood.

There was tribulation this morning at the breakfast table. A poor little German was travelling, and exhibiting to children in the coast towns some *papagaïs* or parrots, canaries, and an *abekât* or ape. The enterprising abekât had devoured the phosphorous heads of an entire packet of matches, and was no doubt being consumed internally. The Norwegian doctor prescribed for him, we got the medicine from the *apothek*, and I poured it down the abekât's throat, while his master held the poor little creature's mouth open. His death meant ruin to the poor naturalist's show, and we were glad that the treatment succeeded.

One day we rambled round the island, and found a beautiful chasm, where ravens hovered, and the waves broke some hundred feet beneath us ; then to a manufactory of guano and codliver oil. The heads and bones of the codfish are steamed, dried, and ground into coarse resin-like powder—costing £10 a ton. The liver is steamed and pressed, till the oil fills immense wooden butts.

Another day we went in a boat to Hornö, a rocky island lying to the north of the harbour, where was a breeding-place of sea-birds. Here we hunted among the rocks and moss for eiderducks' eggs and down. Those birds abound, and gulls, razorbills, cormorants, oyster catchers, puffins, and suchlike swarm. We enjoyed at supper a variety of sea-fowls' eggs.

CHAPTER II.

We sail to Vadsö — The *Perevodtchik* — A Lapp idol — Valit — Voyage to Kola—Vaidda Gûba—Neutral ground—A zealous monk—Peisen Kloster —Trifan's mission—A sacred painting—*Skolte* Lapps—Sibt Navalok— A Viking's grave—Legend of Anika—The Kolafiord—Kola—Bombardment by the White Sea squadron.

AT two o'clock one morning we sailed for Vadsö in the steamer *Orion*. Here we found the treasure, a decent little man with a red beard—our interpreter, we termed him, as he didn't speak a word of English. It seemed we should have to take him for a pleasure journey round the Kola peninsula, in order that he might amuse himself by talking to the Russians; and it fell to my lot throughout the journey to interpret the interpreter—which was the next simplest thing to speaking direct. However, the idea of an interpreter—Russian, *Perevodtchik*— of this kind seemed humorous, and we engaged him, dimly hoping he might prove useful in other ways.

One of the Vadsö whaling steamers returned that afternoon, towing a whale sixty feet long; and at night a second steamer came in with a still larger fish. Poor whales! frolicking about only a few hours before, in the enjoyment of their prodigious strength—gentle, harmless creatures. Vadsö market would be full of whale-beef for a week to come.

We sailed from Vadsö in a small steamer to Mortens Nœs, on the north side of the Varanger Fiord, to visit a Lapp burial-place. We found a few downcast Sea Lapps on landing, and a comfortable wooden house looking out on the mountains of Syd-Varanger. Close at hand there stands an ancient *Bauta*, or *Paata*, or *Pahta*, called by the Lapps Idol stone—*Zœvdse Gœdge :* also Lapp places of worship and burial.

Looking towards the setting sun, and patched with orange lichen, stood the idol stone—a gray slab, slanting a little edgewise. It stood eight and a half feet above ground, and measured two feet nine inches at the base, tapering a little upwards. Its thickness was rather less than six inches. Round the Bauta stone were concentric rings, thirteen in number, of stones carefully placed. The rings stood two or three feet apart, and the outer one measured twenty-five yards across. I could find no trace of cutting either on surface or edge of the Bauta stone. Adjoining the large circle was a smaller one, paved with small stones. It measured thirty-two feet in diameter, and the centre had been opened, probably in the belief that it was a burial-place. I think it was the altar, or place of sacrifice to the idol : and the ceremonies may have been solemnised while the Laplanders stood in the circles round the idol.

Nearer to the farm we found numerous stone circles and mounds—no doubt the place of burial, as the other was of worship. I found one very complete group of rings here. The central ring or mound, measuring six yards across, was encompassed on all sides—save the west—by stone circles of five yards in diameter. At the western side was, in place of a circle, a sort of paved approach. A king and his family lie here, perhaps : and their simple monument has been kept sacred in this cemetery of the Lapps. There were stone rings, more or less regular and well defined, scattered about for a considerable distance. In some of these graves were found the remains of Lapps, wrapped in birch bark. Most of them were empty—the bodies having been probably removed, since the spread of the Gospel, to Christian burial-places.

It is not likely that the Lapps themselves erected the *Zævdse Gædge :* their faith taught them rather to worship strange or supernaturally-formed objects already set up by nature's hand. Their stone idols were, as a rule, of a conveniently portable size. But finding this old Scandinavian monument, they must have taken it for a god, and sacrificed to it. Indeed, one old Lapp woman is said to have offered to this idol within the memory of man.

The Russians claim this monument. In the ancient days when Holy Novgorod ruled from the Neva to the White Sea, there lived a man named Valit, who became chief of Karelia. He went to the Arctic coast to make war on the Mûrmans, who called for help to the Norsemen. Valit fought a victorious battle in Varanger, and on the spot, which that great warrior himself named Babilon, this stone was erected in his honour. Valit

settled on an island in Salimosero, and there ended his
days. In consequence of their defeat, the Norwegians
abandoned Russian Lapland, and thenceforth the Lapps
paid tribute to the Grand Dukes of Moscow and Novgorod.
Verestchagine, the Russian author, learnt this legend from
Feodor Ivanovitch—the deputy sent to Kola in the year
1592, to treat with King Christian IV. about the boundaries.

In the night, we returned in the *Orion* to Vardö.

The Vice-Consul's recommendation ran thus:—
The bearers of this document, the English subjects, Edward Rae and H. P. Brandreth, both for scientific objects
and for pleasure, intend to travel in Russian Lapland:
but do not know the localities. I take myself the obedient liberty to ask most respectfully the Ispravnik Abramovitch Panikarovsky, to give those gentlemen the
benevolent assistance which may be necessary for security
and despatch, to make the journey in the desert parts
of the country where no man dwells. These parts they
purpose to visit. Sure that your Excellency will in all
ways consent to my request, I take with pleasure this
opportunity of, etc. etc.

We had telegraphed from Vadsö, to have our steamer
ready to sail for Kola on the *Orion's* arrival: though we
were not simple enough to expect so much in Norway.
When the *Orion* anchored at Vardö, we found steam was
not up, and only after three hours were we ready to weigh
anchor. The *Pram* steamed out of the north harbour of
Vardö, and turned away to the south-east.

Several of our crew are Russians—as good-natured

and useless a set as ever went to sea. There is a certain antipathy to water in the mind of the Muscovite—whether for toilet, beverage, or travel. Any other nation would have long since explored its own northern coasts and seas. Not ice, nor snow, nor fatigue will prevent the Russian from patiently traversing vast distances by land. His bugbear is water. The White Sea was first opened to commerce by Chancellor and other foreigners: and the only Russian possession beyond the seas, Alaska, was cheerfully bestowed upon the United States.

Our steam yacht, the *Pram*, is small: and we live in the cabin in the stern, surrounded by our effects, which leave very little space for ourselves. The barometer was falling, and wind, hail, and rain came in sudden gusts. The *Pram* did not take kindly to the waves of the open Arctic, but rolled and heaved. Writing, or dreaming on deck, hour after hour passed somehow.

We approached Ribatschi, the north-western extremity of the great lonely Kola peninsula, after many hours' steaming against the tide : and rounding the headland of Niemetski, entered the little roadstead of Vaidda Gûba. It was a busy fishing spot: one or two schooners lay there, and numerous boats. We saw on shore a little wooden settlement. We had put in here to find the Ispravnik, who constantly travels hither to survey with a paternal eye the fishery revenue of these, the Kola and Western Fishing Districts. The former extends from this cape to the Kola Fiord ; the latter from hence to the Norwegian frontier village, Yakobselv.

Fifteen miles south of us lay Henoerne, rocky islands, with vegetation somewhat profuse from the guano of sea-birds—the *Archangelica* growing to the height of nine feet. The Lapps call the islands *Ainak*—the Russians *Ainova*. Hither came Finns, Lapps, Karelians, and Norsemen, in search of eiderdown and birds' eggs. It was a neutral spot, and whoever came first made himself at home. Five and twenty miles south from Vaidda Gûba lies the mouth of the Peisenfiord—the nearest point of the neutral ground between Norway and Russia.

In 1826 Count Nesselrode and Baron Palmerstjerna signed the treaty which put an end to the five centuries' strife between the two powers. So far back as 1326 Norway was mistress of the Kola peninsula : while the Russians collected taxes from the nomad Karelian hunters, as far as Lyngstuen in Norway. The old debateable ground stretching from Bugofiord to the centre of Ribatschi, was by this treaty unequally divided—Russia taking two-thirds of the one hundred versts of coast line, and Norway's authority ending at the Pasvig. Beyond this concession to themselves, the Russians not unfairly claimed a square verst of land lying west of the Pasvig : for there stood the Russian shrine of Boris Gleb. This the Norwegians still seem to grudge very greatly.

The chapel, named in honour of the Muscovite Saint Boris—*Gleb* meaning Shrine or Retreat—was built in the sixteenth century. Trifan, a monk of Novgorod, says tradition, alone hewed and carried the timber, and erected the building : showing zeal and devotion to his faith worthy of Abderrahman Khalif of Cordova, who with his own hands laboured at the building of his wonderful mosque.   Trifan was commanded in a vision by the Saviour to come and spread the Gospel among the savages in a thirsty and inaccessible land.   This apostle to the Lapps also built the monastery at the mouth of the Peisen Fiord ; and such was his energy, that he travelled to Moscow to obtain from Ivan Vassilivitch a faculty to add certain lands to the property of the monastery.

Trifan's fame and sanctity attracted crowds of monks and pilgrims.   The Peisen Kloster became rich and powerful under the privileges of its charter.   The monks had whale and other fisheries ; shipbuildings at the Peisen mouth, and sent 800,000 lbs. of salt yearly to Kola in exchange for flour, wax, linen, etc.   They had considerable herds of cattle, and sent yearly abroad dried fish, train oil, and salmon.   In fact, they possessed the remarkable gift, inherited by the present religious orders in Russia and elsewhere, of profitably blending temporal and eternal interests. In 1590 they were important enough to be attacked by the Swedes, who burnt the monastery and put to death fifty-six monks and sixty-five servants.   Some say two hundred lost their lives.

Trifan found the Lapps worshipping idols, as well as snakes, and other reptiles.   His preaching met with much opposition from the Lapp *Noaids*, or wizards: who attacked him, tore out his hair, felled him to the ground, and threatened him with death should he persist in remaining. Providence alone prevented the threat from being carried out. By continual preaching and gentleness, and by a God-fearing life, Trifan succeeded in softening the Lapps : then he went to Novgorod and returned with letters of consecration from the Archimandrite for his contemplated church. He also brought a builder, who constructed the church on the Peisen Fiord. It remained long unconsecrated; but Trifan at length found at Kola the Hieronomach Elias, and carried him off to consecrate the spot, and baptize the Lapps. Trifan's name is still familiar to the Greek-Catholic Lapps of the Peisen: but their reverence and their disregard for his memory are sometimes curiously mixed.

He took up his abode in a half natural cave, *Trifanraige*, near the entrance of the fiord. This disconcerted the wizards, who hitherto had made the point of Holmengraances dangerous to mariners, forcing them to drag their boats overland across the neck of the promontory, to avoid rounding it. The cave is like that of Adullam—midway up the face of an abrupt cliff. It still contains the shrine, and a small picture representing the Mother of God, and having a white cloth hanging from it, embroidered with a gold cross. Tapers stand before the shrine. Russian Lapps, when going a hunting or fishing, or before rounding the cape, come and offer some trifle to the saint's memory, and one would fancy the shrine would become rich accordingly.

But it does not, because the Lapp, if unsuccessful, returns to the shrine, and recovers not only his own offering, but anything else he may happen to find there. A Vadsö merchant had a picture of St. Michael of peculiar

GROUP OF RUSSIAN LAPPS

sanctity, since presented · to the museum of Christiania. The Russians frequenting Vadsö would constantly come to adore the picture, bowing and crossing themselves, and offering some small gift : but the merchant found that, as a rule, the devotee appropriated not only what his predecessor had offered, but often something that the owner of the house had neither offered nor intended to offer to Saint Nicholas. The Russians called the chapel at Boris · Gleb, *Monastir*, though there were no monks there. It stands by a beautiful birch grove, and contains a few paintings, some very old. The *pope* goes only twice a year from Petschenga to read service and to baptize there.

Ten or twelve families of *Skolte* or Bald Lapps—so-called from the results of scurvy, or some such depilatory disease, which attacked the natives of these parts many years ago—live near the Kloster, in poor huts. There are but few bald heads among them now. Providence in its mercy has restored the covering so necessary in these latitudes. Some of these Lapps are tall, and have reddish hair, suggesting a semi-Russian origin. They, however, singularly enough, have retained more of their national habits and traditions than any of the tribes of the Kola peninsula. In taking a wife, a Skolte Lapp to this day prefers to steal his bride from a stranger or an enemy.

Pasvig is the most easterly Norwegian fishing station on the north coast. *Basse*, in Lappish, means holy, and probably the natives had a place of sacrifice here. At Petschenga, fifteen miles up the Peisen or Petschenga river, is a small village or collection of huts where a Kola

merchant has a store. This is, and always has been, a
rich fishing station. There are traces of an old Norsk
colony. In the year 1612, it is recorded, the monks of
Malmys, Kola, on the feast-day of St. Philip and St.
James, collected revenue from this colony. The monks
of Peisen Kloster, on the other hand, for the privilege of
using the lands and rivers of Ora, Litsa, and Bûmands-
fiord, used to pay a yearly tribute of eighteen marks to
the Norsk crown.

Professor Friis when at Petschenga engaged a young
Lapp to travel with him. The son and his old mother
parted, with the usual ceremony of rubbing their cheeks
together. May God's sun shine for thee wherever thou
goest, she cried. The peace of God go with thee, and bring
thee back unhurt. Then, as the boat sailed out to sea, the
poor old woman followed along the beach, finally standing
on a projecting point, till the boat and her son were lost
to sight.

We put out to sea again, and coasted hour after hour
along the shores of this forlorn Fishermen's Peninsula.
The gray shore rose gently from the sea, and sloped into
brown and orange hills. Behind, rose high purple hills,
patched with snow. In two places we saw lonely fisher-
boats, toiling on the gusty sea. Squalls swept along the
land, driving sleet and hail across our track. We saw,
after many hours, the domes of a little church : and in
another hour, rounding the north-eastern point of Ribatschi,
we steamed into the little roadstead of Sibt Navolok—
Anchor-haven. The Russians call it also *Anikievka:* the

Lapps, *Sabbe Njarg.* In the days of the old Norwegian
colony here, they called it Stangenæs.

The Ispravnik was at Kola—we learned from a
friendly Norse farmer, in whose house we made ourselves
comfortable. The hostess pressed bowls of cream and
milk, biscuits, bread, cheese, coffee, upon us, and eventually
refused payment altogether. We asked the farmer for
old silver in vain : but as we said we loved old things he
took us up over the moss-covered hills to a spot where,
overlooking the little bay and the wild Lapland coast, was
the grave of Anika the giant Viking. There was what
at first sight seemed a circle, but on examination proved
to be a heptagon of stones, having at each angle a small
heap of stones. I found the heaps stood seven yards
apart. Seven spaces of seven yards each must have meant
something—perhaps the days of the week. In sight of
the tomb is an island, half a mile below, Anikief, where
the pirate moored his galleys. The tomb here was opened,
but nothing was found : Anika was buried some hundreds
of yards to the northward, in a stone-covered mound,
measuring seven yards across. Here his huge skeleton
was found : the leg bone from knee to ankle measured
nearly twenty-four inches. The remains were sent to the
Museum in Christiania.

The legend is very familiar throughout Archangel
province and among the Lapps. Anika came yearly to
take tribute of the fishers. None knew of his coming or
going, but he was always seen on the shore when the boats
came in from the sea. He periodically challenged the

fishermen to fight, but his enormous size frightened
them.   For many years he was the terror of Ribatschi.
One day a young man presented himself, and induced the
fishermen to take him fishing with them.   On landing, the
stranger cleaned the fish with incredible rapidity : a fisherman's gloves being wet, the youth, in squeezing them between his hands, crushed them to dust, while the fishermen marvelled at his strength.   Anika appeared, and the
youth spoke boldly to him, and slightingly.   He! he!
laughed the giant : be careful or I'll demolish thee.

They agreed to fight in this ring on the hill, and in
the following fashion.   Each combatant was to turn a
somersault, and strike his enemy in the chest with his feet.
Anika took the first turn, and struck the youth, who did
not budge.   A second blow, and the young man recoiled
a yard : the third time a fathom.   It was the stranger's turn
now.   At his first somersault he drove the Viking back a
fathom : at the second, three fathoms : at the third, he
flung the huge sea robber seven fathoms outside the ring
—dead.   They buried him, and erected the stone heap
over him.   Thank God, each of you, said the youth : your
enemy is no more.   Henceforth none shall molest your
fishery.   God be with you.   Then he disappeared.

We saw two lovely little Lapp calves, with black muzzles
and soft furry coats like sable.   On the hill were black
tern, curlew, Arctic tern, and golden plover, among the
withered reindeer moss of last summer, and that newly
sprouting : bilberries, Alpine lycopodium, Arctic willows
with sweet-scented catkins, and many other Arctic plants.

Late in the evening we weighed anchor, passed Anikief, a small island, where are numerous slabs—tombstones of Schleswig Danes, skippers of Flensborg, who had traded hither when Norway and its dependencies were under the Danish crown. We steamed past Karabella, a better sheltered anchorage than Sibt Navolok. Here we saw a few houses, and several fishing vessels lying at anchor. The wind grows fiercer as we leave the shelter of Ribatschi— blowing heavily from the west, and more piercingly than ever.

At early morning we approach the Kolafiord. Rocky hills line the desolate coast, and rise some few hundred feet. Eastward are the bluff gray cliffs of Kildîn. The wintry wind sweeps along the wild coast. Then comes a storm of hail and driving snow, which whitens the decks of the plunging steamer. The coast is almost blotted out, we have only glimpses of the rocks through a dense curtain of snow : and thus, within a week or two of midsummer, the *Pram* staggers into the smooth waters of the Kolafiord.

The fiord measures here five miles, or so, across. Cliffs and hills line it—as lifeless, and almost as wild, as those on the coast. We ran till two or three in the morning, and ordered the captain to anchor for a few hours so that the Expedition might sleep. The engine drove a noisy jangling screw propeller, close under our pillows in the little cabin in the stern. We approached Iekaterinsk, and here we cast anchor.

When we awoke we were under weigh again, and steaming up the long *Guolle Vuodna* or Fishfiord. Thin starved firs half-clothed the sloping hills—and the *Pram* ploughed up the brackish yellow-brown water poured down by the Kola and the Tûloma rivers. The sun shone brightly, but the wind was freezing cold. We stopped to buy a salmon at the rate of threepence a pound. Learning that the water above us shoaled, we anchored for a couple of hours for the rising of the tide. Then, taking a fisherman as pilot, we crept slowly up past the shallows.

Soon there appear, some few miles away, the green cupolas of Peter the Great's white church in Kola: then the gray houses come in sight. The fiord narrows as we approach the town, and we find ourselves in the fine stream of the Tûloma: which meets the much less considerable stream of the Kola, and forms a spit of low land, on which the town lies. Across the shallow stream of the Kola lies an island with a small yellow church. Round this stand the many hundred gray wooden crosses of the burial-place: a sad-looking little island. The Tûloma rolls past the town on the west—many hundred yards in width, and rapidly widening above Kola. Its banks are sloping cliffs or hills, now clad in the tender green of freshly sprouting birches. The Kola comes down with a rush from a narrow gorge lined with boulders in the cliff of Suolavaréka—*Solavia raika*, Nightingale River, and is quite unnavigable for some distance even by small boats. The summer aspect of Kola, in this amphitheatre of green slopes, with the background of bluish-purple hills, is bright and comfortable. There lies scarcely any snow in sight.

The *Pram* sounded her whistle, and we dropped anchor in the stream of the Tûloma, abreast of the town. It was a rare circumstance, and we could see the inhabitants by the score crowding to the point.

Kola was twice visited by English men-of-war: in 1809 and 1854. On the last occasion the gunboat *Miranda* bombarded the town, and almost destroyed it. In all, nearly a hundred houses, the old battery, two churches, and the Government stores of corn and salt, were destroyed. The inhabitants are said to have shot two English sailors, sent on shore for water, and the commander of the gunboat gave twenty-four hours' grace to the inhabitants to remove what they could.

The people of Kola had heard of disputes between their Government and ours : and their fears suggested, we learned afterwards, that the *Pram* was another British gunboat. If we had chanced to fire a gun, they would have taken to the woods.

CHAPTER III.

Malmys—Walrus fishery—Position of Kola—The *White Sea Peninsula*—
Churches—Persecution of the Lapps—A Kola house—Visit to the
Ispravnik—Plans for journey—A passport—An archæological investigation
—A failure—A naturalist.

KOLA, Lapland's oldest village or town—called in old
Norsk writings Malmys: by the Lapps *Guolladak*, fishing
place: by the Finns or Karelians Kuolaniemi—is over
four centuries old. In 1475 the *Monastir* was founded
on the small island, which is said to have been then connected with the promontory: the Kola river flowing in its
present easterly channel only. In 1505 it had only three
fishing huts: in 1582 it was a small town with over three
hundred houses, and nearly nineteen hundred inhabitants.
In 1582, when Kola was in course of building, the Norsemen sent deputies to protest against the construction of
fortifications. The monks' reply was that they were only
wishful in good faith to protect the fishermen against the sea
rovers. The same year the Danish king demanded tribute
from the monks of Kola. They replied, acknowledging
the king's sovereignty, but asked to be excused from
paying tax, as they had built here as poor people, and
only lived on God's gifts of fishery, etc.

In 1556 Burroughs visited Kola in search of news of the unfortunate *Willoughby*, and sailed hence to the mouths of the Petschora. He found no less than thirty *lodjes* in the Gulf of Kola, destined for walrus hunting in Novaya Zemlia. In 1594 Barents sailed hither—finding numerous Russian vessels. Ever since those days these North Russian vessels have continued to pursue this lucrative trade. Archangel, Onega, Kem, Mezén, and other White Sea ports, have vied with Kola in fitting out vessels for Spitzbergen, Nova Zemlia, and Jan Mayen—despatching them yearly at mid-summer in search of rein-deer, *bieluga*, or white dolphin, seal, and walrus. In the year 1835 no less than eighty vessels, carrying a thousand men, left these ports for Nova Zemlia alone. In 1837 but twenty vessels sailed: and of these only one earned enough to cover its expenses.

The ships carry eighteen months' supply of rye flour, oatmeal, barley meal, peas, salt-beef, and fish, curdled milk, honey, linseed oil. *Kvass*, made from rye flour and water, is the sailors' drink. They break up into parties, erect and inhabit small isolated huts, and kill seals, walrus, deer, bears, foxes. The bulk of the vessels return in the autumn. Scarcely a year used to pass, but some poor sailors were left, castaways, to spend the long dark winter in Spitzbergen. One party of sailors rather than face such a winter sailed in an open boat across to Nordkyn—an eight days' voyage. Kola has abandoned most of this trade in favour of the White Sea towns.

In 1704 Peter the Great built a square battery with

a tower here, and a large wooden church.   In 1780 Kola
was dignified by the official title of town.   A century has
passed, and Kola has shrunk to a moderate-sized village
of perhaps eighty houses and huts, and five hundred
inhabitants.   It is most inconveniently placed as regards
the richest Mûrman fisheries.   It might very wisely be
transferred to Gavrilova or Iekaterinsk, where there is
open water through the winter, and where fish can be
caught in front of the merchants' houses.   It is not even
conveniently placed for the interior.   A few years ago no
steamer ran from Vadsö to Kola, and a letter took four
months between Kola and St. Petersburg.   Registered
letters came only as far north as Kem, and a Kola merchant, if he expected such a letter, must either send a
deputy, or travel himself to Kem to claim it.   The duty
on sugar and salt imported at Kola must be assessed
at Archangel: nevertheless half-a-dozen traders make a
living here.

A few words before we land about this peninsula of
which Kola is the capital.   It has an area of 40,000 geographical miles, and forms part of the *Ouyesda* of Kem, in
the Archangel Government.   It is divided into two *Stanovoi
Pristav,* or bailiffs' districts, and contains eleven parishes,
with twelve priests and twenty-four churches.   In 1834
the population was officially returned at 9134.

Russians	.	.	4970
Karelians	.	.	1950
Lapps	.	.	2214

The latter item is somewhat uncertain.   Many believe

that the total number of Lapps does not exceed 2000. The priest of Lôvosero told me this was his belief.

It is bounded on the south by North Karelia and the White Sea: on the east by the White Sea: on the west by the Norwegian territory and Finland: on the north by the Polar Sea. I have called it the White Sea Peninsula, because, as the map shows, it is the peninsula which contains the White Sea and shuts it off from the Northern Ocean. The coasts are divided into the *Múrmansk*, or *Normansk*—that lying between the Ribatschi Peninsula and Sviatoi Nôs: the Terski, stretching from the entrance of the White Sea to the Varzuga River: and the Kandalaksk coast, extending to the north-western angle of the White Sea. The name Terski may be *Tarje*, promontory, in the Lapp tongue: or *Tershky*, in the Russian—heavy, difficult. This thinly-peopled land compares thus with the other Laplands.

Norwegian Lapland has twenty-six inhabitants to the square mile: Swedish Lapland has thirteen: Finnish Lapland, five: while Russian Lapland has but three. Of the total surface of the White Sea Peninsula, about nine-sixteenths consist of *túndra, i.e,* moor and wilderness: six-sixteenths of forest: and the remaining sixteenth of lake, mere, and marsh.

The churches are distributed as follows:—

Kola has three churches and two priests.

Petschenga—one church and the chapel at Boris Gleb.

Sibt Navolok—one church.

Siem Ostrova—one chapel.

Nuotôsero—one church.

Tûloma—one chapel.

Gavrilova—one chapel.

Lôvosero—one church.

Vrinda—one church.

Ponoi—two churches.

Piâlitsa—one church.

Tétrina—one church.

Tschâvanga—one church.

Vârzuga—one church.

Kouzomen—three churches.

Umba—one church.

Porzha Gûba—one church.

Olénets—one church.

Kandalaks—two churches.

It was by the persevering building of churches, and by baptizing, that Russia gradually won the Kola Lapps to her influence—Norway having made no corresponding efforts to retain them. The priest of Kola received 150 roubles a year until his flock should exceed fifteen hundred : when above that, 200 roubles.

Until dispossessed by the companions of Odin, the Lapps held all the Scandinavian peninsula. In the thirteenth century the Birkyarls, living round the Bothnian Gulf, oppressed them and completed their subjugation. Gustavus I. gave the persecuted savages more equitable laws, and sent missionaries among them. In 1600 Charles IX. ordered churches to be built. Gustav Adolf, his son, had schools built, and some of the Lapp books translated. In 1602 Christian IV., king of Denmark and Norway, persecuted the poor idolaters cruelly. Some of the younger Lapps, taken for education to Sweden, and returning as missionaries, were murdered by their countrymen. In 1716 the pious Westen nobly preached the Gospel in the wildest parts of Lapland. Christianity reached the Norwegian Lapps in the eighteenth, the Russian in the sixteenth century.

One or two hundred people had assembled to see us land. The clean well-dressed women wore red skirts and red or bright coloured handkerchiefs on their heads and shoulders: the children were cleanly, and seemed well cared for: there were a few uniforms among the crowd—gray overcoats, high boots, and the familiar flat-topped caps. The under magistrate was among the crowd. All saluted us with a pleasant *Sdrastvuitje*, and each man took off his cap as we raised ours.

We were taken to a large room in a beautifully clean house, shared, as is the custom, by two or three families. These houses are generally built alike, having inner corridors, closed by small doors thickly padded for warmth. Each room has windows of double glass—perhaps six or eight of them—which give a wonderful cheerfulness, but are rarely opened. We were always at war on this point with our hostess, who protested against our keeping the windows perpetually open, and closed them whenever we left the room. The furniture was neat and clean: in one corner, or more, of every room, stood the *Sviati Obrasi*—the invariable little shrine of silver or brass-covered pictures—with small hanging lamps in front of them. The room smelt continually of incense and tapers. On the walls hung coloured engravings of Pieter Veliki, Nasr ed Din, Shah of Persia, the poor Tsar Alexander Nikolaievitch, and his eccentric father Nicholas.

The following has nothing to do with Russian Lapland, but it is characteristic of Nicholas. He was one day rambling in the fields near Moscow, accompanied by

a gorgeously dressed aide-de-camp, one of the flower of
the nobility.   The Tsar called to a peasant who was
working in a broad trench, Carry me across on thy back.
The peasant bowed to the ground with pride, and reverently carried the Tsar across, returning for the prince.
When half-way over, the Tsar cried, Stop, I will give thee
ten roubles to drop the prince in the mud.   I'll give thee
twenty, not to drop me! cried the aide-de-camp in con-
sternation.   Thirty! said the Tsar.   Forty! cried the
prince.   Finally the Tsar bid ninety roubles: and the
prince, whose uniform and caste were both at stake,
offered a hundred.   *Yezheli on tibia dast sto rublé, toghda
nié bross yevo*, said Nicholas.   If he gives thee a hundred
roubles, then drop him not.

I went to call upon the Ispravnik, an amiable looking
man, who gave me a kind welcome, and kept me drinking
tea and smoking cigarettes for two hours.   He wrote a
letter of recommendation, but expressed himself strongly
about the difficulties of any journey in the Kola peninsula,
the emptiness of the interior and the dangers of the coast:
but he promised to do anything in his power for us.   He
considered the various plans I suggested.   One was to
travel at once to Kandalaks by river, lake, and forest:
but it was uncertain whether the Lake Imandra were yet
open.   Four days before, we knew it to be frozen: our
journey thither need only occupy three days, and a week
would not thaw it.

Then I proposed to move eastward over the *tûndras*
from the northern end of Imandra: transporting our

effects as in similar regions, on reindeer sledges. We
should reach in this way the central lake Lôvosero, and
descend either one of the north-flowing Mûrman rivers,
Tiribirka, Voronje, Karlovka, Yokkonga : the only river
flowing eastward, the Ponoi : or, one of the White Sea
rivers, Varzuga or Umba. The Ispravnik said the reindeer were all sick, and unfit for work. Then I suggested
Lapps as bearers instead : and he said this was the better
plan. There is but one horse in Kola. Dogs draw the
sledges in the winter : as many as twenty-five may be seen
in a train, each drawing his sledge assisted by a man.
The Ispravnik thought there would be no difficulty in
finding men enough to accompany us—even on a short
notice.

I returned to the house of our host the Stanovoi,
Anton Moldvistoff, and despatched the Perevodtchik suddenly down the fiord by boat, so that he might take
advantage of the *Pram's* sailing, and be towed. He was
to go to a settlement of Lapps, and engage them if
possible to come inland with us. Then, seeing that we
must reduce our baggage to more moderate compass, we
set to work and repacked everything—from the commis-
sariat to our personal effects.

We had brought too many comforts with us. Instead
of having several Lapps for one piece of baggage, we
could only have one Lapp for several pieces of baggage.
We were travelling like Soubise, when we should have
travelled like Frederick the Great. How could I fail to
win ? said Frederick, after the battle of Rosbach : Soubise

D

had seven cooks and one spy—I had seven spies and one cook.

This was the letter of Ivan Abramovitch:

FROM THE ISPRAVNIK OF KOLA.

The bearers of this are the English subjects Edward Rae and H. P. Brandreth, who have the intention of travelling in the Half-Island of Kola : and spending some time in the places of Nuotosero, Sviatoi Nos, Ponoi, Kouzomen, Kandalaks, with a scientific object. And herewith I request you to acquaint them with the conditions of the same,

2nd day of June.
ISPRAVNIK OF KOLA,
Monisorovsky.

Rambling one cold evening up towards the gorge of the Kola, I came upon a group of remains. In a quadrangle, measuring forty yards each way, stood square grass-covered mounds, slightly hollowed on top—which might have been the ruined foundations of diminutive huts. Whether this were the old Battery, and the squares represented the soldiers' huts, or whether they were the monks' dormitories in the little early monastery of Malmys, was at the moment not very clear. Close by, were series of rude concentric rings of small stones—much like those at Morten's Nœs — and which appeared to be Lapp graves.

I thought the matter interesting enough to justify an appeal to the Ispravnik's local knowledge. I called upon Ivan Abramovitch, and said : *Ya nasholl Svietskouyou*

batteriou, I have found a Swedish battery. *Etto gdjai !*
Where ! said the Ispravnik, starting as if a body of
Swedes had established an earthwork in front of his
windows. *Podi, smotri:* Come and look. Ivan Abramovitch wrapped himself in his long gray overcoat, and we
went out together to the spot. *Etto batteri*, I said. The
Ispravnik stared all round the horizon, without displaying
in his countenance any token of intelligence or of recognition. I pointed to the green lumpy turf, and Ivan
Abramovitch began to think I had softening of the brain.
Or Monastir ? I suggested. Ispravnik, shaking his head :
There is no monastery here. Lappish burial-place,
there, I said, pointing to the stone rings. The Ispravnik
cleaned his spectacles, and stared at the cemetery lying
on the low ground across the rapid Kola. He began to
have forebodings that I was a *Nigilist*, who had lured him
out to this lone spot in the chilly evening.

Traveller—pacing round the quadrangle : One, two,
three, four—forty. One, two, three, four—forty. Ispravnik, beginning to conceive : *Aha ! Svietskoi batteri !*
The gentle Ispravnik would as readily have accepted the
mounds as volcanic, had I happened to know the Russian
word for volcano. It was clear I could learn nothing
from him ; and taking the battery, monastery, and burial-
place together, I don't think Ivan Abramovitch believed I
was of sound mind.

I have no doubt, now, that this small square marks
the site of the long since demolished fort of Peter the
Great, or a fort of his predecessors the Swedes.

Some little way off lay a bed of perpetual snow, the sole right and appurtenance of an old lady in Kola. The housewives entrust her with their linen, and she brings it here to bleach, while she watches it : receiving some small remuneration for doing so.

This evening the Stanovoi came to me for medical advice. I could not make out what was wrong, and was inclined to think he wished—as many of these poor people did—for some medicine as a treat. I had some thought of applying a synapism, or portable mustard plaster, to his throat, which would have more than entertained him. Kola, I am sorry to say, abounds with drunken men—demoralised creatures, who wrestled in the street, kissed one another, or cursed helplessly in the *vodka* shops. It is a pitiful vice. At the commencement the stupidest of all weaknesses—in the end the most repulsive : reducing a human being to the lowest level of all.

We traded away our mattresses to Stepanina Moldvistoff, our hostess, for some thick warm quilts, which would serve the alternative purpose of wraps or mattresses.

We spent an excellent night on the floor of our room : and in the forenoon the Linguist returned. The Lapps were under contract to a Russian fisher, and could not go with us. We sent him then for Russians, or any outcasts he could find. He came to say no man would go as far as Lôvosero. Get them to come to Rasnavolok, I said : knowing we could, if once there, make it worth their while to go farther. The Perevodtchik came back exhausted : no men would go beyond Kitsa—forty versts from Kola.

The chance was that at Kitsa we should not find people enough to go on, and should be stranded there with our quarter of a ton of baggage, while the porters returned to Kola. I told the Perevodtchik we would have men, and sent him to the Ispravnik for assistance.

In an hour he returned, saying we could have as many men as we wished—as far as Kitsa: but that Ivan Abramovitch himself could compel them to go no farther. This threw the Expedition into a state of mental oppression: it was against all their antecedents and convictions to allow themselves to be defeated. In four or five days a Russian steamer would call at Kola on her way to Archangel, and we determined to go meantime up the Tûloma River to the Nuot Lake. We sent the *Ouriadnik*, the Magistrate's factotum, to engage men and a boat—to be ready to start within three hours—at the beginning of flood tide. The tide affects the river for about twenty versts above Kola.

We learnt that a young Swedish naturalist was in Kola: having spent the winter here and in the Enara district. We went to call upon him, and found him in a small room, surrounded by his specimens. These were beautifully prepared, and packed in boxes. I made a list of those birds which he observed—apart from the classes we saw ourselves. We asked him to call upon us before our departure from Kola, and we had hardly got back to the house before he appeared. A Japanese student at Yale College visited a lady, and was invited to repeat his call soon. He called again in half-an-hour.

After we had had supper together, we gave the poor student of science what he had not seen for months, and what were now a mockery to us—some tins of beef, all our cheese and custard powders, coffee, and some cigarettes. Stepanina came to consult first the Doctor, who proved disappointing, owing to his replying *Horosho!* and *Wollen Sie?* to all her inquiries : and afterwards myself, about her rheumatism.   I was able—unfortunately from ex- perience—to give the good woman some advice, besides one or two remedies.   Shortly before midnight we issued from the house of Stepanina Moldvistoff with a small portion of our baggage.

KRIMIACHA, TULOMA RIVER.

CHAPTER IV.

THE sun was low in the sky as we began our expedition
up the Tûloma with the first of flood-tide. We were lying
in the stern of a small boat, under a little, a very little,
canvas roof: so low, that we could scarcely support ourselves on our elbows without crushing our heads against
the birch-bough rafters. It was a broad clear stream
fringed with larch, mountain ash, pine, willow, alder, and
birch. We saw the redshank, sandpiper, and the shore
lark. Fish jumped frequently. The *njelma* or white
Siberian salmon is found here: weighing occasionally
twenty pounds. The character of the stream continued
much the same.

We travelled all that night, and came in the morning
to the rough oval earth-hut—called a *balagan*—of Krimiâcha, where a Skolte Lapp fisher family lived. These huts
have a flat mud floor and a small platform round, for sitting
or sleeping. The Lapps squat down to eat—as Orientals
do. In front of the hut the river was gliding smooth and

broad like a mirror, and snowy hills lay beyond it, standing
in a cold gray sky above a dull yellow forest of silver birch.
Here we spent some hours, so that the boatmen might
rest.   Late in the day we came to what an American
lady would have called a stylish cascade—a broad and
rather dangerous rapid.   We disembarked, and transported
our luggage by land : while the Lapps poled and dragged
the boat up as best they could, in slack water and eddies
among the rocks.   Onésime Simonovitch, a bright good-
looking little Lapp, and as clever as he could well be, was
our chief boatman.   His intelligence and agility were
singular.   Nikolai Susloff, an elderly and rather drowsy
Laplander, was second in command: then we had an
arrestant or police culprit and a Korelak, or Karelian—
to complete the ship's company.

   At the head of the cataract we met two Lapp boats,
each heavily loaded with three-quarters of a ton of salmon,
bound from Tûloma to Kola : and I was curious to see how
they would bear the passage of the rapid.   The steersman
of each boat sprang on to a rock—shading his eyes, and
taking a brief survey of the track he meant to follow
through the boiling waters.   Then, leaping into the boats,
they pushed out into the stream.   Down flew the boats—
right—left—plunging, swerving, dashing through the
tumbling waters—sometimes seeming to take a final and
fatal plunge : but again tossing themselves pluckily like
ducks after a bath.

   It was a most exciting scene—like watching a run-
away carriage down a hill : far more exciting to me than

the actual descent of comparatively awful rapids elsewhere : and I was quite relieved and drew a long breath
when the boats shot on to the smooth water below.
Apparently, the imposing sight and sound of a falling
river are in the act of descent lost in the interest, and a
certain mischievous enjoyment, of the danger.

We bought a salmon from the Lapps for a small sum
of money. The first salmon fishery is below Krimiâcha,
eight versts above Kola. The Lapps used to fish on
behalf of the priests of Kola. The salmon fisheries of the
White Sea and Mûrman coast were once immense, but
the clumsy defective method of fishing, and the absence
of restriction or protection, has sacrificed the salmon and
the fishers' interests. The fish are very fine : we saw magnificent salmon of over 40 lbs. weight. The fishing
begins here later than in Norway, and earlier than in the
White Sea rivers. Besides salmon, char, trout, gwiniad,
grayling, perch, and pike seem to abound in the lakes and
rivers. There are no falls high enough in the rivers to
impede the passage of the salmon. In the Kola River
they run up to Guollejärvi, in the Kovda to Paajärvi.
They are not often found in the Niva above Kandalaks.

The Lappish name for this stream is *Tûlomjoki*,
Flood River. Great portions of the low banks are submerged in the spring and autumn. There are numerous
grassy and wooded islands : a larger population might
subsist upon the Tûloma's banks. The land and fisheries,
from four versts outside Kola, all belong nominally to the
Lapps. Game is scarce. We saw the golden-eye and

other ducks, geese travelling overhead, a capercaillie, and heard the notes of the sedge warbler and the cuckoo.

At times we would set off a musical box beneath our coverings, and watch the pleased looks of wonder and incomprehension which preceded the boatmen's hearty laughter.

As we lay hour by hour in the boat reading, or handling such things as writing materials, watches, aneroid barometer, cooking apparatus, and suchlike—all of which must have been novel and striking to these and other poor Lapps—we wondered at the good breeding which prevented them from asking the fifty eager questions that would occur to a Russian. The cost and use of each thing the Lapps were happy to know, if we volunteered to tell them, but they were too well-mannered to be inquisitive.

We pushed on as rapidly as was practicable. The current, though rarely swift, made the task of rowing considerable. It was astonishing for how many hours the boatmen, stimulated by promises of additional payment, would continue to row without rest. At intervals we would land and bivouac in the lovely woods, and sit looking from our camp fire on to the smooth broad stream, through the atmosphere of crystal. The merry, good-humoured Lapps would cook their fish, while we made tea for them : and the blue smoke would curl up among the foliage of the larch and birch.

For two days and nights we were on the river. At length we came to the end of our voyage—the Lapp fishing station of Tûloma—*Ultima Tûloma.* We left our

ON THE TUOLUMNE RIVER

boat a mile below the falls, and, loading ourselves with its contents, marched along the banks up to the little collection of huts, the homes of a score of Lapp fishermen. There we pitched our new tent for the first time, hoisting the Arctic ensign above it.

It was on the brow of a high abrupt bank, looking down on the falls of the Tûloma—a romantic and beautiful scene. The river is broken by two or three rock-islands, and it tumbles roughly down among them with an impressive roar that echoes through the woods. A rude stake weir ran across the stream near the falls, and on the bank below us stood a few huts where the salting and cleaning were done. The Lapps were greatly interested in our doings, and came offering to help us, and to chat in a pleasant way.

We clambered down to the water's edge to watch the fishing. They were about opening one of the salmon traps, and hoisted it up with a rude tackle. In the box were three dozen magnificent salmon, some weighing six-and-thirty pounds, and glittering like polished silver. Poor creatures, a Lapp dropped down into the box, and with a club put the salmon to death: a sight very cruel and pitiful. Higher up the island we found a Lapp posted on a rock, with a long kind of boat-hook, which he used with surprising skill—jerking it like lightning, and hooking the salmon escaped from the weir, that were attempting to ascend the cataract. The Lapps said that the salmon, after passing the falls, traverse the Nuot Lake, and even go up the Nuot River to its source in Finland.

The Nuot Lake lies about eight versts above this spot. The river is broken and unnavigable. The Nuot is the second largest lake of Russian Lapland—measuring thirty odd miles by seven. It is full of islands, and has low wooded shores. The lake receives two rivers—the Nuot and the Lût—the former at its southern, the latter at its western extremity. The Lût is rather a succession of swamps than a stream. These stretch all the way to Enara Lake—apparently only sixty miles distant: but the Swedish naturalist told me it had cost him a fortnight, with extreme toil, to drag and float a boat from Enara to the Nuot Lake.

The other swamps important for travellers to know lie, one between the Ponoi and Poûlonga: another between the Ponoi and the Serg Lake: a third between the Mensche Dunder and Kola. Some are bare, others covered with spongy moss, and tall grass, *Carex*, suitable as fodder for cattle. At Mezén, one or two degrees farther south, all through the summer, swamps and ground continue frozen within six feet of the surface. This is a feebly comforting reflection to some few of us. In Russian Lapland it is not so, and travellers, whatever may be their stature, must avoid swamps.

We set off on foot for the Nuot Lake. We were accompanied by two pleasant, intelligent Lapps, who chatted all the way through the forest. Dressed as they were, with tunics and belts, in which hung small axes, like tomahawks, and wearing soft skin boots: they might have been taken for a couple of red Indians. Our footsteps did not sound on the soft reindeer lichen. This vast white carpet was so delicious to the eye, that I could hardly refrain from eating it—or at least from rolling on it. I gathered the blue Andromeda and the wild azalea.

Far in the middle of the wood stood a great granite boulder, twenty feet high, transported, without abrasion, in some great movement in the Ice Period, and deposited quietly here. One of the Lapps told me a long legend about it. It is called *Okladnik Kamen*, or the rock of the burial-place. There was a fight here, I gathered, between the Lapps and the Swedes, or between the Russians and the Swedes : and there was some buried money mixed up with the story. There was an adventurer, Okladnikoff, who founded Mezén, and called it Okladnikova. He may have wandered this way, and crossed swords with the Swedes on this spot. There was no conflict here now, except between Nature and the fallen rotting trees : the forest was as silent as death.

The circumstance showed that our companion Ivan Mikailovitch Titoff had some little historical intelligence— a rare thing among the apathetic hyperboreans. I asked him if this *Okladnik Kamen* were treated as a Bauta Stone. No, he said : but there is a *Pahta kamen* on the Kola Gûba. There are many bears here and on the Kola *tûndra :* but they, no doubt, migrate to the summer haunts of the reindeer.

For two hours we marched through the silence of the woods. From our left came the hoarse sound of the river.

We saw the bilberry and crakeberry in profusion : and
gathered black juicy berries which had lain preserved in
the snow all winter through. We heard the cries of a few
birds, and found the nest of a falcon, or perhaps a fishing
hawk. The salmon in the Nuot Lake are smaller than in
the Tûloma : the finest do not escape the weir. They
cost at Tûloma two and a half roubles for forty pounds.
Then bread was this year correspondingly cheap ; forty
pounds cost two shillings and fourpence. A reindeer costs
from ten to fifteen roubles : a *pulka*, or sledge, seven
roubles. A reindeer will draw a sledge from sixty to a
hundred versts in a day. The dainty reindeer won't touch
other moss than the greenish-white *lichen rangiferinus*,
which carpets these woods : but fish or bread tempts them.
Fastidious animals and human beings often deprive
themselves of pleasures. There was a Count of Paris who
was so particular, that it was said he could only accept
the crown of France on condition that all Frenchmen
became Kights of the Legion of Honour. We could have
no reindeer milk at Tûloma, because it was needed for
the Lapp children : and we respected the Lapps for keeping it for their children, instead of offering it to us for
money.

We emerged from the woods, and came upon the
Nuot Lake, not—so far as we could see—an extensive
sheet of water : so strewn was it with small wooded islands.
We found a Lapp boat, and getting into it, rowed for a
few versts to the northern shore : where stood a wooden
church of good size, and a few farm buildings, on a sunny

clearing by the water's edge. This was the priest's little farm, as it may be called, of Nuotosero. The *pope* was absent: and his boy took us into the cheerless empty church, and into the high belfry. For a great distance round us stretched undulating forest: at our feet lay the Nuot Lake, silvery in the glancing sunlight.

After a rest in the warm sun, we returned to the boat. Again through the woods—a walk shortened by the cheerfulness and intelligence of these most pleasant companions —and we reached the camp, quite ready for our evening meal. We took some photographs of the Lapps, and showed them copies of groups of Samoyedes as the results : but these Lapps were too quick-witted, and laughed heartily at the imposition.

We left Tuloma after a formal farewell to the little colony. We called them together, and I made them a short speech in Russian : finally handing to several of them pocket-knives : but to Ivan Mikailovitch a musical box, which played the air, as I explained to him, of *Prostchaï Ivan*, or Good-bye, John. I showed him how to use it, and said it was to be a souvenir for the community, left in his charge. *Nie ! Ya za derzhou gla sibia— vsiaki morzhat slushat :* No, said Ivan : I shall keep it for myself—but all may listen to it.

Gift deserves gift, says a Lapp proverb : and a fair word an answer. Accordingly, at intervals during the leave-taking, Lapps would disappear, and return with salmon, to press upon us as parting gifts. Our tent was struck, and the baggage packed : the Lapps contending for the pleasure of carrying it to the boat. We pushed off, amid a chorus of *Prostchaïtye* and *Da svidania,* and paddled away rapidly down the Tuloma. Poor honest Lapps—doing their duty in the state of life to which it has pleased God to call them.

We were in motion all through the night, and in the morning drew near to the cataract. Our boatmen asked whether we wished to go down in the boat, or to walk through the woods. We had foolishly descended rapids enough on previous journeys : and, desiring to make a moral stand, told the Lapps we should get out and walk. We then found we had come so near the rapid that, to our inward satisfaction, the stream took hold of the boat, and down we went—safely enough. We take, however, all the credit of our good resolution. On the fourth day we came to Kola.

The Ispravnik sent his cossack to say that he wished to call upon us as soon as we had rested : and the Pere-vodtchik was accordingly set to work to impart to our room more of the appearance of a *salon,* and less of a hospital or store, than it possessed. He was also instructed to rush in with *tchaï* and Laferme cigarettes, as soon as the great man should have taken breath : to have matches at hand : to watch the Ispravnik's cup, seize it as soon as empty, and bring clean cups with hot tea. Meantime to make chocolate ready, and to ply Ivan Abramovitch with it, as soon as the *tchaï* should seem to pall upon him. To hold himself within respectful earshot, and prompt me when at a loss for a word.

Then the Ispravnik arrived, dressed in his becoming full-dress uniform.   Dark-blue trousers, dark-green coat with military buttons—having the single silver star, denoting *Prâprostchik* rank, on his gold shoulder-strap : a flat cap, and long military overcoat.   His small retinue stood at the gate to subdue any chance Nihilist tendencies.   Ivan Abramovitch sat, until I began to think he would never go.   He saw all our outfit—from the cooking apparatus, of which he approved highly : to the tinned and potted meats, of which, poor fellow, he approved still more. The Perevodtchik assiduously supplied him with tea and cigarettes : and we had a long talk over our altered plans. He had never left the province : had never travelled farther than Archangel.   He could not afford to, as he told me.   A poor Russian Ispravnik generally means an honest one.

I asked his permission to take Onésime Simonovitch round the Peninsula with us : but he explained that he was engaged to work the boat traffic in the summer, under contract to the *Stantsia* keeper.   He sent for the man : Românoff Michieff by name, freebooter by profession.   This gentleman asked three hundred roubles for the use of his boat as far as Gavrilova.   We said, Oh.   Then for selling us Onésime, he wanted fifty roubles : this being conditional on our finding at Gavrilova a man to replace him here.   No better, or indeed other, arrangement could be made : so we accepted it, on the pledge that the boat and crew should be ready within two hours.

One of this country's undeveloped resources is lead :

E

of which, Ivan Abramovitch said, ore is found near Pasvig, containing sixty-six per cent of pure metal.   He told me that a Russian professor, who came years ago to Kola, had the misfortune to shoot a Laplander.   I asked how much it cost, and the Ispravnik said thirty roubles.   Then it became clear that the Doctor's gun was one of the articles of baggage for which we could not find transport. Thirty roubles a head for Lapps was out of the question.

At length Ivan Abramovitch tore himself away, and we made him happy by sending the Perevodtchik after him to his house, bearing a box of cocoa for himself and of raisins for his children.   We bought from our motherly hostess a silver cross and chain, and two brass *samovars :* then we went out to watch for the signalling of the steamer *Arkhangelsk.*

It was a melancholy evening.   Gray clouds floated over-head, and rain fell in a gray mist.   Kola seemed deserted. An owl sat on a tall rude wooden cross beside us : a poor priest, and one or two peasants wrapped in sheepskin coats trudged past.   At length word came that the steamer was off the Point, three miles away.   We got into a boat, and were rowed down to the *Arkhangelsk.*   The captain, Braun, received us kindly : and we arranged that he should tow us down to the sea, on his way to Vardö. He recommended us to hasten our preparations, as he must sail in three hours.   It took four hours of incredible trouble to get the miserable rickety old *snéka* ready and manned.

The *arrestant* hesitated, the *Korelak* refused, Nikolai

Susloff agreed at once, Onésime was the soul of the preparations. As the *arrestant* would not come spontaneously, I had to go and engage Feopentovioff, the Ispravnik's *Ouriadnik*, at a high salary, to accompany us: and, as he must not lose sight of him, to bring the *arrestant* whether he liked it or not. Nobody else could be found: so we could not consider feelings which belonged, under the circumstances, not to an individual, but to the State. We were in despair for a fourth man, though we had hunted all Kola through.

I saw on the beach a queer yellow smoky obscure shrivelled little man, staring stupidly at me. Brother, I said, taking him by the arm, come to Gavrilova. *Horosho*, he said quietly: and in ten minutes more we were propelling the lumbering old boat down the fiord. We went on board the steamer, and slept comfortably. We saw *Abrampaata*, a cliff on our left hand, as we steamed away from the anchorage—a sacred rock of the Lapps: worshipped in old days by throwing stones up at its face. When we awoke we were in sight of the sea. As we approached Leshin Point, the *Arkhangelsk's* engines were stopped within a few hundred yards of the rocks. Here the mariner's compass indicates true North. We embarked on the *snéka*, cast off from the steamer, and with a strong wind set sail for the east.

CHAPTER V.

Kildîn Island—The Mûrman coast—A Lapp ally—St. Gabriel's—Fishing
stations—Mûrman fishes—Lôvosero—Investigations—Corruption—A suf-
ferer—Zakkar's Farewell.

THE venerable Laplander Nikolai Susloff had been detailed to superintend the boat's outfit. As we went down
the *Arkhangelsk's* gangway, I asked whether he had filled
the water-casks. Yes, he said. With fresh water? I asked,
having a presentiment. No, he said : with salt water.
We sailed between Kildîn Island and the cold iron coast
of Lapland. Dull volcanic rocks, red and rounded : abrupt
gray cliffs split and fissured, with misty snow crowning
them—rose hundreds of feet from the dark sea. Here
and there green and orange lichen brightened the cliffs.
Gulls rose from their *bazar,* as the Russians call a breeding-place : and ducks flew hurriedly past us. Foam blew
in white streaks, driven by gusts that swept down between
the hills. The island of Kildîn lay to the northward
of us, with a clear table-shaped outline : intensely purple
in the distance, and relieved by brilliant white snow.
On the N.E. side of Kildîn live two Norsk settlers, near
Mogilnyi Nôs, the Point of the Graves. Behind Mali
Olenyi live some Russian fishers.

At intervals we passed a fishing boat as we flew swiftly along the *Mûrman*—corruption of *Norman*—coast. Squalls are sudden and violent here. A short time since, two fishing boats lay quietly at anchor: a hurricane struck them, and the boats disappeared from mortal sight.

Castren had to abandon his contemplated journey to this coast: and could, as he says, only glance at the Lapps between Kola and Kandalaks. We passed Zelénets or Green Point: then Tchorni or Black Point: scudding along to the eastward in deep water.

We left the cigar-shaped Mali Olenyi to seaward of us, sailing through the narrow channel which makes it an island. Next we passed the Tinunko Islands, approached Dolgaia Gûba, Long Bay, and entered Tiribirka Bay. We crossed the mouth of the river of this name, —a good anchorage, and a considerable fishing stream— flowing northward from the common watershed of all the rivers of the White Sea Peninsula. Tiribirka is frequented by three hundred fishermen, with thirty boats: and has a winter population of perhaps eighty.

The wind fell, and we sent the men to the oars: then to light a fire and cook. We had more space in the *snéka* than in the boat on the Tûloma: but far less, relatively, than a dog has in his home—and were cramped enough. Our kennel measured seven feet in length, five in width, and four in height. After dinner we sailed again, and the crew turned over, I can't say in, to sleep. They turned over in the bottom of the boat.

The little Lapp I engaged last at Kola had fallen

asleep, somewhere under a thwart, with his great boots alone visible. He had a small orange-tanned wrinkled face, with dull eyes, yellow hair growing over them, and narrow sloping shoulders. He wore an old yellowish drab soldier's overcoat, and looked as if he had fallen by chance into a pair of boots, whose huge bulgy soles and footprints resembled those of the elephant. The little man looked like a dry fig in a roll of brown paper. He seemed half-tipsy, but was only odd and queer. His gait was one of his best points. He stooped forward, and his arms hung quite loosely at his sides. The crew despised and jested at him : he was an outcast to all but myself. They made sport of the eccentricity and queer ways which endeared him to me : I was his only ally. I asked him his name. *Zakkarandreizitkikoff.* Hadn't he any other names? What was his front name? *Zakkar.* Family name? *Zitkikoff.*

We landed in a small creek on Tiribirka Point. Beside us lay a granite pebble, which had rolled down from the ice-covered ridge above. We found it measured twenty-eight feet, by twenty-one, by eighteen. The men dispersed in search of driftwood. Zakkar Andrei Zitki-koff was to go too : but as I stepped on shore I heard a noise, and profane muttering. Zakkar Andrei Zitkikoff had slipped, and fallen into the bottom of the boat. We clambered up among the granite boulders and snow : finding a small lake, round which we gathered wild flowers, and where we spent a happy hour in throwing stones into the water. Overhead hung cliffs of frozen snow.

Returning, we found an Arctic picture : the boat

moored to the rock : the Lapps hewing wood, or grouped round the fire, cooking their fish and ours. Snow and granite lay all round, and the cold sea beneath. We found granite, gray, blue, white and red, white and green, and blood-red. We had to hurry away, for the tide was ebbing. One man was nearly left behind on the desert shore. It was Zakkar Andrei Zitkikoff.

We finished our meal when under way. I found Zakkar, half-an-hour after the men had finished their dinner, drinking tea absently, and munching black bread. When I put some sugar into his cup, Zakkar Andrei Zitkikoff smiled for the first, and, with one exception, the only time—a quaint comical smile, and doffed his cap. When the wind increased and grew colder and shriller, I passed Zakkar my quilt. He took off his cap, and smiled again. The wind now increased, and blew in gusts. The old *snéka* flew along, her gunwale hissing through the water as though it had been red-hot. In a quick squall the old patched rag which served as a sail blew away from the mast, and the boat reeled. One man got mixed up with the tackle, and was nearly swept overboard : this, of course, was Zakkar Andrei Zitkikoff. Fortunately, the hurricane could not lift him out of his boots, or he would have gone finally.

We passed Oposôva and Zelénetsky. Then, carrying on as well as we could, shortly before midnight we passed the mouth of the Korodok, as the Lapps call the Voronje River : and rounded the rocks lying outside the harbour of Gavrílova.

The Russian thinks much of names. Each Tsar names
a son Constantine, in the hope that he may inherit the
throne of Byzantium.   Each Russian receives the name
of the saint on whose holy day he comes into the world.
Some fisherman, too reverent to give directly to his haven or
village the name of the saint, calls his *Stanovitsche* after
himself—Gavril, the adopted of the messenger angel Gabriel.

In the Cathedral of Tarragona is an old column, having
a capital carved with the representation of three kings
in one bed : one awake and watching, with a pleased,
tranquil face, an angel who is approaching the bed with
the news of Christ's birth.   Here is the legend again in
the white North.   Over the Russian peasants' doors are
carved, together with three crosses, the letters B. M. G.
initials of Balthasar, Melcon, Gaspar, kings of Mesopo-
tamia, Persia, and Arabia.   In the Russian churches is
sung at Christmas a kind of Litany—the Kalenda : and
one part describes the awakening by the angel Gabriel of
the *Tri Karelya*, three kings.

We entered the little cross-shaped harbour.   The gray
rocks were covered with drying fish, and the air was
saturated with the smell.   Heads and refuse of fish tainted
the water, and clouds of gulls were hovering about : some
angry, all hungry, some squawking hoarsely, others with
the snapping bark of a small dog.   We walked round the
harbour, past fish-racks and wooden huts, to the small
wooden house of the chief fisherman, Ivan Retkin.   We
found the family asleep : the house was like a rabbit-
warren—one small room leading to another, and all were

stifling.   Our room was a highway for the family, or rather families : for two or three shared the house.

It was a lonely spot : far out of the world, looking out on the North Polar Sea, the *Sjévernaya Moré*. We sat at the open window : it was past midnight. We looked over the little harbour to the golden sea : only the sea-gulls broke the silence. Our boat lay on the wet sand : Onésime and his crew had their quarters in her. We lay down for the night : young Retkin, in his high boots, slept across the doorway.

Piotri Ivanovitch has much intelligence, and even reads much : he lives here throughout the year. There is far more life here than in Kola. Gavrilova swarms with busy fishers. Four hundred men come here in the summer, using eighty *snékas*. There are but few women : only those who stay through the winter. In winter seven houses only are occupied, by about forty persons. They use traps instead of nets in the winter.

There are forty-one fishing stations on the Mûrman coast : eleven between Sviatoi Nôs and Litsa, the eastern group : seventeen between Litsa and Kola, the middle group : seven between the Kola Fiord and Vaidda Guba, the Kolsky group : and six between Vaidda Guba and Yakobselv, the western group. There are from two to three thousand fishers on the coast, of whom perhaps one-fourth are Norwegians : and there are some of the best sheltered anchorages in the world. The Kola Fiord in January and February never freezes farther than thirty versts below the town : sometimes not at all. Iekaterinsk,

one of the finest harbours, never freezes—thanks to
the Gulf Stream. The midsummer temperature of the sea
on this coast is about 8° Centigrade, or 46° Fahrenheit.

Litsa has many huts, fifty *ketschmari* or *ransiki*, and
a hundred and fifty boats.

Siem Ostrova is an important *Stanovitsche*, having the
advantage that the cod and herrings frequent the coast
more closely than at the western stations.

Gavrilova employs a hundred Russian, and several
Norwegian boats from Vadsö.

Tiribirka, known to the Norsemen in the sixteenth
century as Tiribir, is one of the oldest and most important stations. Great catches of herrings are made at
the mouth of the considerable river the Tiribirka, and
hither most of the Pomorian fishermen come.

Ieretik has several houses and a splendid harbour.

Karabella, visited chiefly by Norsk boats, is a lucrative station.

Vaidda Guba is visited by Kolsk, Pomorsk and Norsk
fishermen.

The chief *Stanovitsches*, Siem Ostrova, Gavrilova,
Tiribirka, have numerous wooden huts, baths, stores,
boiling caldrons : and each has a chapel.

The best fishing years on record have been 1828,
1837, 1840, 1842-3, 1851, 1867-8. The worst have
been 1831, 1844, 1849. In 1854-55 the English naval
demonstrations hindered the poor people's fishing opera-
tions. In 1782-1790, 150,000 *poudov* or, roughly speaking, 50,000 cwt. of salted or dried cod, and 63,000 cwt.

of train oil and various fish were sent from the Mûrman coast to the White Sea ports. From 1826 to 1835 the average export from the Norway fisheries to the Mediterranean was 15,000 cwt.: from the Mûrman fisheries 59,000 cwt.: from 1836-1845, 43,000 cwt. against Norway's 37,000 cwt.: from 1855-65, 106,000 cwt. against Norway's 126,000 cwt.—showing that Norway has steadily overtaken Russian Lapland in the matter of trade with the Catholic countries. From 1865 to 1870 the annual trade between Norway and Russia averaged £125,000: Norway importing as much again as she exported.

There have been as many as three hundred vessels at a time employed here in the shark fishery : some of which, costing four hundred silver roubles, have been known to earn three or four hundred roubles in ten days. The Norwegians taught the Russians this industry. The poor shark—the most friendless of all fishes, and whose only failing is his appetite—is also snared from the edge of the ice at Seredni in the winter. In 1867 a Norwegian named Suul, who introduced this fishery, became a Russian subject, and settled in Kola. A few years later, Ikonikoff, a native of Soroka in Pomoria, joined Suul. The fishery is not fully developed, owing to imperfect tackle and the difficulties of communication.

There have been for centuries whale fisheries on the Mûrman coast. An old charter exempts the Peisen Kloster from duty on whale oil. The Dutch for many years shared the fishing with the Russians.

In 1723, by ukase of Peter the First, a Kola whale fishery was established at the cost of the State : and in 1827-1831 three whalers were sent yearly, supplied with Dutch harpooners.   But as in those five years the whalers took only four whales, the patience of the *Commerce Collegium* became worn out, and they declared the Dutch harpooners to have been suborned by their countrymen. The undertaking was soon abandoned, owing to the expense and loss.   Half-a-century later, Count Voronzoff fitted out a vessel, with White Sea mariners, for the whale fishery about the Kola Fiord.   This expedition wounded eleven whales, but killed none, owing to the defective form of harpoon.   In 1806 a whaler fitted out from Kola was taken by privateers and burnt.   Now, once again, a Russian company—so Ivan Abramovitch tells me—are competing with the Norwegians for the profits of the rich whale fisheries of this Arctic sea.   Every year some dead whales drift on shore near Kola Fiord : the Lapps sell the meat to the Kola merchants for a trifle.

The Mûrman fishes are as follows :—

Gadus morrhua . *Torsk*.	. . .	Common Cod.
„ œglifinus . *Pikshju*	. . .	Haddock.
„ virens . . *Saïda*	. . .	Coal fish.
Sebastes Norvegicus *Morskoi okonj*	.	Bergylt.
Anarrhichas lupus. *Subatik*	. . .	Wolf-fish.
Scymnus borealis . *Akula*	. . .	Greenland shark.
Hypoglossus max-imus. *Paltus*	. . .	Halibut.
Pleuronectes flesus. *Morskaya kambala*		Flounder.

A LAPP VILLAGE.

Pleuronectes limanda	*Tersch*	Common Dab.
Brosimus vulgaris . .	*Morskoi njalim* .	Tusk.
Mallotus arcticus . .	*Moiva*	The Capellin.
Ammodytes lancea .	*Pestchanka* . .	Sand Launce.
Rorqualis borealis . .	. . . . . .	Blue Whale.

Cod are not found in the cold waters east of Sivatoi Nôs, but herrings travel as far as the mouths of the Petschora, the Ob, and the Yenesei.

Not a human being makes his appearance here—or ever a vessel—in the long winter months. There is no post. Sometimes one of the inhabitants goes for necessaries to Kola, and brings letters or news. He must travel for two or three days, in the three hours' daylight, with thirty or forty reindeer. The route is up the Korodok River, a hundred and fifty versts, as far as Voronsky, a *pogost* of twenty Lapps. This takes a day and night. Thence the journey lies over the wilderness, for another day and night, to Kildinski *pogost*—a winter settlement of the Lapps. Thence twenty versts along the Kola river to Kola. Not a tree is to be seen between Gavrilova and Kildina.

The winter journey to Lôvosero is made in about three days. We travelled with Otiets Gorg Kvalovitch Terentieff, priest of Lôvosero, a singular man with an abrupt and impetuous manner of speech. Father George's political eloquence had outstripped his prudence, and, finding expression in some of the journals, had led to Lôvosero parish being assigned to the poor priest for seclusion and reflection.

He readily gave us information about Inner Lapland. The Voronje is navigable, but with toil and difficulty, by small boats. Lôvosero is a small *pogost* of the Lapps, having a church, and lying on the east bank of the Lôv Lake. A stream, practicable to boats, and which is probably the Vârzuga River, leaves the southern extremity of the lake.

Next day there came at our bidding, from the Lapp settlement at the mouth of the Korodok, an aged Laplander in a dirty, odorous, smoked sheepskin coat: accompanied by a younger but even more highly cured Lapp. These were to be our advisers and pilots for the Korodok. It was very hopeless. First the stuffy old Lapp said there were no boats. When we had defeated him on this point, he said there was no river. Eventually he said it was one long rapid—up which no boat could be taken.

Every hour or so—for the interview lasted for half the day—I went out to breathe, leaving Onésime to examine the old Troglodyte. When I gave him some silver, the poor old gentleman cheered up, and gave me details of the river. The Tomânosero, he said, lay thirty-five versts up, and this proving correct, my confidence increased. Then he committed himself to stages and rapids, so vastly distant from one another, that when I added them all together, I found the Korodok must have its source in the centre of the White Sea. Then I disbelieved the old Laplander. *Ti bweel na raiki?* Thou hast been up the river? *Nie bweel.* Never been (!) We paid the two

Lapps for our time and trouble, and sent them away contented.

Then we went to search for a boat, to ascend the river with Onésime and other boatmen. *Traveller:* We want to hire two small boats. *Group of natives in chorus:* There are not two boats to hire. *Traveller:* We will buy them. *Natives:* It is not possible. *Traveller:* One boat. *Natives:* No one has a boat to sell. *Traveller:* We will wait for three days and have a boat built. *Natives:* No man here can build a boat : all are made in Kola. *Traveller:* We will give a rouble to any one who will find us a boat for sale. *Crowd, consulting:* Ask Piotri Ivanovitch Retkin for one of his boats.

I went to Retkin and said we wanted his small boat. Retkin said he could not do without it. I told him that we could not do without it either. He refused point-blank to hire or sell it. Then we knew we must approach him by the circular method. First came the *Ouriadnik* to say that as he could not, in all Gavrilova, find a man to replace Onésime, the little Lapp must return with him to Kola. I took the *Ouriadnik* aside and showed him absently a five rouble note. Onésime must come with us, I said. The *Ouriadnik* turned Gavrilova upside down, but came back in despair. Then we immediately decided to abandon the Korodok, and to sail round to the Ponoi : taking a boat in order to make ourselves independent on that river.

The summer fishing contracts, embracing nearly the whole male population of Russian Lapland, are a traveller's difficulty. I may say that, as far as payment went, we should have rarely hesitated : but no temptation could release a man working by contract. We went after consideration to Retkin, and chartered his large *snéka* to take us to Siem Ostrova : and when he had made all his preparations for several days' absence, and fitted out the *snéka*, we declined to start until he sold us his small boat.

We parted reluctantly with Onésime, and made him happy with various gifts. I paid the hire of the old boat to the *Ouriadnik*, and he drew out a receipt in good Russian.

June 7th. I the undersigned *Ouriadnik* Feopentovioff, give this quittance to the *Gospodin Anglitchanin*, for that I have taken the money from him fifty roubles for the balance of hire from the town of Kola to the Stanovitsche Gavrilova, and for pay of rowers. Herewith I give the receipt for this money, and I shall account for it to Romanoff Stepanovitch Michieff.

Ouriadnik, FEOPENTOVIOFF.

Sitting writing at the window, I heard a sound— *Nozhik !* Knife ! It was Zakkar Andrei Zitkikoff, who unceremoniously demanded a pocket-knife such as I had given to Onésime. I gave him a knife, because I could not collect my thoughts when he was in sight : but he said nothing, and went away.

A child came to be cured of the toothache : and we daily dressed the hand of a poor boy, living in the room next to us. He had torn it with a fish-hook, and the inflammation was spreading up his whole arm. Taking his arm off would be the only chance for him. His brother, one day, grateful for the little trouble we had taken, brought us a beautiful coral-like Arctic mollusk, attached to a stone—the *Hornera Lichenoides* of Linnæus. It was like a miniature fern in ivory. We gave the sick boy a musical box in return. I hear the Perevodtchik asked constantly whether I am a Professor : the Doctor's capacity is taken for granted. The Expedition is variously suspected : few believe that we have come for peaceful and uncommercial objects to the White Sea Peninsula. The Linguist himself, who associates all English travellers with sport alone, is not able to entirely satisfy the public curiosity.

I saw Zakkar Andrei Zitkikoff once again. He was standing silently under the window: and I was on the point of hardening my heart, preparatory to refusing him a second knife. When he caught my eye, he suddenly took off his cap and ducked his head. Then he went away. He had only come to say good-bye.

CHAPTER VI.

WE left the Retkin's house on the third day, each of us
carrying something. The Perevodtchik was armed with
the backbone and one side of the body of a huge salmon,
which at times he shouldered like a battle-axe, and at
others carried under his arm like a gun. We sailed from
Gavrilova, through the ever-hungry swarm of gulls. The
bright sun shone on the crested waves. A *lodje* or lugger
rocked at her anchor, and we could hear the creak of oars.
Two wooden crosses, fixed on a bare pink granite cliff,
struck the eye from every direction. A group of placid
dove-coloured, white-breasted gulls sat beneath them, like
a congregation of Puritan girls with gray gowns and white
handkerchiefs : fluttering when the waves splashed spray
over them.

We turned away to the eastward, and the wind blew
with some force. We were towing our boat, but finding
the *snéka* would not obey her helm, Piotri Ivanovitch and

his comrade Lazari Ivanovitch, with our help, hoisted it on board. Our *snéka* then presented an original appearance, carrying athwart-ships a boat two-thirds of its own length. We looked so singular that we saw a schooner bear down, apparently to inspect and hail us.

We see in the small *navolok* of Podinakta two schooners at anchor, waiting for cargoes of fish, or for better weather. Then we pass in a short time the island of Koussînet, having a large *bazar* of sea-birds—razorbills, little auks, cormorants, puffins, etc. Then Derniznaya Gûba: then Shilpine, where a Russian trader, Matvei Franasovitch Savin, has a *faktori* or store. The coast is lower, and the seas break upon more rounded rocks. We next pass Bieloi Nôs, White Point, where lies perpetual snow. Behind Olényi Island is excellent anchorage, well sheltered from all winds.

A dense cloud overshadows the cliffs, and the weather to seaward looks very mixed. The wind is steady in the north-west, and the *snéka* tears rapidly along. At intervals we see a lonely Mûrman *navolok* such as Tcherbinka or Triastina, indicated by a few wooden crosses set up on the rocks. We watched the gulls pouncing upon the herrings, and the skuas and great northern divers enjoying themselves. There are no sharks at this part of the coast, but numerous seals, especially at the Voronje river.

We noticed that Piotri Ivanovitch was, with the assistance of a clasp-knife, consuming a fish-pie—a huge piece of halibut, *hypoglossus maximus*, baked inside a shell of black bread: called in Russian a *pirôg*, in Karelian *kolybaka.* We determined to ask for some of it. Piotri drew a second one out of a sealskin bag, and made us accept it. We lived for two days upon the hypoglossus maximus pie, in Byzantine luxury. Our attention was directed at this stage of the journey to a monstrous cylindrical sealskin trunk, which had inconvenienced us on the last stage, and which we took to belong to the *Ouriadnik.* It was the Perevodtchik's notion of a moderate outfit for Russian Lapland. We had seen the Linguist with a small carpet-bag, which we admitted to be modest: but here was a case as large as half the body of a walrus. We spoke mildly to the Perevodtchik, and begged him to take an early opportunity of expressing his trunk to the West.

We sailed past Shûbina, where were Lapp huts and about two dozen fishermen: then passed Vrinda and its outlying reef of rocks. There was a large church there. A corvette—carrying the patriarch, priests, deacons, choristers, vice-governor, and many officials of Archangel province, coming here to the consecration,—had a narrow escape in the same gale which nearly lost our Expedition of 1874. The corvette reached Archangel many days after she was given up for lost. The same gale was disastrous to Russian vessels at Vardö : six were capsized, and all lives lost. The storm extended to the White Sea. A vessel lying at anchor in a creek on the Lapland coast, with a cargo of codfish, was capsized in a minute.

The Government seem to contemplate attracting a population to the Mûrman coast by church-building : but a single rapacious trader like Savin will do more to check colonisation than a dozen churches will to aid it. Ten miles eastward from Vrinda lies the *Stanovitsche* of Zolotaia —the Golden. Here are eighty fisher-people and twenty boats in the summer.

We met abroad an engineer of the Russian steamer *Alexei*, wrecked on the island of Kouvshin, at Siem Ostrova, in the autumn of 1876. The shipwrecked crew for many days ate nothing but gulls' eggs. As the fishermen remain at Siem Ostrova until the end of autumn, and, when they go, leave sacks of meal in the huts for the necessities of seafaring men, the castaways must have managed very badly.

I asked Piotri Ivanovitch about the Northern Lights, called by the Mûrmanski *Lunosiânya*, by the Russians *Irisjevernaya Siânya*. The Mûrman fishers believe they are the souls of the dead floating in the air. In Volhynia the peasant mothers throw bread and honey to the first spring swallows.

> *For they think that their dear lost children,*
> *The little ones who are gone,*
> *Come back thus to the heartsick mothers,*
> *Who are toiling and sorrowing on.*
> *And those sunlit wings and flashing*
> *White breasts, to their tear-dimmed eyes,*
> *Bring visions of white child-angels*
> *Floating in Paradise.*

Racing along hour after hour, we sighted at length Karlova, the westernmost of the Seven Islands ; and at length we came among them—Karlova, Litska, Vishniak, Zelénets, Malo Zelénets, Kouvshin, and Gossogorou. Inside the latter island is the *Stanovitsche*. The islands lie in a string, east and west, forming a partially-sheltered sea one or two miles broad and eight miles long: with good and sheltered anchorages. Litska lies more apart—six miles east of the rest. Four miles beyond it is Litsa, a *Stanovitsche*, whither numerous fishing vessels come in the summer. Fifty miles farther eastward stands the light-house of the Holy Cape—*Sviatoi Nôs*. On this part of the coast the tide runs from one and a half to two knots.

Gray huts and a group of crosses stood on gray rocks, upon which the water was lapping. A dozen storm-bound vessels lay in the little harbour, and the few mariners on board stared at us as we sailed past. Our crew crossed themselves as we ran alongside the rocks, close to the *Stanovitsche* of Seven Islands—*Siem Ostrova*, and landed. We sought in vain for a cleanly hut as our home. All were swarming with human beings who spend the summer there: hot with stoves, stifling for want of fresh air: and we were forced to pitch our *barâk* quickly, to shelter us from the bitter, icy North Wind.

The spot we chose, a hundred yards from the sea, and under a cliff where thick snow lay, proved to be the dry-est in Siem Ostrova. Only shallow turf covered the rock, and we had to drive in our galvanised iron tent pegs diagonally, and cross-pin them with others. There our *tchoum* withstood for several days and nights, Arctic gales, Arctic cold, and Arctic rain—a picture of diminutive comfort. The fishermen and boys came up in turns to watch us establish our camp, and stood respectfully round while the Doctor lighted a fire, and the Perevodtchik and boatmen carried up our effects.

22d June.—As I write, I can look out from our snug tent down to the dove-coloured sea. We are encamped in a little amphitheatre of soft brown moss and gray rock, above the huts of Seven Islands. About the tent door are boxes, cooking utensils, sacks, tins, riding boots, etc. Transparent blue smoke floats away from the fire, at which the Perevodtchik has cooked our midnight dinner: and which the Doctor, pipe in mouth, is feeding with silver-birch faggots. The Doctor is a fanatic for fires: he considers the construction and maintenance of a fire preferable to the acquisition of much wealth. He hovers round and cannot leave it: he nurses and feeds it, like a pelican with an only young one. He brought a bill-hook with him—to cut through forests, he said. He also hinted unsuccessfully at jungle. He has already singed the hair off his right hand, and the wool off his sleeve: and his hands are as black as if I had coated them with the mosquito preparation.

Below us, near the water's edge, are rude unpainted block huts, roofed with birch bark and turf. We can see the wreck of the unfortunate *Alexei*. Codfish hangs to dry on long racks: gulls hover round a boat in which the Russians are cutting up freshly-caught fish. Other men are spreading sails to bleach on the snow. It is Saturday evening, and we hear the Angelus, *Vétcherni kolokol*, reminding the fishermen that their six days' toil is over. Our blue Arctic ensign flutters above the little white tent. Against an orange patch in the sky a distant schooner is outlined. Behind the orange cloud lies the chartless Polar Ocean.

Above us, to the right, is a tall rocky cliff, our Royal Observatory. Night and day a grave-looking *moujik* is stationed there, watching for a chance steamer, which may pass miles to seaward—bound to the White Sea. We can see him kneeling there, watching the unsetting sun, with his hands on his knees, like a Moslem at his prayers.

We are enjoying our camp by the snow in the Land of the Midnight Sun. The ground is dry: no dew falls. The moss is a dry cushion. Upon the moss we have spread brushwood, on the brushwood a waterproof sheet, on the sheet a double canvas carpet, on that our ulsters and the Kola quilts. Over us are waterproofs and a familiar travelling companion, a Barbary rug—brown, with elegant red stripes and fringe—altogether highly ornamental. So we fear no cold nor rheumatism. Our effects are stowed for the night in front of the tent: the more perishable ones inside. Our astronomer gets one rouble a night, or two roubles if he sights a steamer: so he is tempted to stay awake, keeping one eye upon our movable property, and the other upon the melancholy ocean.

Piotri, son of Ivan, is much attached to us, and often comes up for a chat. He brought us another very excellent halibut tart as a present. The weather is bad, and threatens to be worse: so Piotri must wait here.

OUR CAMP AT SEVEN ISLANDS.

We have an intimate friend, too, who is dressed like a Kalmuck, in a sheepskin coat and a high fur cap.   He came up with a deputation of citizens on the Sunday afternoon, and we gave him some chocolate.   To eat? he asked.   To eat, I said.   He crossed himself—partly for grace, partly for protection — and then cautiously munched the chocolate.   *Horosho!* he said.

We are in the latitude of Disco Bay in Greenland, of Kolymsk in the Koriak country, and of the North Cape of Asia: in the longitude of Moscow, Azov, Trebizonde, and Palmyra: thirty-eight degrees east of Greenwich: three hundred miles from Nova Zemlia: five hundred from the Kara gates.

Seven-and-thirty miles east of us lies the Arzina—the Riuer or Hauen wherein Sir Hugh Willoughby with the companies of his two ships perished for cold.   The two ships attempting farther north, were in September encountered with such extreame cold that they put back to seek a wintring place: and missing the said bay—the White Sea—fell upon a desart coast in Lappia, and entering into a Riuer were immediately frozen up—since discouered named Arzina Reca—from whence they neuer returned, but all to the number of seuentie persons perished, which was for want of experience to make caues and stores.   These were found with the ships the next summer, anno 1554, by Russe fishermen.

Anno 1556 the Muscovie Company sent two ships, with extraordinarie masters and saylers, to bring home the two ships frozen in Lappia in the Riuer Arzina aforesaid.

But so it fell out that the two which came from Lappia with all their new masters and marriners neuer were heard of : but in foule weather and wrought seams, after their two yeeres wintring in Lapland, became as is supposed vnstanch and sunke. A third ship, the *Edward* aforesaid, falling on the north part of Scotland vpon a rocke, was also lost ; and Master Chancellor with diuers others drowned.

We were in some difficulty about the Arctic ensign, there being no sunset at which to haul it down. The fishermen often came up, and squatted at the tent door, watching our habits and asking to learn a little English. One pleasant man told us that at Kouzomen we should find a party of Kȧnin Samoyedes and reindeer. He brought us a handsome halibut as a present. There also came a good-looking boy in a Samoyede *mȧlitsa*, a native of Mezén, working as a sailor on a Russian schooner.

One morning I set off on foot with the Perevodtchik and a Karelian fisherman, for the Lapp village of Karlovka near the mouth of the Karlovka River : seven versts away, I was told. It blew a heavy gale in our faces, and we were four long hours in getting to the river. Crawling down precipices, dragging ourselves up cliffs, fording streams, staggering across swamps, or from one boulder to another—we were very grateful to come to the end of the journey. We saw among the cliffs two immense Arctic hares. They seemed to be as large as young reindeer. They had patches of gray near the shoulders and ears, but were otherwise quite white.

At the river Rièska, on a tongue of rock, I found

what appeared to be a Lapp *Paata*. There were stones
of a considerable size, placed on the smooth rounded
granite and moss, in the form of a rude ring. At
intervals there came storms of driving hail, snow, and
rain, then the sun would issue from the clouds and shine
brilliantly. I saw, while lying on the soft white reindeer
moss, a coloured rainbow extending from the zenith:
and within the rainbow to the North, 45° above the sea, a
horizontal ring of pure white light—which hung steadily
while the gray clouds drove past it. We were on a cliff
facing Kârlova, a long island two miles from the coast,
one of the Seven Islands. Under its lee were nine
Russian *lodjes*, sheltering from the gale.

The granite became more and more precipitous,
assuming almost the forms of dolomites. The Karlovka
runs in a deep bed. The huts, four in number, lie on the
western bank, and stand a half verst from the sea. There
are here eighteen *Lopparee*, who have some reindeer. A
beautiful fawn-coloured reindeer with dark horns and
black muzzle, accompanying a white calf, came grazing
beside us while we lay at luncheon on the moss.

The land of Lappia is an high land, hauing snow lying
on it commonly all the yeere. The people of the countrey
are half Gentiles: they liue in the summer near the
sea-side and vse to take fish, out of the which they make
bread.

The Lapps of the Karlovka are chiefly occupied in
fishing salmon, of which they take a considerable quantity
in the river. The Karlovka rises in a small lake fifty

miles inland. It is a fine stream, but is barely navigable
for boats up to the *pogost*. I took a photograph of the
really beautiful spot from the cliff above : then we went
down to the river. By the river bank among the rounded
stones, carried down and accumulated by the stream, appeared to be stone rings, very numerous. Some had
been opened, and of others I was told the stones had been
used by Russians in building fires, while fishing at the
river's mouth.

We wished to go back to Siem Ostrova by boat : but
as a sea was breaking on the river bar, the Gentiles said
it would not be possible to get out for hours—that is,
until the tide should rise. I was too tired and hungry to
wait for hours, having shared my biscuits, brandy, and
chocolate with the men : and we could get nothing eatable
from the Lapps. The gale was in our favour, and we
set out homewards on foot.

I never so much repented the grudging a few hours'
waiting. Exhausted with the storm, cold, hunger, and
unexpected exertion, I fell upon the snow every few
hundred yards, and was perpetually going to sleep. We
crossed—how, I don't remember—the faces of almost
perpendicular snowdrifts, where a slip would have pre-
cipitated us a hundred feet down among the boulders.
After many hours, we crawled down on to the shore.
The falling tide had left a beach on which we could walk.
White shells in drifts, coloured pebbles, and bleached
driftwood were all that lay on the white sand. An Arctic
beach has little life ; this was the shore of a dead sea.

I must have looked like the native of such a shore as I came into camp, and dropped on to a mattress, with my eyes dim and the gale still singing in my ears. The Doctor made me a bowl of consolidated German army soup, of double strength, and restored my forces.

One morning I was helping the Perevodtchik to feed the fire, when he let a log of wood fall on my fingers. He said he hoped I was not hurt, and I said mildly that anything which squeezed the blood of the fingers into a bubble must hurt. In his agitation he handed me directly afterwards a frying-pan, of which the handle was to all intents and purposes red-hot. I laid it down on the ground, after it had taken the skin off the thumb and two remaining fingers. The Linguist said he felt very sorry, and I could only tell him that I felt sorry too.

The heavy rain which fell at intervals reduced our neighbourhood to a swamp: but we had hit upon the one naturally drained spot. We had, in spite of wind and snow, a constant group of respectful visitors, who would ask the Perevodtchik and myself sixteen or seventeen hundred questions in a day. The Doctor afforded them great hopes for some time, as he always amiably replied to their questions—*Horosho.* Mûrman : Where do you come from ?   Doctor : *Horosho.*   Mûrman : What are you cooking there ?   Doctor : *Horosho.*

The Doctor's interrogative *horosho* means no fewer things than the following :—What do you think of this sort of thing ?   Shall I do it thus ?   How do you like the biscuit ?   Not bad, is it ?   Will the fire last for half-

an-hour, if I leave it? Don't we look snug in here?
First-class tent, isn't it? Is it going to be a fine day?
Those eggs are sound, aren't they? Is that driftwood
dry? Each separate meaning he conveys by gesture
and the use of the comprehensive enquiry—*horosho ?* If
the Doctor would only apply his mind to learning
twelve words of Russian, he could talk politics and
ornithology.

We were asked whence, why, how we came: whether
for geology, fishery, timber-surveying, or what: and innumerable other questions. It is the foolishest occupation
on earth, minding other people's business. Still we were
very friendly with the poor people, and would always
humour them within reason—even if they came ten times
a day to the tent door.

Strolling out one afternoon I found close to the tent
a titlark's nest with four eggs, among long dry grass: and
a black rat, *Mus lemnus*—called by the Finlanders, and
also, curiously enough, by the Americans, *Mink*—ran out
of a hole in the grass. Not a good neighbour for eggs
or young titlarks, I should have thought: only the *mink*
feeds only on grass and reindeer moss. These Lemming
rats cross the country in the Bothnian basin in thousands:
travelling straight across rivers and swamps. They are
the prey of the white fox.

A great bee, *Apis arctica*, hummed about the cloud-
berry, which was forming into beautiful white blossom:
and I gathered the *Diapensia Lapponica.* I saw bilberries
between Siem Ostrova and Karlovka, which had lived

fresh and juicy under the winter's snow—enough to fill a
boat. White gulls had deserted the stormy water and the
floating relics of fish, and were crowding on the snow,
which lay a hundred yards from our tent.

In August 1611, on the four-and-twentieth day, the
boat's crew of the English ship *Amitie* reached the Seven
Islands. Here wee found many fishermen of whom wee
enquired after Cool—Kola—and Kildina, and they made
signs that they lay west from us—which wee likewise ghest
to bee so—and with that they shewed vs great friendship,
and cast a codde into our scute: but for that wee had a
good gale of wind, we could not stay to pay them for it—
but gave them great thankes, much wondering at their
great courtesie.

Poor sailors and fishermen, gone over two centuries
ago to their account. I wonder if any one—encamped
where we are now, two centuries hence—will know or
care that the Doctor and I came to the Seven Islands.

I asked the Perevodtchik to be so kind as to keep
a minute record of the journey: and I often watched him
biting his pencil end, at a loss for ideas. He was to make
a clean copy on his return home: and after a month or
two I received a neatly-written MS., which a neighbour
had translated for him into English.

After photographs were taken—he writes—of the tent
at Túloma, with Laplanders and the waterfall, Mr. Rae and
the physician went with Laplanders seven versts, to the
Laplanders' winter quarters. On their return presents
were distributed, whereas the Laplanders paid (or gave)

us salmon, accompanied us to the boat, and gave us many congratulations with on the journey.

Then the secretary goes on to Tiribirka Bay. We set the course for Gavrila, but before we arrived, a storm arose, and took the sail from us. At last we arrived at Gavrila. One day a tipsy Russian came up to me, and took me for a Jew who had escaped from Kem: but this was cleared up in this way—a Russian from another place who knew me from former years came up, wherefore he saluted me, and mentioned my name. Then all commenced to make inquiries if we were functionaries, if we were in the service of the State, how far we intended to travel, until we were quite annoyed thereof, and gave them evasive answers, wherefore they left us as they could not get any information.

Piotri Ivanovitch came to wish us good-bye. Poor Piotri, he told the Perevodtchik a sad love story. It was of years before, and Piotri was well off, and envied by his neighbours: but, as the little secretary expresses it: There rested always a sorrow over him.

CHAPTER VII.

A naughty boy—Camp life—Origin of the Lapps—A piece of mischief—An ornithological discovery—Temperature—*Parahod*—Holy Cape—A risk.

A BOY came one evening with a cap full of cormorants', puffins', eider-ducks' and gulls' eggs. He appeared to be the naughty boy of the village. He would whistle, and look at me with a knowing confidence, as if to say it was not so long since I had been a naughty boy with weaknesses too.

Naughty boy: I want to sell the eggs. Traveller: How much? Thirty-five kopecks, to buy half a *botelka*. Traveller: Rum? Naughty boy: I often drink it. Traveller: How many summers hast thou? Fifteen, give me some tobacco. Traveller: To smoke? Naughty boy: I smoke whenever I can. Traveller: It is wrong to smoke and drink——here is a knife instead of money. Boy, confidentially to Perevodtchik: How much is it worth? Perevodtchik: A rouble. Boy: Dost thou want more eggs? Traveller: What eggs? Boy—imitating exactly the cry of a tern: Little ones. Traveller: Are they good to eat? Boy—smacking his lips: *Horoshohoroshô!*

In an hour he was back again with a cap full of terns' and puffins' eggs, and on his knees in front of the tent.

G

I gave him a pair of scissors, which he again submitted to the Linguist's valuation. *Stoyt aneeli polbotelki ?* are they worth half a *botelka ?* Yes, said the little man impatiently: *Oubiraïsa !* be off! I saw the boy afterwards kneeling and endeavouring to cut the long grass with the scissors. I sent for him another day, and he came to kneel as usual at the tent door, chewing a piece of grass between his replies.

Traveller: Thy name? Naughty boy: Lavrenti Petrovitch Balakin. Born? In Kem. Been to school? No. Read or write? No. Go to church? Yes, every Sunday. Why? *Boghou malitsa*—To pray to God. *Kak znayesh Bogha ?* How knowest thou of God? From my father and mother. Dost thou believe in a future life? *Ya vierou posslai smertje shto paydou Boghou*—I believe I shall go to God after death. Did he know good from bad? Yes. His occupation? A fisher. His pay? Only food in return for his work. Would he live here always? He did not know where else to go. What would he do with twenty kopecks? Buy biscuit—no, rum. Had he smoked and drunk for long? Yes. His food? Bread, fish, tea. Had he seen *Anglitschani* before? No. Traveller: What dost thou think of us? Naughty boy: *Nie shto*—Nothing at all.

His body was swaying curiously about as he knelt, and he began to answer at random. He was drunk already. Poor fatherless boy: no one to teach him: no one to show him a good example. Many of the Russians here were the worse for drink. They could buy rum for a shilling and fourpence a bottle, and did so only too freely.

I dressed a fisherman's hand this day, and bequeathed a large roll of diachylon plaster to the *Stanovitsche*. Flesh wounds are frequent among the fishermen, from the use of hooks and knives.

The weather at Seven Islands does not improve, though it changes. The wind goes to the north-west, but still brings sleet and rain. We spend the hours in the little tent, which keeps us famously warm and dry. The Arctic is a dull gray beaten up into white, and the Seven Islands stand coldly and sullenly in it. It rains and blows all through another night, and as we lie awake we hear the moaning of the winter sea.

We have not seen the sun since we encamped here : but the few days spent in this dreary and forlorn spot, with gale, cold, sleet, rain, and the noise of the sea, have been among the very happiest of our lives. We cannot explain why : unless that the Doctor and I in our secret instincts enjoy and appreciate the primitive life of our nomad predecessors who have long since vanished from the earth.

The camp will be struck on the arrival of the *Arkhangelsk*. I saw but two women in the *Stanovitsche* : none stay here : they must have come from the vessels. We pack, of course, I mean the Doctor packs, the fire with turf, which smoulders slowly all through the night in spite of rain or wind. In August 1611 the weather here was tempestuous, foule, cloudie, mystie, snowy, and dismall.

Some little way from our tent I found what seemed to be a Lapp burial-place. The Russian dead have been buried, probably for centuries, on Gossogorou, the

little island which helps to form the harbour.   There the
wooden crosses stand thickly.   When the Lapps came to
this region, it is hard to say : but that they are the original
inhabitants I have little doubt.   On the banks of the
Yokkonga, sixty miles eastward, have been found stone
knives and axe heads.   We find traces of their past strewn
all along this Arctic coast ; but none of a lost civilisation.
I think the Lapps never had any civilisation to lose, but
are very much now what they were when they used their
stone implements in the forests of the Yokkonga.

In form and feature the Russian Lapps vary much
from those of Norway, and from the Samoyedes of
Siberia in Europe, only a hundred miles distant.   Their
average intelligence is far greater, and their features have
but little of the Mongolian type.   Intermixture with the
Russians may have modified the race characteristics
among a large proportion, but the Lapps of pure descent
are distinguished by the same energy and vivacity.   I
should take them, accordingly, for a race distinct from
Norwegian, Lapp, or Samoyede, who much resemble each
other.   They seem to interrupt the links of continuous
relationship extending among the Arctic tribes from the
Atlantic to the Pacific.   Only, their traditions and
religious observances are, or have been, very similar.
Possibly the paucity of reindeer, and the absence of the
accompanying habits of life, may have imparted a necessary energy to these people : and made boatmen and
fishers of them.

Early one morning I was awakened by a loud voice

and the appearance of an ugly face at the tent door. It
was a boy of dirty looks, who greedily and impudently
demanded twenty kopecks. Fancying he must be in
want, I was about to give him money, when he thrust
himself inside, and begged more rudely than before. Then
I told him to go away, and at last he went. So did the
Expedition's *palernik*, omelette pan, and all our eggs:
the former perhaps borrowed to cook the latter. A
Chinaman in San Francisco stole a few yards of indiarubber hose. Its proprietor dragged him all the way
down the street, striking him at intervals, until quite out
of breath. Then the Chinaman turned placidly round
and said: What for? You no likee lend 'um?

One morning when I arrived at the tent, writes the
secretary, Mr. Rae asked me to fry a little salmon. I
therefore ask, If you have taken in the pan, for it was not
outside. No, said Mr. Rae, the pan is outside with the
eggs: you will be kind enough to look. I seek round the
tent, but find nothing. A boy was suspected: I therefore
went out to examine how it be, but find no boy according
to the signal.

I determined to open one of the Lapp graves, and
taking two boys up to the spot, set them to dig.
Though my hopes were raised by the appearance of layer
after layer of stones, we came upon no traces of the
Laplanders. While the boys were digging, my attention
was attracted by a little bird which ran about the moss
within a few feet of us.

It was of the size of a small titlark, snipe-shaped,

having a black bill three-quarters of an inch long, slender
black legs, black eyes, brownish head, snowy breast,
faintly speckled throat, wings speckled like those of the
golden plover, and tail short like a starling's. I could
not hear its note. It ran quietly and seemingly unconcernedly about : often picking up small seeds, or approaching us. At last, within three yards of us, I found its nest :
a simple little hollow on soft moss, with a few dry *maroschka* leaves, and containing two eggs. One was broken
and much incubated, the other entire. This I brought
home. The eggs were slightly over an inch long, brownish
in colour, pointed at one end, and at the other covered with
close brown blotches.

I supposed the bird to be the little stint, not before
known to breed in Russian Lapland. The bird made one
or two quick little runs towards the nest whence I had
taken the egg : finally snatching up one-half of the
broken egg and flying off with it. Afterwards it carried
off the remainder—whether to clean the nest or to save
the egg from us, was not clear. I sent the egg to Henry
Seebohm, author of that pleasant book, *Siberia in Europe*,
who confirmed my opinion.

The little stint, he says, seems a very quiet bird at
the nest—quite different from Temminck's stint. When
you awake a colony of the latter birds, they fly wildly
round and round, crying vociferously or hovering in the
air trilling. We saw none of these habits in the little stint.
Its eggs can hardly be mistaken for those of Temminck's
stint, but are in every respect miniature dunlin's eggs.

The average size of the twenty eggs we obtained of the little stint is about $1\frac{1}{16} \times \frac{3}{4}$ inch—a trifle smaller than the eggs of Temminck's stint. The ground colour varies from pale greenish-gray to pale brown. The spots and blotches are rich brown, generally large, and sometimes confluent at the large end.

It rains and blows again : our tent has withstood for several days and nights gales, rain, squalls, and snow, in turns. Not a dry or quiet hour has there been at Siem Ostrova. The wind moves from the east to the south, but does not improve the temperature. All winds are cold on this coast. The north wind comes from the polar ice : the east wind from the Kara Sea, Siberia, and the Ourâl : the south from the White Sea, the half-frozen lakes and the *tûndras* behind us : the west from the snow-covered fjelds of Norway.

In the afternoon a boy, one of my excavators, came to say that there were persons who knew where our *palernik* was : and that they wanted twenty-five kopecks for the information. I set out with the boy, and he drew the omelette pan from behind some rocks, a short distance from the camp. This was the only instance of theft that we have met with among the Russian peasants. It may have been only spite.

In the night the Perevodtchik came running up, shouting *Parahod!* steamer! In ten minutes the tent was struck : rugs, quilts, boxes, and fifty other things were packed up : and men were carrying them down to the Expedition's gig, which lay afloat in readiness. In half-an-hour after the *Arkhangelsk* was sighted we were afloat in one boat, and the Perevodtchik and the baggage in another. The worthy Dane, Captain Braun, welcomed us and had our boat slung up on deck.

We nearly had to deplore the loss of our baggage and the Perevodtchik, who persisted in hanging so closely to the *Arkhangelsk's* gangway ladder, that at every roll of the steamer our gig was swept under it by the swell: and thrice the gunwale was under water. We roared to him to let the boat fall astern, and eventually secured him and the baggage. We were soon off to sea, and saw the last of the friendly little *Stanovitsche*.

It is very shameful that the poor Mûrmansk fishermen should be deprived of all medical assistance. The captain told me he feared a doctor sent here would infallibly take to drinking. I said he might be kept on board the steamer, and travel backwards and forwards among the fishing stations. It is hard that not even an apothecary's assistant can be found on these thirteen hundred miles of coast between Vardö and Archangel. A poor sick or wounded fisherman, if he would save his life, must sacrifice the bulk of the earnings which should keep his family from hunger in the winter months, and travel to the hospital in Archangel.

An inspector was appointed two years since to report on the matter. After enjoying himself for a month at Tiribirka, this gentleman returned to Archangel to draw out a report, and his pay. Captain Braun sees many cruel cases of suffering here.

As we dined, it occurred to us that on that day a very agreeable event was taking place at the Doctor's home : and after dinner I rose, and had the happiness of making a speech in broken Russian in honour of the good friend whose wedding day it was. At breakfast time we rounded the Holy Cape, and steamed into the White Sea.

At this cape lyeth a great stone, to which the Barkes that passed thereby were wont to make offerings of Butter, Meale, and other Victuals, thinking that vnlesse they did so, their Barkes or Vessels should there perish : and there it is very darke and mystie.

The Lapp witches of the Yokkonga used to frequent the promontory to assist in the worship of the Paata of the Holy Cape : and they would sell a fair wind to the English sailors who traded to the White Sea. ·

This was a wide-spread superstition. In the Capitularies of Charlemagne at Aix-la-Chapelle were penalties against *tempestarii*, such as raise storms and tempests : in the ancient Norwegian statutes were similar provisions. An Icelandic chronicle relates how the Bishop of Skalholt allayed a storm with holy water. Mela tells how on the Iles de Sein, off the Brittany coast, lived priestesses who had the winds and tempests at their disposal.

We passed Tri Ostrova at noon on a beautiful sunny day. Von Baer, the naturalist, after his visit to Novaya Zemlia, was by thick fog driven into Tri Ostrova. Dreary and desolate as these shores had seemed on his northward journey, he was now charmed with their green slopes.

A boat's crew from the *Amitie*, abandoned on Novaya

Zemlia in 1611, reached Kânin Nôs, and boldly crossed the White Sea. Hauing a good north-east wind wee set forward in the name of God, and when the sunne was north-west wee passed the point, and all that night and the next day sayled with a good wind, and all that time rowed. The next night, after ensuing, having still a good wind, in the morning about the east-north-east sunne, wee saw land on the west side of the White Sea, which wee found by the rushing of the sea vpon the land before wee saw it: and perceiving it to be full of clifts and not low sandie ground with some hills, as it is on the east side of the White Sea, we assured ourselves that we were upon the west side of the White Sea, vpon the coast of Lapland : for the which we thanked God that He had helped vs to sayle ouer the White Sea in thirtie houres.

Late in the day the good captain stopped the *Arkhangelsk* off Karabelni Nôs, and we embarked with our effects in the family canoe. The Perevodtchik's heart failed him when he saw our skiff afloat. We left the steamer, he writes, in a poor boat: all on board the steamer said we had too much luggage, and that we could not reach shore : but we pushed off and commenced rowing towards the shore, which we also were happy to reach. The Perevodtchik rowed, the Doctor sat in the bow, with an umbrella hoisted as a sail, and I wielded a paddle in the stern. The wind rose and began to blow very stiffly, and the boat to leak freely: but we came in this way into still water behind a reef of rocks, and so into the mouth of the Ponoi river.

CHAPTER VIII.

THE coast consisted of undulating tableland or *tûndra*, with patches of snow, rising from the sea a hundred feet or more. We were on the extremity of Karabelni Nôs, and saw before us a majestic stream, a mile and a quarter in width. Granite cliffs rose abruptly from the water's edge to a considerable height: and between them the great stream of the Ponoi, reinforced by the ebb-tide, was pouring down at the rate of four miles an hour. Accordingly, we rounded a reef of rocks and drew the boat up. The *Arkhangelsk* had disappeared on the horizon, and we were outcasts on a strange shore.

Seeing some human beings on the cliff, the Linguist and I hastened towards them to ask for rowers. As we approached they retired, and finally we had to run over the *tûndra* to come up with them. They were three boys, who seemed to come from nowhere and to know nothing: so we returned to the boat. On the cliff stood a few

wooden crosses : beside them a lonely grave.   Some poor
mariner cast up by the sea, sleeping where the Ponoi rolls
past, the winds always blow, and the snow always lies.

We gathered some driftwood, found a cleft in the
rocks to shelter us and the fire : then made ourselves as
comfortable as we could, intending to await the flood-tide.
Here we were, on the dreary Terski coast, stranded between the White Sea and the ebbing river, with only the
fire and our provisions to cheer us.   While in the middle
of a comfortable meal, we sighted a boat making for the
sea, borne fast by tide, stream, and wind.   We sent the
Perevodtchik to make violent signals with an open
umbrella : and at last, attracted by our boat, fire, and
umbrella, the stranger came sailing straight to Karabelni
Nôs where we were.   A handsome young Russian and a
boy were on their way out to the salmon fishery, which
extends from the river's mouth some miles to the north
and south of it.   The salmon, travelling from river to
river, keep of course to the coast, and here the Ponoi
fishers snare them.

The young Russian agreed to await slack water and
help us as far as Lachta, a *navolok* three miles, or more,
up the stream.   After some hours we set forth, towing,
poling, rowing—with much difficulty and little progress.
Three hours later we found ourselves aground on a stony
bank in the middle of the river, half-a-mile from either
side.   The Doctor and I, wearing fishing-boots reaching
to our hips, attempted to walk on shore.   Within a
hundred yards of the right bank we found the water

deepen : a false step would have taken us into a violent current and deep water. It seemed absurd, in the lonely night, to be walking about in the Ponoi river, far from our boat, with the tide very near the turn. Signalling for the boat, we got across, and walked to a bay on the river, where we found the huts of Lachta, and numerous boats on the sands.

Every human being came out of bed to stare at us. We looked into the huts : they were uninhabitable — swarming with human beings, sleeping like cattle together. It was impossible to spend the night here, and only with difficulty we found a boatman to take us to Ponoi. We told him that if he would only get ready quickly, we would make him a present of our boat.

We left our pleasant young Russian roubles enough to make his face light up, and set out for Ponoi, sheltered from the piercing cold of the night by quilts and rugs. We saw a merlin, then a golden eagle : and on an overhanging cliff the nest of a *kanyúk*, or sparrow-hawk. We were many hours in the boat, and left it, with the double object of lightening it and warming ourselves. The banks were fringed with towering ice-blocks and boulders : the great cliff sloped, wall-like, almost perpendicularly behind them. It was impossible to walk on or beneath the ice: and we scaled the cliff, only with exhausting efforts, and found ourselves on the wide lonely *túndra*.

So lonely it was, that even the lonely river seemed more genial. No bird, or animal, or human being could we see : and it seemed as if the Doctor and I were the last creatures in a deserted world. From the upper edge of the cliff projected frozen snow, like eaves, which only waited for a confiding and inquisitive traveller, to crash down into the river. At times we crossed ravines upon a hollow snow-crust, under which we could hear running water. We saw our boat below—an atom floating on the broad stream. A few hundred yards away from this great sunken river one would not know of its existence. It was the grandest river I had seen. We seemed reduced to the importance of insects. At last we found a zigzag sheep-track, and, beneath us, the rough gray roofs of Ponoi village.

Ponoi lies on a platform left when the original convulsion split the *tûndra*, and the two great cliffs formed and fell apart. On the grassy bank stood a few dozen unpainted wooden log houses and huts, and two churches with green cupolas and belfries. The boat, with the Perevodtchik and other luxuries, had just reached the bank, where logs of timber and a few boats were lying. We walked, on a rough planked way, to a large new wooden building : the house of the merchant Sabotchakoff. This gentleman, like Savin on the Arctic and Karelian coasts, sells to the fishermen and Lapps, at enormous prices, stores and necessaries.

We were taken into a small close room, with a stove and double windows : where we found our host's nephew, a hard-faced individual, with a loud voice. He was a gentleman with a simplicity of manners amounting to the grossest rudeness, hurling rough and impertinent

THE RIVER PONOI.

questions at us, like the wolf who insisted upon picking a quarrel with the lamb. As this wretched human being's house was necessary to us, we determined to wear him out by innocent candour.

Host, roaring as though he took us to be deaf: Where do you come from? Traveller: From Lachta. How did you get to Lachta? By boat. Host, irritably: Of course: but from where? From Karabelni Nôs. Host: From where, before that? and so on for half-an-hour. Host: Where are you going to? Traveller: Up the Ponoi. Host: You can't. Traveller: Oh. Host: There are rapids. Traveller, getting tired: Don't understand. Host: Waterfalls. Traveller: How much does that cost? Host, in a voice like a cataract: I said waterfalls! Traveller: How many people are there in Ponoi? Host, keeping to the point: Why are you going up the Ponoi? Traveller: Who told you that? Host: Why do you want to go up the Ponoi? Traveller: I don't understand. Host, brutally: You do understand. Traveller, pleasantly: Can we have some milk? Host, beside himself: What the *Sataoui* do you want on this river? Traveller, beginning to unpack: We have plenty of biscuit.

I thought we should never get rid of this inquisitive boor: but we fairly wore him out, and he went away cursing our stupidity. He seemed to fear we had come to prospect for timber and minerals, or to compete with him in plundering the poor fishermen. Mercifully, he was called away for a week: and we never saw, nor hope to see, him again.

We spent an entire day in Ponoi, endeavouring by direct, and indirect or corrupt means, to engage a crew to explore the river with us.   None had ascended the river, and, like the unknown elsewhere, it was taken to be terrible.   Once get an idea of danger into these Russian peasants' heads, and you cannot get it out if you cut them in pieces.   An active obliging man, promising fairly in the morning, and undertaking to collect a crew, comes in the afternoon very drunk on prospective credit of our pay. I went from hut to hut negotiating for boatmen, and incidentally amassing old silver crosses.

At length importunity and subsidy secured us a crew. One lovely summer evening we embarked, in two boats, having abandoned the secretary and much of our baggage, with detailed instructions for their return to Norway in the event of our failing to reappear after a given number of days.   We pushed out on to the broad stream : and after paddling for a short way, the ascent had to be made by towing.

We are sitting side by side in a frail skiff, warmly covered up : one handsome young boatman is staggering at the tow-rope, over huge stones, and under ice and boulders : another is poling in the stern of the boat.   Our baggage is in a second boat far astern.   It is midnight. The soft northern sunlight lingers on the top of the great purple cliffs which close in the river.   Rosy flame dwells upon the snow.   The banks are lined, above the boulders, with ice—huge uncouth masses twenty feet high—heaped on either bank when the winter ice broke up.   The great stream is in half shade, but glances in reflection of the light above.   Three or four hundred feet, steep as Dover cliffs, tower the great banks on either side of us.   The stream is over a thousand yards broad.   Two lazy Lapps propel our second *lodka :* and we wait at intervals for them.   One Lapp is drunk : but as we forbade *vodka* in either boat, he will improve.

The current is strong, and we progress but slowly. The Doctor thinks—or, what is equivalent, smokes : while I scribble.   We are afloat on the mighty Ponoi, the mysterious river, almost uninhabited, and unknown.   The Lapps who in winter time frequent its banks abandon it in the summer : and from Ponoi to Kamensky there lives scarcely a human being.   The fishing seasons are uncertain, and the yields precarious : so the few Lapps of Kamensky alone inhabit in summer the Upper Ponoi.   The river freezes, of course, completely over, and the ice extends far out into the White Sea.   The ice above will be fatal to our chance of ascent : leaving no foothold between it and the strong current, for towing.   We have brought one musical box with us which plays, '*Way down upon the Ponoi River.*   This cheers us, and reminds us of the family plantations and of the old folks at home.   Salmon leap constantly near the boat—small fish of perhaps three pounds' weight.

We went on for some hours.   At one halting-place I asked how many days' bread they had.   One loaf each. *Slûshetye niviertsi !*   But listen, you idolaters ! I cried : I told you we were going for many days.   How far can

you go with a loaf each? Two days' journey. Can
you get any on the river? No. How far can we go in
two days? Yevsie Feôdoroff Matrokin: To the cataract.
Traveller: And what will you do beyond the cataract?
Erasim Filippoff Andreanoff: Nothing. Traveller: How
do you mean? Artimon Kapidonoff Gubuntzov: We are
not going beyond the cataract—the boat can't go. Traveller: We can drag the boat overland. Vassili Dimitrieff
Kariloff: *Spassibogh!* Thanks—forty men might do it.
Traveller: How many hours from here to the cataract?:
Artimon Kapidonoff Gubuntzov, Yevsie Feôdoroff Matrokin,
Vassili Dimitrieff Kariloff, and Erasim Filippoff Andreanoff,
together: Nine hours. Traveller: Mnyeh!

Truly there is much that is mysterious about the
Ponoi. We would have given these sulky, stupid boatmen
in a few days more than they would have earned all
summer through. We don't like sulky, discontented people
about us: they oppress our freedom of thought. Under
the circumstances, I sent one boat back to Ponoi, with
sealed directions in Norwegian for the Perevodtchik. This
morning at four o'clock, writes the zealous little man—to
whom, to do him justice, day and night were alike: two
men came back with the luggage and letter from Mr.
Rae, saying that I should procure men and a boat to take
us to Kouzomen: could I not get here, then I ought to
go to Lakta. I immediately departed from Ponoi in order
to hire a boat.

Only a day before, a post-boat sailed from Ponoi for
Kouzomen. Sometimes one does not go for two or three

months. The men said one would go again soon. But the Russian soon is not sudden enough for us.

These boatmen devoured their black bread without a spasm of conscience : crossing themselves before tasting it : like a Russian in the cathedral at Moscow, who was seen crossing himself devoutly with one hand and picking his neighbour's pocket with the other. The remaining boatmen chatted pleasantly with us. Six months ago they paid for bread a shilling and ninepence a *poud*—40 lbs. Now they paid half-a-crown. Within eighteen months Russia was for the first time in her history importing wheat : and bread cost in St. Petersburg itself over four shillings a *poud*. In Ponoi no meat or fish, tea or sugar, can be bought : only salt-fish, salt reindeer-flesh, and *vodka*.

We saw a nest of a *kanyûk*, sparrowhawk, round which the parent birds were curiously swooping, attended by a small bird. Then we came upon a rough-legged buzzard teased by two ravens, who were hoarsely threatening him. Then a solitary black crow went down the river on some matter of business, and strings of geese flew overhead. Salmon leapt more frequently.

Above us, on the brink of the cliff, was a ledge of snow, pure white against the sky, ready to fall into the river on the first warm day. Huge blocks of ice lined the shore, blue and white, or brown with sand. A few versts higher, the river winds, so that we might be in a land-locked Norway fiord. Stopping for supper, we shared our chocolate with the men, who pressed upon us in return some excellent black bread. We went on shore, and

I found the *Ranunculus 'Lapponicus* and the cinquefoil.
Artimon Kapidonoff returned with a handful of wild
onions. As in the Tûloma, we found gold-like glittering
particles of mica in the sand. We heard the cuckoo constantly here and on the Tûloma. The *kukavka* comes
here in the early summer—not in great numbers, however.

The river still winds, always deep between the cliffs.
We took soundings at one point. The stream measured four
hundred yards across. For three hundred and fifty yards
of its width the soundings averaged four feet, for the last
fifty yards eight feet. Ten feet was the greatest depth.
The current ran at three miles an hour: the volume of water
was consequently about seventy thousand tons a minute.
We stopped near some floating timber, and went on shore.

There was a little camp of the raftsmen. Six
tchouma had stood here: but there were only two now.
Each was a conical birch-bark tent: a heap of ashes lay in
the centre, and five people would sleep in one, the boatman
said. A rough pillow and a heap of reindeer skins lay on
one side. There was a copper pot containing a small
flounder and a handkerchief with salt. These objects
Artimon Kapidonoff carried off. At Kamensky, near the
head of the river, grows timber of a considerable size,
which is cut and floated down the river. The largest
trees I found here measured eleven inches in diameter.

Artimon wears a white linen jacket and rarely
anything on his head, while we are shivering in pilot
jackets, fishing boots to our hips, and Lapp *shapkas*.
The *shapka* is the softest and most delightful head-dress

SUPPER ON THE PONOI RIVER.

possible : made of dark-blue cloth, decorated with patch-
work of red and yellow cloth and beadwork, having a
border of reindeer fur, and lined with soft wolf-skin
which stands in a fringe close round the face and over the
eyes, making one feel rather like a Skye terrier.

We poled, and pulled, up numerous rapids : at length
we came to a broad sweep of the river, lined with solid
ice, and here we drew the boat up.   Artimon found a
floating tree nine inches thick, and cut through it with a
small axe as quickly as if it were sugar-cane.   Then he
shaved off some thin pieces to use as tinder : while Vassili
Dimitrieff thrust a pole into the ground to carry the borrowed copper pot which he previously scoured with sand.
The Doctor armed himself with an axe, rubbing his hands
at the prospect of a fire.   Then he photographed the rest of
us, seated beneath the blocks of ice.   We had a comfortable supper on the lonely Ponoi at six in the morning.

The ice lay curiously.   The edge of the crust stood
out a straight layer a foot and a half thick, fifteen feet
above the river's present level.   On this layer stood a bed
of snow, which had fallen when the river ice was only
fifteen inches thick, and frozen on it.   Beneath the crust
was solid pack ice.   While the Russians had fish and
bread, we had devilled biscuits and pâté de foie gras :
our relish for the latter being impaired by a solitary goose
which flew round and overhead, croaking dismally as if
he had a presentiment of what we were eating.

We could hear the heavy roar of the fall, hidden from
us by a bend of the river.   It was a wild, impressive scene.

At the foot of the cliffs clung a shelf of ice twenty feet
thick. The Ponoi ran at our feet, brown, and broken by
the fall: a few trunks of fir lay stranded on the beach.
We pushed on to the formidable cataract. The Ponoi
ran swiftly in a bed two hundred yards broad, the same
steep bank towering on either side. The river burst
through huge boulders: and masses of ice thirty feet thick
lay piled up by the torrent's edge.

It was a fine scene—an Arctic river. The descent is
not nearly so dangerous, to all appearances, as that of the
Muonio-koski in Swedish Lapland: but the difficulty of
ascent is greater. In the case of the latter cataract the
boat is dragged through the woods: here nothing short
of strong tackle could haul a boat up the cliff's face:
and from Ponoi to the falls there is not a single ravine
up which a boat could be taken. The Ponoi shuts itself
up in its wide gorge. Of course, it could be done—like
most other things: but the absence of supplies on the
higher river makes the ascent, to ordinary intents and
purposes, impracticable.

We clambered about the ice blocks for some time,
and then paddled away down the stream. When in sight
of Ponoi, we turned aside to examine a net belonging to
Artimon Kapidonoff. One poor little salmon trout was
caught in it. Will you sell it? I asked Artimon. No,
he said shortly. Why not? I asked. *Ya tibia dayou*,
I give it to you, he said. Shall I do whatever I like
with it? Certainly, said Artimon. I took the salmon
trout and flung it into the river. Artimon Kapidonoff

ICE ON THE PONOI RIVER.   BELOW THE FIRST CATARACT.

looked at me for a moment, and said nothing. Two days afterwards he came to me and asked: Why did you throw the fish away? To save its life, I said. Oh, said Artimon: I thought it was from superstition.

Once back in Ponoi in our room overlooking the river, we set to work to engage a crew for the voyage round the Terski coast. Our boatmen said in the village that they had been generously treated: and we found less trouble accordingly. The *Starschina*, too, in consequence of my slipping rouble notes into his hand at intervals, and giving him knives and pairs of scissors for his wife, was devoted to us. Still it was very very slow. A man would come in the morning, and promise to do something, or to get somebody else to do something: then would come at noon and say he had changed his mind. I have spent ten hours in a day talking to a succession of these tiresome imbeciles without tasting food.

Every visitor, whether he came to terms or not, used to shake hands with me whenever he came, or went, or promised, or received anything: and I used to be much worn out and soiled after a day's work of this kind. By midnight on the third day at Ponoi, we had, after innumerable negotiations and arguments, engaged a crew, and solemnly bound them by contract. The *Pravlennik*, a tall, dark, needy-looking man, prepared the bond.

CONTRACT AT PONOI.

1879, *June* 14*th*.—We, the following peasants, Pavel

Ivanovitch Dosegitch, Nikolai Kuzintzoff, Artimon Gubunt-
zoff, Yevsie Matrochin, Filip Afanasievitch Iekaterinoff, have
concluded the following contract with the English subject
Edward Rae :—That we have agreed to take him to
Kouzomen by boat, past Pjâlitsa, for fifteen roubles each.
And if we should take him well, then the same English
subject will add five roubles for each.   From Piâlitsa to
Kouzomen, if we do not wish to go farther, the same English subject will be bound to pay the smaller sum agreed,
and will not be hard upon us.   Herewith it is promised
that the engaged men will not, after bringing the same
Edward Rae to the before-mentioned places, have any
further claim upon him.

The marks of the five peasants, they being illiterate,
affixed in the presence of me,

Pravlennik GREGORI DOLILOFF.

Subscribed with my own hand at Ponoi.

EDWARD RAE.

A few recruits were taken even from Ponoi for the
Turkish war.   The captain of the *Curfew* told us the son
of the ship's stevedore in Archangel was drawn for service.
Alexander catch him : as the father expressed it.   We
bought some Lapp mittens from a poor old woman in
Ponoi : and as we gave her more than she asked, she went
off to the church to return thanks and to pray for us.

In the winter Ponoi is covered up to its chimneys in
snow, and sledges travel unconsciously over the roofs of

the buried village.   So do the wolves, who abound on the high *tûndras* of the Ponoi, and come, desperate, poor animals, with hunger and cold, in search of food.   They are often seen in the village, and carry off reindeer.   No one but myself seems to extend any sympathy to the wolf.   Having been intimate with a wolf, and enjoyed what I am sure was his strong affectionate instinct for me, I speak with sincerity of him.   Not long since a Russian peasant was acquitted who, to save his own life, had thrown from his sledge his children one by one to a pack of wolves. The Doctor and I do not care for wolves in packs : they lose their individuality,

In good weather the natives dig themselves out again, to be buried once more by the next fall of snow.   The reindeer are turned loose now : to return in the autumn with their calves.   Sheep are fed in the winter upon pine bark.   The timber about Kamensky is cut by the Ponoi people, who travel up in the winter, and go fishing on the coast during the summer.   The best timber lies fifty versts below Kamensky : the logs varying from thirty to forty feet in length, and sometimes reaching twenty-five inches in diameter.   The lake of Sergosero, near Kamensky, has salmon, perch, trout, and pike.

Lunelsky has about thirty Lapps in the winter.   Several families of Lapps live in Ponoi, and about a hundred pass through in September on their way from the fisheries. I was told here that on the upper river were many *beboor*.   This would be interesting if we could find any one who would tell us what a *beboor* is, and what it principally lives upon. The Doctor thinks it may be a hippocampus or a mormylus.

Several sick people came for advice and medicine. Even a herb doctor would be a Providence here. Vaccination was introduced with difficulty into the Russian provinces: I quote from a Russian author. One would think that vaccination was a simple thing. The *Tchinovnik*, or official, would go for the doctor. They would lay out all the instruments—a turning-lathe, different saws, bores, anvils, and knives as large as if they were going to cut up an ox. Next day, when all the old women and children were assembled, all these tools were set going: the knives were ground, the lathe squeaked, while the children screamed and the old women groaned. Then the *Tchinovnik* would accept from each, a couple of roubles as the price of exemption.

The Ponoi fishermen catch seal, walrus, and salmon. When there is abundance of fish they work steadily: but otherwise will settle down to drink. A man may earn in a whole season not more than thirty or forty roubles: with good fortune he may gain three roubles in a day.

There are a hundred and fifty people here. Their chief complaints are from intemperance and bad habits: disease in the bones is prevalent. Occasionally a native lives to the age of eighty: but rarely. The priest spends the summer in salmon-fishing near Lachta. The people go regularly enough to the church.

The people of Ponoi, generally speaking, are poor, and terribly drunken. There seemed to be a drunken man in

every second house. The *Tiflis Gazette* of July 29, 1880,
states : Nineteen members of the sect of milk-drinking
Sabbatarians arrived at Tiflis with their families under
military escort : the adult males being in chains. The
sectarians state that they were condemned by the Kazan
Tribunal to deportation on account of their having sought
to disseminate their doctrines.

This last paragraph does not require italics. In fact,
the stronger a sentence is, the less it needs the weak
emphasis of underlining. The dialect of the Russians of
Ponoi is peculiar. Many of the villagers came to see us
leave. Several kissed our hands in thanks and muttered
a prayer as they said good-bye—not an ordinary Russian
custom, in our experience. Then they stood on the bank
and cried *Tchas slivui poot !*—A fortunate journey.

One golden midnight we pushed out on to the great
stream gliding silently down to the sea. We paddled
away, close under one cliff. The ice had dwindled away
since our voyage up : it was melting fast. The dark
igneous rocks were wet : and the water, dripping from
every snowdrift, splashed over delicate green ferns, moss,
and lichens. We saw a very beautiful waterfall, a hundred feet high. A brown eagle flew overhead : then a
vulture : then eider ducks paddled out of our track. The
cliff grew more abrupt. We passed a frozen waterfall,
which, like an undermined flying buttress, was sliding
bodily from its hold on the rock. The wind blew straight
against us : it could not have come much more direct
unless it had been blown through a tube. Burst and

shivered rocks were ready to fall—split by the irresistible
action of frost.

Yevsie, one of our boatmen, was a Lapp of Yokkonga, the *pogost* lying fifty miles to the north-west of
Ponoi. There are two hundred Yokkongski Lapps: their
dialect is distinct. The dialects of the Kola Lapps are
three: that of the Ponoi and Yokkonga: that of Karlovka, Lôvosero, Voronsky, Kildina, Maselsid: and that
of Petschenga, Mutka, Yekostrova, Babinsky, Nuotosero.
The dialect of one group is not easily comprehended by
another. The Yokkonga rises in the Peninsula's almond-
shaped central plateau—sixty miles long by ten wide—
which is the watershed of all the chief rivers. For this
reason all the rivers having an equal descent are alike
difficult to ascend. Yevsie knew two hundred versts of
the Yokkonga. He described it as a fine stream, as broad
as the Ponoi, and containing much salmon: running
through several lakes and having many rapids. He never
heard of stone knives among his people.

Yevsie had spent, until the last three years, the whole
of his life at Yokkonga. There are about eight *isboushki*
or wooden huts, a small church, and forty *gamme*—some
built of old boats. The pinewood used in the *pogost* is
cut a hundred and fifty versts away: birch-trees grow
close at hand. The Yokkonga Lapps own a few hundred
reindeer, which they use with *sâni*, sledges, like those of the
Norwegian Lapps. The priest of Ponoi visits Yokkonga
once in a year: in the winter, when the snow makes travel
easier. The Lapps get their bread from the Russian

Edw Pae 1881

A LAPP BUNTING ON THE SNOW.

traders on the coast in exchange for fish. They drink and smoke much. Curiously enough, among our crew of four Lapps and Russians, only one smoked.

I asked Yevsie for a Lapp proverb. After some thought he said in Russian: *Svoyevo narodou skarey vierout.* One trusts most among one's own people. Afterwards he said in Lapp: *Aktierro sonli pweram tattili yennik kidki wala.* One available kopeck is better than much money one cannot have.

The Laplanders are a nation of a very confined intellect, live mostly in places apart from others, and are not enlightened.—Extract from the Perevodtchik's *Day-book round the bay of Hvidsö (White Sea).*

We reached Lachta, and went to the log-hut of Vassili Feodoroff Makaroff, agent of the merchant Sabotchakoff. He assured us he could not spare his *yolle* for the voyage: that he couldn't trust her with our crew: that he couldn't spare his own men, and so on. We perseveringly met and combated all his objections, among other things offering to buy the boat: and he seemed amused by our pertinacity. At last we diplomatically asked him for coffee, and this awakened a cordial feeling. He agreed to take a fair sum—fifty roubles, I think—for the hire of the boat: and of this we must have recovered at least two roubles and a half by ravages among Makaroff's Russian sweetmeats. A Dutchman in New York took a friend to breakfast at a restaurant, and when he received his bill he came out storming at the landlord. My vrendt, said his companion: do not get angry. Got is goot. De man is boonished already : I have my bocket full mit sboons.

Lachta is deserted in the winter : and is merely a summer station for the fishers.   It stands, like Ponoi, on the southern bank of the river.   A fishing boat came in, and for a rouble we bought a number of beautiful fish. The annual production of train-oil on the Terski coast is, so Ivan Abramovitch told me, ten thousand *poudov*, or 400,000 lbs.   Northward from the Ponoi mouth are found large quantities of haddock, cod, flounder : and southward, salmon, very abundantly.   Our crew was reinforced by Makaroff's skipper and a *mousse*.

We drifted away from Lachta, without wind, as the tide was falling.   Ere we reached the river's mouth, the wind sprang up, and the *yolle*, a small open cutter, flew out of the river, and scudded down the Terski coast of the White Sea Peninsula.

CHAPTER IX.

The last of the Ponoi—The White Sea coast—Lapp costumes—A storm—
A harbour of refuge—Terski Villages—Matthias Alexander Castern—A
dispute—The Terski fisheries—The Terski rivers.

WE left the broad Ponoi, on whose stream we had navi-
gated for four days : passing Karabelni Nôs, where we had
landed as castaways.   The wind, as we had calculated,
went round to the north-east, and freshened rapidly, while
the *yolle* flew through the water.   The shore gradually
became sloping *tûndra*, bare of trees, and almost bare of
snow : in colour, dull greenish brown, and scarcely undulating.   We coasted along : keeping a few versts out from
land.

We had seen water-casks, anchor, ballast, fuel, fish,
stores, etc., put carefully on board.   Russian mariners do not
trouble. themselves much about such things till they find
the want of them.   Also a half cask for our morning tub,
we had secured with especial difficulty : and the poles for
a temporary *tchoum*, in which the Doctor and I could
reside if storm-bound.   We had sent our own tent home-
ward by the *Arkhangelsk*, to economise transport over
land.

In six hours after leaving the Ponoi we sighted Sosnov-ka, and in two hours more came abreast of the island, and crossed the polar circle. Forty miles from the Ponoi—that is, south of Sosnôvets or Fir Island—we found the northern limit of trees, dull dark patches of fir. This line, or tree border, runs north-west with a curving line through the heart of the Peninsula, to the north of the water-shed lying between Imandra lake and Kola. It divides the Peninsula into two very equal parts—the forests practi-cally abounding on the southern side of the water-shed only.

The White Sea is gray, and beginning to rise : the change of tide will raise it. At Sosnôvets the tide runs north for five hours' ebb, and south for five hours of flood, at a maximum speed of two and a half knots : the extreme rise or fall of tide here is seventeen feet. Beyond Sosnôvets and Piâlitsa—that is, within the throat of the White Sea—the rise or fall is six feet, and the speed is only half a knot.

Beyond the White Sea, thirty-five miles away, lies Zolotitsa—the golden village—on the *Zimni Bérek*, or Winter Coast. Here the Mezén fishers begin their walrus and seal catching at the end of January. The fishermen here talk, not by the time or the hour, but by the tide. So many tides ago : or, at high water : or, at the begin-ning of the flood. In the long winter the White Sea is covered with an unsightly and fearful mass of drifting ice : surging up against the coasts with the flood, and out to sea again with the ebb.

Edw Rae 1881

A LAPLANDER IN SUMMER DRESS.

Our little *kayûta* is comfortably arranged, and we lounge there—writing, sleeping, or watching the sea and the shore. Artimon is busy with an awl, soling one of his boots in a neat and clever way, while he makes Stepan Gregorivitch Potkoff, who acts as *pôvernik*—that is, *mousse*, cook's boy, or galley-slave—laugh almost to suffocation. Yekim Afanasievitch and Yevsie Feôdoroff, the Yokkonga Lapp, are a heap of boots and yellow homespun in the bottom of the boat.

Rain clouds swept heavily over sea and land, and the wind fell. We wear Lapp *shâpkas*, which we bought in Ponoi : mittens, very thick and warm, woven by the Lapps of Ponoi, and only inconvenient for fumbling in a pocket, taking dust out of the eye, or for buttoning a coat. Then the mittens must come off. The Lapps in winter wear, besides the *shapka* and *rûkâvitsi* or gloves, a fur *mâlitsa* or long robe, and loose boots. In the summer they have a homespun tunic, with a belt holding a knife : and peaked boots bound tightly round the ankles with parti-coloured cord.

The women wear head-dresses very similar to those of the men in the winter, and like those of the Norwegian Lapp women in the summer. They wear boots like the men in all seasons. In summer, dark-blue cloth dresses, decorated with bright colours at the breast, and in winter reindeer skin *mâlitsi* bound round the waist. The babies are strapped into their cradles, like small mummies, or Indian papooses. This keeps their little hands from mischief : and in the summer season the defenceless baby

I

attracts the mosquito, which would otherwise annoy the parents.

How little man needs. We are here squatting under a round-topped canvas roof, measuring six feet square, and a yard and a quarter in height, in the stern of a small open boat. We have something soft to lie upon : consolidated German army soup, black bread, fish, and tea, for food : it rains thickly and threatens to blow heavily : but we are as happy as the day is long. The white man has too many luxuries at home. The sweet smell of the silver-birch fire comes from the bow of the boat. Yekim Afanasievitch and the *póvernik* are cooking fish-soup for the ship's company.

At eight o'clock in the night we passed Poulonga : it came on to blow, and at half-past nine, by the Doctor's watch and chain, we were abreast of Piâlitsa. We had run in twelve hours a hundred and twenty versts—at the rate, that is, of six and a half miles an hour. Then the barometer dropped suddenly, and it blew a gale. The sky became dark, and it was drenching wet.

We drove on through the storm, which howled frightfully. In two hours we ran nearly twenty miles, which in an open boat is considerable. Drenched and cold, we swept along over huge waves, with a double-reefed mainsail: amid hoarse blasts of the North-East wind, which shook the heavens, and seemed as if they would strip the sea of all floating things and blow them into space. We attempted to run in closer under the shore, but a heavy surf kept us out.

Purchas' poor pilgrims were no better off. The thirteenth day of September, the sunne being south, there began a great storme to below out of the south-south-west, the weather being mistie, melancholy, and snowie, and the storme increasing more and more.

A storm becomes more solemn and impressive when you watch it from a small boat, which an instant's carelessness would destroy. We know the sound of a White Sea gale : it is unlike other gales, seems not to know its own mind for many hours together, and has paroxysms which would give it an honourable place among hurricanes. At three in the morning we found deep water in a small bay called Moski, ten miles east of Tétrina : and here we dropped two anchors and rested. Westward of Piâlitsa the coast rises, having an outline of rounded, wooded hills, and a level beach. I told the men to take the boat elsewhere as soon as the tide began to ebb : then we slept. When we awoke we were riding with two anchors in the little *navolok* of Tétrina.

It is a small village, down by the shore, with about sixty gray wooden houses and huts, a white painted church, and three hundred and fifty inhabitants. In the afternoon a *moujik* ventured his life in a small boat to come alongside and merely put the eternal questions—*Otkouda vui eedyotai? Vui kto ? Gdyai vui eedyotai ! Zatchem vui eedyotai !* Whence come you ? Who are you ? Whither go you ? What do you go for ?

I have a new silver watch which causes me much thought and computation when I have to consult it. The minute hand works by the hour, and goes regularly round : the hour hand is governed by no laws of rotation, or by any fixed astronomical principle.   Thus, while the minute hand steadily runs through the twelve hours, and keeps fairly enough the apparent time at Greenwich: the hour hand occupies either eleven or thirteen hours for the equivalent, according to its convenience—and generally points midway between two hours.   I bought it for this journey : and it is not unlikely to pass into the Pere-vodtchik's possession at the end of it, if he conducts, not us, for the poor little man can't do that, but himself, well. The sleeping-bag is a comfort in narrow little cribs open to the air like this : but for a country of piercing winds, I prefer a reindeer-skin sleeping-bag.

Tétrina is the largest of the Terski villages.   Piâlitsa has about twenty-five houses and a hundred and seventy settled inhabitants, Tschâpoma, forty houses and two hundred and fifty : Kouzomen and Varzuga, each fifty-five houses, and two hundred and fifty occupants.   On the Kan-dalaksk coast, Umba has seventy houses, and four hundred and fifty inhabitants : Kandalaks itself, seventy-five dwell-ings, and four hundred.   On the Karelian coast, Knashja has twenty-two houses, with a hundred and twenty natives : Kovda, sixty houses, with four hundred.

Some of these villages are two centuries old, or more : but their population has varied little.   As all the wood for building must, under the State regulations, be brought from Kovda—hundreds of versts in the case of some villages—the lack of expansion is not surprising.   Thus the population of Terski Lapland, exclusive of Lapps, does not exceed probably three thousand four hundred

souls. Tetrina is in the latitude of the North Cape of
Iceland, and of Obdorsk in Siberia.

Poor Castren sailed from Archangel, in a corn-laden
vessel, for the Mûrmansk coast, but in a sudden gale the
ship was driven to Moski, where we anchored yesterday.
The skipper was a *Raskolnik*, or bigoted old believer,
and relied on fine weather because the day following
was the feast day of his saint. Suddenly black
clouds appeared in the north. Before the crew could
weigh anchor, the vessel was enveloped in thick mist and
the storm raged terribly: the vessel broke from her
anchorage with a crash, and the *Raskolnik* swore aloud
at Castren, the ship, and the particular saint: as he had
lost his good anchor, which had cost him a hundred roubles.

They tried to run into the mouth of the Tschâvanga
but were driven to sea. Towering waves rose foaming,
and rolled one after another on deck: the seamen could
not cross the deck. Two English sailors were once
lashed to the rigging of their vessel in storm and rain.
Said one to the other: Don't you pity poor devils caught
out at a picnic in weather like this?

Castren's ship was next driven towards the Solovetsk
Islands, and all hope was given up. Then the wind
changed once more, and the ship drove to the Winter
Coast. Finally, Castren, who had been already prostrated
by fever, reached Archangel, glad to escape with his life.
From one of the Russian fishermen, Castren heard the
story of Anika—described as an English viking.

The White Sea *lodjes* are so built and rigged that

they can only take advantage of winds that blow from half the points of the compass. All others drive them whither they please. The compasses are almost worthless: never adjusted, and as often as not hung between iron nails and rings. The mariners strive never to lose the land, otherwise they have no idea of their position. There is no lighthouse west of Sosvôvets on the north coast, or north of Solovetsk in the western part of the White Sea. When a crew are storm-bound they carve those crosses which we see at intervals along the shore, and set them up in honour of their patron saints.

June 27th.—Departed from Lachta. It was still, and we rode at anchor for about a half-hour: then it commenced to blow well up. At 4 o'clock P.M. we went by Saasnaava light, the wind blew hard, so we must shrink the sail. *June 28th.*—I was awakened by the boat's being in a terrible movement: by looking out I saw it was breaking on all sides. The dreg was taken up, but the storm had grown stronger, so we must seek harbour at Derevna Tétrina: the sea is lying in a fearful hurricane. *Extract from Day Book round the Bay of Hvidsö.*

The barometer did not recover, and the storm blew furiously all that afternoon and night. We lay at Tétrina: for the frightened crew would not sail. I tried persuasion, bribes, threats: for we could have made a wonderful run to Kouzomen. At ten o'clock at night I compelled them to sail, in spite of the savage protests of Feodor Ivanovitch, in whose charge Makaroff had placed the boat. In two and a half hours we had run thirty versts.

Then Feodor Ivanovitch grew hungry: and while we slept took the boat into a creek, and sent the men on shore in our diminutive dingey or corracle for firewood. This sacrificed some hours of favourable, if heavy wind: and I accordingly addressed Feodor Ivanovitch for upwards of ten minutes. I told him we should have been in the Ponoi yet, if we hadn't driven him to sea: or at Kouzomen if he hadn't been afraid of a little wind at Tétrina. Little wind! he cried. *Ourakán!* It's a tempest! Tempest, I said: you are afraid of salt water. This made him frantic, and he got the anchor up: and we beat against wind and tide, both of which had by that time gone against us. Then he ground his teeth, and said that the boat was not a steamer: so we sailed into another creek near the mouth of the Tschâvanga, and prepared for dinner. Feodor Ivanovitch had lost us two days for the want of a little nerve.

The coast here had a sandy and stony beach: behind were sloping sand-hills, half covered by dull green turf. We saw groups of wooden crosses by the shore: but over the broad, gray, stormy sea we could see no sail nor trace of humankind. We ran from Tschâvanga after many hours' patience, with a strong north-easterly wind, in smooth water, close under the low shore. The wind was the very breath of ice, the disembodied spirit of the Pole. We passed along near the shore. Woods lined it, gray and blasted with winter's touch. There are pearl-fisheries on the Terski coast: I have bought some of the pearls in Archangel, and they are fairly good.

Many huts, still untenanted, stood at intervals on
the beach, with salmon fishers' apparatus. We saw the
herring gull in numbers here. The Mûrmansk fisheries
open while the White Sea is still covered with ice. At
Lachta we saw kelts which had spawned in the Ponoi, and
were on their way to the sea : they are salted and sold to
the poor. In the year 1826 1,200,000 lbs. of salmon
were sold at Kouzomen, and 800,000 lbs. at the Ponoi
fisheries. Want of restriction and indiscriminate weirs
have sacrificed the salmon and reduced the yield : 800,000
lbs. is now a good catch for all the rivers together. All the
salmon fisheries of the Kola Peninsula are supposed to
belong to the Lapps, but have been sold—too often for
a nominal price—to Russian traders, who contrive always
to keep the poor Lapps in their debt.

Herrings swarm, not only along this coast, as well as
from Kola to Sviatoi Nôs, but for fifteen hundred versts
farther, to the delta of the Petschora, and even to the
mouths of the Ob and the Yenesei. A million pounds
have been taken in one season at the Dwina mouths.
They are salted, of course, and are so cheap that the pigs
are fed with them. At Soroka and other villages of
Pomoria, the cattle are often fed upon smoked herrings.

The Tschâvanga is one of the greatest rivers on this
coast. The others are the Vârzuga, the Umba, and the
Niva. In the winter the inhabitants of these gray huts
take vast quantities of seals : 400,000 lbs. of train-oil,
Ivan Abramovitch told me, are yearly sent to Archangel.
They also hunt bears and shoot wild geese and ducks.:

in the winter they make casks and repair their houses. Wolves are seldom seen here.

Walrus is no longer found, or very rarely, in the White Sea. Even Walrus Island, *Morjovets*, is deserted by those poor persecuted animals. The ivory boxes, which for an unknown period have been carved and made in Archangel, are of walrus, or even of mammoth ivory : of which caravans used to come to Archangel earlier in the century from Vaigatz, the sacred island of the Samoyedes. There was found a deposit of these mammoth tusks also at Kastinskoy. As in Siberia, so round the White Sea shores, the wolf and reindeer have replaced the mammoth.

CHAPTER X.

Kouzomen — Feodor Andrevitch — Samoyedes — The Varzuga river — Village of Varzuga — A pioneer — A contract — Yekim's journey — Sergosero — Kamensky — The Upper Ponoi — The Bolshoi rapid — A letter from Lachta — Overtures for photography — White Sea midnight.

TOWARDS midnight we entered a broad, shallow stream. On our right hand lay the low shore, with a few small houses, a church, and the apparatus of a fishing village. To our left, across the stream, which is half-a-mile broad, stretches the river's right bank — a bare, tapering spit of yellow sand three miles in length. On this sandbank, facing the river northward, and having the sea behind it, stands Kouzomen, with its gray houses and numerous boats. One or two Russian *lodjes* lay in the placid stream: it was night, and scarcely any people were to be seen.

We landed and went to the little house of the *Starschina*, Feodor Andrévitch : finding one of his two rooms full of citizens drinking tea and vodka. Feodor, an oily, apologetic man, was not accustomed to lodge guests, but the travellers seemed to promise a favourable opening for spoil : and after a short consultation, he offered us an oppressive welcome. The guests were all more or less intoxicated, but the Starschina's head was clear enough.

We handed Ivan Abramovitch's letter to him, the *Stanovoi*
being absent: and he assured us that the friends of his
friends were his friends' friends—or something about as
sincere.   Then with pleading gestures he asked his dear
friends and fellow-citizens to be so uncommonly kind, as
to excuse his displacing them by two English travellers
recommended to his hospitality.   Patting one on the back,
and stroking the hands of another, Feodor Andrévitch
patiently endeavoured to rid himself of probably good
customers for his surreptitious *vodka* store, without giving
them offence.

His task was a delicate one, for each tipsy guest had
instinct left enough to want to know all about the two
strangers before leaving : and the *Starschina* feared that,
growing impatient, we might go elsewhere.   They tried
the Doctor : the Perevodtchik, who was instructed to be
deaf and dumb : tried me, in vain.   Whence come you ?
Whither go you ?   What on the earth do you come for ?

Eventually the plausible Feodor Andrévitch, promising
to ascertain the minutest details relating to us, and to
report fully on the morrow to his dear friends and neighbours, fairly stroked them out of the room.   Before going,
the tallest guest rose, a glass of vodka in his hand.   Feodor Andrévitch, he said, *Za vashai zdarova.*   Feodor
Andrévitch filled a glass, raised it, acknowledged the toast,
and I saw him put it behind him on a little table.   Each
man severally having shaken hands with us, wished us
welcome to Kouzomen, and *Do svidania*—Au revoir.

We established ourselves in the room, opening all the

windows: and our pretty hostess, Kovronia Feôdorovna
Obrévitch brought the steaming *samovar* and *tchainik*.
The Linguist made us some pancakes, and we lay down
on our quilts on the floor to sleep: after arranging to take
Yekim Afanasievitch and Artimon Gûbuntzoff, in the
Starschina's boat by the early morning tide, up the river
to Varzuga. I also asked for some Samoyedes living here,
tending the reindeer of the trader Sabotchakoff.

At five in the morning they came, four in number, and
I took some photographs of them. There was an elderly
man with a fine head and white hair straggling over it :
a younger man, baptised as Vassili Ivanovitch Rôgoloff,
twenty-four years old : a little woman, his wife, and a
little child, their daughter, all natives of Mezén *Ouyesda*
and of Kânin Tûndra. They had come from Kânin a
year and a quarter before.

The quaint old Dutch traveller Le Brun, who visited
Archangel in the beginning of last century, relates how
he came to a wood outside that city, where, he says : We
saw several of the people called Samoeds, which in the
Russian language signifies Man-eaters, or such as subsist on
devouring their fellow-creatures. There are very few of
them but what are perfectly wild, and extend themselves all
along the sea-coast as far as Siberia. As to their diet
they feed for the generality upon the carcasses of oxen,
sheep, horses, or any other carrion they meet with in their
way, or what is given them by strangers. In one part of
their tent was heaped up a profusion of raw horse flesh, which
the reader may easily imagine was a most shocking sight.

The Samoyedka wore the *pânitsa* of her country-women, a soft warm jacket and short skirt of fur patch-work : and *dorbouri* or fur boots. The men wore the *mâlitsa*, a long tunic with a fur collar, made of reindeer skin with the fur inwards. The *mâlitsa* of the elder man had the *panda* or striped fur border, as may be seen in the frontispiece : the younger man's had none. Their boots were similar to those of the woman. The old man's gloves were sewn to the cuffs of the *mâlitsa*, as is often the case : a passage being left for the hand indepen-dently of the glove. These were not good examples of the beautiful Samoyede dress, and the poor people them-selves looked shabby and forlorn.

We set off at eight in the morning, the Perevodtchik constituting himself one of the crew. We had given up the idea of crossing to the Ponoi and descending it, as it would have involved either sacrificing for an uninhabited river what was of more importance elsewhere : or, travelling round and round in a circle, with all the risks and chances of another sea-voyage from Ponoi. Besides, on reaching Ponoi, we should find the only even partially safe boat at Kouzomen : or, if she had made a remarkably fast passage back, her owner probably unable to spare her from his salmon fishery for another voyage of uncertain length.

We sailed and rowed up the shallow sandy bed of the Vârzuga : finding constant shoals. This huge bed of sand appears to have been gradually accumulated by some easterly current, across the old mouth of the river—

diverting and prolonging its course for three miles or more to the eastward. We passed several islands. The larch and birch were clothed in fresh and lovely green, making the river's banks feathery and soft. Above them rose dark, tall, pointed firs. The Vârzuga has none of the grandeur of the Ponoi : beyond the fine broad sheet of water and its sunny smiling banks, it has no beauty.

We went on shore, and I gathered a bunch of forget-me-not—*nézaboudka*—of lovely shades of blue : a more universal friend, perhaps, than any other flower : conveying the same tender, friendly meaning in many different regions and many different tongues. By the river-side I found, too, the black-fruited honeysuckle and lovely white silky cotton-sedge. Mosquitoes, young and inexperienced yet, were beginning to find their way into existence. On the cold Mûrman coast we had seen none, and at the cataract of the Ponoi, where they were generating, they were a cloud of almost imperceptible insects.

An eagle passed overhead, then a gerfalcon : a string of ducks at times spluttered across the water. The sun shone brilliantly, but the wind was piercing cold. The region had not yet shaken off winter's grip. The ice which had lately passed down to the sea had left traces on the banks, and at places piled up mud.

We met occasional fisher boats with pleasant, well-mannered Russians in them : boats laden with moss for house-building : then a boat in which a *moujik* and his wife were towing a raft of timber. The inhabitants of this coast are remarkable for their good looks, and the greater proportion of them for their agreeable manners and hospitality.   There was but a slight current : altogether two rivers, rising so near one another, could not be much more unlike, than this pleasant broad stream with its green banks, and the stately Ponoi with its towering cliffs.

We came, after three hours' journey, to a point on the right bank, from whence we could hear the sound of a rapid : and here we landed.   We walked through a much thinned pine forest.   Some of the stumps measured eighteen inches in diameter : but in Vârzuga village we saw timber logs twenty-four inches in thickness, and as much as eighteen *arshin*, or forty-two feet long.   A raven sat on a log, and croaked at a dragon-fly which was hovering in its nervous, fussy way over some oak fern. The sun's heat in the sheltered wood at noon became great.   Mosquitoes abounded, and took an interest in me, when, after a march of a few versts, we came in sight of Vârzuga, and I stopped to photograph it.

We crossed a meadow, a field of delicious clover, and reached the village, which lay on both banks of the stream. On the right bank stood a queer old Tartar-Byzantine church—wooden, of course.   The village was full of busy sawyers and wood-cutters, and on the river were many rafts and boats.   We crossed to the left bank in a skiff, which a drunken boatman came very near upsetting, and went for milk and *tchai* into a peasant's house.

The heat was great, apart from the huge stove : and

the room smelt as one that has not had a window open
for years.   I do not remember seeing a window open in
a Russian peasant's house, whatever might be the heat,
unless we opened it ourselves.

We sent for a man of whom we had heard at Kouzomen,
Gavril Pietroff Tschunin, who had been to Sergosero and
to Kamensky on the Upper Ponoi.   I had secretly decided
to send, at the charge of my privy purse, an expedition
overland to Ponoi, to confirm what I was confident
about, namely that the journey was practicable.   This plan
had to be subject to the faith or fears of the Ponoi boatmen, and I felt I must approach them gently.   Filip
Iekaterinoff, familiarly called Yekim, was the firmer man of
the two: and I had left Artimon with the boat near the
rapid, lest he should undermine Yekim's courage.

Gavril Pietroff presented himself.   Hast thou been to
Kamensky in the summer?   I asked.   I have been there
in summer.   How many days from Varzuga to Kamensky?   Gavril reflected.   Two and a half days, he said.
How many days did I tell you, Yekim?   Three days,
said Yekim.   How many days for the whole journey from
hence to Ponoi?   Seven, said Gavril.   How many did I
tell you?   I said to Yekim.   Nine, he admitted.   This
had some reassuring influence on Yekim's mind: he agreed
to make the journey if Artimon would go: and I bought
Gavril's boat for the expedition.

On a hot afternoon we left Varzuga in two boats, for
the rapids, which we successfully descended.   Beside us was
a boat, beautifully steered by a woman.   We found Artimon

asleep on the bank. He refused point-blank to go overland to the Ponoi: so we all embarked, and the men paddled down the river. At night we came to Kouzomen in warm, bright sunshine. It was a wonderful Arctic night.

Next day came Yekim with Artimon to say he had determined not to go to Kamensky without his companion. I had promised them twenty roubles each. I took Yekim aside. You will do better to go alone, I said confidentially. Why? You get double money. Forty roubles? said Yekim. I nodded :—And the boat at Varzuga too.

Artimon tried to shake Yekim's faith. He had heard alarming stories about the journey and its dangers. It might take them many days to reach Kamensky, and weeks to reach Ponoi. I appealed to Yekim to repeat Gavril Pietroff's assurances : but was amused to see that Yekim, having once figured to himself the forty roubles, grew less eager about Artimon's company.

I pictured the risks and horrors of the wintry White Sea : how it might take a month to reach Ponoi, if they ever reached it : how they would travel by sea at their own expense, by land at mine : how my offer gave them as much each as they would earn in the next six months. All this even Artimon mournfully admitted, but the negotiation lasted all through a long and weary day. Finally, I induced Yekim to undertake the journey alone.

Quite worn out, I drew up a contract : and next morning Filip Afanasievitch Iekaterinoff came to sign it and to say farewell. I gave him categorical directions as to the details he was to observe and note. I paid him

K

twenty roubles in advance, and was a little puzzled about
paying the remaining twenty.   Finally, I sent for Feodor
Ivanovitch, though I had been at war with him, and en-
trusted him with the money, to be handed to Filip
Afanasievitch on his completion of the journey.   Feodor
Ivanovitch undertook this, and honestly fulfilled his trust.

CONTRACT FOR THE PONOI EXPEDITION.

In the year 1879, June, 18th day, I, the undersigned
peasant of the Archangel province, native of Kemskawo
Ouyesda, inhabiting the Ponoi district of the Kouzomen-
Varzuga parish, Filip Afanasievitch Iekaterinoff, make these
agreed terms, for that I, Iekaterinoff, undertake to carry out
the journey from Varzuga to Sergozero, accounted thirty
versts.   Therefrom to set forth on the journey as far as
the river and the town of Ponoi.

And I engage to give a detailed description of everything upon the journey to Ponoi : and therefrom to write
directly to the British Consul in Arkhangelsk, and record
to him all the circumstances of the journey.   For this
journey I am to receive forty roubles, whereof I have taken
twenty roubles.   Twenty roubles remain to be paid on my
arrival at Ponoi by the Kemsky peasant, Feodor Ivanovitch
Simeonoff.   For this quittance I subscribe with my own
hand,   FILIP AFANASIEVITCH IEKATERINOFF.

If I, Iekaterinoff, should fail to carry out this undertaking, I agree to pay back the received twenty roubles,
sending them to the English Consul in Archangel.

Filip Iekaterinoff subscribes with his own hand in presence of me.

Starschina FEODOR ANDREVITCH.

This was the contract, and the sequel was satisfactory and interesting. Filip Afanasievitch sent the manuscript of his journal to the Consul in Archangel, who sent me a literal translation.

JOURNAL OF FILIP AFANASIEVITCH IEKATERINOFF.

To the British subject Edward Rae, travelling in Russian Lapland, from the peasant of the Kouzomensk district, Filip Iekaterinoff.

I have the honour to inform you that I, in consequence of your having engaged me for a route from the village Varzuga, of the Kouzomensk circuit in the Kem district, as far as Loparsk-Kamensk parishes, lying in the Ponoi circuit of same district, started the 21st June from Varzuga as far as Sergozero.

The road was two versts from Varzuga by water as far as the rapid Porokushki, on the River Varzuga. This rapid is swift, not high, sloping for one hundred fathoms : it is possible to pass with a boat. Further proceeded on River Varzuga by a straight channel of two versts as far as the rapid Stoodeno, which is also swift and sloping : it is likewise passable in a boat. This rapid is fifty fathoms long.

From here, as far as the mouth of the River Sergi, originating from Sergozero and flowing into the River Varzuga, by a straight rapid channel of three versts in

length : then on the River Sergi by a straight rapid channel
of ten versts, as far as Sereshnoi Fall, which is falling from
the height of three fathoms vertically : its ascending is impracticable.   Half-a-verst distant from this fall there is
another called Nadpadun : then comes a channel three
versts long, in the course of which there are rapid places.

There is a sloping, quiet rapid called Bashenka : it is
passable with a boat.   This rapid is followed by a channel
of two versts long, with strong current.   Then comes the
Krasnoy rapid : its ascending with a boat is combined
with great trouble : from Krasnoy is a quiet channel of three
versts in length : then not a large rapid, called Dvinskoy,
of one verst in length, swift and stony, the banks of which
consist of rocks.

From the Dvinskoy leads a calm channel of eight
versts, to the Klobuk rapid, one hundred fathoms in length,
sloping, stony, and very swift : going up is possible, though
difficult.   From here comes a channel of five versts with
strong current, as far as the Bielonoska rapid, also sloping,
but swift : its going up with a boat is possible.   Then a
channel of ten versts, whereof five versts strong current and
five versts quiet, as far as the Lake Sergozero.

The banks of this channel are flat, and are covered
with a dark and gloomy forest of pine and red-pine.   To
approach the lake one must pass swampy ground with
great difficulty, as one's feet are sinking down almost to
the knee.   This route I accomplished in thirty-six hours.

From Varzuga as far as Sergozero by water the distance is forty versts.   There originates from Sergozero

the River Sergi, from the origin of which I proceeded on
the left bank upon moss, overgrown with small bushes for
the distance of twenty versts.

On the banks in that place were living temporarily
Russian fishermen, who brought me to the island called
Kuropteff, distant from the shore two hundred fathoms,
occupied by Laplanders, fishermen, who are living at
different times of the year either on the island or on the
shores of the lake for fishing, and nourish themselves with
dried fish and reindeer flesh dried in the air: they eat
very little bread, and do not keep many reindeer. A
family is living here consisting of six members.

On this lake there are six islands covered partly with
pine, partly with red-pine forest. The lake is twenty versts
in length, fifteen in breadth, and fifty in circumference: on
its shores trees are growing. Into the lake are flowing
two rivers, Sinka and Pikomka, deep enough but narrow,
originating from the lakes of similar name. From the
island to the continent the passage is three versts.

From here there is a summer road leading to the
Kamensky parishes, following which, on the extension of
about sixty versts, there are large forests, sometimes inter-
rupted by swamps: in the middle of this road there is a
rather high hill of one hundred and fifty fathoms in height
and two versts in circuit, called the Vonzuya.

From the Vonzuya, four versts before reaching the
Kamensk parish, is a hill with a comb-like ridge of one
hundred fathoms in height, called by Laplanders Kelchal-
pahke: it has no Russian name. Here is the first Kamensk

summer parish situated on the river Ponoi : in this parish
there are two huts, in which are living two families, consisting of three males and four females.   Ten versts up
the river from this parish is another parish, containing
four huts, with four families, consisting of ten male and
nine female persons.

Ten versts farther up the Ponoi is a third parish of one
hut with one family—man and wife.   These Laplandish
families are living badly, subsisting only on fish in a dry
or raw state, and possess one hundred and twenty-five
reindeer.   Around these parishes is forest and good grass.

Down the Ponoi from the first parish there is a calm
channel of seven versts ; here the Ponoi runs through two
lakes, which are stony and shallow, and it is very difficult
to cross them.   Here is a parish consisting of two huts,
with two families, consisting of eight male and seven
female persons : they possess fifty reindeer.   They nourish
themselves as above mentioned, and sometimes use bread.
These lakes are five versts in length and one and a half
versts in breadth : there is no forest near them, only
meadows with good grass.

Ten versts farther down the River Ponoi are two huts
with two families, consisting of three male and three
female persons.   Seventy versts farther down the River
Ponoi, the River Lebyashja flows into it from the left side,
on the banks of which from time to time are living fishermen, Laplanders, and where I engaged a guide to take
me in a boat as far as the village Ponoi.   The river, a
hundred and fifty versts before reaching the village Ponoi,

flows slowly, calmly, and in some places exceptionally rapidly : its banks are low.

From the left and right sides of the River Ponoi besides the Lebyashja, many other small rivers and rivulets flow into it. The principal and largest of them are : Atcha-rick, Tomba, Kolmack, and Purnatch. From the Purnatch and Tomba, forty versts before reaching the village Ponoi, there are swift large rapids, to ascend which it is quite impossible, and going down scarcely possible with great danger. The banks of the River Ponoi as far as Tomba are low and covered with red-pine trees, and nearer to the village Ponoi hilly with fir forest : the hills are stony and steep.

At the time of my voyage the water in the river was very high, which made it most difficult to go down the rapids. Fifteen versts before reaching the village Ponoi there is a rapid, called Bolshoi, which is known to you.

At Ponoi I arrived in the night of the 30th June. In all I was on the voyage nine days : one might have made this journey in a shorter time, but there were no people who had spare time, they were all out fishing. The whole distance from Varzuga through the Kamensk parishes, as far as the village Ponoi, is nearly four hundred and twenty versts.

To the guide from Varzuga to Sergozero I paid four roubles twenty kopecks : from Sergozero to the Kamensk first parish four roubles : from the first to the fourth parish three roubles : from the latter as far as Ponoi twelve roubles : in all twenty-three roubles twenty kopecks.

For the passage to the village Ponoi I was obliged to buy a little boat for ten roubles—which makes a total of thirty-three roubles twenty kopecks, which money, independent of the payment of forty roubles, I have the honour to beg you to send me to the address of the chief of the district at Ponoi—for transmission to Filip Iekaterinoff.

I remain respectfully, always at your service,

Peasant, FILIP IEKATERINOFF.

I wrote to Makaroff at Lachta about flint implements and embroidered birch-bark and reindeer-skin coverings : and from his reply it would not appear that I had inspired him with much confidence :—

VILLAGE PONOI, *2nd August.*

To the British subject EDWARD RAE.

I hasten to inform you, Mr. Rae, that I received your letter from Kouzomen of the 20th June, and present you my deep respect. As to sending out to you ancient stone goods and other things, I cannot execute your desire at present for the reason that it is combined with outlays, and the Laplanders do not give away such things without money. I remain, with due regard,

VASSILI MAKAROFF.

We passed some days in Kouzomen. I used to learn from the Samoyedes : or for a rest go out and use Feodor Andrévitch's axe, helping him to build an addition to his log-house. He used an axe with perfect skill, making it serve the purposes of saw and plane. One day Kovronia brought her child to ask about some of its simple ailments. Then she wanted to buy one of our enamelled iron plates, which we couldn't spare : then a pocket-knife and a box of matches, both of which I gladly gave her. She used to buy fish and cream for us, and help the dilatory Perevodtchik to cook our simple meals.

A small steamer calls here on her way from Umba to Solovetsk every ten days : as punctually, that is, as the weather allows.

One day the Perevodtchik came in. He said that a certain Simeon Petrovitch had seen me photograph the Samoyedes, and wished his own portrait taken. Ask Simeon Petrovitch what he will pay me, I said. The little man burst into the preliminary of a smile, but seeing me unmoved he was overcome with fear : and hastily transformed his expression into one of ludicrous solemnity. I heard no more of Simeon Petrovitch.

Another day I was seated writing, when there entered a gentleman with a long Sunday coat, a pewter badge of military service, tall boots newly greased, and a lately-washed countenance. He said he wished to have his portrait taken. It was not convenient, I said. But he wanted it at once. I asked his name. Dimitri Makivoff. Are you a Samoyede ? I asked. Dimitri, scarcely containing himself : I am Russian ! Ah, not a Samoyede ? Dimitri, suffocating : I am a Russian—was a soldier ! Then he added the Russian words for abomination, malediction ! and rushed out of the room.

Late one night we walked down to the beach for fresh air. We passed two white wooden churches with red roofs. Round them, out of the bare yellow sand, rose a thick crop of wooden crosses—an unenclosed burial-place. We walked over the dry flat sand for a mile, and came to where lay the delicate summer sea, flushed with pale pink. Rounded waves curled and broke musically, and white foam swept silently on to the smooth sand. The sea became, as it sometimes did towards midnight and dawn, smooth and white as milk. Behind us northward lay Kouzomen, a low line of black dots in intense shade, under a delicious pink sky: and on the horizon lay the misty golden light of the scarcely obscured midnight sun.

The beauty of the white sea and the sky seemed to mock by contrast the darkened clouded lives of the natives of this Peninsula: life seems one long Arctic winter to them. Some of us have sorrows harder to bear than theirs: but they do not know, poor people, of the country where there shall be no winter and no night. Perhaps for some of them the time and the knowledge are not postponed for long :

> *The sad dark clouds of life shall rise, and there*
> *Reveal the white sea of Eternity.*

THE NORTH SEA: MIDNIGHT

CHAPTER XI.

Samoyede studies—Characteristics—Worship—Superstition—Religion—A
Recognition—A risk—The bear—Weariness—Samoyede gods—Wizards
—Sacrifices—Burials—Samoyede Folklore—Story of the thirty old men
—Marodata—Tanako—The one-armed servant—Samoyede song—
Connections of the Samoyedes—Departure from Kouzomen—Vassili
Ivanovitch Rogoloff.

THE younger Samoyede, Vassili Ivanovitch Rogoloff, used
to spend the days with me. I was at breakfast the first
time he came: he took a seat, and with a bow and motion
of his hand begged me to continue eating. I offered him
a plate of pancakes—made, like the black bread, with
coarse rye flour: and he tried to excuse himself, though
probably hungry, poor fellow. Finally he accepted the
dish, crossed himself, and began to eat. Perhaps he did
not like the look of the Perevodtchik's black pancakes.
Ultimately he grew to respect me as the introducer of
pancakes, *blini*, to the White Sea. There was urgent
necessity for the introduction of something: for the biscuits
and jams were rapidly dwindling away. We expect to
see the *blin* in every *isba*. Sir Walter Raleigh introduced the potato to Great Britain, and we popularised the
pancake on the White Sea shores. Vassili stopped care-

fully whenever he thought I wished to ask him a question. It was a rare thing for us to get a warm meal—what with prescribing for sickness, making contracts, buying old silver, learning Lappish or Samoyede, making plans, gathering information, bargaining, and holding interviews enough for directing an army in a strange country.

Vassili Ivanovitch had never been taught, but he had a superior intelligence and swift perception, combined with much dignity and unaffected courtesy. One of the most striking characteristics of the Samoyedes is this quiet dignity. They are calm and unruffled by passing circumstances: accepting stoically, and not with the morbid It is written, of the Mussulman, or the cynical indifferent *Eh mon Dieu*, of the Frenchman—whatever befalls them. Agitation and emotion are almost unknown to them. They are Nature's philosophers, and have by nature all the tranquillity and composure of good breeding.

Vassili habitually used the word Christian curiously. In helping me with translation he would say for, In Russian—*Pa Khristianski*, Among the baptized. Early in our intercourse I received very agreeable encouragement by hearing Vassili say in an undertone to his wife: *Kak skoro on ponimayet*, How quickly he understands. One must be dull to fail to understand with a teacher so intelligent.

I asked him of his religion. *Maya viera tozhe samaia shto drugovo narodou.* My religion, he said, is the same as others' teaching. He did not care to speak of his religion, but talked readily about that of his countrymen.

His father, who, with his wife and second son, was tending reindeer at Bâbosero, was still a *Tâdibe* or magician. His drum and clothes were with him : also wooden *hahe* or idols, as many as two reindeer could carry. I asked Vassili of the prayers to the *hahe*, and record his replies as I heard them : they are not all consistent, but I quote them literally—not as a general statement of the Samoyede belief, but as an example of the extent to which the views of a very superior Samoyede, regarding his people's faith and practices, are defined.

Did he pray to the *hahe ?*   *Niet : anee tchertovskoi vieri.* No : they are of the devil's faith. When does a *Tâdibe* operate ? When his son is in pain : when another Samoyede is sick. When reindeer are sick ? I asked. They cannot personally help the reindeer in sickness, but pray for them to the *hahe :* and when wolves come the *hahe* can drive them away from the reindeer.

When the Samoyedes lose anything they use the divining drum at once, so that the thing may return. If a man steals anything, and hears the drum, *seytchass* he brings it back. Many, however, are so obstinate that the drum and such like means do not answer : then all the tribe must go together and find the missing object.

If no *hahe* is at hand, if all are far away, a sick Samoyede cries, *Ya! Hahe! Pomilui, ya bolin.* Be so good as to help me : I am sick. *Pomagi mnya k'zdarovyou.* Help me, that I may be well again. *Ta padaryou tibia shtoto posslai.* I will give thee something by and by. If anything happens to a Samoyede, he prays : and thinks he will get better the next day, or after the next, but at no fixed time. If good comes, he thanks the idol.

When the *hahe* is appealed to for a sick reindeer, the *Tâdibe* takes blood from it and smears the *hahe*, praying for its recovery. When a reindeer is missing, all the idolaters assemble round the *hahe*, and while the idol is smeared with blood by the *Tâdibe*, one cries: I pray thee, *Hahe*, that thou wilt secure the reindeer, so that it may not go astray: I will smear thee with blood: I will bring thee meat: I will cook meat for thee. Then the meat is cooked, the idol is anointed with fat, the meat is left, and the devotees go away. When they come again, the meat is always gone. Who eats the meat? I asked. The *hahe*. Not some other Samoyede? No, the *hahe*.

When a man is sick, an unregenerate Samoyede, he stands in front of the *hahe:* his hands and arms straight by his side as in military position, thumbs in front of his hips, and so repeats his prayer. He does not prostrate himself, so said Vassili, as the Laplanders of old. However, I saw a Samoyede, wishing to show me the ancient method of devotion, crawl on hands and knees before an idol.

Many Samoyedes in Kânin Tûndra are unbaptized: all of these pray to the *hahe:* many more pray to the *hahe* than to God. It would be a heavy sin for a baptized Samoyede to go to the *hahe:* he prays to God for his reindeer or for anything belonging to him, as well as for himself or for his health.

When a Samoyede prays to God he says: *Pomagi*

mnya Bozhe, naïti moyo olenya. Help me, God, to find
my reindeer again. *Ya kouplou tibia svaitchou: ya
prinyasou tibia miri.* I will buy lights, and I will bring
Thee incense. After the reindeer is found: *Gospod Bozha
blagadaryou tibia: blagadaryou da Troitsi*—Lord God,
thanks to Thee: thanks to the Trinity. One old Samoyede woman having lost a reindeer calf, and having vainly
applied to the *Tâdibe*, went to the church at Pustosjersk,
and promised the God of the Russians a silver rouble if
He would undertake to recover the missing calf.

I asked Vassili if he remembered any stories his father
had told him. He said his father never used to talk with
him. Did his mother? No: only of the present—of what
they have, and what they want. Did he know of any
Samoyede writings? No: no Samoyede could write.
Had they proverbs or common household expressions?
No.

I asked what he thought of the Northern Lights. He
said, I do not know whence they are. God sends them.
I believe they are hurtful, and bring sickness or evil to
people, loss of reindeer, or perhaps death. I asked him
if he fancied they were the souls of the dead. He said
his people did not think so.

On the second day Vassili stopped and said: I remember seeing you before. Where? I asked. At Schoina,
in Kânin Tûndra: I do not recollect the other *Anglitchânin* so well. My wife Piribtyah remembers you too:
she taught you our language at Mezén.

I then recalled the poor little woman with a shrill

voice and dull eyes, whose patience I had tried in that dreary village in Siberia in Europe. I remembered, too, a beautiful midsummer night, when, after a long sledge journey, we reached the hospitable Samoyede village of Schoina. Vassili and his neighbours had offered us a kind and courteous welcome, cooking reindeer flesh for us, offering us their fish soup, and trying to make us comfortable.

I asked him what the Samoyedes thought of us. They were displeased that the strangers should go into their country: they were frightened. The news spread all over Kânin Tûndra. What did the people say? I asked. They said: Why do the strangers come to our *tûndra?* they have no occasion to. Why do they photograph our reindeer? I asked Vassili what they thought about the photograph. They believed their reindeer would die. They feared for a long time afterwards that something terrible would come to them—cholera, loss of reindeer, or death.

Did we run any risk from their fears? How do you mean? Would the Samoyedes have hurt us—with knives, or sticks? No, he said with some hesitation: but they thought of binding stones to you and casting you into the sea. As we were warned at the time, we ventured perhaps too much, in going, with the enthusiasm of young travellers freely among the Samoyedes on the *tûndra:* for the peaceful, apathetic Samoyede, when labouring under fear or excitement, becomes once more a savage.

The Samoyedes suffered during the years 1831 and

1833 from a plague, which first destroyed twenty thousand of their reindeer: and then, in consequence of their eating the diseased meat, attacked themselves. They attributed the latter ill to intercourse with the Russians, however. Great numbers of them died, and now there remain— scattered along the Siberian *tûndras* from the Mezén to the Khatanga, from Kânin to Taimurland, from the 45th degree of East longitude to the 110th — only about 10,000 of their race, possessing, in all, perhaps 70 to 100,000 reindeer.

Of these, the Russian settlers, grasping and crafty, are gradually getting possession. On the Petschora about two-thirds of the reindeer have passed out of the hands of the Samoyedes, who are now, like Vassili and his father, employed only as shepherds. What precious stones and silver they had have gone the same way, and it seems likely that before very many years the Samoyedes will, as a distinct race, have almost disappeared. Is it strange that the poor people suspected and dreaded strangers of whom they never saw the like before: and who, for all they knew, might be only an aggravated form of Russian trader, or the authors of some new pestilence?

Did Vassili think his people would hurt us if we returned to Kânin Tûndra? No, he thought not. We had better take money with us: but we should be wise to take no *vodka*. His people were honest, and, when sober, not dangerous. He told me he had seen stone knives in Kânin, years ago: and many of his tribe have silver crosses.

L

The bear, Vassili said, was a good animal : an oath taken on the snout of a bear was sacred. This might easily be. The Doctor would keep any oath he might happen to make over a bear's snout, and would be pleased to have a friend to hold the bear. Wolves are good animals when they don't eat the reindeer.

Vassili was to go to Bâbosero, in a day or two, a journey of two days eastward through the woods. He gave me an account of Bâbosero and the adjoining lakes. They lie as near together as the English Lakes, and as a herdsman must accompany the reindeer in their wanderings, no doubt the district was very familiar to the Samoyede. He displayed more geographical intelligence than all the Russian peasants I ever met put together.

I made studies in Samoyede long and exhausting to Vassili, his wife, and myself. Their little child would come in from time to time, as if to appeal for her parents' release. Piribtyah had less endurance than her husband : his patience and courtesy often made me feel ashamed.

I gave him constant cigarettes, refreshment at intervals, and sent him for an occasional rest. We compiled a vocabulary, which would serve an ordinary traveller in the Samoyede country. I have included the results of Piribtyah's former teaching—of which Seebohm writes in *Siberia in Europe :* we went through most of the vocabulary given in the *Land of the North Wind*, and found it on the whole correct.

There can be no such thing as strict accuracy of grammar or expression among an illiterate people : nor can there be among these simple creatures any consistent or fixed appreciation even of their own forms of superstition or belief. Local practices have been perpetuated, and it would be difficult to take any version of the Samoyede belief as universal. I have, as an instance, quoted a man far superior in intelligence to any Samoyede I ever knew. But, having no object in arriving at a common view of such matters, each Samoyede, if questioned separately, will give more or less his own disconnected impressions of his faith.

To sum up, the Samoyede religion can only be regarded as idolatry, with a slight varnish of Christianity: Our Lord being only considered as a kind of Russian *Noum*. The Samoyedes are too ignorant to understand otherwise: but Russia will not educate her own peasants, much less the savages inhabiting her borders. I will therefore say what I believe to be the still prevailing faith, whatever may be the practice, among the greater part of them.

Those who have come much in contact with the Russians have discontinued in cases some of the old practices ; but I do not believe they have replaced them by substantial progress in a higher direction.

The chief deity is Yliambertje, supreme and absolute. Next come the *Nouma*—inferior spirits, who can be persuaded, and propitiated by prayer or sacrifice, and to whom the Samoyede applies for relief when suffering under some infliction of Yliambertje : or of whom he asks health, means, success in hunting, etc. The *Nouma* are represented by *hahe*, small natural objects of wood or stone:

and in default of either, earth or snow, rudely representing
sometimes human or animal forms.   They are roughly
decorated, and generally carefully put aside.   Each tribe
used to have a special sledge for the transport of these
idols.   They can be approached by the Samoyede himself: while access to one of the *Nouma* must be through
the mediation of a *Tâdibe.*

The *Tâdibe* of the Samoyede is, or was—for, like
other superstitions, this is slowly fading out—equivalent
to the extinct Laplandish *Noaid,* to the Siberian *Schaman,*
the Esquimaux *Angakok,* the American Indian Medicine-
man, the *Marabout* of Barbary.   His incantations and the
use of a drum have the effect of summoning the deity.
I have seen one of these drums, and, unlike those of the
Laplanders, which were covered with figures and rude
characters, they have no ornamentation whatever.

Armed with this drum, and covered with a cloak of
reindeer skin, adorned with red cloth: a polished plate
of metal shining upon his breast, the *Tâdibe* takes his seat,
and beats the drum, at first slowly, then faster as his
excitement increases: he and his assistant chanting mono-
tonously.   Then the spirits are understood to appear:
the *Tâdibe* pauses from time to time to listen to their
words.   Suddenly the song changes to a wild howling, the
drum is furiously beaten, the *Tâdibe* foams at the mouth,
and writhes upon the ground, till the noise ceases, and the
spirit's decision is given.

A story is told of three Samoyedes and a Russian
upon the Timân Tûndra: one of the Samoyedes was a

Tâdibe, and in his spiritual exaltation challenged the others to discharge a loaded gun at him. The first Samoyede fired, and the ball rebounded, so they say, from the *Tâdibe's* body. The gun was again loaded, and the second Samoyede fired, with the same result. Astonished at this, the Russian loaded, aimed, and fired. The *Tâdibe* fell dead on the spot. They relate many things of the *Tâdibes* of old times. They flew, they swam under water, they mounted into the clouds, descended into the earth, and assumed whatever shape was agreeable to them.

The *Tâdibe* is generally a man of the world, and when consulted in cases of loss of reindeer, of sickness, etc., he begins by shrewdly informing himself of the circumstances of the loss : when and where it happened, whether the Samoyede has reasons for thinking it was a theft : what neighbours he has, whether any of them is his enemy, and so on. This is all before he betakes himself to the drum, and he has probably by that time ascertained from the simple Samoyede what he pretends to learn from the *Noum.* The questions to a sick man are : When he was taken ill, what he had partaken of, whether he had been quarrelling, whether he had an enemy likely to injure him.

If the spirit can do nothing, the *Tâdibe* begs him to go to *Yliambertje,* and prevail upon him. *Yliambertje* dwells in the air, and sends forth thunder and lightning, rain and snow, wind and storm. The stars are considered as his property, and are called *noumgy.* The rainbow is the border of his *mâlitsa,* and is call *noum-panda.*

Panda is the name of the patchwork border, of alternate stripes of white and dark fur, which every complete *målitsa* bears. The idea was suggested to the Samoyedes by the rainbow. The sun is respected almost as much as *Yliambertje*, and by some the earth, sea, and Nature are regarded as divinities.

Everything that happens upon the earth, *Yliambertje* sees and knows. He sees the good that men do, and gives them health, prosperity, and long life. But when they commit sin, he throws them into poverty and suffering, and sends them an early death. The Samoyedes believe that in this life men are requited for their works, good or evil. A suspected thief is brought before a *hahe*, which has been smeared with blood, and is asked solemnly whether he is guilty. An oath of innocence if taken thus may be relied upon, for no Samoyede dare perjure himself under such grave circumstances. However, crime and dishonesty are very rare among them.

The sacrifice to the *hahe* is generally a reindeer, of which the hoofs, hide, and head are hung near the idol : its countenance is smeared with blood, and part of the fat is thrown into the fire. That is the *hahe's* meal. The Samoyede's own share is the whole of the effective portion of the reindeer.

I speak of all this in the present tense, rather than in the past, for though superseded in places, and in part, by a faint approach to Christianity : these idolatrous practices are still openly maintained by the remoter tribes, and must therefore still be considered as characteristics of this un-

LANOVICH ROGOLOFF A SAMOYEDE OF MALAYA ZEMLIA

fortunate race. I hope I have made it clear that they are partial, and that among the Russianised Samoyedes open evidences of the old life and faith are becoming more and more rare. The change is not to be attributed to any special effort of the Russians, but to the effect of example and the insensible influence of civilisation.

The Samoyedes reverence their dead superstitiously, and honour their memory long. The graves of the unbaptized are furnished with a knife, an axe, a lance, etc., for the maintenance of the dead in the other world. When a *Tâdibe* died, the custom was to fence in the spot of burial, and lay the body on a wooden framework, stretched out at full length, carefully dressed, with his bow, arrow, and hatchet : and to fasten up two live reindeer to the tomb to starve to death. Le Brun says that the children who happened to die before tasting meat, were tied up in a cloth and hung to a tree. Those that died later were placed between two boards and buried in the earth. Parents' bones were preserved, and never interred, unless they were very advanced in years, and then they were thrown into the next river : as Le Brun was informed, so he says, by credible eye-witnesses.

When it was known that we were about to travel to the country of the Samoyedes, a gentleman wrote entrusting me with a commission. It was to procure an authentic Samoyede skull, for which I was authorised to pay £5 : but I regret that my efforts did not bear fruit. The constant daylight in the Samoyede country was an impediment to anthropological research.

Here are a few literal examples of Samoyede stories, and a song which Piribtyah and Vassili sang to me.

First Samoyede Story.

By a lake were thirty hills, thirty islands, thirty streams, thirty graybeards, thirty iron tents, thirty gray-headed women, and thirty sledges—one for each. There they lived : there were their tents set.

The thirty old women each bore a child. The youngest bore the smallest. Said each old man to an old woman : Is it a boy, a girl? A boy, said the old woman. Then I shall try to get him a wife, because it is a son : where may Bolshaya Zemlia be? The old woman replied : I know not. If thou dost not know, I do. Near the head of the Great Land's mountain ridge will I get the boy a wife. Thereupon they went to sleep.

The sky grew gray, the day broke : they harnessed the thirty reindeer, set the thirty old men on the sledges : but over each cradle a cross stay. The old heads were white as leaves. The gray-headed old women took their seats—on the gray old men they sat down : thirty reindeer they harnessed.

They wandered, they went to marry their sons : came to the mountain ridge in the Great Land. One old woman went to negotiate about the marriage, saying : For a son seek I a wife. The stranger promised a daughter. The marriages took place. They killed a reindeer, its flesh to eat. At the wedding they ate ; the thirty gray-beards, however, could eat no flesh—ate only the fat.

The wedding was over. They went home to their country—left the thirty reindeer behind for the daughters-in-law. Themselves without reindeer bound the sledges together, loaded their companions on them, went: themselves drew their companions along. They came to the Little Land, came to their tents. There lived the thirty gray old men : there they live to this day.

Second Samoyede Story.

Marodata harnessed two reindeer, followed his father's sledge track. He went forward, approached his father. Said the father : Whence comest thou ? Where the three men came from. The father asked : Whither ? Nowhere —after reindeer. The father said : Reindeer—what for ? thou hast plenty already. The other said nothing : drove his reindeer on.

Farther on he found the train of Wahapta, his elder brother : remained standing near him. Wahapta the elder brother said : What for—these reindeer ? Thou hast already as many as sense requires, shouldst thou use them. This one scorned his companion's word : went farther. The day became evening : near the tent he remained waiting : lay down to rest.

The next day they struck the tent. Yambhan bound a great reindeer to Marodata's sledge : he gave him cloth and a woman's dress. Yambhan's wife said : What for— the cloth ? Why, these reindeer ? To the beast she gave a blow, let it run loose. For the cloth I don't care, said

Marodata: but the woman will I take.   He bound the
woman's reins to his sledge, returned to his tent.

He wandered: there met him his elder brother's
sledge.   His brother spake: Why hast thou stolen a
strange man's wife?   The elder brother smote the younger
with the driving pole, so that the staff broke in pieces.
The younger went towards his tent: reached the tent.

Day dawned.   Then said he to his servant: Go we to
my elder brother's tent: make the bow ready.   Yesterday
he struck me: to-day kill I him.   The father came up
from one side, broke the arrows, and said: Should companions shoot one another dead? art thou become mad?
The arrows were broken: the son abandoned his intention.

Third Samoyede Story.

Tanako's daughter had hunted courageously: she
watched awhile and fell asleep.   As day broke, the
maiden awoke alone: her companions had vanished.   She
looked round the tent: there was no one to be seen.   On
the heath she donned her snow-shoes, and made ready:
went forth on foot—for her reindeer were seven days'
foot-journey away.   She found a trodden spot—found a
tent-place: there was a man dead: he was her younger
brother—was her father's child.   There wailed she much
and wept.

The tents had wandered farther.   Again went she for
seven days.   There was a tent to be seen: she came to
the tent.   Then said her elder brother: Where hast thou

left the brother? The brother is slain by death: I have not killed him—here she wailed. The wolf has strangled the wild reindeer: there are traces to be seen. The servants went on watch: they fell asleep.

At night came robbers: surrounded the tent. Man, thou diest while thou sleepest. But the father sprang from his couch: climbed out by the chimney. The robbers shot arrows. He lacked bow, knife, axe. They fought all night: he overcame one robber: slew him, tore his heart out: the robber was dead. He slew another: slew his fellows—twice seven in number: put all to death: tore all their hearts out. Then he stopped.

He sat down on a sledge: took the pole in his hand: drove with reindeer to the watchmen. Struck one with the staff—he was dead: struck the other—he was dead. Other robbers came, and met with the same fate. Again came robbers. Let us steal his bow and sling: in an earth-hole let us live. They stole the bow and sling: lived in a cave. His reindeer went over to them: they caught them, killed them, nourished themselves on them. Bones and horns were heaped up tent-high.

Three years they lived so: then spake the leader: His bow will I steal: maybe now am I strong enough to kill my father—shall undertake it. The father sat backwards: the son shot two arrows at him. Began to shoot again: could not kill his father. But the father caught him by the bow. I am getting tired of this, said he to his son: be thou master here, and for whatever thou sharest with me I shall be grateful.

Fourth Samoyede Story.

There lived once seven brothers, seven rich men in the land: and had reindeer over and above—so many as they could wish. Also, to tend the herds, they kept a servant, whose sister led the sledge-train. So once went the seven brothers on their light sledges—always forward, without looking about them.

But the long train followed, and the servant drove the countless herd behind. He sat himself on a cross-board, on a bad pack-sledge, which had no seat. He used, too, a single reindeer for his sledge.

This servant had but a single arm, which grew in front of his breast, and with which he guided his light sledge. As driving-staff he used a tent-pole, which he supported against his chest and the back of the sledge when he wanted to drive: for he had but one hand, and that already held the reins.

The seven brothers went always forward, without looking round, and crossed seven rivers. Then they reached a very steep cliff which they must traverse. But as the servant came to the cliff, behold! there fell down from the height a man through the frame of his bottom-less pack-sledge, so that his reindeer stopped suddenly in its course.

But the servant said to the man: Why fallest thou right through my pack-sledge? Is the space not wide enough for thee on the Tûndra to fall on one side? The stranger answered: Do not get angry, wait: I tell thee a sensible word: give me that straight-horned deer

Said the servant: No, but thou canst catch that outside stag.

How shall I catch him? said the other. I don't understand how to catch him. Stupid! said the servant: wandering about the earth's ground, and not understanding how to catch a reindeer! Then the stranger asked to have the reindeer harnessed for him, and disappeared.

Suddenly there came a fearful storm and whirlwind. Beyond the river the servant saw a sledge appear with a dark and monstrous man on it, bearing a driving-pole a hundred fathoms long. The reindeer drawing him reached with its horns to the stars: when it snorted, it blew mist and darkness before it, seven days' journey on.

Then thought the servant in his mind: He looks angry and fearful: won't leave a poor wretch like me alive long. The monster proves to be the stranger whom the servant had befriended, and they live happily together ever afterwards.

Such are the stories, half-real, half-imaginary, to which the Samoyede loves to listen in the dark winter nights when the winds sweep over the snow.

SAMOYEDE SONG.

Oka yali manyan toukon—A manyan wao !
　　　　　　　A manyan wao.
Yali, oka yali ! Man pwuthyou—A manyan wao !
Lana pwitha pwanunganya—A manyan wao !
　　　　　　　A manyan wao.

Dawanawa Kânin Tûndra—A takkan wao.
Pwitha harwamas hamgatha—A takkan wao !
Blina Vassili ortagou—A manyan sawo !
                    A manyan sawo.
Pwitha damas yângou vodka—A manyan wao !
                    A manyan wa-a-a-o !

The translation is as follows :

Many hours we been here—Ah, bad for me !
                    Ah, bad for me.
Hours, many hours !   Am tired—Ah, bad for me !
Long talketh he—Ah, bad for me !
                    Ah, bad for me.
To Kânin Tûndra came he—O, bad for him !
What sought he there ?—O, bad for him.
His pancake hath Vassili eaten—Good for me !
                    O, good for me.
Vodka he giveth not—Ah, bad for me !
                    O, woe is the Yellow Man.

To the European ear this ballad sounds perhaps best in Samoyede. The air was original, not exactly soothing, and not founded on any principles of harmony. Taken altogether, it was about as good as if the Samoyedes had asked the Doctor to stand up and compose words, while I improvised a melody.

These stray Mongols extend, under the name of Samoyedes, from the White Sea to the Obi : Ostiaks from thence eastward : Yakuts, Tungûsi, Koriaks, on the

Yenisei and Lena rivers, to the borders of Northern China : with habits and modes of life only varying with the conditions of climate and existence : all nomads, supporting themselves by their reindeer, horses, or dogs, as the case may be. Much alike in costumes, in dwellings, in faith, and more or less alike in language, these scattered races have evidences of a common origin.

The Tungûsi are Mandchous proper. They split into two great tribes as late as the seventeenth century : and this migratory, illiterate race, towards the middle of that century, placed a Mandchou emperor on the throne of China, whose descendant still reigns, and whose language is still the court tongue in Pekin. There is, therefore, an affinity between these poor Samoyedes who are living in darkness and the shadow of ignorance, who feed like savages, who wander homeless over the wildernesses of Siberia—and the witty cultured Chinese, who regard us all as barbarians.

The origin of the Samoyedes and their kindred Siberian races is doubtful : but their life being primitive, and without evidence of development, it is difficult to realise their having led a different existence to the present, or consequently their having inhabited a region different in conditions to this. Climate has varied in these latitudes : but it is difficult now to conceive any other inhabitant for it than the existing races. At the period of the dispersion of the races of mankind from Lower Asia, these Mongols may have found their way up gradually through Central Asia to the Altai Mountains, and thence drifted

northwards to spread along the shores of the Polar
Sea.

Vassili was relieved when our long conferences had
come to an end. I gave him a pancake, a pocket-knife,
a box of cigarettes, a pair of scissors for Piribtyah, and
some roubles.

At midnight the Perevodtchik disturbed us to say the
steamer had been sighted: she had arrived from Umba,
and we could see her smoke over the low stretch of yellow
shore.

In the early morning we set off on foot, each bearing
something, for the shore. We met the mail officer carrying a few letters to the house of the *Stanovoi.* He
showed us one directed to me—care of the official, but
refused to part with the letter except to the *Stanovoi :* so
the Perevodtchik was put upon his trail, and directed not
to lose the mail officer out of sight for a moment.

Vassili Ivanovitch Rogoloff was with me—we were
like brothers: only if any thoughtful Russian had seen
Vassili yesterday and to-day, he must have felt some little
shame at the result of his countryman's intercourse with
the poor dependent savages. Vassili was tottering under
the burden of a light box and two little parcels : and was
repeating himself in a helpless, maudlin way. He was
smoking one of my cigarettes: he smoked one like a
gentleman yesterday, and displayed a calm, patient,
intelligence. To-day he repeats dreamily what the
Samoyedes of Kânin said of us.

Why do you come here to bring evil to reindeer, and

sickness and death to us? Why come? *Z'tchem prîshli?* *Z'tchem?* But I, Vassili, go to Kânin with you. I say *Dobri loudyi*, good people. Samoyedes say: *Anglitchâni* not good to come to our Tûndra. I, Vassili, say: Have come to look. *Dobri loudyi.* My brother been to Pietimburgha—I been Piet'mburgha—Vassili been Pie'mb'rgha, Vassili Ivan'tch Rog'loff.

We arrive at the beach and await the loading of the boats and the return of the mail officer. *Moujiks* stand respectfully round us: but Vassili is close at my side, like an old friend and fellow-grammatist—his cap on one side, and his face grave. As I write, he looks over my shoulder, then looks round and says *Horr'sho!* He nudges my elbow confidentially, but I cannot catch his eye: he having one and a half bottles of vodka on his conscience. He explains to the crowd that I am a Norwegian: when I correct him mildly, he says: *Niet, niet, Anglitchânin.* An old woman arrives to offer me a cross—asks three roubles for it. Vassili nudges me: he murmurs confidentially, Two and a half—then to the woman authoritatively, *Dvas polavina.*

At this stage the Samoyedka heaves in sight, tacking over the waste of sand. Poor Piribtyah too is a victim to the poisonous *vodka.* Vassili goes to meet his wife: he knows she bears the remains of one bottle of *vodka.* They seat themselves on a tree trunk cast up by the sea. I join them and we sit together. The handsome boatmen and our pretty blue-eyed hostess Kovronia, in a sheepskin jacket and hood, stand apart waiting for the boats.

M

Vassili offers me a cigarette from the box : then offers me *vodka.* As I decline, he pours a glassful of the spirit down his throat : Piribtyah does the same. Vassili smacks his lips : Come to Kânin Tûndra, he ejaculates : all the Samoyedes will make you welcome. *Dobri loudyi. Vui Anglitchâni*—takes off his cap—*Zdrazhe-layou*, Welcome ! When you come to Kânin Tûndra ask for Vassili Ivan'itch Rog'loff.

He tries to stand on the round tree trunk, but it rolls : he raises both his hands and smiles apologetically. I go to *parahod*, he sings : I accompany Englishman, I take him to Kânin Tûndra. He wrinkles up his lips to his nose, and sings : I see good *Anglitchânin*, gave me *blini*—*A manyan sawo, A manyan sawo.* Takes off his cap and bows to Piribtyah : Farewell to thee : I go to *parahod. Amanyan sawo.* He smokes a cigarette three inches long, but the tobacco has all fallen out, and I can see the sunlight through the paper.

Piribtyah is seated meantime on the log, her head moving to and fro. She sleeps, then sings a little, and sleeps again. Vassili seizes the bottle and empties it into his throat. They had finished three bottles between them that morning—thanks, alas ! to my money : but how could I refuse the poor creatures money for their services ? A Samoyede when sober has too much dignity to beg : the only thing he will ask for is *vodka*. He sees your money, your food, your knife, but he asks for none of them. Drunkenness is the only habitual vice in his pure and simple life.

Vassili asked me for more money for carrying the small parcels : but I was too disheartened to consent. Consequently, he said he would not wish me good-bye. *Niet diének, nie prostchai !*   No money, no farewell ! Vassili was a materialist.   All our friendship wrecked over a twenty kopeck piece !

We push off in the boats, and see the last of the poor Samoyedes.   Piribtyah falls.   Vassili raises her and takes her by the hand.   He falls, and she tugs at him to lift him.   They trudge and totter over the desert of sand, and we lose sight of them in a cloud of dust and sand drifting with the wind.   Poor souls, their sins are few. They have hardly the consciousness of sin—hardly a conscience at all, with its awful responsibility.

CHAPTER XII.

A *passepartout*—A rich establishment—Coming events—The White Sea monastery—A misunderstanding—The God-worshippers—Selfishness—History
of Solovetsk—Its churches—Sacred paintings—Devotion.

Padorostni from the Government.

IT is permitted to Edward Rae and Henry Pilkington
Brandreth to use at all stations boats, horses, and men
who keep the stations for the Governor, without delay.
For assurance of this, subscribed with the State seal.

GOVERNOR IGNATIEFF.

Ministry of the Interior,
Archangel Government,
    1 2*th June.*

We were rejoiced to find a packet of letters from the
Consul, one containing the *padorostni*, others from England : and we read them as the *Onéga* steamed gaily over
the White Sea.

Workmen from the Terski and Kandalaks coasts frequent Solovetsk for the purposes of building schools and
churches and doing general repairs. They come from

June to September : and receive no pay : only their food
and the absolution and thanks of the saints.   The *Onéga*
carried numerous barrels of herrings from the Terski coast
for the use of the pilgrims.   Every *Boghomôlets* who visits
the monastery receives free food and lodging : but leaves
in return a *gratificacion* for the Holy Church.   Women
may not remain in the island longer than three days at
a time.

The monastery earns much money by its steamers,
which sail in the summer months every three days.   In
fact, it is vastly wealthy.   It has its bakery, brewery, and
other establishments.   Four thousand pounds' weight of
bread are daily baked in the summer season, and this
scarcely suffices for the pilgrims and the monkeys —
as the captain of the *Onéga* inadvertently called the
reverend fathers.   There was no inn, he told us, where
we could buy *vodka*.

Our storm on the Terski coast blew at Solovetsk, and
all round the White Sea with great fury, out of the North
North East.   The squalls on the White Sea, as the captain
said, are frightful.   Seals abound on the Terski and
Karelian coasts.   The ice on Imandra broke up at the
usual time, that is, in the beginning of June : and, what
was very rare, it came floating down to Kandalaks, there
being not enough heat to melt it in the lake.   In 1867
the lakes were covered with ice till the end of June.   This
part of the White Sea in winter is frozen for some versts
round the coast, but outside that, is drift-ice travelling
with the course of each tide.

Many Karelian and Terski peasants volunteered here for the Turkish war, but not many were taken. A good number went to Archangel for the local defence. At the battery at Krepust, near the bar on the Maimouks channel of the Dvina, four thousand soldiers, with artillery from Petersburg, assembled when the English fleet was expected. The miserable bars, channels, and mudbanks of the Dvina are protection enough against any fleet.

The peasants here must pay eighteen, twenty, twenty-five roubles a year to the Government: and they often have no bread in the house. There are symptoms of a change of thought among them. They even make bold to ask, Why the war? Why not a Constitution? Why, indeed, no modification of the system which presses so heavily upon the poor people, refusing them almost the recognition of manhood. The King of Italy pardoned the pastry-cook who attempted his life: the White Tsar had Solovieff beheaded. Poor Tsar! sitting on the safety valve, where he might have reduced the pressure instead. There are two exiled gentlemen, *buntovtchiki*, at Kem, sent to reflect on the vanity of entertaining progressive opinions. All political prisoners are not Nihilists, though they are often confounded with them. But if anything would convert a *buntovtchik* into a *nigilist*, it would be the harsh repression which political opinions receive.

At midnight we were off low rounded islands, thickly wooded. In the centre of the largest stood a white light-house. Westward on the horizon lay, faintly outlined, the coast of Karelia. In the North the sun had dipped:

we were 1° 30′ below the Arctic circle, but the flaming sunlight illumined the white Inland Sea. In the whole heavens not a cloud was to be seen.

We rounded the islands to the westward, and entering Solovetsky harbour, which lies at the southern end, came in front of the remarkable Byzantine group of sacred buildings. We entered the harbour at two in the morning, and moored alongside of two steamers—one, the *Kem*, a branch steamer sailing to Soroka and Onega: the other the Imperial gunboat *Polarnaya Zvisda*, Polar Star, carrying recruits for practice.

The monastery was very like Troitsa—white churches, green cupolas, surmounted by gilded Russian crosses and chains: towering old gray walls, formed of gray granite stones, the interstices covered with orange lichen, like gold settings. On the ramparts stood circular towers, covered with red conical roofs: under the walls stood delicate silver birches. Outside the walls and on the low granite quay, stood one or two shrine-chapels, white on a background of rich green turf and feathery birch woods.

All this group of buildings and colour stood reflected in the glass-like water of the harbour: a most beautiful scene—very unlike the White Sea. Near the quay, outside the monastery walls, stood a great white hospice: on each red mooring post stood a cross. Everything was neat and picturesque. The trees were trim and park-like: there was no look of the rugged North. The walls were an interesting. picture, and the whole place had the brightness and cleanliness of a Dutch town: Solovetsk is

one of the few tidy spots in Holy Russia. Gentle musical
bells chimed the quarter hours, and the whole scene was
romantic and charming. To *Solavietski*, the Islands of
the Nightingale, comes the sweet bird which sings in the
woods of Granada on Easter Sunday—to join in the
singing at the White Sea Monastery on Ascension Day.

We wished to detain the mail steamer, but the captain
would not even consider it. First I thought of a personal
subsidy: then I offered the equivalent of first-class
passage money of twenty persons. Eventually I left the
Perevodtchik to make what terms he could. Judging by
his own account, he seems to have got a little mixed. He
bargained for payment of so many roubles for so many
hours: and as we did not detain the vessel so long, the
little man maintained he would only pay in proportion.

The captain said, writes the Perevodtchik, that he did
not care for any account of the hours — the full sum he
would have: he would say I was a liar, that I had
not interpreted aright. Even Mr. Rae thought it to be
my fault, but I was sure of it.

We landed. On the mooring posts, on the quay at
our feet, were huge gulls, the *Larus canus*, as tame and
self-possessed as pigeons or barn-door fowls. Their plum-
age was lovely and soft—dove-like and white. At three
o'clock we entered the low, old gateway as the rich
morning bells were ringing in the belfries. Here, in the
courtyards and gardens, were the gulls again, thousands
of them, swarming everywhere: quarrelling with pigeons
and sparrows for grains or odd trifles. They perched

within a foot or two of the passer-by : squawked, cooed, squealed, gaped, as tame as flies. It might have been a vast aviary : railings, grass, pavement, steps, teemed with gulls—old and young.

In rude holes or nests lay one, two, or three young gulls—gray, furry, spotted things, very simple looking and droll indeed : almost tame enough to be stroked. They were as much cared for as sacred storks. The old gulls assumed airs of sanctity : but if we pretended to stroke a young one, they were furious in a moment. They were as arrogant as if the monastery had been built for their convenience. It was good to watch them open their mouths, say nothing, but look on the ground as if praying.

We went from one church to another. Here were crowds of *Boghombletsi*, God-worshippers : the same sheep-skin coats, the same stuffy bundles, the same patient faces that throng the shrines of the Holy Land. Here was a Laplander, regenerate and of the orthodox faith, come to leave his mite for the saints. All were wrapping themselves up closely in the biting frosty air. A white-tailed sea-eagle flew overhead. I found in the little woods outside the walls the lovely white star on its slender stem—the chickweed winter-green, *Trientalis Europœa :* and within the monastery the bird-cherry, in full blossom.

I sought long for old silver, but in vain. In a ware-house upon which I chanced, I found and bought thirty of the beautiful embroidered towels which the peasants bring to hang on the shrines : and which the monks trade away for the benefit of the saints. A boy had taken some trouble for us, and I gave him half a rouble. He went straight to the nearest priest, showed him the coin, and bowed low while the priest gave him absolution. I was told it was forbidden to mention money within the monastery walls.

One would respect this delicacy if there were more sincerity in it. The monks of Solovetsk have a reputation for getting rather than for giving. Almost at their doors live the harmless Karelians, whose families starve in the summer, who travel to the Arctic coast to earn their bread, and suffer and die by the hundred for the want of some little medical help. Three hundred miles away lie the *tûndras* of the Samoyedes : and, with all the priests and steamers, these poor savages have remained almost untaught. A *vodka* manufactory was established in Malaya Zemlia six years before either a church was built, or a mission sent.

In reply to a proposal I made to him, the Consul in Archangel wrote me thus : No mission would be countenanced unless proceeding direct from the synod. I make no doubt a good, kind, and honest priest might do good : but should the man, as you say, not be suitable, they would only be perplexed.

Solovetsk would never think of furthering any mission : their system being to take all they can get, and give nothing. Besides the long-robed gentlemen there would, if anything, only strive to instil superstition into the poor

creatures' minds with a view to enriching the monastery's treasury—already full to overflowing. Any proposal on your own part would not find favour in the sight of Government.

The churches were like all other Russian ones, imposing and gaudy. They were crowded with meek and reverent worshippers, and the music and singing were, as usual, sweet and rich.

> *The hushed low voices and the silvery bell,*
> *The incense-laden air, the kneeling throng,*
> *I knew them all: and seemed to hear the cry*
> *Of countless myriads, rising deep and strong—*
> *Help us, we faint, we die.*
> *And from those myriads kneeling, prostrate, bowed,*
> *A low moan rises to the throne on high:*
> *Not shut out quite by error's thickest cloud—*
> *Help us, we faint, we die.*

We saw some unexploded shells, and a piece of wood struck by a ball from one of the English guns when our fleet bombarded the monastery in 1854. Their only gunner having been killed by the bursting of his gun, the fathers formed in procession and marched round the walls, bearing aloft the sacred relics of their founder, while the shells flew harmlessly over their heads. We saw also a great picture of the bombardment, and an obelisk commemorating the event. We spent many hours here, and examined all parts of the monastery, going on board the *Onega* tired out.

Solovetsk was founded in 1429 by St. Sabbatheus, assisted by two other holy monks. Zosimus, one of them, became abbot, and the monastery grew in wealth and power. Novgorod, the great and rich, made large grants of land, and the citizens gave gold, silver, and rich vestments. It was the offspring of the old capital of Russia, that foundation of Ruric the Norseman in the eighth century—the Lord Great Novgorod, as the city was reverently called. This rivals Japanese ceremoniousness to travellers : Will the imperial strangers partake of my honourable rice—and my lord their dog, what will he eat ? Who can resist God and the Great Novgorod ? was a common saying.

The saintly founder's remains are in the Cathedral of the *Preobræstchenia*, or Transfiguration. In 1485, and again in 1538, the monastery and its churches were destroyed by fire : in 1552 they were rebuilt in stone. Between 1590 and 1594 the monks built, of granite boulders, a wall four fathoms high, three fathoms thick, and over four hundred fathoms long. In 1667 the monks rebelled against the Patriarch Nicon and the Tsar. Their leaders were imprisoned, but the monks took arms, and for nine years defended the monastery against the Streltsi. It fell at last, through the treachery of a monk, when many of the rebellious monks were slain and others exiled. The monastery was then held for a year by a garrison of three hundred Streltsi.

In the sixteenth century Sylvester the Monk was banished here by John the Terrible, and here was buried.

So was Abraham Palitsin of Polish fame. Nicon the Patriarch took the cowl here : and Simon, the deposed Tsar of Kazan, was sent here by John the Terrible, and forced to become a monk.

Peter the Great and his unfortunate son Alexis visited Solovetsk in 1702. The small chapel facing our steamer marks the spot where he landed. Within the walls are models of his two vessels—one an English-built yacht.

The celebrated fortress monastery has six churches : The Cathedral of the Transfiguration contains the shrines of St. Zosimus and St. Sabbatheus, which are of silver, weighing 180 lbs., and made in Amsterdam in 1660, by order of the Boyar Boris Morozoff. The *ikonostas* was erected by Peter the Great. Near the cathedral are two chapels with tombs of saints. The Church of the Assumption was built of stone in 1552, that of St. Nicholas in 1590, that of the Annunciation in 1596. The Church of the Metropolitan Philip in 1687, and re-built in 1798. The Church of St. Onuphrius the Great, built in 1667, with a belfry a hundred and twenty feet high, stands outside the monastery walls.

The sacristy is full of treasures—gifts from sovereigns and nobles : vestments given by John the Terrible, shrines of silver, a cross of gold and pearls, a rare copy of the Evangelists, and such things as justify what many people call dishonesty on the part of collectors or antiquaries. There are the Psalter of St. Zosimus, a picture of the Virgin, brought to the island by St. Sabbatheus, and the armour of Abraham Palitsin : the swords of Princes

Shinski and Pojarski: various original charters from Novgorod city, and many miscellaneous old weapons.

I was disappointed with the pictures at Solovetsk. In some of the old Russian churches they are full of beauty and feeling. There are myriads of these idol paintings—for to the masses they are little else—in this huge empire. At the time of the foundation of the Russian Church, prohibited by their faith from the worship of carved images, the early Russian Christians brought from the holy places of pilgrimage pictures of the Messiah, of Virgins, and of saints. They protected all but the faces from the wear of devotees' lips, by plates of precious metal: and their descendants, who, void of original genius, have a remarkable talent for imitation, closely and successfully copied the originals.

Some of these pictures have the feeling and colour, in fact, almost everything but the originality of Cimabue, Giotto, and Fra Angelico. One of the most revered subjects is the Virgin with the bleeding cheek. A priest once struck, it is said, a picture of the Virgin: and blood issued, and continued to flow from the Virgin's cheek. Another much venerated subject is the Virgin with three hands. A monk was painting a picture of the blessed Lady bearing in her hands the child Christ. On returning to his work one day, he found a third hand had been added. He painted this over, wondering much. The same thing happened thrice: then the monk recognised that it was the work of angels.

I have many old Sclavonic pictures—careful reproductions, in many cases, of older Byzantine originals : some worn with kissing, others smeared and smoky from the use of tapers.

Poor, reverent, credulous, worshippers ! This empire, founded in the days of Alfred the Great, by nomad Sclavonians, ought to have become great in the world's history. Enthusiasm, obedience, devotion, on such a scale as among the Russian people, constitute a prodigious force for good or evil.

A Russian officer told his troops they were to capture a stronghold. It is impossible, they said. He ordered them to advance, and they took the place. Why did you say it was impossible ? he asked the soldiers afterwards. So it was, they replied. Then how could you take it ? *Ti nam preekazall !* You ordered us to. This obedient devotion was worthy of Cœditius. Soldiers ! said he, before a desperate action : it is necessary for us to go, but it is not necessary for us to return.

Count Golovkin was about to sell his serfs in order to pay his debts. Deputies from among his peasants came to Moscow, beseeching an audience of their lord. They begged to know why they were to be dismissed. Because, said the Count, I must pay my debts. How much? exclaimed the deputies, all at once. About thirty thousand roubles. *Spassi nas Bogh ! Nie prodai nas ! Mwee dienghi prinisiom.* God help us ! Do not sell us ! We will bring the money.

CHAPTER XIII.

AFTER four hours' steaming, we entered the fiord which
leads to the capital of Karelia. The shores were rocky,
low, and covered with woods. The water, brought down
by the broad River Kem from the Kuitta and the lakes of
Finland, had the transparent brown of a moorland stream.
Steaming past a grass-grown battery, a few salmon weirs,
and two ships loading timber, we proceeded for several
miles, and anchored three versts below the town. Kem was
in sight—a pleasant-looking little town, or large village,
standing where the Poudaz and Kem Rivers met and broke
in a broad rapid. We could see three churches with conical
steeples, not the cupola of the orthodox churches : and all
round lay gently sloping land, richly wooded.

Kem is of older date than most of the North Russian
towns. The traditional founders of Kem and settlers of
this region are the Tchudes—a branch of the Finns,
connected with the Yugrians and Esthonians. Their

reputed descendants the Karelians have their villages distinct from those of the Russian settlers: the latter adhering
to the coast, and the former to the interior.   Sjögren, a
Finnish writer, thinks the Karelians or their predecessors
once extended all through the Kola district to the
Northern Ocean.   They have the legend of Valit, the
conqueror of Lapland, whom they claim as a countryman.

In the fifteenth century Kem belonged to Martha, the
Possadnitsa of Novgorod, who gave it to the monastery
of Solovetsk.   In 1580 the Finlanders attacked and took
it, the *Voyevoda* of Solovetsk and many Streltsi being
slain in the defence.   In 1590 the Swedes captured Kem
and its entire district.   A wooden fortification, built by
the monks in 1657, was destroyed by floods.   One
grotesque hexagonal battery, built by the Streltsi at the
command of the Empress Katharine, is in sight now:
slanting painfully to one side like the tower of Pisa, and
apparently ready to fall into the river.   This absurd old
block-house fired on the English war vessels in 1854.

The inhabitants of Kem are almost entirely *stareveri*,
heterodox Old Believers, to whom the greater part of the
White Sea fishing stations and vessels belong.   Their
fishers sail for the northern coasts in clumsy *lodjes*,
snékas, and *kotschmaris*, that is, *chassemarées*.   In summer
the town is almost deserted by the male population: the
wives remain behind for necessary work, and occasionally
make pilgrimages to the monastery of Solovetsk.

After the custom-house officers had kept us waiting for
four hours, we determined to go on shore in one of the

N

steamer's boats.   Half-way we met the customs' boat and were peremptorily recalled.   The *Pristavnik*, a small, fat, pompous, fussy, old man, in the Russian official uniform, pryed into every corner of our portmantcaus.   This self-important little insect, probably bullied by his wife, was the embodiment of inquisitiveness and suspicion.

In a voice intended to alarm and subdue, he demanded full and complete papers : of course he meant papers, small, bearing the inscription—

ГОСуΔAPCТВЕННЫІЙ   КРЕΔІТНЫІЙ   ЫІΛЕТЬ.
ОΔІΛНЬ РуВΛБ

and embellished with a double eagle and the Imperial crown : but we were vexed at the delay and recall to the steamer, and were determined that he should not have a kopeck if we kept him in hopes all through the night. I leisurely handed him our passports.   Where is the endorsement ? he growled.   I pointed to the special Russian *visé* obtained in England.   Where do you come from ?   Vardö.   Where is the Vardö endorsement ?   I showed the Vardö vice-consul's endorsement, and began to suspect that this aggressive little turbot could neither read nor write.

But after Vardö ?   From Kola.   Where is the Kola Ispravnik's certificate ?   I gave him Ivan Abramovitch's letter, which rather took him aback.   But how do I know that you have the liberty to travel here ? he exclaimed, as he felt his importance was dwindling away in the eyes of the deferential minions in uniform.   He looked

round as if to say: This will be too much for the stranger.
I gave him the *padorostni* from the Governor of Archangel, which scotched the little *Pristavnik*. But his
opportunity came.

Ti kto ?—What are you ? he suddenly asked the Perevodtchik. A Norwegian, may it please you, replied the
Linguist. Give me your passport. The Perevodtchik
said reverently that he had none. No passport ! shouted
the little man. What papers then ? None : you see
I am only the Perevodtchik : I am of no consequence.
Papers of no consequence ! roared the *Pristavnik :* how
dare you ? *Da, ya nie shto :* I really am of no importance,
said our unhappy secretary. Where do you live ? Why
do you come here ? Who saw you last ? What do you
mean ? blurted out the little *Pristavnik*, looking indig-
nantly round. I told the Perevodtchik to disarm him
by saying I was a professor engaged in a scientific work
of a mixed nature, and he my assistant. This would give
the Expedition an unpolitical and unwarlike character.
But it was in vain.

The Perevodtchik's heart grew heavy as there whirled
through his mind, like scenes in a nightmare, the pitiless
Pristavnik, the *Pravlennik*, the Ispravnik, their offended
dignity, their small salaries, their few opportunities : their
misplaced conviction that he was indispensable to us, and
that we would redeem him from captivity by rouble notes.
Then the rapacious Cossacks, detention, various accumu-
lative fees, loss of the Englishmen, his return to Vardö an
unsuccessful man. For the Perevodtchik had lived for

some years in Russia, and knew all this, as he should have known that to come to Russia without full papers was an inexcusable stupidity.

The *Pristavnik* took our papers for endorsement by the *Pravlennik :* then told the Perevodtchik to find identification, or remain under arrest. Identification in Kem! Tears rose to the little man's eyes, and I was very sorry for him : because, as I was obliged to tell him, we could not delay our journey.

The *Pristavnik*, who now entertained definite hopes in the direction of our exchequer, became very polite. He offered to take us up to the town in his official boat, but I thanked him, and said we had our own.

We proceeded up the stream and landed near the rapid, with the dejected and almost despairing Perevodtchik. We went to the *Stantsia*, a white wooden house, with numerous little windows looking out over the Poudaz River. One-third of Kem lies between the two rivers : the remainder on the north bank of the Poudaz.

A Cossack accompanied us, having one eye on the Perevodtchik, and the other on the small rouble notes with which I was making disbursements. The Cossack, though orthodox in point of discipline, was heterodox in matter of coinage. The *Potchtovoi*, or posting master, keeper of the *Stantsia*—which was also styled in large letters, KEMSKAYA POTCHTOVAYA KONTORA, Kem Post-office—declined to receive us. He was an Old Believer, of the first water, a *Raskolnik*, who would have turned us away had we not produced the Governor's letter.   Then he agreed to find a room for us.

A gentleman now made his appearance, in a red cotton shirt and a flat cap: having a wide countenance shaded by yellow hair.   The heterodox Cossack had meantime taken our crushed secretary away.   *Samovar?* the stranger inquired.   *Seytchass*, I said: Directly.   *Seytchass* is supposed to represent something quite sudden. It is, however, only the Norwegian *straks* in disguise: and is about as forcible as by-and-by.

I asked for milk.   There is no milk in the house, said the Korelak: and I don't see a cow anywhere.   The idea of catching sight of a cow and hurrying out to milk it was so genial and original, that I asked the Korelak his name: Stepan Petrovitch Makuskin.

The prevailing idea in the Russian peasant's mind concerning travellers is the *samovar*.   The first questions asked are of course *Otkouda?* Where from, etc?   But the *samovar* comes next, and appears to comprehend meat and drink, though it only represents hot water.   Bring eggs too, we said: and a salmon.   There is no salmon in the house.   Then buy one.   *Horosho*, he said.   The variety of expression that this word is capable of is infinite. *Horosho*, slowly: I will see.   *Horosho*, quickly: I understand.   *Horoshâw!* My word!   *Horôsho:* Very excellent. *Horosho*, impatiently: Don't bother me.   *Horoshohoroshâw:* O goodness!

At this moment I caught sight of two cows, and hailed Stepan Petrovitch.   I see them, he said: *Seytchass, sey-*

tchass. Stepan hastened out and returned with a bowl of warm milk. The Karelian customs are excellent. Our jam is rapidly failing us, and this occasions a want of confidence between the Doctor and me. He makes raids upon it under the impression that I blame the Perevodtchik. I consequently appropriate the chocolate in the silent night : and the Doctor suspects our late secretary.

We bought at Solovetsk what we call maccaroons : pink, sickly-looking biscuits, tasting of peppermint and smelling of the monastery. An old lady was taken to an ancient church. How solemn it smells! she said. We determined to buy more confectionery here. An Old Believer named Vôronoff had some, Stepan said. His shop was closed, but we went to his house, some distance away. It was one in the morning, and Stepan went up to his room, but the bigot refused to get out of bed to assist us. In no country does a traveller receive from the Government so many facilities for travelling, and from the people so few.

This anticipates. We are waiting for the *samovar.* Stepan arrives. From one pocket he produces a small packet of tea : from the other a great lump of sugar, wrapped up in a fragment of an Archangel newspaper. The *samovar* is not due yet. All that takes place when the *samovar* is wanted is this : Stepan goes to the kitchen or common room, and asks Feôdora Martinovna to get the *samovar* ready.

So Feôdora gets the brass implement down from its shelf. Then, having no sand in the house, she goes down to the river bank, and has to answer, in crossing the road, six or eight questions about the *Anglitchâni* in the *Stantsia*. Then she conscientiously scrubs and cleans the *samovar*. Meantime Stepan Petrovitch goes out to select a dry log, and with an axe shaves off some thin strips of pine : or he tears some bark from birch logs, to light the charcoal.

Then Feôdora takes from a box, of which the key was in the top of the house, two tumblers, and searches for a cloth to wipe them with. Then a tray has to be found : but there being no sugar, Stepan goes out and buys some : and the sugar basin being lost, a saucer is cleaned instead. Tea is put into the *tchaïnik*, and the *samovar* is ready. So that it really occupies one or two Russians for three-quarters of an hour to get hot water for a traveller, without their having been quite idle during any part of the time. The traveller who knows this will not give himself up to impatience, or the representative Stepan Petrovitch to abuse.

We had entertained hopes that we should lose the Perevodtchik : but as we sat by the open window at supper we saw him approaching the house alone. We knew then that he was once more at large, and that the reactionary Cossack had released him. It seemed that by a singular happy coincidence a Norwegian was found, and induced to say he remembered the Perevodtchik : also a Russian, to state that he had been in Vadsö, and was familiar with the detained. I did not ask the expense of this : but in the East a witness costs about

twenty-five piastres, and in this country I should not
hesitate, in case of need, to give a higher sum.

We rambled about with Stepan in quest of *sviati
obrasi* and silver crosses, going with him from house to
house among the Mirsky, or Orthodox families : for a
Stareviernik will not sell a cross.   I succeeded in getting a
dozen old crosses, but no *obrasi*, though we saw many of
them.   The devotion of the *Raskolniki* to these images
is intense.

Their Idoles have their hearts, on God they never call :
Unlesse it be Nikola Bogh, that hangs against the wall.
The house that hath no god, or painted saint within,
Is not to be resorted to : that roofe is full of sinne.

An Old Believer will stand for hours crossing himself
before one of these painted saints.   He will not attend
the Orthodox Church services, but has his own priests,
and gives himself up to prayer and contemplation : believing that this life's affairs are as far removed from those
of the other life, as earthly meadows from the vault of
heaven.   To please God, man must turn his back upon
the world : pray for persecution, treachery, hatred, ill-will,
and thereby earn a martyr-crown in heaven.   A few
weeks ago the Tsar released from prison three *Stareviertsi*
bishops, who, for the tenacity of their convictions, had
remained in prison since 1856.

There is a wide belief among these heterodox ascetics
that Nicon, the famous reformer, founder of the Orthodox
faith, lived three whole years with the devil in a cave : and

A KARELIAN STANTSIA.

there, under the Evil One's dictation, perverted the old
writings of pure teaching.   When ready, Nicon prepared
to visit the reigning Tsar, Alexei Mikaïlovitch, to prepare
him for the new teaching.   The latter, being warned in a
dream, shut himself up in a strongly-guarded castle.   A
blow from Nicon's cloak opened the doors of the fortress :
the Tsar was convinced, and the present Orthodox Scrip-
tures were adopted.   The *Stareviertsi* won't read them, but
retain the old legends and monastic works written in
Sclavonic.

· The very method of crossing among the Orthodox is
an offence.   What says the fiend - inspired innovator ?
Cross thyself with the thumb, the forefinger, and the
middle-finger. · Here thou seest the devil's play, for well
must thou know the forefinger represents the Earth, the
middle - finger Heaven, and the thumb God.   What a
diabolical reasoning—a Trinity composed of God, Heaven,
and Earth !

This is not all.   As the three Persons of the Godhead
are of equal rank, so must the benedictory fingers have
the same height.   But the middle is higher than the index
finger, as the heaven is above the earth : if, then, the two
fingers are held at an equal height, the dwelling of God
must lower itself to the sinful earth.   The heterodox say,
therefore : Cross thyself with the thumb for God, the third
finger for the Son, and the little finger for the Holy Spirit.

An Old Believer is highly sensitive to pollution.   He
cannot tolerate that even one of his own family should drink
from his cup or use his spoon.   Castren says the Faithful at

Knashja took such exception to his horse's drinking out of the village well, that it at once became unclean, and he himself was exposed to difficulties in consequence. He acknowledges, however, the kindness and willingness of these silly fanatics. The *Stareviertsi* are respectable, good old-fashioned people, partly corresponding to the worthy Friends of England and America. Poor Castren— enthusiast and genius—he was seriously ill at Kem : contracting the disease which his own courage and energy could only battle with for a few years.

The Raskolnik town has seven hundred inhabitants, of whom but two hundred are Mirsky or Orthodox. The fishing here consists of salmon and salmon-trout : *navaghi*, small cod : *njelma*, or white Siberian salmon : and small flounders. A beautiful salmon of 18 lbs. cost us two roubles and a half, which was dear for Kem. *Njelma* costs in the season threepence a pound : they occasionally reach the weight of 40 lbs. The fishery is carried on in winter as well as in summer : the fishers hew holes in the ice to lay their nets. Starting from Kem or Soroka, they often travel sixty versts over the ice in a small sledge or *pulka*, drawn by a single dog. Corn comes from Archangel : the yeast used here is made from beer or *kvass*. The peasants of Karelia, as a rule, are so poor that they must mix birch-bark and even straw with the rye-meal : only a few of those in better circumstances can use unmixed flour. We found this bread difficult to eat, but rather better when dry and old.

The River Kem is the line which divides Karelia from

Pomoria.   The journey overland to Uleaborg, by river, lake, and forest, takes fourteen days: the return journey, with the current of the Kem River, nine.   The *Ouyesda* of Kem embraces a wide district, having a population not far short of thirty thousand.   Of these not four hundred can read and write : and in Karelia and the Pomorsk villages, there are at least fifteen hundred souls unable to support themselves.

In spite of this pitiful fact, less than forty crimes have been committed in the Kemsk *Ouyesda* in five years : and of these only five were thefts : one, murder : one, house robbery : one, disobedience of officials : one, harbouring a deserter : and twenty-two, unlawful wood-cutting.   Fifteen hundred starving creatures—and in five years twenty-two had cut wood in the Government forests.

It is true that these persons had no other means of warming their children in the dreadful White Sea winter. Also, that the Government have in these regions twenty thousand square miles of untouched forest : and that they levy the manhood tax upon each individual whether he has bread in the house or not.   But dishonesty is so repugnant to the mind of a Russian official, that he must carry out the law even at the sacrifice of his own generous and merciful instincts.

Heaven knows, if the Doctor and I had been the odd two of the two-and-twenty, and we had been in Karelia starving for five years—or, for the matter of that, in England—we should have helped ourselves to firewood or food, and thought it no sin.

Apart from unlawful wood-cutting, among twenty thousand poor hard-living peasants there are three crimes annually : and of these one theft. Drunkenness does not exist among the Karelians : but we saw a low Russian drinking-house in the chief street of Kem, said to be the only one in the *Ouyesda.*

The Karelians are peaceable, domestic, forgiving. Mixed with the Russians, as in parts they have been for centuries, they have lost with their original Lutheran faith much of their energy and independence. Their language is closely allied to the pure Finnish—is, in fact, only a dialect of it : and it is hard to tell where a Karelian ends and a Finn begins.

The entire population extending from Kem to the Arctic coast in 1861 was this :

	Russians.	Karelians.	Lapps.
	17,600	14,637	2,000
Horses .	2,251	1,822	5
Cattle .	4,121	4,835	96
Sheep . .	10,636	6,720	319
Reindeer .	7,233	1,916	4,181

Possessing respectively.

CHAPTER XIV.

Appearance of Kem—An inflammable village—Old silver—An acquisition—
    Departure from Kem—An escape—Ianotka's after career—A launch—
    Pongamo—Government posting stations—Stray Lapps—A deserted *isba*
    —Wild flowers.

THE village of Kem is old-fashioned and picturesque.
Quaint old dark block-houses slant forward and sideways,
with heavy projecting gables : green trees rise between
them. Shops are scarce, and are dotted about in ordinary
houses : a signboard rudely painted in the Russian fashion
being the only outward mark of a shop. The streets are
simply green grass, with planked side walks : there is no
vehicle traffic in the summer, and the snow is the paving
in winter. As the Kemski always use the side-walks, the
streets might as well as not be planted with vegetables.
The ground is uneven, and the old dark houses form a
succession of picturesque perspectives. Kem has the look
of a town of Old Believers. All about the place is water.
First the large river and the Poudaz, then two smaller
streams, and numerous pools and inlets of the sea. In
some enclosures potatoes were springing up. In most of
the windows were roses, geraniums, scented geraniums,

fuchsias, musk, or some such sweet flowers.   In one window lay a colossal Russian cat.   At the northern end of
the town stood several painted Norwegian-looking houses.
One of these, of considerable size, would cost about two
hundred pounds.

Two hundred versts up the Kem River large timber
grows : some of the wood measuring sixty feet in length
and twenty-two inches in thickness.   A schooner lay in
the fiord, which had brought rye-flour from Archangel, and
was loading firewood for Vardö.   The forests in Syd
Varanger have been so much thinned that cutting is forbidden, and it is cheaper to import Russian wood than to
buy Norwegian.

Milk and eggs are plentiful in Kem.   I saw some
lovely calves, with coats as dark and glossy as sable.
Mosquitoes hovered about us, not very venomous yet, for
the summer was late.   In the past winter the snow lay a
yard, where it usually lies a foot, deep.

At midnight I had a steam bath, and afterwards went
out to photograph the Pomorsk bank of the river, the long
wooden bridge, and the rapid.   A thick mist was rising
from the rapid, and faint sunlight came from behind the
trees.   A watchman was on his rounds, and a watch-
woman : both on the look-out for fires.   There are eight
watchers in this inflammable old village.   In the summer
months the women undertake the duties of the more sensitive sex, and are referred to indifferently as *tcholoveka*,
men.   This is one of the few spots in Europe where
woman can rejoice in the right of sharing man's occupations.

I had, of course, a prolonged search for old silver. Mr. Howorth, the learned author of the *History of the Mongols*, suggests that the Northern silver art has an Eastern character and an Eastern origin. He accounts for this by the progress of Arab civilisation northward—both east and west of the Ourâl Mountains, on both sides of the Caspian, and as far as the White Sea : by the constant intercourse of the Eastern traders with the cultivated communities of the Khazars and Bulgars on the Volga : by the incessant presence of Norsemen in Eastern and Southern Russia : by the evidence of *samani* and other Oriental coins found all over the North of Europe. He might have further instanced the Oriental origin of Odin and his adventurers, and the maintenance of a Scandinavian or Varangian body-guard at Mikkelgard or Byzantium.

For years past I have been struck with the similarity between Northern and Eastern silver. In the study of old silver—at the sacrifice of, at all events, too much time—I have collected in Syria, Egypt, Barbary, Algeria, on the one hand : and in Denmark, Iceland, Norway, Sweden, Russia, Lapland, and all round the White Sea, on the other. The more the silver ornaments are seen together, the more the Northern and Eastern types seem to harmonise. An Icelandic belt will have a purely Eastern design : Kabyle neck ornaments strung together with Lapp belt plaques, will suit perfectly : certain classes of filigree-work approach one another so closely that some of the beads may have been brought, for all I can tell now, either from Russia, Iceland, or Barbary.

Certain classes of work are, of course, distinctive of the Christian countries. Spoons, drinking-cups, crosses, reliquaries, are not found among the Mohammedans : nor are charms, amulets, and the variety of elaborate and often ponderous necklets or bracelets, worn as much for security as ornament in the East, found among the Northern people. It is suggestive that, among the honest Scandinavian races, tankards, cups, spoons, and suchlike easily convertible and portable objects should have abounded : while among the Russians crosses hung at the neck : and among the Orientals, rings, bracelets and anklets, worn about the person, and rarely out of the owner's sight, should have predominated.

The presence of Byzantine art in Russia is easily accounted for : but there is a vast amount of pure Eastern design and workmanship which found its way to Scandinavia, independently of Russia or the Eastern Church. The subject of Oriental art in the North is worthy of study and development, though the practical pursuit of specimens is laborious and not inexpensive.

There are numerous bears in the neighbourhood of Kem. A short time since a bear devoured seven sheep close to the town, but none of the Old Believers would venture out to do battle with him. Kem is full of sledge-dogs. I once possessed a handsome Karelian sledge-dog. I possessed him for about six hours and a half. He was wolf-like, and of a light buff colour, having black patches above his beautiful eyes and about his muzzle. I saw him lying near a peasant's house, as I was buying an old

cross.   After the purchase the Korelak held up a black
kitten at the window.   Will you buy that? he said,
laughing.   Traveller: No, will you sell the dog? Korelak: Yes.   Traveller: How much?   Korelak: A rouble
and a half.   Traveller: Good.   This was a short introduction.   Ianotka, after receiving a blameless character, was seized and bound: and when we sailed in the
morning he was, reluctantly, put into the boat.

Instead of being awakened at four o'clock by the
Perevodtchik, as stipulated, I had to awaken him at half-
past five, and to tell him that we had missed the tide.   In
the vexation which this caused me, I forgot myself, and
called the Perevodtchik a skunk.   We started on a brilliant
summer's morning, and after being rowed for a few hours
by our four boatwomen, we were deserted by the tide,
and lay stranded for some hours on the mud in a broad
channel.

The first thing the young ladies had brought on board
was a *samovar:* the last were cups, saucers, and a teapot.
The Doctor and I wondered, seeing them partake of *tchaï*
before they would consent to start, whether we should have
to make afternoon tea, and ask each of them whether
she took sugar and cream.   Our ancestors used to take
sugar and cream without giving any trouble.   The four
young ladies talked from the minute they appeared on
the river bank to the moment of the final *Prostchaïtje:* at
least, they stopped talking only when they wanted to sing.

We were sitting in the warm sun drinking tea, having
made enough for the whole ship's company.   The dog,

whose family name was Makuskin, had been reserved all
the morning, pleasantly mannered, but refusing to eat or
to make friends.   At 10 A.M., while on the mud-bank,
we took the opportunity of breakfasting.   Ianotka Rae,
late Makuskin, cheered up a little, and ate bread and
salmon.   He was apparently beginning to understand that
he must make the best of me.   At 10.29 A.M. I heard a
cry, and saw that the dog had stepped out of the boat,
and was moving slowly away on the sticky mud.

Stepan, who, I ought to have said, had come as our
korseka or steersman, sprang after him, and his haste
accelerated the dog's pace.   *Sobâka, sobâka !* the women
shouted, but the *sobâka* seemed to have an instinct that
it was now or never.   The Perevodtchik, who felt that
any misadventure owing to our missing the tide, would
be laid at his door, had hurriedly taken off his boots and
joined in the race.   The dog was steadily gaining.
Ianotka ! Ianotka ! called the women : but Ianotka had
gained the land, looked round once for his bearings, and
careered into the woods.   The women said it was an
island, and that Stepan would catch the dog.   There was
a quarter of an hour's silence.

11.30 A.M.   Some creature was sighted, half-a-mile
away, cautiously feeling its way across the mud.   It was
the Karelian sledge-dog, Ianotka Makuskin, late Rae, who
had found he was on an island, and must make for the
mainland without loss of time, as the tide would rise soon.
The Perevodtchik did not appear.   Stepan had seen him
last in the woods.

Would he never return, or would he limp back with some self-inflicted wound which should move me to tears and compassion? At length he appeared, travelling towards the boat like a fly on a plate of honey. I asked him agreeably to let us have breakfast. The Perevodtchik almost kissed my hand, for he knew that we had spent five hot hours on the sandbank, and lost the dog and the ebb-tide, thanks to his unpunctuality.

I considered that the dog's intelligence and love of home entitled him to his liberty : but on second thoughts, believing he might be made happier, fed better, and worked less, than in Kem, I afterwards arranged to have him sent to England. Ianotka has now been a resident in Cheshire for two years. At first shy and suspicious, he now trusts, and is popular with everybody. Gentle and polite, but no fonder of one than another, he is a thorough Russian. Often trying to escape at first, and still fond of roaming, he has not lost his Arctic instincts. A month after his coming, while still furtive and strange, he picked out in an excited and noisy crowd a lady who had been kind to him a fortnight before. He has a tutor to take him out for exercise and teach him English. He understands I am his master. But that we talk to one another in Russian, and that he knows I remember his giving me the slip on the White Sea shore, I should have no special hold upon him.

We proceeded up the Karelian coast, which was low, wooded, and had numerous outlying islands. Ducks, geese, gulls, etc., were very plentiful. Landing on an

island, we found several nests of eider, teal, and other
ducks : also an orange star-fish, which we never saw on
the Mûrman or Terski coasts. We saw for the first time
the black and gray Lapland crow, *Corvus Lapponicus.* In
a blaze of light the sun slowly dipped for an hour, leaving
a sky of purple and flame colour. We were approaching
the Arctic circle again.

We awoke to find the boat on the beach, and the crew
asleep round a fire. We had awakened the Perevodtchik
to cook for us, and to make tea for the rest of the Expedition, when we noticed that the tide was leaving the
boat. Arousing the whole party, we made violent efforts
to launch our great heavy boat, in vain. Here was a
second tide rapidly slipping from us. We dragged every
movable thing out, but the boat would not budge. With
half-a-dozen strokes Stepan cut a young birch-tree into
lengths for rollers : with indescribable difficulty we raised
the lumbering boat to admit the rollers : and, using oars,
masts, poles, and branches as levers, we thrust the boat
into the water.

Then we came to the small village of Pongamo, lying
on a stream near the sea coast. Encouraged by the
promise of a special rouble, Stepan had the new boat prepared within an hour. We spent the time in a clean
room, whither the priest and several of the neighbours
came to stare at us and ask questions. I bought some
crosses, and Stepan ranged all over the village in search
of old Karelian tankards without finding any. Then
Stepan demanded the boat hire. This journey of thirty

hours cost, by the Government tariff, one rouble and a
half, or three shillings—that is, about three halfpence per
mile for hire of boat and crew : the traveller being expected to give a few kopecks to the boat people by way
of *vodkou*.   The poor hard-working women and Stepan
were quite surprised when we gave them a present of
eight roubles, and a packet of tea to cheer them on their
journey back.

Our *padorostni* enables us to claim these posting boats
on the same terms as the Government tax officials and
others, for whose convenience the system is maintained.
The *khozeyn*, or master, receives, at Keret for example,
eight hundred roubles a year : for which he undertakes all
the duties and charges of the summer boating and winter
sledging of his posting station.   In summer he maintains
two boats, each with a steersman and a crew of four
women, who receive about twenty roubles each for the
season, and their food when on service.   In the winter he
must keep two horsemen, four horses, and several reindeer, all of which are at the disposal of the traveller who
bears the Government letter.   From a traveller unrecom-
mended, the *khozeyn* may extort whatever terms he can.

The winter track through Karelia from Kem to Kandalaks lies inland : it is fairly well kept, and cleared of
snow.   In summer, lakes, rivers, and melting snow make
it impracticable.   In the winter the traveller journeys for
hundreds of versts through black woods rising from the
sheet of snow : while the winds moan through them, the
wolves howl through the long night, and the awful

Northern Lights flash like diamond vapours, or shiver in the heavens like curtains of flame.

On the Letna Raika, twenty-three versts north of Kem, live in winter two Lapp families. They stray thus far south of their hunting-grounds in quest of wild reindeer, which frequent this country in herds of two or three hundred. The Lapps pursue them in a *pulka*, drawn by reindeer and accompanied by dogs. Within the memory of man, Lapps lived habitually on the Kouto and Pää lakes: but, with the exception of these few souls near Pongamo, none now live south of Babinsky. There are about a hundred souls in Pongamo, of whom ten are Korielski. There is a newly-built wooden church of fair size. All our boat people, and the women and girls we meet on this coast, have blue eyes.

We set out in a new but smaller boat, having an excellent hard-working crew: Tekla Dimitrievna, Petrovna Kovronia, Feôdora Andréevna, Peterina Alexandrevna, being our ladies' names: and Karili Dimitrieff the name of the gentleman who undertook the laborious task of steering. It rained thickly as we left Pongamo. We made steady progress up the coast against a head wind.

The White Sea traveller must study the tides, and may make them useful allies. Between Kem and Pongamo the ebb-tide helps boats northward: from Pongamo northward the ebb sets to the south. It may be taken for granted that to travel southward in these regions by boat is easier than to travel northward. The prevailing winds are the North, and its cousins the North-east and North-

LAPP SUMMER ENCAMPMENT.

west.   The latter blows here sometimes for two long summer months as steadily as a trade-wind.   We landed on a small island, and made ourselves at home for a few hours in a ruinous *isba*, awaiting the flood-tide.

It was a gray sea, a gray rock, and a gray sky.   Our log-hut measured twelve feet each way and five in height : an opening in the roof operated about as effectually as, or very little better than, modern ventilating shafts or costly flues elaborated with huge mental effort in our own country.   That is to say, where the smoke should have gone out it came in, and where the cold air should have come in, the smoke tried to go out.   In the case of the hut, about three-fourths of the smoke did not go out, but was inspired into our systems through mouth and nostrils.

The whole party had streaming eyes, and could barely eat for coughing.   At times we were obliged to lie flat down to avoid the denser smoke at the top of the hut. The Perevodtchik, with an enthusiasm inspired by three roubles and a half per day, stood gallantly to his fire-irons, and evolved out of the flame and smoke a dish of fried salmon, a black pancake, and a tin of soup, which we salted with our tears.

The island had a pretty little wood, in which the ground was carpeted with cloud-berry, *Rubus chamæmorus*. I found also the branched dog-violet with huge blossoms, the heart's-ease, the delicate oak fern, the Alpine cerastium, and the lovely *Antennaria alpina* or pink and white everlastings of Switzerland and the Pyrenees, all recalling a different climate and different scenes.   Wild flowers become companions, sometimes sad ones, in a traveller's memory.   Perhaps in these Northern solitudes they have a beauty greater than elsewhere.   The Son of God saw in the wild flowers which then as now made beautiful the plains and woods of Palestine, a perfectness exceeding the utmost glory of man : and the lovely Arctic plants and fruits, in which the Creator alone can take pleasure, are lavished by millions of acres in these regions where no soul or animal lives to consume them : and here they spring up, blossom, ripen, die, untouched and unseen.

CHAPTER XV.

Kalgalaks—A pleasant evening—Literary possibilities—A fishing spot—Somostrova—An anxiety—Qualities of the peasants—Keret—The Korelak—
A selfish priest—A human spider—Suggestions—Wonders.

WE reached, after thirty hours' journey, the village of
Kalgalaks, which the river of the same name divides into
two parts. Two hundred blue-eyed good-looking cleanly
people live here : two dozen Korielski among them.
About forty men go each spring to the Mûrman fishery,
and five for seal, whale, and walrus to Nova Zemlia. The
river is navigable by boat for about thirty versts. While
we sent as usual the last boatman to hasten the next
crew, and the Perevodtchik to cruise about for old crosses,
the priest came to read the Governor's letter on behalf of
the *Stantsia* keeper, and to endorse the travellers' record
book. We paid here for a pail of milk, some eider-duck's
eggs, a famous loaf of bread, and some flat fish, seventy
kopecks, or one shilling and fivepence. Two old *lodjes* lay
high and dry, and an efficient one was loading wood some
way down the river, where the water was deep enough.

Leaving Kalgalaks, we proceeded up a succession of
salt water lakes connected with the sea, and opening out

among lovely park-like woods of fir and larch. For two-
thirds of our journey we did not come in sight of the sea.
We saw shoals of little fish, *kolugha*—not good to eat—
and a small fish, *jalésina*, having a spike at each side and
on the back. We saw a white-tailed sea-eagle crossing
over the woods, a teal with a very young brood, many
strings of ducks, several geese, and a few divers. Our
Karelian boatwomen were so good-looking, and their
dress was so brilliant and pretty, that we stopped near a
small rapid to photograph them. As they rowed they
sang—not very perfectly, but the boat-songs were picturesque and interesting.

We stopped at a small *isba*, Varovnia, and went in to
cook our breakfast. It was near midnight. Again a low
warm cabin, but not so full of smoke. Going in I found
a woman and four girls, and I said I had the honour to
be their servant. They pleasantly replied: *Milostje
prossim*, Welcome. Our boatwomen were there too, and
as they sat round the cabin in the firelight it was quite a
picture. Of eight faces six were pretty, and all were
modest and pleasant. The Perevodtchik cooked salmon-
trout, and made tea for us.

Our crew expressed anxiety as to their portraits: I
said they could not see the results then, but that I would
send them from England. They were delighted with
some English portraits: my mother was *krassiva*, beautiful
—my father *maladiets*, young. In point of complexion
they slightly, but firmly, preferred light hair to dark: and
after ascertaining my forlorn and solitary condition of life,

they expressed a strong wish that I should attach myself
to some lady with a fair complexion.   I promised to see
what could be done immediately I returned to England.
On leaving, I spontaneously and delicately offered to the
young ladies the usual modest souvenirs, which they
received with many expressions of pleasure.   Their
names were, Dâria, Anna, Maria, Harâtina, Féodosia.

I found near the *isba* two long obelisk-shaped stones,
lying across one another.   They once stood upright, but
now lay among the stones that had helped to support
them.   I found, too, a plant which puzzled various people
for a time—and which I consequently thought of naming
after the Doctor the *Pilkingtonia impenetrabilis :* but I
afterwards identified it as the *Ledum palustre.*   The
Melampyrum pratense, or cow-wheat, grew also here, and
the mouse-eared cerastium.

It was stormy and high sea, writes our secretary, before
we went in at an *isba* where there were five women who
were fishing little fishes.   It must not be thought that the
authors of *Round the Bay of Hvidsö*, and of *The White Sea
Peninsula* are the only members of the Expedition who
reduce their experiences to writing.   The Doctor is dili-
gently engaged upon his journal, and illustrates it by
pencil drawings : nor has he travelled and written without
encouragement.   One of the reviewers of the account of
our journey to the Samoyede country wrote as follows.
Mr. Rae seems to be a young man who has little to do,
and to succeed in doing it : we should prefer to have had
Mr. Brandreth's account of the journey.

We came in the morning to the Russian village of
Gredina.   There are no Karelians there.   About thirty
fishermen go yearly to Novaya Zemlia for whale, *bieluga*,
porpoise, and walrus : and twelve men to the Múrman
coast : all returning in October.   They rarely if ever write
home, and their families are often in want during their
absence.   Poor women, half-starving sometimes, rarely
coming to beg, waiting for the autumn and the husbands
on the far-off Arctic coast, who too often would never
come back.

A clearing on the forest's edge, a small box-shaped
log-hut with blue smoke wreathing from it, a few racks
for drying nets, a boat drawn up on the shingly beach,
another afloat, an apparatus for drawing the salmon nets,
a cross standing on a rock, a sea-eagle sailing overhead, a
sunny sky and a sunny sea, a background of spruce and
birch, a strip of fir near the beach—gray and blasted as
if by some poisonous breath : such was one out of many a
fisherman's *isba* on this western shore of the Inland Sea.

We were rowed along, hour after hour, day after day,
changing our crew from time to time, landing to light
fires and cook our meals : with never an hour's fair wind
since we left Kem.   We came to Somostrova, a lovely
spot, midway to Keret, finding a superior *isba* and a
respectable set of fishermen.   We meant to sup in the
boat, but were driven into the hut by a cloud of mosquitoes
—so young and credulous, however, that instead of following us, they haunted the boat expecting us back.

In front lay the crescent-shaped *navolok* or haven, in

A LAKE SCENE IN RUSSIAN LAPLAND.

lovely calm sunlight. Behind, through a delicious strip of forest, lay small and beautiful lakes, with rocky banks and fresh green foliage of larch, spruce, fir, and silver birch. We never tire of these trees : they supply a want in the Northern landscapes, as no other trees could. Near the hut stood three crosses, carved with Sclavonic characters, and having at each side the emblems, the spear and the sponge. Outside the wood I found the sweet *Primula farinosa* or mealy primrose, the *Primula Scotica* or Scotch primrose, and the heath-like blossom of the *Andromeda polyfolia.*

The Perevodtchik gave us some anxiety to-day. He had a pain. I hunted for chlorodyne for a long time : and found it when I was on the point of trying some mosquito lotion in despair. He said it was not bad : but he fell asleep immediately afterwards, and lay with a very drunken look, doubled up in the bottom of the boat, and we entertained fears for him. Shortly after, he came with a dejected face, and asked me to give him *kastor olen*. Rather wondering, I said that I had none. Seeing me puzzled, he explained : For cooking. I thought the chlorodyne had taken a curious effect, and would have asked him to go and lie down again, but he explained further, *kostroula.* This was familiar enough, the Russian word for a cooking-pot : he had used the Norwegian word for the first time.

In the *isba* a fisherman was busy making a cask in the cleverest way : his only tool was an axe. Using an axe and kindling a fire are the only duties in which a

North Russian peasant loses no time. In all other occupations of life he will dawdle till your soul becomes
oppressed. There are two things in life that we cannot
replace, a lost friend and a lost day. The Russian will
rob you of the latter as if life were to last for ever. In
all the dozens, hundreds, of Russian peasants' huts, cot-
tages, houses, that we have visited, we have seen but one
clock going. This was an old English clock in the
Stantsia at Keret.

The poor people have other qualities, however, that
entitle them to respect. We have wandered again and
again among the peasants, leaving our effects unwatched
and unsecured : and with the exception of the small theft
or piece of spitefulness at Siem Ostrova, we never missed
so much as a piece of sugar. Of the class immediately
above the peasants, those who are in the position of
making bargains or receiving money otherwise than as
wages, we have a different opinion. As to the miserably
underpaid *tchinovniks* or officials : if they attempt to add
to their incomes, they are hardly to be blamed.

We sailed from Somostrova : I say sailed, for here we
found our first fair wind. We sailed through sounds and
bays and lovely lakes, all shining in the midnight sunlight.
We saw widgeon and mallard in numbers. Sea-eagles
flew leisurely from rock to tree, flapping their wide wings :
fish leapt, and the boat spun through the quiet water with
a musical ripple. At length we reached the open sea, and
ran before a strong east wind. At first I devoted my
abilities and patience to managing the foresail : afterwards

taking the helm for the rest of the night while the poor boatwomen slept.

After sailing swiftly for many hours, we ran along a narrow river-like sound for some miles, and approached Keret. It lies at the foot of a long cataract. Many little wooden warehouses cluster on the river bank. Above them tower the new white church, and a large house of the merchant Savin.

The interior of the village is most quaint and picturesque, old dark wooden gabled log-houses project and recede from the planked pavement. It is a village as old as Kem, and much of the same character. The house doors are of double width, and are singularly low. As we were anxious to take advantage of the heavy easterly wind blowing, the Perevodtchik was sent to prepare a boat to take us to Umba, across the Gulf, while we went to the gloomy house of a *Raskolnik* close by.

In Keret there are about twenty Karelians, most of whom go to the Arctic fisheries. In the interior live many Karelians, not in considerable villages, but in small scattered settlements by lakes or rivers. Such are the hamlets of Novaya on the Tchornaya Raika, forty versts west, where are five or six houses and forty inhabitants : Tikshya, eighty versts distant : Niska, on the Pää lake : Oulangansu, on the same lake: Skita, Loggûba, Suolapoha, and Lampahaïs on the Tuoppa Lake—all twenty or thirty versts apart, dotted about between this place and the Finland frontier, a hundred miles to the westward.

The Korielski all live by fishing, in lake or sea.

Those who hire themselves for the summer's work on the Mûrman coast make a contract with a *khozeyn*, and generally receives in the autumn in advance ten or twelve roubles as earnest money.   This man will give to a set of four fishermen their food and one-third of the result of the fishing.   The hundred and fifty men who go from Keret frequent chiefly Vrinda and Shilpine.   The Korielski hunt the bear, wolf, fox, and deer, with dogs, of which they keep great numbers.   These dogs make it impracticable for them to keep poultry.   Having but few reindeer, they cannot afford to eat them.   They eat miserable bread : during the constantly-recurring famines it is made more of birch-bark than anything else.   They are stupid too.   In the famine of 1867 they refused to give up their bread and fish for fresh meat.   The Korelak is idle, and will only work when in want of food : so, it may be fancied, when the thriftless, indolent father goes to the northern coasts, after living through the winter on his previous summer's earnings, how poor his family are.   Many Korielski and Finns go to Vadsö for the summer fishery.   The Norwegians are jealous of them, looking upon them partly as Russian pioneers. But where the poor people find justice, medical help, and free fishing, it is not surprising that they congregate. They spend little in Vadsö : almost everything comes home to their poor families.

The priest of Keret came at our invitation to drink coffee with us.   He told us the fishermen generally take their boys with them to the North, leaving one or two to help the mother. So that in the summer months the school, which is free to all, but not compulsory, is quite deserted. In the winter, when the men and boys are at home, perhaps fifty children attend the school. I asked why the people of Keret and elsewhere, who travel yearly backward and forward, do not take their families and settle where fish and employment are so abundant: rather than live on as at present, half-starving here, and toiling on the long journeys over the snow each autumn and spring. Some of the Múrmanski travel a thousand versts to the sea, from Pomoria and Onéga, and even farther— setting out in the end of March. It is a strange sight to see old and young, parties of twenty or fifty, drawing clothes, bread, anchor, chains, etc., on hand sledges.

He said they were fond of their homes, and that life would be hard in the winter on the Arctic coast. I said not so hard as here : the sea being open, the climate less trying : in Gavrilova, Kola, Tiribirka, people lived in comfort. I added that if the Múrmansk summer population were to settle there, there would soon be steamers and a telegraph line as on the coast of Finmarken. I asked if he had ever tried to persuade the people to settle on the Múrman coast. He said, Yes. But as the emigration of half his flock would reduce his comforts and advantages, and might involve his following them to the lonely Winter Sea, I imagine the priest was not importunate in his persuasion. I am sorry to say I think it more likely he would work upon their superstitious fears to detain them in Keret.

P

No doubt the present absence of communication, the poor facilities offered to colonists, the weakening religious fasts, amounting in all to something very like half the year, the absence of legal protection, the scarcity of vegetable food, the lack of Government encouragement, have chilled what energy for development these poor people might have possessed. And men like Savin, a wealthy trader, who has a huge house and store here, tend further to burden the Mûrmanski.

This philanthropist has accumulated a large fortune by selling to the fishermen here and at Shilpine necessaries at an enormous profit, taking in payment fish, at a very low price. He sends fish by shiploads to St. Petersburg and elsewhere, and has seal fisheries all along this coast. No doubt he has a hold, too, upon many of the fishermen through the Russian trader's favourite habit of getting his dependent into his debt : so that private competition would not benefit those who dare not avail themselves of it. We found the price of sugar at Savin's store was thirty-five kopecks a pound : in Archangel it was about twenty. An occasional economy of this gentleman is to engage, as seamen on his foreign-going ships, deserters at four roubles a month, or less than £5 a year wages.

I wrote to Mr. Shergold, Consul in Archangel, suggesting the establishment of Government stores, which, by exacting a fair profit, would enrich and encourage the population of what is now a wretchedly poor district : thereby directly and doubly benefiting the Government itself.

The Consul wrote me as follows : Your remarks about the food monopolies are true enough : but there seems no help for it.   The authorities here know it well enough, and are fully aware of the ruinous effect it has upon the poor population of the Mûrman coast : but, notwithstanding repeated representations to St. Petersburg, made by different Archangel governors, things are allowed to go on in their old way.   However, in my next interview with the Governor, I will lay the case before him.

I also wrote begging the Consul to use his influence to have some medical assistance sent among the fishermen : saying, that so soon after the close of the great war, there were probably numerous unemployed surgeons at the disposal of the Government.   Mr. Shergold replied : As to doctors, you seem to be greatly mistaken.   There is no abundance of them : on the contrary, a great want, and besides, no doctors or surgeons are to be persuaded to take up their residence in those out-of-the-way regions.   Such a place like Onéga, for instance, lying close to Archangel, is often left without a surgeon : the salary allowed by Government being so trifling that no surgeon deserving the name of such could be found to go and live there.

I am confident that if the Government were in earnest enough to offer a small salary, there would be found dozens of poor Norwegian or German, if not Russian, medical students or apothecaries, glad to go for experience to the Mûrman coast—at all events for the summer months when most needed.   Soon after interesting himself so kindly for these poor people, this popular and amiable Consul died.

I asked the priest of Keret to urge that medical help should be sent to the Mûrmanski, telling him of their wants and sufferings. For hours I talked to him, begging him as priest of a hundred and fifty of the fishermen, to write to the authorities of the province, or to urge Savin, in his own interests, to set up an apothecary's shop on the coast. Finally, the priest half promised to write a letter to the Archangel newspaper *Vedomosti.* I was disgusted : but as it was not polite to ask questions alone of our guest, I told him about our country.

He asked for Her Royal Highness Maria Alexandrovna, Princess of Edinbourghi, and wished to know what Edinbourghi was. I said it was the capital of the northern half of Velikaya Britannia, and told him what a noble manner of city it was. Then I told him how a railway ran round Londongorod, underground. How that city measured forty versts round. How our railway trains ran at the rate of seventy versts in an hour. How our steamers, carrying half a million *poudov*, could travel four thousand five hundred versts in seven days—till the priest began to think that Velikaya Britannia was a very remarkable country.

CHAPTER XVI.

A misconception — Laziness — Return to Keret — The rapid — A difficult opera-
tion — An apparition — Kovda — Public baptism — Prejudices — Rusânova
— Kandalaks — An unexpected meeting — A beautiful panorama — A
wrangle — Transport — An inventory.

IN the forenoon the Perevodtchik announced that he had
personally superintended the preparation of the boat, and
that it was ready. This gave us misgivings : and when I
offered to pay the hire from Keret to Umba—forty
miles direct across the Gulf—the *Raskolnik* told me
we must travel to Umba in five stages, *viâ* Kandalaks,
i.e. somewhere in the neighbourhood of two hundred miles'
voyage. In any case, the boat provided by the Linguist
was not good enough to take the Expedition over the sea
forty miles in an easterly gale, and no other boat could be
hired or bought : we therefore decided to go to Tchornaya
Raika, Black River, and try to find a better boat there.

I first sent for the Perevodtchik, and told him he was
a *sumaschetche dourak*, a helpless buffoon. He looked at
me with fear, or at least with a certain feeling of incomprehension : and I then told him that Umba was straight
across the Gulf, and that he should ask questions when he

didn't know things for certain. We went on board the boat and fell asleep. Late in the day we awoke to find the crew and Perevodtchik asleep, and the boat lying moored to a tree three versts from Keret. The crew had slept all the afternoon.

I called the *korseka*, and told him he was a miserable outcast : and the Perevodtchik that his imbecility would end in making me ill. Young man, said Diogenes, when his patience was sorely tried, I am not angry yet, but I am in some doubt whether I should be so or no. I envied but could not quite imitate Diogenes. As we might now reach Kovda too late for the *Onéga*, we returned to Keret.

We spent two days there. We sent for a Karelian sledge and dog, to see the method of harnessing. A padded leather collar is pushed over the dog's head : the traces are fastened to it and round the dog's middle. We photographed the poor dog, who had lost one eye, and was at first timid and suspicious : but was reassured by salmon steak. Many of the bystanders were ambitious, but as we did not want them in the picture, we encouraged them to stand still, and left them outside the photograph. We often chose this way of affording harmless enjoyment to inappropriate persons.

We went to see the rapid, which by the removal of two small rocks might be made practicable, though not very safe, to boats. We walked out to some rich ground overlooking the river, where was abundant grass, and where potatoes were sprouting thickly. We gathered some marsh marigolds with immense blossoms, and some blos-

som of the *brosnitsa*, *Ledum palustre*, which grew in profusion, the *Pyrola uniflora*, winter green, some sorrel, white
clover, and enormous dog-violets : then we walked up to
where the Keret expands into a smooth broad sheet
of water.

The graveyard has some of the rudest and quaintest
graves possible : and more than the untidiness of an
Eastern burial-place.　We saw a poor half-blind idiot and
gave him a few silver pieces : but were beset immediately
by other boys, also idiots, to expect money to enable
them to idle about in perfect health.　We dressed the
eye of a poor man who had been struck with the branch of
a tree, and who, we feared, must lose his eye.　The Karelian
women rarely smoke.　One told me, with something of
contempt in her manner, that she had heard that women
in Archangel smoked *papyrosi*.　We had eaten but little of
our English meat for weeks, and, curiously enough, had lost
our taste for it : preferring soup, salmon, and eggs daily.

Our hair had grown so long, that it became an
anxiety.　I knew I could trust myself to cut the Doctor's,
but hesitated about trusting him.　At last I determined
to confide to the Doctor the delicate task.　We chose the
largest and sharpest pair of scissors brought for the
Lapland ladies, and the Doctor began.　In less than five
minutes my head had the appearance of having been
gnawed by some herbivorous animal in a hurry.　With
incredible pains, and by means of two mirrors, I partially
repaired the ravages.　Then I resolved to cut the Doctor's
hair : not from any small motive of self-enjoyment or re-

venge, but from a sense of my obligations as a citizen and
a fellow-traveller. I imagine I must have used a certain
originality : for after ten minutes' work with the scissors
the Doctor looked as I had never seen him look before.

One morning we were aroused by the quaint sound of
a horn. In the street was a fantastic mediæval-looking
man, wearing a hood, which covered all but his features,
and reached down to his waist. His tunic was bound
round his waist with birch-bark, his shoes were curiously
plaited in birch-bark, and he was blowing a birch-bark
trumpet. I took the unusual step of hailing the birch-
bark man, and of addressing him in Karelian : Who are
you ? Where do you come from ? Where are you going
to ? What are you going for ?

The birch-bark man replied in Karelian to the following effect : I am the man with the birch-bark horn,
who summon the maidens all forlorn, to milk the cows at
five in the morn. I asked him promptly what he would
take for the trumpet. He said he must use it that day,
but would make another for me in the woods. In the
evening he returned with a horn made from silvery birch-
bark. He also gave me his own, and when I asked how
much I should give him, the poor fellow at first said :
Nothing at all. I asked him to get us a little bear, but
he said he knew of none at the moment. This birch-bark
trumpet will serve as a post-horn to announce our arrival
in various places, to amuse bears, or to summon cows
when we want milk.

At midnight one of our Karelian boatwomen came to

report that the steamer had arrived. Our effects were
soon stowed in the boat, and we and the Karelian post-
horn were rowed down the stream to the *Onéga*. In the
early morning we sailed, passed the Arctic circle, and came
before noon to Kovda, on the beautiful gulf of Kandalaks,
the only romantic and picturesque corner of all this dreary
White Sea. We landed in the mail-boat.

Kovda lies on the east bank of the Kovda River,
where that stream pours, in a powerful rapid, two hundred
yards broad, into the gulf.

The Kovda is rich in salmon : indeed, the chain of
lakes through which it runs—the Tuoppa, Pää, Kouto,
and others—have abundant fish. They are deep : deeper
than the lakes of the Kola Peninsula. The salmon
fishing begins in the Kovda River on August 12, while
in the Kola, 3° farther north, it opens on the 16th of July,
and in Syd Varanger, again farther north, in the middle
of June. The Koutoyärvi is but a short distance from
Kovda—one and a half hour's journey. Round this
and the other inland lakes stand comfortable Karelian
villages. The sociable, tipsy, thriftless Russian will not
shut himself up as a squatter in the lonely backwoods.
The Finn, Quain, or Karelian prefers solitude and independence. Better, he says, under one's own roof to drink
water out of a sieve, than, in another man's dwelling,
beer out of a silver tankard. I could hear of no such
tankards here, though they abound in the inns on the
western side of Finland. Indeed, I felt ashamed here
more than once to have asked for them, when a poor

Karelian would answer my inquiry with a mournful, almost reproachful, ejaculation : *Serebro !*   Silver !

At the feast of *Maknaveidan,* the 1st of August, as well as on the 6th of January, Old Style, public baptisms are held here : where adults and others burdened with their sins can be rebaptized, and consequently feel freed from sin.   The priest comes with the crucifix to the river bank, and, having said mass and sung, the cross is dipped, as Christ was, thrice in the river.   Then all the candidates, clad in large gowns, plunge into the river, or, if in winter, into an opening cut in the ice : then, covered with furs, they run into the warm church, where they bow and cross themselves until they are dry and the priest collects the absolution fees.

This and other superstitions linger in Karelia.   A student of the Finnish language was believed, with his ink-bottle, to have poisoned the wells, and the people compelled him to swallow his ink to prove its harmlessness.   It is just a question in some places whether our photography is tolerated.   People are apt to look askance at the instrument : old Staroviertsi women grumbling and hinting at sickness and misfortune if this were to be tolerated.

The houses of Kovda were old-fashioned and picturesque : there was the usual wooden paving.   One old house stood curiously in the middle of the rapid.   Two or three schooners were here for repairs : one old vessel had come to be broken up, and lay on her side as if exhausted by a hard life.   There was a charming view of the high,

purple hills, some snowy, which hemmed in the Gulf, and
the rapid broke musically past the village.   Delicious wild
flowers abounded with ferns and moss by the river-side :
and, on the outskirts of the wood lying behind the town,
I discovered for the first time the delicate *Linnæa borealis*,
or thyme-leaved bell flower : and, for the first time near
the White Sea, the grass of Parnassus.

Boats shot the rapid or skimmed across it : others lay
at anchor.   I asked for old silver crosses.   A man standing among some peasants said mockingly that I might
perhaps like to buy a great wooden cross near us : the
only example of irreverence to the cross that I ever noticed
in Russia.   On many houses seals' skins were pegged up
to dry.   We saw one of the inoffensive creatures swimming about as we entered the harbour.   The white dolphin, *bieluga*, and the seal abound here.

I share my cabin on the *Onéga* with a young Russian
Nadliessnik, or forest inspector.   I wrote to Mr. Sharvin, one
of the founders of Rusânova, the little timber port across
the White Sea, about the timber riches of Keret and Kovda.
He replied : It is my intense desire to make use of some
of the advantages the place possesses, and I wait for the
moment when my designs may be realised.   Our saw-mill
here was last year burnt down, and on its place we have
built a much finer one.   This will lead to the arrival of
more ships, and lay foundations of more improvements of
the little City of the Future.   Immense flights of *dikiye
outki* are now travelling in the neighbourhood of Rusânova :
they are not afraid now of being fired at without missing,

by their enemy the Doctor—to whom please transfer *mes
salutations favorables.* Energy and enterprise of men like
Russânoff or Sharvin may transform Keret or Kovda.
.Already a Norwegian has a considerable trade with the
latter place.

At Kovda the *tchinovnik's* two sisters came on board :
they might have parted from their brother last week
instead of last winter. I have often been struck in these
regions by the absence of any evidences of family or other
affection. One might easily take the natives to be without feeling. You will not forget me, said a French husband, as he was leaving home : or cease to love me ?
Never ! sobbed his wife : and she tied a knot in her pocket-
handkerchief accordingly. The *tchinovnik* and his sisters
played cards and smoked cigarettes all the way to Kandalaks. Twenty miles south of that place we passed Knashja,
a dirty village of a hundred and twenty inhabitants.

Opposite to Kovda, on the northern coast of the Gulf,
lies Umba, with its fine broad river, having at the village
a depth of twelve fathoms. It is said that some of the
inlets on the Kandalak coast have a depth of sixty
fathoms. Turnips and radishes may be seen in Umba :
corn ceases to grow at the 66th parallel of N. latitude.
Umba has two hundred reindeer. On the islands here, as
well as on the mainland, are numerous lodes of silver, lead,
copper, and calamine or zinc ore. In 1734 mining oper-
ations were undertaken, but were abandoned in 1742.
At night we reached *Kantalahti,* Kandalaks, a village
of five hundred people : standing at the head of the long,

KANDMAKS

tapering gulf of the same name. I asked the captain to see Stepan Makuskin on his return to Kem, and to send the dog to Archangel. Stepan is on board, said the captain. Stepan was sent for. His face was hot and grimy. It appeared that on his return, his master learning the amount of our gift, declared it belonged to him as *progonye dienghi*, boat tax : and would have arrested Stepan, had he not disappeared, and engaged himself as fireman on the *Onéga*. I wrote a letter, stating how much I had given as *progon* and how much as present, much relieving the poor fellow's mind.

The captain's boat put us on shore, and we walked to the *Stantsia*. Leaving the Perevodtchik to engage baggage-carriers and to cook, we went out to see the river. There are no shops here : *vodka*, fish, and of course bread, can alone be had. Sugar, coffee, or tea must come from Kovda. Many Karelians live eastward from Kandalaks, on the coast towards Umba and Kouzomen.

It was midnight. We went to the burial-place on the hill behind the village. It was a lovely panorama—a vast amphitheatre. On one side the Niva or Swift River, at our feet one half of the gray wooden village, on the tongue of land beyond the river the other half. A red and yellow church stood on the point. Beyond lay the Gulf, broken with islands and inlets, losing itself in a line of hazy coast. Behind us, to the left, came the swift gray river, with a hoarse roar, down from thick pine woods. To the westward, under the shining sky, was an amphitheatre of blue and purple mountains, rising from the

White Sea Gulf, which shone like the silver of a salmon's back. Round all its margin were soft, purple reflections.

The graveyard was on a grassy hill : all was silent but the river. A quaint old church stands on the hill, and a belfry still bearing marks, I am ashamed to say, of English shot. The village was bombarded in 1854, and one half burnt : a cowardly unEnglish cause of suffering to helpless, harmless people. We ascended the belfry among the rich-sounding bells, while swifts came sweeping through like bats. It was a beautiful, peaceful scene— our last sight of the familiar White Sea.

The Perevodtchik, I found, had collected the men, but only to talk with me. After arranging terms, we had a long and tiresome wrangle about the weight each should carry. At length, in disgust, I told these foolish, greedy *moujiks* that they should go with us on Government terms. I had promised them thrice as much. Now they had to go, and to carry forty pounds' weight for three kopecks per verst.

The Perevodtchik, of course—unlucky little creature —was to blame for the dispute. Usually abrupt and not polite to the peasants, he received a reprimand on the subject only a day before : and consequently I found him to-day beseeching these cold-blooded and stupid ruffians, *Gospoda, gospoda ! bweetye stol dobrim* : Gentlemen, gentlemen ! be so uncommonly kind. I consider that the Linguist's first exercise in politeness very nearly cost us fifteen roubles.

I tried to hire or buy a horse here, having been unwell

for two days, and not able to face a march of fifteen miles : but the horse, one of the only two that Kanda-laks possessed, was neither to be bought nor hired.   The reindeer are sent in summer time to the White Sea islands near, or I should have felt inclined to try if one would carry me.   The Doctor and I even talked of engaging a cow : but the only old lady who owned one sent an indig-nant reply to our overtures.   I therefore hired four men to carry me.

I had feared the transport even of the ruins of our baggage overland to Kola might become a serious ques-tion : but for a statement volunteered by the Doctor at Keret, and verified by an inventory I took myself, of the contents of the Doctor's shooting-coat and pilot-jacket pockets :

A large bath sponge.

Three pocket-handkerchiefs.

A pocket-comb and glass.

Two pairs of leather mosquito gauntlets.

A pair of Lapp mittens.

A tobacco pouch.

A supply-bag for ditto—capacity, about $1\frac{1}{2}$ lbs.

Three clean collars.

A spare scarf.

Passport.

Diary-book.

Six boxes of matches.

A slab of chocolate.

A bundle of rouble notes.

Two captain's biscuits.

A bundle of letters and documents.

A watch.

A rough towel.

A spare pair of thick woollen stockings.

A comprehensive pocket-knife.

Three pairs of scissors—for gifts.

Two pocket-knives—ditto.

A woollen muffler.

A shooting-cap.

A light waterproof overcoat.

A bundle of rope.

A bill-hook.

This saved me from some pre-occupation. The Lapland bearers use a slight wooden frame, with cross-netting, like a Canadian snow-shoe : strapped upright on their backs, and having the box, portmanteau, or bundle, made fast to it. In this fashion the Lapps will carry a weight of eighty pounds from morning to night.

CHAPTER XVII.

Through the forest—Arctic *flora*—Neglected advantages—A travelled native—
Mosquito precautions—Imandra—Sashyeka—Babinsky Lapps—Habits of
the Lapps—Resources—Miron Yefimovitch Arkipoff—A storm on the lake
—The Island of Graves—The Ritual of the dead.

AT length we set out, a party of about sixteen persons,
including two Lapp women. Our way lay past the old
graves on the hill, and their decaying crosses, then into
the woods of pine, fir, and brilliant green larch. We
saw no more of the White Sea. At times we saw the
Niva gleaming through the trees. The wild flowers
were more lovely than ever, springing from the soft moss
and rejoicing in their new and delicious existence. Silver
birches, with delicate foliage, rose from a silvery carpet
of reindeer moss.

We filed in a long procession through the woods:
coming, after an hour and a half, to the Plosa Lake,
a long narrow mere, out of which the Niva whirled,
surrounded by steep fir- and larch-covered hills. For
considerable distances through the swamps runs a wooden
track—three roughly-hewn planks side by side, supported
on cross pieces. In many places the wood has rotted

Q

away : it was old when one of my companions was young, thirty years ago. In default of the planks, one must flounder through saturated sponge-coloured moss on either side.

Then we reached a smaller lake, finding also a boat, and parting with some of our carriers. I had spent a good portion of the journey in defeating the efforts of these gentlemen to transfer what articles of baggage they could to the shoulders of the two women and a good-natured boy. They were some of the worst specimens of Russian peasants that I have seen. We rowed for five versts along this pretty lake, then set out as before in Indian file through the lovely forest.

The *maroschka* luxuriated in the warm sunny moisture, and surpassed itself in great blossoms, like white wild roses with yellow hearts : its blossom ordinarily is scarcely larger than that of the strawberry. My carriers gathered for me the dwarf cornel, *Cornus Suecica*, the *Draba hirta* or whitlow grass, the *Vaccinium vitis Idæa* or red whortle-berry, the wood geranium, the *Saxifraga Arctioides*, or yellow mountain saxifrage, all in full blossom. Field violets, heart's-ease, exquisite oak and beech fern, moss, and innumerable flowers, glorify the summer time in these Arctic woods, and help the tired traveller to forget his fatigue, himself, and space.

Again we reached a lake, the Pinosero, near to where the river issues from it: we traversed the lake for five versts, and found once more the rapid Niva. This stream seems to have no falls, but to consist of little else than one long rapid. Of its length from Imandra to the sea, two-and-twenty miles, lakes occupy about six : and the river descends in sixteen miles, according to my aneroid, about five hundred and fifty feet.

I saw noble pines upon its banks, which, if cut and tossed into the river, would, with a little labour on the smooth water of the lakes, reach Kandalaks almost without assistance. None is cut here : yet the Government, who are lords of these huge forests, might here find revenue for themselves, and work and wages for the often starving Karelian peasantry. Fish on the coast for the seeking, timber for the labour of cutting : and the peasants are eating birch-bark bread and their wives begging piteously in the summer months.

If the natives will not work on their own initiative under Government encouragement, they should be set to work in the interest of themselves and of the common weal. Lapland abounds in minerals : but if the natives have not the heart to work for timber which they see, no wonder they will not work for something which they don't see. If a juster proportion of the profits of the vast fisheries went to the peasants who risk their lives and health in fishing : if all who will not fish, or who are unemployed, were sent to hew timber, and were fairly paid : if the communications and means of life were made easier, as they readily could be : there are in Lapland the elements of wealth and comfort for more than her population. The Government must do something more than build churches if they wish to give this province a chance.

Norway has no more than this country—simply fish
and timber : but she has individual liberty, active economic
intelligence, and an honest administration.   Telegraphs,
steamers, churches, schools, medical dispensaries, abound
on her Arctic coast, which is identical in climate with that
of the Kola Peninsula, and no more accessible.   The Norwegians, too, are a less clever race than the Russians.   Of
the present scanty population of the White Sea shores, the
Russians are, speaking generally, the traders, fishers, and
speculators, the Lapps and Karelians the hunters and
fishers, the Quains or Finns the agriculturists.

I talked for a long time to an ex-marine, who had
been round the world in the frigate *Sevastôpol.*   He had
been for two years at school, for four at sea, and was now
working in Kandalaks.   He was a clever, amusing fellow
and talked of all manner of things : laughed heartily at the
ironclad *Peter the Great*, which had made the fortunes of
three different contractors, and could not venture out of
sight of Kronstadt.   In addition to his own language he
knew two words of Norwegian, which he imagined assisted
and encouraged my feeble intelligence.   He had been to
the Amûr River—*ikke god,* not good.   General Heimann,
who captured Kars, was since dead—*ikke god.*   Government forbid the cutting of timber, but the peasants help
themselves—*ikke god.*

We came upon a ptarmigan—Lapp, *tcherûna*—almost
under our feet : the devoted old bird covering the retreat
of her fluttering, frightened brood of fifteen.   I saw a few
butterflies of sober colours : dull grayish black, shaded

into coffee-brown on the wings. Afterwards the *Papilio Æmilia*, dark brown with red spots: and a few specimens of the *Apis Lapponica*, the bee-fly, as an Icelander termed it. The bee-flies were not numerous.

We wore with much success our mosquito-puzzlers: the woods abounded with these insects, but we could look at them without bitterness. We gave the Canadian veils with the tar and oil a good trial on this journey. Their drawbacks are these. Many a mosquito settles before he is aware how sticky and unpleasant you are. Then he buzzes and flutters on your countenance till you are compelled to mash him, and either leave his remains there, or fumble about for him with your clumsy gauntlet.

Then in pawing over your face you absorb or remove some of the tar: and if you do not recoat yourself, the next mosquito settles triumphantly on the spot. Then apart from the risks of conflagration with cigarettes, and going about smelling like a Guy Fawkes ready for a bonfire, you perhaps want to use your handkerchief, or your nose tickles: then you remove some of the combustible coating, and must smear yourself again. Then a light gauze veil resting against the sides of the face tempts the mosquito to settle at those points, and convert your flesh to his private benefit. As to keeping your hands tarred, it is not seriously possible.

We have tried as a protective coating, aromatic vinegar and oil: but the acid evaporates in spite of the oil: and we prefer of the two the smell of the tar. Certainly the strong acetic gives the mosquito convulsions, but there is no enjoyment in that : if he would go away, that would be enough.   I once gave a mosquito some aromatic vinegar : and his sufferings seemed fearful.   He spun madly round on one wing as though he had drunk liquid fire, and his other wing appeared scorched and withered.   Of course I quickly put him to death.   I now regret the process of his end.

This lotion, as also aromatic vinegar with alum and glycerine, or carbolic acid and oil, are excellent remedies for stings.   For protection, we prefer the cage-shaped, dark gauze veil, with whalebone hoops which isolate it from the cheeks, ears, and nose.   A clean white handkerchief round the neck, and the collar of the coat turned up, are additional comforts and protections.   There is no sense of imprison-ment : the net is almost as transparent as glass, and one becomes insensible of its presence.   As to our gauntlets, I should have no hesitation in watching the Doctor attack a wasp's nest with them.

We had travelled for a long time through the forest, when suddenly we saw a great blue sheet of water in front of us, and a beautiful ridge of purple mountains, half covered with perpetual snow.   We had come, before we were aware of it, upon the Lake Imandra, sixty miles long and ten wide, lying over five hundred feet above the sea. The stately Umpdek Dunder, seventy miles in length, stretches northward along the east side of the lake.   We had come from Kandalaks, thirty-three versts, in ten hours, including stoppages : which is very good travelling for Russian Lapland.

Before us were the huts of *Nièshka*, or Sashyéka, one

SASHYEKA.

of the stopping - places on the long track followed each
spring and autumn by the fisher people.　We had seen
the homes and families of the Mûrmanski, and were now
following their path to the Winter Sea.　We had come
again among the *Laplandsi:* and it was a relief to hear
their merry chat after the wranglings of those greedy boors
of Kandalaks.　For hours together, as they carried me,
their only talk had been of kopecks and roubles.　They
divided, subdivided, and squabbled hundreds of times over
the roubles I had promised them.

By the margin of the lake stood the two buildings of
Sashyéka, an *isba*, and a *balagan* or earth hut.　In the
former we found the Lapp family asleep on the floor,
lying on their faces on reindeer skins.　They awoke, and
helped the soldier to make a fire of birch logs.　The rest
of our party straggled in one after another, crossing themselves devoutly, and bowing towards the corner of the hut.
I looked towards the corner shelf for the saint or *Obras :*
only a cup and saucer were there, but they seemed equally
to afford religious satisfaction to our devout companions.

The woodcut represents the Hotel d'Angleterre where
we were lodged, and the whole of the population and
shipping of Sashyéka.

I told our host he much resembled our friend Onésime.
He is my brother, said the Lapp : my name is Larivan
Simonovitch.　He is one of the best men in Lapland, I
said.　Yes, said Larivan, he is a good man.　This Lapp
had a short well-shaped sinewy body, a clever face, a
tanned complexion, a fine head of hair, a thin dark

moustache and small beard.   He wore a home-spun gray
tunic with a belt, and the usual Lapp cap.   He and his
brother were perfect specimens of small men.

A Norwegian Lapp resembles a big man above the
waist, and a small man with bow legs, below : or a small
man whose waist has slipped down, to the disadvantage of
his legs.   The Norwegian Lapp has a dull apathetic look:
he takes no interest in anything that does not concern
himself.   The Russian Laplander is quick, bright, and animated : whether his intelligence is quickened by an almost
exclusive fish diet, or not, I cannot say.   He is capable of
cultivation, as I do not consider his neighbours are.

Larivan and his family were natives of Akkala, or
Babinsky, an old village lying thirty versts due west of
Sashyéka, and the most southerly settlement of the Russian
Lapps. *Akka* in Lapp, and *Baba* in Russian signify equally,
old woman.   The winter settlement is Akkalaver Pogost,
where are three *isboushki* and one *balagan*, on the banks of
the Yuni River—a stream flowing all the way from the
Finland frontier, a hundred and twenty miles away, into
Imandra.   The Lapps of Akkala have seven hundred
reindeer, which they send in the hot season to islands on
the lake.

In old days the magistrate of Vardö came all the way
to Akkala to collect tribute for His Majesty of Denmark.
His last journey hither was in 1613.   At that time there
were eleven tax-payers in Akkala.   The unfortunate Lapps
have gained nothing by the discontinuance of these financial visits.   Besides the manhood-tax of ten roubles

a year, they pay one or two roubles each to avoid the
conscription.   They pay to this day ten roubles not only
for themselves, but, until the ensuing census, for their dead
relatives.   In 1872 a Lapp named Gregori had paid for
ten years ten roubles a year on behalf of his dead father,
and expected to do so for three years more.   In most
districts is a yearly census, and this hardship may have
been occasioned by the Lapp's omission to register before
the *Ouyesdni Natchalnik* his father's death.

The fishing-places of the Lapps are looked upon as
properties, and are hereditary—some of them from remote
times.   The Lapps are known as Pasvigski, Petschengski,
Nuotovski, Lovoserski, Terski, and so on : from the river,
lake, or district where they have their winter abode.
None of the Greek Catholic Lapps are strictly nomads,
though they flit three or four times in the year from one
spot to another.   In the spring from the winter *pogost* to a
balagan, near some lake or stream, for fishing or bird-catch-
ing: at mid July to the larger lake fishery: in August again
to fishing and fowling, or hunting reindeer, martens, squirrel,
otter, bear, etc.   Finally, at Christmas, back to the *pogost*.

Here stand their small chapels—simple wooden huts
surmounted by a cross : and only when firewood and rein-
deer-moss become exhausted do they change their homes.
Then the chapel is moved too, and reconsecrated.   Their
herds being small, they do not exhaust the moss so
quickly : consequently they need not remove so frequently
as the Norwegian Lapps.   They have not, as the Finns
and Russians have, bath-huts.   Their food is very very

simple—curds, fish, and soup, often made with fish and powdered birch-bark. For one-half of the year they are forbidden by the Greek Catholic faith any but fish diet. They cannot afford to eat reindeer, so this is not as serious a deprivation as, in this hard climate, it might seem to be. But the Samoyedes of Malaya Zemlia and the Terski Lapps, by special dispensation of the Church, are permitted to eat ptarmigan during fast time. Seeing that in the whole of Terski Lapland and Malaya Zemlia there are two or at most three priests, the Lapps might, without much risk, dispense with the dispensation. A Lapp said that if he might eat on a fast day an egg, he did not see why he should not eat the bird that laid it.

In the western parts of the White Sea Peninsula are swan, geese, ducks, and other migratory birds: ptarmigan, wood-grouse, and capercaillie. Eastward and in the interior game is scarce, unless on the rivers. Nature is so bountiful in providing fish that the Lapps are to a great extent independent of reindeer: the White Sea, the great lakes, and the Icy Sea are better than gold-fields to them. The Lapps hunt the bear on snow-shoes, bravely, coolly, and skilfully. They honour the bear: but wolves they call creatures of the devil, contaminating even the gun they are shot with. So that a Lapp always uses a club to despatch the wolf, and sells the skin to Russians.

The reindeer they mercifully kill by plunging a sharp-pointed knife into the back of the head, separating the spinal marrow. The reindeer instantly drops and dies without a struggle. These poor savages teach us humanity.

But, it is said, the process suffuses the meat with blood
and spoils it.   The Lapp also teaches us anatomy.   At
once plunging the knife behind the shoulder into the heart,
the blood flows straight into the stomach.

Imandra, together with the other lakes, is generally
covered with ice from the end of October until the first
half of May—sometimes longer, even up to the end of
June.   The White Sea closes and opens much at the same
periods.   Snow generally falls with the first frost : Heaven
in its mercy makes this provision, so that the shallower
lakes may not freeze to the bottom, destroying the fish :
and also that the *débâcle* in the spring may be accelerated
by the melting of the snow.   Imandra was once called
Lower, as Enara was called Upper, Imandra.   It abounds
with wild-fowl, swans—which the Lapps of Sashyéka
much pursue—trout, and fish of various kinds.

I noticed at Sashyéka and afterwards at Yekostrova,
some fine wolf-like Lapp dogs.   There are occasional
herds of wild reindeer on the Umpdek Dunder, also round
the shores of the lake, which are a close fringe of forest.
I wished the soldier to accompany us to Kola, but having
no passport he had to return at once to Kandalaks.   There
was a Lapp in the *isba*, rather deaf.   Larivan hailed him.
Will you go to Kola ?   I will, he answered briefly.

Miron Yefimovitch Arkipoff had a remarkable head, a
great shaggy tangled mass of fair hair and beard, a quick
and humorous eye, and moved like a Jack-in-the-box, or
as if he had swallowed a spring.   He was a natural
humourist.   The ends of his great moustache would curl

up towards his eyes, his nostrils would dilate, a savage
frown settle upon his features: and Miron was on the
point of uttering some quaint piece of humour, that would
convulse every one about him.

We sailed in the night from Sashyéka—a warm sunny
night. With the morning came the wind, in gusts and
squalls. Our wretched Lapp canoe was pitching and
driving into waves which looked as if they would over-
whelm her. Larivan Simonovitch and his Lapps were
shrieking to one another, struggling in fear and with wild
energy to gain the shelter of some islands: but the
northerly gale rose higher and higher, and it looked as if
our boat would not reach the shore. To our right was
the solemn Umpdek Dunder, to our left the Tschûnin
Dunder, looking down upon us through the gale.

We struggled past Mogylni Ostrov—the Island of the
Graves, a burial-place of the Yekostrov Lapps—and got
under shelter. This is one of the most forlorn spots on
earth. The crosses are rotting, and the graves barely
distinguishable. The Lapps only dig six feet deep: consequently, unless on an island, the dead are not secure
from the bears. Among the trees we saw a pretty group
of reindeer, belonging to Larivan Simonovitch. He called
to them, and the reindeer appeared to know his voice.
At length we landed, wet and tired, in the little haven of
Tschûk Suolo or Yekostrova: and spent some hours in the
isba, chatting with the Lapps. Three miles only separate
Imandra at this point from the Piringa Lake. The Piringa
River enters Imandra at Yekostrova.

YEKOSTROVA, LAKE IMANDRA

Larivan's wife had an infant two weeks old.   I learnt
that the child must be taken to Kandalaks, the district
place of registry.   Its mother would take it soon, under
escort of the *Stârista* who would pass this way.   The
Lapps have occasionally large families.   After a death,
the deceased remains in the hut with the rest of the
family for three days.   I asked, Why?   Only because
the priest forbade an earlier burial.

Should two Lapps be on a journey, and one die, the
survivor must try to find a witness, unless the deceased be
his father or relative.   In such case he is beyond suspicion.
If no witness be within reach, the Lapp straightway digs
a hole in which to place the body, and utters the words
S'mirom s' Boghom, At peace, with God.   Adding the
simple reverent prayer : *Pomeni Gospod, tsartsvoye nebjes-
noye*, Remember me, Lord, Thy Empire is in Heaven : or
this, *Gospod nie sabout menya da smierti*, Lord, forget me
not, until I die—a brief and touching ritual of the dead.
Then he fills in the earth, leaving Nature to cover over his
friend with moss and wild flowers—

> *And from his ashes may be made*
> *The violet of his native land.*

I have heard gentle lips express the wish that from
our ashes might always grow sweet flowers or apple-trees.

CHAPTER XVIII.

Lapp sayings—Folk-lore—Ivan, son of Kupiska—The King of the Lapps—A
story of Yokkonga—The priest's wedding—The fox and the bear—The
salmon and the trout—*Jetanas*—The giant's life—The giant and his boy—
The Stallos—The fisher Lapp—Patto Pwadnje's revenge—Stallo's marriage
—The beaver traps—The Sea Folk—The Goveiter—Dog Noses—Ruobba.

I ASKED for Bauta stones, and the Lapps promised to
show me one on the journey to Rasnavolok. It proved
to be a simple boulder on the edge of a little creek, sacred
for some reason or other to the Lapps. I induced the
Lapps with difficulty to tell me stories. They said at
first they did not remember anything of old times. I
asked Miron whether his father or mother had ever talked
to him of old times. Never, he said. Shortly afterwards
he corrected himself. I do remember something from old
times. How old? I asked. About three years.

The Lapps told me a long story, among others, of a
bear hunt : and I spent two hours in trying to explain
what I meant by proverbs or common sayings. Then
they gave me the following. *Shiga olmitch apas olmitch
ey andan*, A good man, good : bad man don't give
nothing, no matter. Otherwise : From a good man you
get something, from a mean man nothing.

Bochts olmitch, pwads yanni.
Rich man, reindeer plenty.
Shilé olmitch, shilé doddal.
For fisherman, fisherwork.

The Lapps are gentle and friendly among themselves,
hospitable and affectionate. Castren knew a Lapp woman
who for thirty years had never received from her husband a harsher name than My little bird. They are
neither mercenary nor deceitful. They are strangers to
cruelty or crime, and spend their harmless lives in providing for their daily wants. In the lonely winter nights,
or, in the summer nights, squatting round their forest fire,
they tell one another simple tales : some original, others
as old as those of the Arabs, Germans, or Norsemen.
Professor Friis, in his excellent book on Lappish Mythology, relates much of the Lapp Folk-Lore, which is not
easily learnt from the Lapps themselves, until confidence
has been established between them and the traveller. I
take the following from *Lappisk Mythologi.*

Ivan, the Son of Kupiska.

A Story of Akkala.

There was once a Lapp who died, leaving all his property to be divided between his son and daughter. To
the son he left also a large dog. The children sold the
property, gave the money to the church, and went out
into the world to seek their fortune, followed by the dog.
They came to a lonely house in a forest, inhabited by

three robbers.   The sister was frightened, but the brother
commenced to fight with the oldest robber.   The dog
seeing that his master was about to be beaten, caught the
robber by the throat and killed him.   The second robber
was disposed of in the same way, but the girl asked Ivan
to spare the third as he was very young.

In the absence of Ivan, an attachment sprang up
between the robber and the sister, who determined to take
Ivan's life.   Pretending to be ill, she sent her brother on
various dangerous errands to procure medicine.   With the
assistance of a bear and a wolf, whom he had trained,
and of his faithful dog, he always succeeded : until one
day he lost the three animals in a hole in the mountain.
On his return home Ivan was shut up in the bath-house,
and fire was set to it.   The three animals, however, escap-
ing from the mountain, appeared and tore the robber to
pieces.   Ivan reproached his sister, and went to the nearest
town.   Here a merchant took a fancy to him, and Ivan
married the merchant's daughter.

The King of the Lapps.

A Story of Koutokeino.

The King of the Lapps one day lost his way in the
mountains and met a large party of Tschudes.   They
inquired if he knew the Lapp King.   He replied that
he did, and, moreover, promised to bring the king to a
meeting, at an appointed spot on the ice of a neighbour-
ing lake.

The Lapp King went home, collected his men, and made them turn their boots inside out, so that they would not slip on the ice. He also had a great tree cut, and the bark stripped off. Then the King with his men came to the rendezvous: hurled the tree along the ice, and most of the Tschudes were thrown down. The Lapps then ran among their enemies, who, in ordinary boots, could not move easily on the ice, despatched them, and took much booty.

The Lapp and the Tschudes.

A Story of Yokkonga.

A man had three sons and a daughter. One day the sons went out hunting, leaving their parents and sister at home. Before long the dogs announced strangers, and, to the man's dismay, they proved to be Tschudes. He, however, invited them pleasantly into the hut, and asked his wife to bring food. Appearing anxious at the wife's absence, he sent the daughter out: finally, he found an excuse for going out to ask the cause of the delay. Then fastening the door, he took a long lance, went on the top of the hut and looked through the smoke hole. The Tschudes struck at the door threatening vengeance, but the Lapp with his long spear ran them through, one by one. When the sons came home and saw what their father had done, they praised him. My sons, he replied, when death threatens, then comes wisdom.

R

The Priest's Wedding.

A priest who was about to marry, invited as guests all the wild animals of the forest.

The bear came first, but met on the road a boy. Where are you going? inquired the boy. To the priest's wedding, replied the bear. Don't go, said the boy: you have such a fine coat that they will kill you. Whereupon the bear turned back. Next came the wolf. He also followed the boy's advice, and turned back. Then the lynx and the arctic fox came, and all followed the boy's advice, and did not go to the wedding. But the horse told the boy that he was too swift and strong to be kept prisoner, and went on: as did the cow, the goat, the sheep, and the reindeer. As the boy had warned them, they were all made prisoners and tamed.

The Fox and the Bear.

A fox being hungry, laid himself down on the snow and appeared to be dead. A *raide* or Lapp sledge-train soon came past, and the driver seeing the fox, and believing him dead, picked him up and put him on a sledge. The fox, however, requiring to be placed on the last sledge, fell off as if by accident. The Lapp picked him up again and placed him on the last sledge, which was loaded with fish. The fox managed to unfasten the sledge from the train, and possessing himself of the fish, started for his cave, there to enjoy the stolen food.

On the way he met a bear, who asked where he had

got the fish. I put my tail in the pond, said he, and the fish clung to it. Can you get fish to hang on to my tail? asked the bear. Yes, grandfather, said the fox: follow me. They came to the pond, and the bear put his tail through a hole in the ice as directed, the fox telling him not to stir. When the fox saw that the tail was frozen in, he shouted: Come out, Lapps, with bows and lances: the bear is frozen to the ice! Out rushed the Lapps, and when the bear started up, his tail gave way. Thus the bear has a short tail to this day.

The Salmon and the Trout.

A salmon swimming up the Tana River met a trout, who challenged him to race up the cataract. The salmon laughed, knowing well he was the best swimmer: then went with a rush up the rapid. The trout caught hold of his tail, and when the salmon reached the top of the fall, he turned to look for the trout. The trout shouted: I have won: I am higher than you.

Jetanas, or Giants.

The Lapps have many tales of these monsters of human form: and in some parts names of places, mountains, etc., are still associated with them. A mile below Karesuando a large stone projects into the river. The Lapps say it was placed there by a giant who wanted to step across: it is therefore called *Jatuni-suando*, giant's stepping-stone. A Jetanas could take a Lapp between his fingers and put him in his pocket.

The Quest of the Giant's Life.

A young Lapp whose father had been killed by a giant, and whose mother had been compelled to marry the monster, sought for revenge. He asked his mother to find where the giant had hidden his life. This she did, with difficulty. On an island surrounded by a sea of fire was a garden: in the garden a house: in the house a sheep: in the sheep a hen: in the hen an egg: within the egg was the giant's life. The young Lapp took a bear, a wolf, a hawk, a gull, and crossed the sea of fire in an iron boat.

The bear and the wolf rowed: hence their brown coats, for the fire-waves washed over and burnt them. They came to the island and found the house—the bear breaking into it with his paw. The wolf caught the sheep, the hawk the hen: but the egg dropped into the sea. Then the sea-bird dived and brought it back. The egg was burnt, and the young man returned home in time to see the giant in flames, at the point of death.

The Giant and his Boy.

A boy once served a giant, who, wanting to try his strength, took him into the forest. The giant proposed that they should strike their heads against the fir-trees. The boy anticipating this, had made a hole in a tree and covered it with bark. They both ran, the boy burying his head in the tree, while the giant only split the bark. Well, said the giant, now I have found a boy who is strong.

Then the giant wished to try who could shout the loudest. The giant roared till the mountains trembled and great rocks tumbled down. The boy cut a branch from a tree, saying he would bind it round the giant's head, for fear it should burst when he shouted. The giant prayed him not to shout ; and said they would try instead who could throw the farthest. He produced a great hammer which he threw so high into the air, that it appeared no larger than a fly. The boy said he was considering which sky to throw the hammer into, and the giant fearing to lose his hammer, asked the boy not to throw at all.

In the evening the giant asked him when he slept the soundest, and he answered, at midnight. He then went to bed, but getting up before midnight, placed a log of timber in the bed, and concealed himself. At midnight the giant came with a club and aimed heavy blows at the bed. In the morning when the boy, in reply to the giant's inquiries, said he had felt some chips falling on his face from the roof during the night, the giant thought he had better send him away. This he did, giving him as much money as he could carry.

The Stallos.

These were somewhat more human than *Jetanas*, but much larger than ordinary men, and were cannibals. They wore coats of mail, and were very rich. Their wives were all short-sighted : and carried iron tubes wherewith to suck blood out of their victims. They often challenged

the Lapps to fight : the two antagonists revealing mutually
where their property was concealed, and the survivor
taking all. A Stallo was always accompanied by a great
dog, who guarded him while he slept. If a Lapp succeeded in killing him, he must also kill the dog : otherwise
the latter would lick its master's wounds, and bring him
to life.

Stallo and the Fisher-Lapp.

Returning from his nets, a Lapp, one day, found a
Stallo on the beach. There was nothing for it but to
fight. The Lapp, finding himself in imminent danger,
promised various offerings to the gods, but Stallo also
made promises. At last Stallo promised to offer the
Lapp's head to the gods, if they would give him the
victory : but the Lapp, who was not a cannibal, promised
Stallo's axe and the whole of his body for an offering :
after which he succeeded in killing Stallo. This axe, say
the Lapps, was found many years afterwards under a
stone in Luleå.

Patto Pwadnje's Revenge.

Patto Pwadnje, an old Lapp, had several children,
some of whom disappeared in a mysterious manner. At
last he discovered the cause. A Stallo living in the neighbourhood laid traps, by means of which the children fell
into the river and were drowned. Patto Pwadnje resolved to be revenged ; and, pretending to have fallen
through the traps, he lay down in a shallow part of the
stream, awaiting Stallo's approach.

When Stallo saw Patto Pwadnje he laughed, pulled him out of the water, and took him home. As he appeared to be frozen, Stallo put him up the chimney to thaw, and then went out to prepare for cooking him. Meantime Patto Pwadnje climbed down, picked up an axe, and when Stallo appeared knocked him on the head.

Stallo's Marriage.

A Stallo sought the hand of a Lapp girl in marriage. The girl's father not daring to object, the day was appointed. During the meal a son of the Lapp took what appeared to be a red-hot kettle, put it on his knees, and ate out of it: and his would-be brother-in-law, not wanting to appear less brave, took a kettle off the fire, placed it on his knees, and was frightfully burnt. To conceal his anguish he went out, and shortly afterwards died.

The Stallo's father, unaware of this, and induced to go and play blind-man's-buff on the ice, was led by the Lapps into a hole, and drowned. His wife, who was in the house talking with the other women, heard her husband's cries. Suspecting something wrong, she seized her tube: but as it had been placed in the fire, she sucked into her mouth cinders and flame, and was so burnt to death.

Stallo and the Beaver Traps.

A Stallo went out to catch beavers. Having set his traps, he arranged a cord which would ring a bell. Then he kindled a fire, and lay down to sleep. A Lapp who had watched him pulled the cord, and the bell rang. Down ran Stallo to the lake, only to find that he was mistaken. Meantime the Lapp threw Stallo's coverings into the fire: and when Stallo came back he was vexed with himself for having, as he thought, in his haste thrown the coverings into the fire. The Lapp rang the bell a second time. Off started Stallo, and when he returned, the fire had gone out. Commencing to freeze, he called on the moon to help him, but in vain: before morning he froze to death.

Cacse-haldek or Sea-Folk.

A Lapp boy was invited by an old stranger to go fishing. Soon a dense fog settled on the sea, and they pulled long until they got out of it. At length, before them lay a town. The boy asked what place it was, and the old man replied: It is our town. The boy was frightened, for he saw then that his companion was not a human being.

However, he went out fishing with the old man's sons, and received for his share of the fish a hundred dollars. In the streets of the town were goats: and great hooks attached to fishing lines hung down from the skies. Occasionally a goat bit at a hook, and was pulled up out of sight He asked the old man what this meant, and he told him that the goats were fishes, which real people above the sea were catching. In a few days he was taken back to his home through the same fog; but told to reveal nothing of what he had seen.

Saivo Fish.

An old man and a young one went out a-fishing. The old man believed in Saivo people: the young one did not. The old man said he knew where to get plenty of fish: but they must be silent, so as not to offend the Saivo people. The young man promised this, and they put out their net. When they drew it in it was full of fish. The young man, in spite of his promise, spoke, and all the fish slipped out of the net. The old man said that he might get angry, but was induced to try another haul.

This time also the net was full: but again the same thing happened. Now the old man got angry, and wanted to go: but the young man promised not to utter a syllable. He kept his promise, the net was safely landed full of fish, and from that day the young man was convinced.

Goveiter.

A Lapp accidentally built his hut above the Goveiters' subterranean abode. He was tormented by them, until at last he removed his hut. The following day, while looking after his salmon nets, he heard some one on the river side opposite singing a song, thanking him for having moved his hut. Finding a salmon in the net, he placed it on a stone outside the hut, but returning in a few minutes, he found the fish gone.

Next day he saw his child sitting on the spot whence the salmon had disappeared, playing with silver money.

A search was made and a lot of money was discovered. In the night a Goveiter came and thanked him for having removed the hut, saying he had taken the salmon but paid him well as a mark of gratitude.

Bædnag-njudne, or Dog Noses.

These were savage spirits, having the forms of men, with dogs' noses, and but one eye in the middle of the forehead. They were cannibals, and very dangerous. A little girl once came to the house of a Bœdnag-njudne, finding only the wife at home. Taking pity on the little girl, the wife concealed her. The husband came home. It smells people, he said. The wife tried to persuade him that he was wrong, and contrived to let the girl escape : but Dog Nose, with his keen scent, discovered her track, and went in pursuit. The girl concealed herself underneath a bridge, and Bœdnag-njudne lost the track.

Ruobba, the Giant, and the Devil.

A man had three sons, who went out into the world to seek their fortunes. The eldest came to a king's palace, and was engaged by the king to watch a tree on which grew golden leaves, which were being constantly stolen. In the evening he watched, and saw how the leaves grew gradually larger : then heavy drowsiness came over him, and he slept. In the morning the leaves had disappeared, and the young man was beheaded. Next came the second brother, but the same fate befell him. Lastly came the third, nick-named *Ruobba*, or Dawdle, from his lazy habits.

He seated himself on a branch of the tree, and had
nearly fallen asleep, when he heard a curious sound in the
air.   He saw two men coming towards the tree, who
proved to be none less than the devil and a giant.   They
had only one eye between them, and when the devil handed
the giant the eye, Ruobba quickly took it out of his hand.
The giant asked for the eye, thinking the devil had kept
it : but the latter declared that the giant had taken it.
The giant was exasperated, and they fought till they were
both dead.   Ruobba received next day half the kingdom,
and the king's daughter for a wife.

The page of the history of Lapland is almost a blank.
In an Icelandic chronicle I have read how Grymer, a
Swedish nobleman, wooed the daughter of the King of
Sweden.   The King promised the princess' hand on condition that Grymer should overcome Hialmar, son of Harec,
King of Lapland.   The two armies met.   O Grymer, said
the Lapp warrior : let us be friends.   I will give thee
the unmixed juice of the grape, I will seek a Swedish
wife, thou shalt marry a fair maiden of my country, and I
will give thee the Principality of Biarmland—so we do not
fight.   Grymer refused with bitter words these peaceful
overtures, and in the combat Hialmar was slain.   His
father, wild with grief, sent to ravage Sweden, and that
country became a sheet of fire.   Charles sent his son Eric
to meet the invaders, but he was slain.   Grymer then set
out to meet Harec, disarmed him, then sparing his life,
sent him back to Lapland contented.

CHAPTER XIX.

The Umpdek Dunder—A novel bird—Rasnavolok—An unprofitable sacrifice—
Pleasant companions—Arctic solitudes—Journey to Lôvosero—Talk with
a Lapp—The Russian Lapps—The Northern Lights.

WE left Yekostrova with cordial farewells, taking Miron
with us, as we heard that the succeeding stations were
badly provided with carriers and boatmen. It was a long
tedious journey among the islands on the west side of
Imandra, and against a head wind, all the way to Raika
Taivola. Here we spent some hours with axe and auger,
raising the roof of the diminutive cabin, under which we
had been cramped and uncomfortable.

There were fine pines standing by the lake. The *isba*
faced the blue water, and far away beyond the lake rose
the fine blue Umpdek Dunder—the *Khivenski Gory* of the
Russians—with a pale cold mist clinging round its snowy
summit. Pines grow freely all round Imandra, and indeed
much farther north. At Pasvig in 69.30° north latitude,
and on the Tana River in 70° north, pines grow readily.

There were eight Lapps at Raika Taivola, decent hospitable people. I wished to leave the auger behind as a
souvenir, and offered it to one man, on condition of his

equalising matters by giving his brother one rouble out
of the present of money we gave him at the same time.
Though the auger was worth, he admitted, three or four
roubles, he could not see how it was worth his while to give
one rouble away.   Finally, we gave it to the other, who
readily accepted the condition.

Among the Mûrmanski, whom these small huts serve
in spring and autumn, exist strict principles of priority
and etiquette.   He who has carried no wood for the fire
will be shut out from it.   He who cooks the bread soup
gives way to him who cooks the fish soup.   The man
takes precedence of the woman, the woman of the boy.
The servant gives way to the master.   Masters and servants must arrange in what order each puts his pot on
the fire.

Rambling by the lake, my attention was drawn to the
note of a cuckoo, *geeka* the Lapps call him, who appeared to
have been at a convivial meeting.   Kuk-kuk-koo ! he cried
feebly at intervals, from among the lovely silver birches
which were mirrored in the lake.   This stuttering or convivial cuckoo being, as far as we knew, of a novel species,
I determined to name him after the Doctor—*Cuculus
Doctor*.   We took our leave of the Lapps and of the
cuckuckoo, and paddled away northward.   Still among
islands closely wooded, no great expanse of Imandra was
to be seen : it might be a group of small lakes.   The pure
glorious summer atmosphere reduces space, and distances
are hard to judge.

We came, upon a delicious Sunday morning towards

five o'clock, to Rasnavolok, and rested.   The *isba* stood,
with one or two earth huts, in a small clearing on the bank
of the *navolok* or creek.   We had still the lovely trees
reflected in the lake, and across the lake the soft light and
shade of the Umpdek Dunder.   The *isba* was, as usual,
a rough-hewn timber hut, measuring about sixteen feet
square and six feet high.   It had in one corner a fireplace
of considerable pretensions made of rough stones, in which
the Perevodtchik hastened to kindle a fire.   Two or three
Lapps who had been asleep on the rude bench which
runs round these huts, good-naturedly set to work to carry
water from the lake, and to cut firewood.

Then a drowsy Lapp brought us a salmon-trout, and
we fricasseed an unfortunate hen we had bought at Keret,
and transported with us for two hundred versts.   We had
bought two : and after the word had gone forth for their
execution, my heart smote me, and I hurried out to save
the poor fowls' lives.   In the case of one I was too late.
We now found that the unhappy bird had long since
passed the meridian of life, and even with our best arctic
appetites we could make no impression upon it.   The
secretary, whose instincts were more or less wolfish starved
and ravenous, could scarcely succeed with this fowl.

Afterwards a tall handsome elderly man came in to
offer us welcome.   He was unlike a Laplander.   He wore a
conical striped woven nightcap, and a gray home-spun suit,
with the usual Lapp moccasins.   He brought his young
and pretty wife, Maria Ivanovna Arkipoff, a cousin of Miron.
Two other women came in their Sunday dresses—red and

A RUSSIAN LAPP.

yellow short gowns close to the figure, Lapp boots bound round the ankles : on their heads close skull-caps, worked with silver-gilt thread, and red and yellow handkerchiefs. At Rasnavolok the Gavrilova and Sviatòi Nôs fishermen branch off to the North-east.

We set out from Rasnavolok with our good-looking crew : our host, Miron, Maria Ivanovna, a pretty girl Nastasia Kotéovna Arkipoff, and a middle-aged Lapp woman. A beautiful south-easterly wind blew, and our boat sped under sail over the ruffling waters of Imandra. The pretty Maria Ivanovna pointed out to me with a smile the Doctor, who was asleep with his mouth open. I then perceived that Maria Ivanovna was somewhat frivolous in character and deficient in reverence.

We had seen the last of the great lake, as we landed near a small *isba* by the mouth of the Koro stream. It strained our consciences to see the little Lapp ladies load themselves with their share of our baggage and trudge away merrily into the forest.

Still lonely woods : pines and silver-birches, with sprouting foliage, and their dead leaves still lying on the moss among fresh ferns. Now we saw a woodcock, and now a whimbrel in these almost lifeless woods. At times we chattered and laughed : at others we marched through the white solitudes, hearing only the crushing of dry boughs under foot.

These great lonely spaces are impressive to a degree : the Arctic silence is as it were the dawn of creation, and as if life had still to be called into existence. Mankind might inhabit some other globe, or might have existed only in a dream. Forests are lonelier than the sea. We saw no bears, reindeer, nor four-footed creatures : indeed, only vegetarian bears could find a livelihood here. Travellers are scarce, and ill-fed.

We left the three *isboushki* of Ratlombal to our left. The journey from here over the *tûndras* to the Umba Lake and Lôvosero occupies, so I learnt here, four days. Lôvosero has in winter about sixty Lapps : in summer, since many descend the Korodok to the sea, only about thirty. A Lapp told me that it was practicable to ascend the Umba River to Kânosero from its mouth in one day : thence in two days to Umbosero. Thirty versts below the latter lake are four rapids—one a difficult one. Some few fishermen frequent an island near the north end of Umbosero.

We came in two hours to a small lake, and blowing the Karelian post-horn, embarked in two boats. Then we traversed forest for an hour, and sailed out on the Pières Osero—a sheet of water surrounded by rolling hills thickly wooded. We spent two hours upon this lake.

Miron began to hesitate at this point of the journey and wanted to return home. When Diogenes' only servant ran away, a friend asked the philosopher how he could bear to lose him. What! said Diogenes : can Manes live without Diogenes, and not Diogenes without Manes? However, in this case we could not live without Miron, who had accordingly to be humoured into compliance.

I asked Miron how long he would remember me. For years. If I were to give him no present would he remember me still? Yes: but the larger the present the longer the memory, said Miron laughing. For how much a year would he remember me? Miron said he would remember me without money. Would he give me food, should I come to his house without any money? It is the custom of the Lapps, said the others quietly, to offer food to every one who visits them.

I asked Miron if he could tell me anything old: something that his father's father knew. Miron said simply that his grandfather was dead, and he couldn't talk with him. He added: We do not mark what is past. We have nothing worth remembering. If I go to Kola, what good to remember that?

I asked the Lapps if they believed all mankind came from two human beings, or from many. We do not know, they said. Have you heard your fathers say? I have something like that in my memory, said Miron. I said that if the original couple had four children, each of whom had descendants, the world might be well peopled. True, true, said Miron. I pointed out how Miron had four grandparents and eight great-grandparents, and asked if he were pleased to have had so many relatives. *Nié znayou shtobi snimi dyélat*, Miron said: I don't know what I can do with them. Miron had never received a letter in his life.

These were the best examples of Lapps we had seen: in speech, manner, and behaviour: quiet, modest, digni-

S

fied : their voices were soft. They had not the falsetto voices of Onésime and Larivan, and none of the Karelian blue eyes. The least mixed races of Lapps are said to be those of Southern Finmark and of Terski Lapland. I asked our host if either of his parents were Russian. No, he said briefly : they were *Laplandsi*, and my fathers' fathers too. The suggestion of Russian birth did not appear to be agreeable.

The Lapps, like the reindeer and the arctic dogs, are fond of their country. Ianotka howls when the church-bells remind him of the rich Russian bells in the home of the Old Believers by the White Sea. Prince Yablonovsky took in 1850 a girl from Russian Lapland to St. Peters-burg. She there received a superior education, was kindly treated, and seemed happy. Two years afterwards a party of Samoyedes with their reindeer were brought to St. Petersburg : the Lapp girl saw their tent, sledge, and reindeer, and disappeared to her home. A young Lapp entered the Swedish army, served for twenty years, and became captain. But his home instincts were too strong : he returned to his country.

The Lapps of Finland and of these regions have in the last three centuries diminished, while those in Nor-way have increased. No priest here speaks their tongue, no zealous missionary comes to welcome their children to school : no encouragement to thrift or energy ever reaches them. They are an old and primitive race. They have not, nor do they appear to have had, development or civilisation. Probably they were among the first inhabitants of the Frozen Zone, when at the end of the glacial period these regions became habitable.

I measured our friends of Rasnavolok. The elderly man stood five feet ten inches in height, and was, I believe, the tallest Laplander living. Miron measured five feet four inches : Maria Ivanovna four feet nine inches : Nastasia, the girl, four feet four inches and a half. The mean height of the Norwegian male Lapps is said to be four feet eleven : of the females four feet ten inches. The mean cephalic index has been found to average 87.15 in the men and 87.64 in the women. The *annularis* is as a rule longer than the index-finger—an evidence, it is supposed, of low culture.

There came a rain-cloud and squall over the mountains. To our right, on the edge of the lake, was a square verst of forest scorched and blasted by lightning. Electric storms rage here in the winter with great fury. I asked the Lapps their belief regarding the *Vose gaes*, or Aurora. Formerly it filled them with terror : and the Lapps would howl and shout during the grand phenomenon, which their ignorance connected with their own petty existence.

The Lapps told me they believe the Northern Lights bring wind and storms, woe and sickness. They are evil omens for mankind. The Lapps recognise, they said, hands and feet in them, and supernatural forms. I wished to ask, but could not, what they thought of a comet.

Six years ago the Northern Lights consumed a reindeer at Maselsky. A man of Karelia on a Saturday

afternoon was in the bath-house.   The Northern Fires
came, and a loud cry was heard.   The priest ran to the
bath, and found the man cut in two.   On another occasion, so it had been reported to Miron, a Laplander was
in the bath, replacing his clothes ready to go out.   The
Vose gaes flashed in the heavens, and again a cry was
heard.   This man was found with a cord round his
neck—hanged.   No human presence was visible.

Miron's face lighted up with a quaint earnestness, and
he shook his shaggy beard to emphasise his faith in the
preternatural energies of the *Vose gaes*.   Poor Lapps,
timid, credulous spiritualists—as many more civilised
people are : no wonder witchcraft and superstition still
chain their simple minds.   Castren was caught in a snow-
storm.   Probably, said his Lapp guide, the *Seida* wishes
to exact an offering from us, and through this storm to
show his power.   Then the Lapp drank to the *Seida*, to
assuage his wrath.

Whether it were a whistling wind, writes the Solomon
of the Apocrypha : or a melodious noise of birds among
the spreading branches, or a pleasing sound of water running violently, or a terrible sound of stones cast down, or
a running that could not be seen of skipping beasts, or a
rebounding echo from the hollow mountains—these things
made them to swoon for fear.   For the whole world
shined with clear light, and none were hindered in their
labour.   Over them only was spread a heavy night, an image
of that darkness which should afterwards receive them.

The timidity of superstition, which in the case of our

afflicted countrymen restricts itself to a childish dread of omens, presentiments, ghosts, and suchlike, has upon the mind of the Lapp an effect amounting to hysteria, and almost to mania. A Karelian, journeying by water, met a boat containing a Lapp woman with a baby in her arms : beside herself with terror at the Karelian's strange dress, the woman cast the child into the lake.

A man sat chatting in a circle of Terski Lapps. A sudden sound was heard, and the Lapps fell prostrate on the ground, as still as corpses : rising in a minute unconcernedly as if nothing had happened.

A merchant suddenly displayed a knife to a Lapp woman : she flew madly at him, and attacked him, then sank senseless to the ground. Another suddenly waved a white cloth before a Lapp woman, and she tried to tear his eyes out : all curious manifestations of failure of the faculties and of self-control. Cover the agitated Lapp's eyes with your hand and the ecstasy passes.

Authors who refer to the Lappish mythology are Schefferus, 1673 : Tuderus, 1773 : Fjellström, 1755 : Hogström, 1747 : Lindahl, 1750 : Jessen, 1767 : Læstadius, 1831-3 : Lars Læstadius, 1840 : Ganander, 1789 : Castren, 1853 : Professor Friis, 1871. To the two last-named authors, I have chiefly referred, for my sketch of the Lapp mythology. Professor Friis seems in a great measure to have used Scheffer as his authority.

CHAPTER XX.

Mythology of the Lapps—The Noaïds—The *Kobdas*—A self-sacrifice—The Lapp divinities—Tiermes—Sun-worshippers—The formation of a soul— The *Haldek*—Heaven and hell—The flood.

THE wizard songs of the Lapps, and their numerous ballads mentioned in the Kalevala, have faded out of recollection : and a song or two about a bear hunt, or about the Pæive Barnek, Sons of the Sun, are all that a traveller is likely to hear among the Russian Lapps. The mythology of the Lapps, handed down by the missionaries sent among them, would have been more complete had they treated the Lapp wizards or *Noaïds* more tolerantly, and not driven them into reticence. The *Noaïds*, like the Druids—the persecution of whom deprived us of much knowledge of the mythology of our forefathers—alone were familiar with their traditions : and with many of them their knowledge was buried.

These wizards even seem to have remotely assisted in introducing Christianity. They adopted each new-comer's faith, and afraid to give offence to some unknown Almighty, tried to gain the favour of Rist Ibmel, the Christians' God, as well as of their own traditional divinities. The ability

of a *Noaïd* determined the number of his followers. Some
were very famous, and are still remembered : Guttavuorok,
for instance, who could assume four different forms. In
trances the *Noaïds'* souls were supposed to take flight on
a bird or fish to Yabmi Aibmo, the Country of the Dead,
where they gained the knowledge desired.

As I have just instanced, the nervous system of the
Northern races is very feeble, and ecstasy comes to them
without much provocation or effort. Lapp children, if
unusually nervous or excitable, were sent to *Noaïds*, in the
hope of their becoming adepts. One of the Norway kings,
Suttorm the White, sent his daughter Gunhild to Motle,
king of the Lapps, to have her instructed in magic.

No one knew the form of instruction. Inspiration
came partly in sleep, partly through assistant ghosts,
Noaïda Gagge, who must introduce the candidate to the
Country of the Dead. All the *Noaïds* sat cross-legged
in front of the *gamme :* then the novice sang, accompanied by the oldest *Noaïd*, and drummed on a magic
drum. If during the subsequent trance the *Noaïda Gagge*
crossed their bodies and entered the hut, perceptible to the
novice alone, this was the sign of his initiation.

One *Noaïd* could harm men and animals : another
could find causes of ailment and their remedy : a third
could change himself into animal forms. The Greenlanders believe the same of the *Angakok*, the Samoyedes
of the *Tâdibe*, and the Siberian races of the *Schâman*.
Noaïds must be perfect in form and constitution : when
old and toothless they lost their virtues.

The *Noaïds* were also the medicine men of the Lapps : and some became skilful by experience and the study of nature. Like the familiars of Odin, who had bitter, favourable, and medicinal *runes*, the *Noaïds* had cabalistic words and tokens. Dangerous illnesses were attributed to the influence of dead relatives—to their impatience to meet, or their wish to punish, the living. Thus, to seek conciliation, the *Noaïd* must travel to the Country of the Dead. For this and other services he was well paid.

The *kobda*, or drum, used alike by all the Turanians for divining, was beaten by the *Noaïd* like a gong, slowly and gradually, to a low chant, *Goy, Goy, Goy*, and this summoned the familiar spirits. Spaces, painted on the parchment with reindeer's blood or a decoction of alder-bark, were set apart on the *kobda* for various deities : for the sun, stars, and planets, living creatures, Lapps, their abodes, reindeer, Christians, etc. The interest and value of the *kobda* depended, of course, much upon the *Noaïd's* skill in drawing, and knowledge of mythology.

This is a fair example of a *kobda*. The horizontal lines divide the oval into spaces which represent Heaven, the Earth, beneath the Earth. Professor Friis interprets the drum more or less as follows :—

1. The moon.

2. Thor with a hammer and a pickaxe.

3. Freya, with emblems of plenty — apparently a flowerpot and a tankard.

4. Freya clothed in a fishing-net as the patroness of fishery.

A LAPP KOBDA OR DIVINING DRUM.

5. Thor's servant.

6. Freya's little boy: who appears to have gone wrong.

7. Ducks.

8. The cuckoo.

9. The Morning Star, the Evening Star, and the Moon Star.

10. A cock.

11. The cat.

12. A bear—which appears to have come out of a Noah's ark.

13. A hare.

14. A reindeer.

15. The ship *Ringhorna*, in which the sun and moon are sailing over the sea by night.

16. The ox.

17. The sun.

18. Heimdal, the messenger of the gods, disguised as a Saivo bird visiting Yabmi Aibmo.

19. The waves of the Central Sea.

20. The cow Audumbla, on board the *Ringhorna*.

21. An alligator.

22. Yabmi Aibmo, the Country of the Dead.

23. Three judges.

24. The swallow, herald of the sun's return.

25. The swan, mourner over the sun's departure, and the singer of Sorrow's song.

26. The sun beneath the earth in the winter.

27. The melancholy hog whom the sun slew.

28. The crane, which comes in the spring to give an account of the birds of passage.

29. The ferryman bearing a soul to purgatory—to the apparent satisfaction of a neighbour.

30. Charon and a passenger.

31. The moon below the earth tossing the sun with its horn.

32. Twelve judges.

33. Thor's dog Starbo, in search of the absent sun.

34. Lower Yotun, or Niflheim.

35. The great worm Yormungad, whose coils represent the sun's course through the year.   Three coils show the sun to be in the third month.

Some of these interpretations are hypothetical : and I should be inclined to modify them.   The drum being divided into three spaces—Asgard or Heaven, Midgard the Earth, and Niflheim beneath the Earth—I should take the spiral animal to be the great serpent of Midgard : described in that marvellous Icelandic poem, the *Voluspa*, as encompassing the earth, and as long enough to stretch from Heaven to the region beneath the Earth.   Thor once went out in a boat with the Giant Eymer to fish for the great serpent : and this may be the meaning of the two men in the boat, No. 30.   Otherwise it may be the Ship of Death, *Naglefara*, of which the Giant Rymer was pilot.

No. 23, I should take, not for the dog Starbo, but for the squirrel which runs up and down *Ydrasil*, the great ash-tree of Midgard, seeking to sow dissension between the Serpent and the Eagle.

I think the ship *Ringhorna* was the *Skidbladner* of Odin—so great that [it would carry all the gods, and so small that it could be folded into a pocket. No sooner were its sails unfurled, than a favourable gale sprang up, to waft it whithersoever the gods wished to sail.

The unnumbered animal flying near the sun I should take for the black winged dragon, which flew round and round the Abode of the Dead, devouring the bodies of prisoners in Niflheim—the prison-like construction at the foot of the drum.

Heimdal, the Mercury of Asgard, had acute faculties : he could see by night a hundred leagues, and could hear the growth of the grass on the earth, and of the wool on a sheep's back.

Nos. 24 and 28 I should have taken rather for Thor's two ravens—*Hugin*, Thought, and *Munnin*, Memory, which were stationed at either side of his head.

No. 27 I should call the boar *Skrimner*, on whose flesh all the gods supped each night, and which became entire again each morning.

The cow *Audumbla*, depicted in the ship *Ringhorna*, is the *Oedumla* of the Scandinavians. A breath of heat spreading over the gelid vapours of chaos formed a man Ymir, and this cow. *Oedumla*, nourished Ymir and supported herself by licking rocks covered with salt and hoar frost.

The figures 32 may be the twelve apostles, introduced, like many Christian saints, to the Lapp mythology in later days. And the three figures, 23, so much resemble a

Trinity on an old silver plaque I found in Lapland, that they may be an archaic suggestion of the Christian's triple divinity—dwelling like departed souls in bliss, close beneath the surface of the earth.

I have not heard the oval form of the *kobda* accounted for. It is so like the section of a skull that it may have suggested the head of the *Noaïd* and the various inspirations contained therein. The *Goy, Goy, Goy,* I think, must have been the *Noaïd's* adjuration of Goya—that is, Freya or Vanadis, the Goddess of Hope.

The *kobda* must be made from a birch, pine, or fir tree : grown in a spot where the sun had never shone, and standing apart from other trees. The trunk in its growth must have twisted contrary to the sun's course : so as not to give offence to the Sun God. The *kobda* varied from one to three feet in diameter. The Kemi Lapps are said to have had a drum so huge, that they could not carry it on a sledge, and accordingly burned it whenever they migrated.

Vaïnemoïnen and Ilmarinen, two kings of Finland, went to Lapland in order that Ilmarinen might receive as wife the fairest girl in Lapland. She was daughter of the Lappish king, who as a condition demanded a *kobda* of singular properties. The two kings set to work and made one. It proved so wonderful and lucrative, that they resolved to get it back. They seized it, but on their return journey were overtaken by the Lapp king in the form of an eagle. In the struggle for its recovery, the drum was spoiled. Ilmarinen was a great hero : immortal-

ised as Ilmaris on the Lapp *kobdas*. The hammer used
in divining was small and T-shaped: a brass ring, which
hopped on the parchment as the hammer tapped it, was
the direct mouthpiece of the oracle.

A wizard's son was sick. Forbidden to use the drum
himself, the father sent for his wife's brother. Drum as
he would, the ring drifted into the Abode of the Dead.
After the promise of a female reindeer, it travelled to the
Christians' region. The father next promised a male deer,
then a horse, to the *Noaïd* of the Kingdom of Death, if
only the ring would jump to the place of the Lapps: but
all in vain. He then saw certain death for his son.

His brother-in-law now went out, hung a stone round
his neck, and fell upon his face in prayer. The stone
intelligibly answered that a man must die in the son's
place. The father gladly offered to do so: and the
ring at once leapt to the Region of the Lapps. The
son recovered, but the poor father fell dangerously ill:
and the next afternoon went with his unfortunate soul to
Mubben Aibmo. The son in gratitude killed a reindeer,
so that his father in the Abode of the Dead might ride
whither he pleased.

The Runic tree was as much venerated by the Lapps
as the *kobda*: it was a sort of household idol, kept sacredly
in the recesses of the *gamme*. No woman must approach
it. If within three days she crossed the path by which a
Runic tree had been transported, she must expect misfortune or death, and speedily make expiatory offerings.
Svitsch was a reindeer offered at a moment of imminent

danger: *pomitj*, a reindeer offered for the repose of a dead Lapp's soul.

At death a guardian angel would come to bear the soul away on a reindeer: not travelling direct to heaven, but for seven weeks wandering to each spot where the departed had in life done evil or good. The soul was thereby reminded of its earthly life, good and bad, lucky and unlucky, of joy and sorrow: and would, if regenerate through this purgatory, at its completion be fit for access to heaven. The Greenlanders had a grotesque and ludicrous goddess, whom a released soul must visit on its journey to heaven. If the soul could not keep its countenance in spite of the appearance of the goddess, it was lost.

The Lapps believed the universe to be filled with supernatural beings: in heaven, above heaven, and below it: above and beneath the earth. Each mountain, lake, river, and spring had its *Halde*, or divinity.

Radien Akke was supreme in power and majesty. His wife was the almighty mother Kwarve Adne or Freya. As patroness of reindeer breeding, she was often drawn on the *kobda* with a horn upon her head.

Radien Kjedde their son was the active creator of everything: Radien Njeida was their daughter.

The god of heaven and air, the oldest and most familiar of the gods, was Yumala, who was at the same time the god of strangers: Ibmel of the Northern Lapps, Yibmel of the Southern: Yummal of the Esthonians: Yuma of the Tcheremiss: Yumala of the Finlanders:

Yumal of the Northern Tschudes : Yeu of the Syriänen: and Yûm, or Noum, of the Samoyedes.   He was god generally of the agencies of nature.

Tiermes was the thunder god, known to the Samoyedes, Ostiaks, and other Mongolians as Father—a term of deep veneration.   The Lapps, and the Norsk farmers to this day address thunder as grandfather.   The matter-of-fact Julius Cæsar, in his Commentaries, mentions a Gaulish god who presided over winds and tempests. Lucan gives this deity's name, Taranis.   *Taran* signifies thunder—*taranis*, thundery, in Welsh to his day.   Tiermes ruled over the weather, wind, and sea, man's welfare, life, and health.   He is drawn with a hammer, and also for a weapon, the rainbow—hence called *Diermes Davge* or grandfather's bow.   His dog, Starbo, protected the *Noaïd*, in Yabmi Aibmo, from the evil spirits.

Agya, probably Tiermes in a modified form, governed the skies.   His arrows were of red-hot copper : his weapon a rainbow : his voice the thunder : lightning was the fire he struck when in want of light in his heavenly abode.

The gods had also their wizards, *Varalde Noaïde*. These were generally drawn at the head of the drum. The storm god was drawn with a shovel, wherewith to shovel wind, and a club with which to drive it back.   The Lapps worshipped him on the *tûndras* and mountains, where the reindeer were exposed to his power.   The *Noaïd* would pray to him for a storm to blow upon an enemy.   They would make three knots in a cloth, says Scheffer : unfastening one when they asked for a moderate breeze: two when their enemy must use a double-reefed sail : three when they prayed for a tempest.

There were gods of fruitfulness of earth and sea, and *Ailekes Olbmak*, or holy-day divinities. Sunday was the best day for oracles and hunting : Saturday the next, Friday the next. Friday and Saturday were unlucky for woodcutting, as blood would flow from the trees.

The great gods used little winged gods, flying between heaven and earth. The sun, moon, and stars were in a degree worshipped by the Lapps, as by the Samoyedes, Ostiaks, Voguls, etc.: and associated with the gods. Ursa Major was Tiermes' dog. The three stars in Orion, Freya's distaff : the Milky-way was the road of winter. An old Samoyede woman told Castren that each morning she bowed to the sun, saying : When thou, Iliambertje, arisest, I arise : when thou goest down, I also go to rest.

The Esquimaux thought the sun and moon were once human—a brother and sister. The third star in Orion's belt was a Greenlander, lost while out seal fishing. The Aurora was composed of souls of the dead floating in space—dancing and playing ball. Snow was the blood of the departed. Souls rested on the skins of young white bears while on the journey to heaven. The moon needed food, and during an eclipse was suspected of casting about for seals : so the Greenlanders made noises to drive the moon away.

All this is more poetical and less childish than the horror of going to sea on a Friday, of breaking a mirror, of being one among thirteen at table, of having snowdrops or peacocks' feathers in one's room, of passing under a ladder, of seeing a crescent moon through a window, of nightmare apparitions called ghosts: and suchlike imbecilities.

The sun and moon had children, described on the *kobdas*. The morning and evening stars shone for the *Noaïd* on his journey to the Kingdom of Death. When the ring settled upon the morning star, it promised fruitfulness and plenty: on the evening star, want and famine. There was a moon-star, *Manno Naste :* and a child-star, or *Manna Naste*. When the latter issued from the moon, a woman would bear a son : when the contrary, a girl.

When a child was to be brought into the world, Radien Akke authorised his son to make a soul, and sent it to the assistant god, Mader Akke, who ran off with it round the sun and through all the sun's beams. Then he delivered it to his wife, if destined to be a boy : to his daughter, if a girl : and at length it reached the mother.

Sarakka, one of Mader Akke's daughters, was greatly revered. Her abode was by the hearth, and to her the Lapps offered something at each meal. After they adopted the Sacrament and the Lord's Prayer, they had a sacrament in honour of Sarakka ; and each child christened and baptized was rebaptized in honour of Sarakka, receiving likewise a Lapp name.

Leibolmak, or willow-wood-man, was the god of hunting and of wild animals. Barbmo Akke was the god of birds of passage. Barbmo was a land where the sun always

T

shone, where the birds remained during the northern winter.   Barbmo Akke received from Guorgaf, the crane, king of the birds, a reckoning of the birds born or lost during each migration.

Tapio was the god of reindeer : Kakke Olbmak, the god of water.   Samoyedes and Ostiaks offer to the River Ob, which is sacred in Siberia, a reindeer.   The Tartars, before eating, throw food into the water.   The Lapps pray to the water god : Send fish to my hook.

A *Halde* was a ubiquitous terrestrial deity, appertaining to every feature in Nature.   Before pitching a tent, the local *Halde* must be conciliated.   The Doctor and I must have found our way at Tûloma and at Seven Islands to the hearts of the local *Haldek* : for happier days we never spent.   *Haldek* could, for a consideration, be engaged by by *Noaïds* to watch a Lapp's reindeer on earth.   The Greenlanders were careful in their provision of local deities.   There was a god whose function it was to watch foxes when they went down to the beach to devour dead fish—an employment as close as that of the gentleman who said his occupation was to blacken glasses for eclipses.

To this day a deserted child is called *apparas :* and the Lapps believe its spirit goes about *tûndras* and woods seeking, with cries and wailing, for its mother.   If encountered, it will reveal its mother's name : and the traveller should at once give it a name, for, unbaptized, it will never find repose.   Læstadius says Lapp children · · thus put out of the way have been found with their tongues cut out, lest they should betray their parentage.

Yabmi Akko, the Mother of the Dead, was worshipped in hope of a long life. Rote or Rutu was the Evil Spirit, the Loke of Valhalla, who haunted men with ill intent from the cradle to the grave. Inferior evil spirits were numerous. Gadflies and magical darts were superhuman means of human revenge. An enemy's picture was sometimes drawn, and shot at with sharp or blunt arrows, according to the hatred he inspired.

Saïvo Aibmo was heaven, where good men and animals passed their life after death. The souls lived close under the surface of the earth, with ordinary human occupations, only in a happier and more perfect state of being. They were regarded as rich and fortunate: and compared with them the poor Lapps on earth were miserable beings. In each great hill lived four or five spirits. Lapps would make offerings to their dead relatives in Saïvo, and could even visit them in company of the *Noaïds*. There were Saïvo fish, birds, and reindeer, of which only the most eminent *Noaïds* could obtain possession.

Yabmi Aibmo, the kingdom of Rutu, Prince of Evil, was the place of darkness, pestilence, and wailing: whither went such as had been guilty of anger, theft, swearing, quarrelling—the only sins considered serious by the Lapps. A sick reindeer was believed to have been milked by Yabmi Akke. When a child cried much, its name must be displeasing to some spirit, who wished it called after himself. It then received an additional, a Saïvo baptism, to assure the dissatisfied spirit that he was not forgotten.

Lapp *Bassek* were holy places, cliffs, rivers, and such-like.   Even spots in which they had been lucky or un-lucky in hunting, the Lapps would call *Bassek :* in each *Basse* was erected an idol, or *Seida.*   The Terski Lapps, for success in hunting, would offer a perfect reindeer, skinned without a knife, and then frozen stiff : while they stood round and chanted.   They had great autumnal and winter feasts, in which they offered various gifts : to Rutu a horse, to others black cattle, and so on.

A Lapp bought from a peasant a black cow, and offered it to one of his gods.   Ten days afterwards the peasant found the cow tied up and emaciated.   He re-leased it, and several times sold it to the same Lapp.   At last the poor Lapp perished in a snowdrift.   This happened in 1790.   They have still an elaborate cere-mony in hunting the bear.   They pray and chant to his carcase, and for several days worship before eating it.

The Lapps remained heathen long after their pro-fession of Christianity, owing to foolish efforts to teach them religion in languages which they did not understand. Rastus, a rich Lapp had an idol—within the memory of man—to which he used to offer brandy and reindeer blood.   One day Rastus had failed to bring his usual offering, and two of his reindeer were killed by lightning. Enraged, he hastened to the idol, cut a limb from the reindeer, and, striking the Bauta violently with it, ex-claimed : There, thou hast what thou hast slaughtered, but from this day thou hast never an other offering from me !   This completed his conversion.

The Lapps believed Scandinavia and all the world to be an island, which lay drifting on the sea. Their sacred mountain was Sulitelma, *Suolicielbma*, the Island's door. Yumala had once turned the whole world upside down, so that the water covered the earth and drowned all but a boy and girl, whom Yumala took in his arms, and carried to the top of a high hill, *Basse varre*, Holy Mount. When danger was past he let them go their ways separately. After three years' wanderings, they met and recognised each other. After another three, they met as strangers: then they married, and mankind are their descendants.

Of the four millions of inhabitants of the polar regions, the great majority entertain to this day superstitions and belief of which the foregoing are fair examples: and as for us who live elsewhere, we are only at the threshold of knowledge, and must remain so until the great veil is lifted.

> *We have but faith, we cannot know,*
> *For knowledge is of things we see.*

We shall then discover, says the heathen Seneca, the secrets of nature: the darkness shall be discussed, and our souls irradiated with light and glory: a glory without a shadow: a glory that shall surround us, and from whence we shall look down and see day and night beneath us.

CHAPTER XXI.

Maselsky—The snowy mountain ridge—Education—Wild flowers of the Kola
River—A Lapp gentleman—Tschongai—A profession of faith—Kola—
The route from the White Sea.

THERE runs into *Guolle Yaur*, or Fish Lake, from its
southern extremity, a tongue of wooded land, dividing it
into the form of a lobster's claw. The other chief lakes
of the Kola Peninsula are Imandra and Nuôtosero:
Buerinskosero, opposite to Sashyéka: Kolvitsosero, beyond the Umpdek eastward: Kânosero, on the Umba:
Umbosero, that river's source: Lôvosero, the central lake:
Porosero and Kolnosero, two of a chain of lakes through
which the Yokkonga runs: Yenniosero, the origin of the
Arzina River: Sergosero, in the marshes between Vârzuga
and the Ponoi.

On a brilliant, cold, windy afternoon, we reached
Maselsky—a little settlement midway along the east shore
of the Guolle Lake. Here, in a snug little *isba*, a bright
crackling birch-fire awaited us. Our Lapp *khozeka* had seen
our boat approaching—the comeliest, pleasantest hostess we
had seen yet. Soon the salmon-trout were spluttering in the
frying-pan, and we were restoring our energies with food.

The winter settlement of these Lapps is Maselsîd, five miles away, where are ten *isboushki*, and in winter forty or fifty Lapps. We despatched two Lapps thither that they might bring winter garments, and in the afternoon they returned. Miron and Maria Ivanovna put on the *mâlitsi*, caps, and boots, and I took their portraits.

On the edge of the wood I found the cattle trefoil: the bog whortleberry: the pretty arctic raspberry, *Rubus arcticus:* and the pale butterwort, *Pinguicula lusitanea:* the latter was not growing in the rich tufts of lower latitudes.

From the little hut we could see westward, across the rippling lake, the fine snowy group the Mensche, Tschyne, and Volsche Dûndri, standing three thousand feet above the sea. They look down, on their westward slopes, upon the valley of the Tûloma and the Nuôt Lake. Our route from the White Sea to the Arctic lay almost due north: we were travelling along the 33rd meridian of east longitude.

We parted very regretfully from the charming Lapps of Rasnavolok. They were examples of untrained intelligence of a high order, and of instinctive good breeding.

The Lapps expressed their wonder that there should be anything in this country interesting enough to bring us from so far. I tried to explain that the Doctor and I acquired at school such geographical ignorance, that it had been necessary for us to spend much time and money in correcting it.

We saw many a prostrate tree, uprooted by the arctic hurricanes which sweep through these forests. A reindeer

trotted along the beach beside us as we left Mâselsky,
probably for company.   We landed on the northern shore
of the lake : our crew, pleasant and willing like the last,
loaded themselves with the baggage—our food chests had
grown painfully light—and away we went in Indian file
through the forest.

Then lake for an hour—forest, lake—lake, forest—for
hours, till we came by boat cold and hungry to the *isba*
of Angasgory, where the Kola River leaves the lake.   Here
we failed to get any fish, and we had little left otherwise.
The poor Lapps had nothing.   They were hungry : so
were we.   On perceiving this, the Lapps and the Doctor
were nearly moved to tears.   We gladly shared what we
had with them, and all lay down on the floor round the
fire to rest.

I went out into the white birch wood among the reindeer moss, to see the source of the Kola River, and gather
wild flowers.   I found the small white Alpine cerastium,
the deep violet Pyrenean butterwort, the *Campanula Zoysii*
or Scotch blue-bell, the smaller gentian, the *Pedicularis
Lapponica*, or smaller liquorice, and the pale marsh violet.
Among the reindeer moss I gathered some huge *Cladonia
deformis* or cup moss, and on the white carpet beside it,
in brilliant scarlet spots, the *Cladina cornucopioides*.

The stream here is narrow, and falls in a rapid from
the smooth lake—disturbing the silent woods into echoes.
We began a midnight march from the *isba*.   We could
hear the murmur of the river.   The flowers were asleep :
only the sleepless mosquito watched.

HALT IN A SILVER BIRCH FOREST. RUSSIAN LAPLAND.

After two or three changes we came upon the Kola River, and for the first time descended it. We left it, returned to it, and travelled down as far as the hut of Kitsa. Here we made a long halt for food and a night's rest: five-and-thirty versts still separated us from Kola. To our left, hidden by trees, lay the Pwads Waïve, or Reindeer Head: the plateau separating the Kola from the Tûloma River.

In the morning, having found Lapps enough, we released Miron. Under our arrangement we owed him six roubles. I paid the other Lapps first: giving one or two roubles to each beyond their pay. Coming to Miron, I gave him a single rouble. Miron rose, bowed, took my hand, and sat down again—quite content, poor fellow—and not thinking me capable of treating him unfairly. In a minute I gave him another rouble. This was a welcome surprise: he rose, bowed, and thanked me pleasantly.

After an interval I did the same again, and again, till Miron's eyebrows rose, a comical look came into his face, and the other Lapps began to laugh heartily at him. At length I gave him a three-rouble note, and Miron threw up his hands. *Davolno, davolno !* Enough, enough ! he exclaimed. Poor Miron: a gentleman himself, he believed the Englishman was the same: and with nothing in his pocket, and a wife and four children in Kandalaks, he could trust a stranger's honesty and cry enough, when he thought he had received more than he was entitled to for his work. We were sorry to part: I think Miron was exceedingly fond of us.

The Lapp girl, who had accompanied us from Mâselsky, wore her Sunday dress—a bright and pretty one—and I asked her father if I might buy her belt, from which hung numerous brass charms.   He said that having himself given it to her, he would rather she did not part with it : knowing, at the same time, that he might have five times its value for it.

The Russian Lapps have no silver now—sold, stolen, or buried long since.   A Lapp of Ieretik, Ingier by name, is reputed to have, besides two thousand reindeer, a quantity of buried silver.   The Skolte Lapps are said to have silver buried too.   The Ispravnik of Kola tried to persuade the Lapps, but in vain, to place their money in the Archangel banks.   Within the last few years only, the Lapps of Finmark have had the faith to place money in the Government savings banks.

For four hours and a half on this the last day of our overland journey did we trudge through the forest on the eastern side of the Kola River.   We saw a woodcock, and a three-toed woodpecker, *Picus tridactylus*, amusing himself on a tree.   I found the snakeweed here, and the globe-flower.

For some versts after leaving Kitsa the track was rough and steep, and as each of us carried something it was exhausting.   Brandy, chocolate, and biscuits encouraged us from time to time : and after noon we staggered into the *isba* of Tschongai, a woodcutter's hut.

I had a long talk with a young Lapp of Mâselsid. I suppose his views are a fair example of the extent of a Laplander's religious knowledge. I asked whether he knew what would become of him after death. He would cease to live—nothing more of him—*nie tchevô*—no matter. Would he never meet his dead friends? No.

Did he know what God was? Yes, he had been taught to pray to Him—that is, to the *Obrasi*. But, I said, the *Obrasi* were not God, and were only good to recall God's presence and existence—as reindeer, rivers, and trees were. It was not right to pray to them. *Aito mnya prioutchili, y nie magou ad viknût* — I have been taught, replied the Lapp, to pray to them : and I cannot give up doing so.

Did he know what a cross meant?—No. I told him that *Khristos* had once come to live in this world, and had been put to death upon a cross. *Ya niekoghda nie slishol ab aitom : ya raskazhou k'mayim drougam*, I have never been told of this : I will tell my companions. He added, that whenever he worshipped the *Obrasi* he would try in future to remember God. Poor Lapp boy — almost as ignorant of evil as of good—one of the simple souls of whom little will be required.

We passed, as we paddled down the rapid and pretty Kola River, some droll little fishing rafts composed of three logs about eight feet long. On one of these almost submerged vessels a Lapp was busy, setting his lines. A butterfly flew across the river to remind us that the summer had come. Six miles distant, to our right, lay the *pogost* of Gilda Sid, or Kildina, the winter home of fifty Lapps, and a station on the winter track from Kola to Gavrilova.

We passed, as we descended the river, a considerable landslip. Silver-birches and all the lovely undergrowth lay piled up in a ruin by the river's brink. We landed at Muotkek, or Sashyok, four versts from Kola : and set off for a smart walk to the end of our journey.

In an hour we stood on the cliff of *Solaviaréka*, looking northward to the town of Kola, three hundred feet below us. To the left was the splendid Tûloma, sweeping down among green hills. From the right of the cliff came the rapid Kola : and the rivers met below the little gray town. Two or three *lodjes* lay in the fiord, which disappeared towards the sea in soft blue haze. It was a very lovely view : a delicious breath came from the coast, thirty miles away, and the landscape, under a cold sunny sky, was bathed in silvery light.

Route from the White Sea to the Kola Gulf.

	By Land. Versts.	By Water. Versts.
Kandalaks to Plososero .	13	...
Tinda Taivola	4	4
Pinosero .	4	5
Sashyéka	7	...
Yekostrova . .	...	35
Raika Taivola .	...	25
Rasnavolok . .	...	25
Kouringa . . .	...	12
Kouringsky Taivola . .	4	...
	32	106

| | By Land. | By Water. |
	Versts.	Versts.
	32	106
Pieres Osero .	...	12
Mâselsky	1	5
Kolosero . .	...	10
Angasgory .	4	...
Polosero . .	...	12
Mordosersky Taivola . .	4	...
Mordosero . .	...	15
Plososero . .	4	...
Kitsa . . .	...	3
Tschongai . .	17	...
Solovara Taivola	...	15
Kola . .	3	...
	65	178
		65
		243

CHAPTER XXII.

Onésime—The *Masslinitsa*—Obtainable necessaries in the White Sea Peninsula
and Karelia—Negotiations with Laplanders—Michieff—An enquiry—
Baseball—An international cricket match—Farewell to Kola.

WE had come from the White Sea to the Arctic. Since
leaving Kola we had made the circuit of Russian Lapland
and sailed half round the White Sea. We scrambled down
the face of the cliff, and trudged into the village.

From a crowd of men, a small dark Lapp sprang forward and grasped both my hands. It was Onésime. I
expected you this evening, he said. Only last night I
told these men you had promised to be in Kola on this
day. Then we walked to the house of Stepanina Moldvistoff together : Onésime's arm round my waist and mine
round the little Lapp's neck: as though we had been
long separated brothers. Half-an-hour after he had left
us in Stepanina's care and disappeared, he returned bearing a salmon nearly as long as himself. From Onésime,
he said, handing it to me with a bow and smile.

It was the *Masslinitsa* or Butter Week : the three
weeks' Fast of St. Peter was over, and it was less difficult
to get solid and sustaining necessaries in the village.

Even here the reaction from the long fasts is considerable: and the arctic peasants have their carnival.   Numerous marriages take place in the *Masslinitsa.*

Milk, cheese, and butter are forbidden in the fasts:
and in no part of the world are religious restrictions more
scrupulously observed than in this country.   The Russian's
instinctive obedience serves the Church well.   He pays
much money for intercession.   Each new-built house, each
newly-entered shop, must be cleansed or blessed with a
religious ritual, at a moderate cost.   Constantly the priest
and sacristan come to purify houses with holy water.

Day and night, from the cradle to the grave, the
Russian lives as in the sight of God.   He rises from sleep
with a prayer on his lips, and as he lies down to rest a
blessing fills his heart.   Eating or drinking, he remembers
a saint's presence: day and night he thinks of his
guardian angel !   *Slava Boghou*—Praise be to God, is
ever on his lips.   A peasant was accused of having given
a false name.   How could I do that ? he exclaimed, in
reverent horror ; I should lose my guardian saint.

Does this external service penetrate the life of the
Russian peasant : does this constant adoration of saints
and images, this uninterrupted muttering of prayers, beget
correspondingly the Christian virtues ?   By no means.
This familiarity with holy things and intimacy with pro-
tecting saints, etc., encourage the notion of easy remission
of sins ; and the Russian peasant, though good-natured,
hospitable, and obliging, is as fond of taking advantage of
his neighbour as if he had no other idol than money.

It has been reported to us that a Russian walrus fisher
was engaged to sail to Nova Zemlia, for so many roubles
a month, and two pounds of butter a week.   No sooner had
the ship sailed than the fast began.   The butter accumulated, and on the night the fast ended the fisherman went
straight to bed and ate the six pounds of butter.   There
are people who are of opinion that Lenten fasts are best
observed in the mortifying, not of the palate—which is
easy, but of the tongue and all its works—which is less
easy.

Necessaries obtainable in the different parts of Russian Lapland.

Kola. Flounders, salt-fish and salmon, milk—good and
plentiful, tea, sugar, eggs, white bread and biscuits, flour,
pancakes, fowls, mutton.   Black bread is universally obtainable.

Tûloma. Salmon, reindeer milk, when not needed for
the Lapp babies, wild duck, geese, capercaillie.

Kola, Gavrilova, Siem Ostrova. From the Russian
steamer calling three times a month, tea, coffee, tobacco,
white bread, biscuits, cheese, spirits, meat, potted meats,
and butter can be had.

Gavrilova. Tea, sugar, salmon, halibut, cod, herring,
haddock, milk, eggs, the latter scarce in fast time.

Siem Ostrova. Salmon from Karlovka, halibut, haddock,
eggs of eider, puffins, guillemots and curlew, tea, sugar, etc.
No milk.

Ponoi. Sheep, milk, tea, sugar, eggs—scarce.

Ponoi River. Only the produce of rod and gun.

Lachta. Salmon, salmon-trout, pike, biscuits, tea, sugar.

Koúzomen. Sheep, eggs, various fish : also potatoes, beef, and white bread from the fortnightly steamer.

Kem. Milk, salmon, sweet cakes and sugar, tea, eggs, butter, beef, mutton, fowls : in winter reindeer meat.

Keret. Groceries, milk, salmon, fowls.

Kovda. The same.　Cloudberries in autumn.

Kandalaks. Milk, salmon, fowls.

Karelian Coast. Plentiful fish : also mallard, teal, widgeon.

Imandra District. Bread scarce, salmon trout generally obtainable : at Måselsky and Rasnavolok sheep.　Game— ptarmigan, curlew, golden plover—but scarce.

We cannot look back without wishing we had then the information we have now.　A bag of white flour for pancakes or cakes would have comforted us : and con- solidated German army soups and fluid beef, supported by captains' biscuits, chocolate and jams, were the only positive necessaries of life required to go out from England. Everywhere we found timber, brushwood, driftwood, or turf.　The latter burns fairly well, and one can make a noble oven with stones.

Stepanina had not expected us so soon.　The room smelt of incense, tapers were burning before the *sviati obrasi :* and the windows had been sealed from the moment of our crossing the good motherly hostess's threshold.　While Stepanina was cross-examining us

U

about the journey, the little girl Maruscha was preparing
the *samovar* and the steam bath.   Before many hours, the
smallest details of our travels had been extracted from the
Perevodtchik and were in the mouths of all the villagers.
Ivan Abramovitch had gone to Archangel.   The *Arkhangelsk* was not due for several days, and we determined
to make the voyage to Vardö by small boat.

Unwilling to have further dealings with Michieff, who
owned the old *snéka* which had nearly drowned us off
Gavrilova, I sent Onésime to cast about for some other
craft.   He found four Skolte Lapps of Titovka in West
Bumand Gûba, and after long negotiation we made an
agreement to sail with them to Nova Zemlia at the neck
of Ribatschi.   Then came difficulties, as natural in
Russia.   They could not get, they found, permission
from the *Pravlennik* to embark a barrel of meal they
meant to take home with them.   I had three interviews
with the *Pravlennik*, and after confidential financial
arrangements carried him off prepared to sign anything
—down to an order for the Laplanders' exile.

Then the question of price was reopened.   I offered for
the few days as much as the *yolle* would earn in a
summer: and the Laplanders said they would consider.
Onésime was sent to watch them, lest they should consider some *vodka* at the same time.   I went from one
point to another: I offered to buy the boat at double its
value, to make them a present of it afterwards: at last
I offered to buy the Laplanders themselves: and when
this final effort of finance failed, I sent for Michieff.

Edw: Rae. 1881

LAPP IN SUMMER DRESS.

I scored one for the Expedition by showing him the *padorostni*, which he did not expect to see: but he claimed that the Doctor, myself, and the Perevodtchik independently should pay for the boat, as though each of us had hired it.   I represented that the latter was Perevodtchik, and not *popootchik* or comrade: and as I volunteered to leave him behind, Michieff ceded the point.

He had been so dishonest and rapacious, and his boat was so unsafe, that I inserted in the *Stantsia* record-book a rectificative note, describing the facilities afforded at this station to Government travellers.   We were getting rather worn out with knaves and simpletons: our patience had become strained : we grew discouraged and ceased to laugh : the Doctor's best jokes lay neglected.

While talking to Michieff I saw Stepanina, the Perevodtchik, and a pretty woman enter the room.   I didn't see him, said the Perevodtchik impatiently: or hear of him, at Ponoi.   I asked what was the trouble.   The woman asks after her husband, *Starschina* at Ponoi, said the little man.   I haven't heard from him for a year, said the poor woman : and I don't know if he is alive.   I hoped you might have seen him at Ponoi, or brought me a letter.

I saw you on the beach as we sailed from Kola, I said : why did you not ask us to inquire for your husband ?   I did not know you were going to Ponoi, she replied.   I asked the secretary who had collected our crew for us at Ponoi.   It was the *Starschina*, said the Perevodtchik : I remember now.   A stout man with a large beard? I asked. Yes. Not unlike Michieff there? Yes, yes! cried the poor wife. Then I said he was well, and would have given us a letter had he known we were coming to Kola. With this small consolation, and with much gratitude, our visitor withdrew.

When the herring season begins at Kola, the water is so full of fish that the townspeople bale them out in front of their houses, and wade up to their knees in herrings. They hardly know what to do with them. Hastily curing them with coarse salt, they send them to Archangel, to be sold for a shilling a firkin. With better salt and more care, they might gain a million roubles a year, where they now gain one-fifth of it.

On Sunday afternoons there is the usual Russian gathering on the plain under Solaviaréka : when the inhabitants of Kola have races and play ball—or, in winter, sledge in couples. We were sitting one evening in the delicious Northern sunlight by the open windows, when we became aware of a game, *palant*, resembling base-ball or rounders, in which the Kolski youth of both sexes were rejoicing. It seemed an opportunity for a frolic, and I went out.

Calling them together, I asked if they would like to learn *Angelskaya igra*, an English game. They said yes, and one of them brought an axe to Stepanina's wood heap, where I fashioned a bat and wickets. The Doctor joined us and picked an eleven for himself. Having the honour and the happiness to be at the time captain of an English cricketing team, more or less widely and honour-

ably known as the C.I.C.C.: I chose my side, and the
match partook of an international character.

Among the players were a few girls, excellent at
base-ball: but feeling shy about the new game, they
sidled away, reducing the strength of each side.   All
Kola collected round us, at doors and windows, or in
groups: and at the different events in the game roared
aloud.   It was surprising to see how readily and intel-
ligently the young Russians and Lapps took to the
game, and how good-naturedly, when put out, they left
the wickets and joined in the general laugh.   Running
was compulsory at each stroke, to make the game
livelier : and the runs were scored by notches cut in
the wooden wall of Stepanina's house, which served as
Pavilion.

The C. I. won the toss, and Alexei Stepanovitch was
sent to the wicket to face the bowling of the All Lapland
captain.   The first ball was neatly hit to square leg: at
the second the enthusiastic batsman uprooted the whole
of his wickets.   He was succeeded by Varsonovi Pivoroff,
whose first hit, three to long-off, was greeted with much
cheering and cries of *Bross nazat !*   Throw it up ! *Bierzhi
yeshtcho ras !*   Run again !

The next ball was sent in the direction of the first:
but Leonti Yargine, who had been especially posted in that
region, received and retained the ball, to his extreme
astonishment and to the universal delight.   The C. I. captain added two to the score : Maxime Sinikoff was bowled
after making three : and Samsoun Sinikoff failed to score,

having returned the ball into the bowler's hands. The feature of the innings was the careful and masterly play of Spiridion Tonikoff, who made four singles without a mistake. The innings closed for sixteen.

Erasime Tcherkess commenced the innings for the All Lapland, but was run out without scoring. Andrei Moldvistoff and Leonti Yargine succumbed to the bowling, after scoring two and three respectively. The Doctor, after returning the first ball to the bowler, who failed to profit by the chance, played an effective innings of five: and was enthusiastically received when he retired, bowled. The three last wickets were disposed of for four runs, bringing the All Lapland total to eighteen.

The C. I. followed, with fourteen for their second innings. The second innings of the All Lapland was a remarkable one. I refer the reader to the score.

The match was attended, from beginning to end, with shouts of *Horosho! Horosho igrali!* Good! Well played! and loud laughter. Heads were out of every window: *moujiks* and women were grinning from ear to ear at each hit or blunder. When the result was made known there was cheering such as Kola had probably never heard before.

Thus was the *Angelskaya igra* introduced into Russian Lapland. It might have been the introduction of a Constitution, to judge by the popular enthusiasm.

In an hour or two, after everybody had dispersed and gone to bed—that is, at one o'clock in the morning—our attention was directed to a noise in front of our windows.

The members of the late C. I. and All Lapland Elevens were engaged in another single wicket match. Unable to sleep, they had got up to plunge again into the fascinating game. They appointed captains, chose sides, and played as well without us as with us. Now and then a difficult question arose, and they detained me at the open window for appeal as umpire. On the whole, it was a great success. Cricket had become the rage in the White Sea Peninsula.

C. I.

	First Innings.		*Second Innings.*	
Alexei Stepanovitch,	Hit wicket, bowled Doctor	1	Run out .	0
Varsonovi Pivoroff .	Caught Leonti Yargine, bowled Doctor .	3	Do. .	4
Rae	Run out . .	2	Caught and bowled Doctor .	0
Maxime Sinikoff .	Bowled Doctor .	3	Bowled Doctor	1
Samsoun Sinikoff.	Caught and bowled Doctor	0	Do.	5
Spiridion Tonikoff.	Run out .	4	Run out .	2
	Extras . .	3		2
		16		14

ALL LAPLAND.

	First Innings.			*Second Innings.*	
Erasime Tcherkess,	Run out . . . o			Bowled Rae . o	
Andrei Moldvistoff,	Bowled Rae . 2			Do. . o	
Leonti Yargine .	Do. . 3			Run out . . o	
Doctor	Do. . 5			Bowled Rae . o	
Nikita Tonine . .	Run out . . . 2			Caught Ste-panovitch, bowled Rae o	
Karlo Ploginoff .	L. b. w., bowled Rae . . . 2			Run out . . o	
Vassili Yargine .	Thrown out, Spiridion Toni-koff . . . . o			Bowled Rae . o	
	Extras . . . 4			o	
	18			o	

In the morning, write the *Pilgrims*, we saw some trees on the Riuer side, which comforted vs and made vs glad as if wee had come into a new world. In the evening wee got to the Salt Kettles, which is about three miles from Koola, and with the west-north-west sunne got to Iohn Corneli-son's ship, wherein wee entered and drunke: and wee reioyced together at that time, giuing God great thankes, and wee were all exceeding glad that God of His mercie had deliuered vs out of so many dangers and troubles, and had brought vs thither in safetie.

The eleuenth, by leaue and consent of the Bayart, Gouernour of the Great Prince of Moscouia, we brought our scutes into the merchant's house, and there let them stand for a remembrance of our long, farre, and neuer before sayled way: and that wee had sayled in those open scutes about four hundred leagues to the towne of Koola.

On the present Expedition we have sailed three hundred and fifty leagues in open boats as small and ill made as the poor Dutchmen's scutes.

We left the White Sea Peninsula with sad impressions. It was the scene of so much unnecessary poverty and suffering—the fruits of Government neglect, of ignorance and superstition : it seemed to be the abode of fatherless children and widows, and all that are desolate and oppressed.

CHAPTER XXIII.

The Kola Gûba—The Mutke Gûba—Difficulties and studies—A Lapp artist—
Novaya Zemlia—Zakkar—*Culex pabulator*—Pursuit of the Perevodtchik
—Farewell to the Lapps—Astray in the swamps—Vaidda Gûba—A
swift voyage—Studies of the midnight sun—Departure from Vardö—The
last of the Arctic—Greenwich.

WE left Kola in Michieff's disgraceful old *snéka*, at three
o'clock one glorious sunny morning.   It was a dead calm.
Our crew consisted of Onésime, Nikolai Sûsloff, a boy, a
pretty fair-haired blue-eyed sunburnt young woman, a
little girl, and, of course, Zakkar Andrei Zitkikoff. Onésime
was the only able-bodied member of it.   They pulled
slowly down the fiord.

Morning came, then noon, then afternoon, and we were
still in the Kola Fiord, thirty versts from its mouth, and
thirty from the town.   We steered to the Varlamo
Islands, in the hope of adding to the strength of our crew,
and found two Lapps fishing.   One was sick, another
would not go.

We passed Seredni Zaliv, or Middle Bay, where the
steamer *Onéga* comes to lie up in the winter.   In the
month of April she begins a fortnightly service between
Vadsö, Vardö, and the Lapland coast stations as far as

Siem Ostrova. When the White Sea opens the *Arkhangelsk* comes out to take her place. Steamers come at intervals in winter to Seredni Zaliv to bring supplies, which are sent by sledge to Kola.

If less money were devoted in Russia to personal and more to national objects, Seredni might become the port of winter supply not only for Kola, but for Karelia and all the White Sea regions. Reindeer transport would be economical, and the traffic would afford employment to many poor souls who are hungry through the winter now.

We passed St. Katharine's, and late at night reached the mouth of the fiord, having made the journey from Kola at the rate of 1·23 miles an hour. Like Purchas' Pilgrims, we set sayle out of the Riuer of Koola, and with God's grace put to sea to sayle homewards, and being out of the riuer, we sailed along by the land, west and by north.

A southerly breeze sprang up, and we hoisted our tattered old sail. We rounded Cape Pogân, and made our way all through a long sunny night up the East Bûmand's Fiord, or Mutke Gûba. We passed Ieretik, where is a fine natural harbour which would shelter a fleet, and where two Lapp families live—one, that of the wealthy Ingier, who owns two thousand reindeer. Then we sailed past Ora Fiord, a lonely, dismal fishing station. A Norsk settler is here, and does the baking for the Lapps, some of whom bring flour from long distances to be baked.

At Ieretik two Kolski have a store. In Mutke Pogost are six settled and three nomad Lapp families. In Peisen

Fiord, seven nomad and three settled Lapp families—all
Lutherans, but distinct in no other way from the Russian
Lapps of the Orthodox Church.   These Lapps live in the
summer on the shores of the Mutke Gûba or on Ribatschi,
for the benefit of the reindeer.   No wolf has been seen
here for ten or twenty years.

In 1700 there lived on this fiord, at Davve Mutke,
where we shall land, Lutheran Lapps who knew the Lord's
Prayer and Creed : and who seem to have paid tribute at
the same time to Norway, Sweden, and Russia.

We passed the inlet of Litsa.   At this place is a fine
anchorage with deep water.   The tide in the Mutke Gûba
flows for two hours and ebbs for eight : its extreme speed
is two knots.

In the morning we landed on the bare rocky island of
Kouvshin, to search for water, of which we had run short.
Then we set off again, a fresh wind sprang up, and we
scudded due westward up the Gulf.

On the Arski Islands, off the mouth of the Ora Fiord,
grows the cloudberry in great profusion.   The fruit is sent
to Archangel, where one *anker*, eighty pounds, can be
bought for four roubles.

On one cliff we saw a herd of reindeer, emerging from
a valley to breathe the easterly wind and escape the mosquitoes.   We watched them marching in single file round
and round a bare rock.   The heat was very great until the
wind came, but now we spun along before half a gale.

On our left was the stern rocky Mûrman coast : on
our right, seven versts distant, were the somewhat less

FACSIMILE OF DRAWING BY ONESIME SIMONOVITCH—A RUSSIAN LAPP.

rugged shores of the Ribatschi Poluostrov. At Eina, in the mouth of the river of that name, is one of the few good anchorages of Ribatschi.

Our meals in the boats were matters of difficulty and of arrangement. When the wind was ahead, we were set on fire or suffocated in the *kayûta*: if it came from aft, the steersman could not see his course: if it came abeam, it set fire to the sail. When we gave anything to eat or drink to the Russians or Lapps—not only here but in these parts generally—they would receive it in silence: but after eating or drinking, would hand back the cup or plate with a quiet *Blagodaryou*, Thank you.

I used to study Lappish. Onésime, who was one of the most intelligent Lapps I ever met, was one of my teachers. When we came to verbs or constructive words, however, the difficulty of arriving at a coherent or systematic result was evidence of how limited a vocabulary is in use among primitive people.

I asked Onésime to make me some drawings, and this clever little man, who had never had a pencil in his hand before, drew a reindeer, a man, a gull, a bird on a tree, a Russian *isba*, a Lapp *balagan*, a boat, and a salmon. Curiously, as he drew the man he held the paper in the ordinary way: but for all the other objects, at right angles to him. The salmon, reindeer, boat, and gull he drew as if they had been erect: the tree as though it grew horizontally.

The Lapps draw signs, as the Arabs use seals, for their signatures: a practice inherited from old times. As

in the case of Odin, whose experts alone were familiar
with the Runes, so I think the art of drawing figures and
signs was confined to the *Noaïds*, who gave to each Lapp
a mark of identity.   These marks closely resemble figures
on certain of the *kobdas* representing deities and Russian
saints who, in process of time, were admitted to the drums.

| Nikita Katijei | Kostloska | Trofim | Pietr | Seder | Nikofor | Gregori |
| Fedota. Arkipoff. | Afana. | Mashjnikoff. | Mashjnikoff. | Arkipoff. | Gavrilov. | Titoff. |

Each Russian receives the name of the saint on whose
holy day he comes into the world : and the signs above of
the Lapps baptized as Peter, Nicholas, etc., probably cor-
respond with those saints' representations on parchment.
The mark of Gregori Titoff might suggest the monogram
of the Sultan, or the French riddle of G crossed by I—
translatable as *J'ai traversé Paris.*

We passed, to our left, Mutkovski Pogost on the
Titova Bay—a settlement of fifty Lapps, having twenty
huts and a church.   South-west, twenty miles farther, lies
the *Stanovitsche* of Petschenga.   We tore before the strong
easterly wind, for which we had longed for two days, up
the northern extremity of the cross-headed Mutke Gûba.
Madde Mutke lay ahead of us, Davve Mutke or Novaya
Zemlia to our right.   The strip of land connecting
Ribatschi with the mainland is contracted at these two
narrow points.

To Novaya Zemlia we proceeded, at the instance of

the secretary, who assured us there were thirty or forty
Norsk boats engaged in fishing on the west side of
Novaya Zemlia.   Thirty or forty boats were ample, so,
rounding Cape Tri Koróvi or Three Cows, we steered for
Novaya Zemlia.   The mail steamer would leave Vardö
on the following day at ten in the morning.   It was not
over-wise to cross sixty miles of open sea in an undecked
boat in threatening weather : but we meant to chance it.

We passed the cliff of Roka Paata.   The inlet contracted as we ran in : the water was still deep.   There are
admirable anchorages here, thirty-six miles from the open
sea, in six fathoms of water.

Of all the men I ever knew, I think I prefer, in
memory only, Zakkar Andrei Zitkikoff.   Hitherto in receipt of an income of about five roubles a month, he had
been tempered from head to foot in the furnace of the
miseries of human life : but since receipt of our gift
at Gavrilova, he had lived in affluence.   From that period
was diffused in his mind the serenity characteristic of
persons who enjoy incomes without effort of their own.
He had not only volunteered, but had insisted on coming upon this cruise.   In fact, I think he would have
paid something for coming, so great a fancy had he taken
to me.   He used to exchange confidential looks with me
—we had formed a kind of tacit Association.   The
American lady is reported to have said of the hippopo-
tamus : Oh my, ain't he plain !   Zakkar Andrei Zitkikoff
was even ugly.

His voice was hoarse and abrupt.   He used to make

cigarettes of Russian newspaper, with tobacco and other
dust. I found him one afternoon sitting at a very smoky
birch - bark fire which he had kindled, almost to our
suffocation, at our feet. He was boiling some tea for
himself—using his pocket-knife first to stir the fire then
the tea.

Other friends had come with us all the way from
Kola, and only vanished when a high wind came. These
were the mosquitoes : insects about which there exists
much prejudice. We are intimate with the mosquito, and
from behind our gauntlets and veils we watch him with
tranquillity.

I smear my hand with tar and oil, and watch his
dainty and troubled air as he approaches it. He considers man a good thing, and tar a good thing : but he
dislikes them together. I offer him sugar or jam : but he
prefers man. He does not care for man like cucumber,
with oil and vinegar. Vinegar makes him sneeze, and
brings water into his eyes : tar makes the mosquito sick.

I watch him settle on the tiller near my head. He
raises his legs in turns, like the fingers of a pianist.
He lifts one in the air and works rapidly with the
others. He takes two or three experimental paces, and
then beats time with his two antennæ, like the con-
ductor of an orchestra. He examines the tiller with his
proboscis, and finds it is not tasty : then he sits down
on two hind legs and looks about him. He elevates his
proboscis like a telescope, as if to look out to sea, then
smooths it down with his forefeet.

ATTITUDES OF THE MOSQUITO.

He is a seafaring mosquito : in rough weather he feels no qualms. When the North Wind doth blow, he sheltereth below, or else to the shore he doth go. When hungry, he has a thin light body, with a fur cape on the shoulders : but after man, he looks like a little sodawater bottle full of claret.

I must say I have grown to like the mosquito, and to appreciate the humorous side of his character. I believe he has no other friend. I have studied him as *Culex pabulator, Culex volans, Culex repletus*, and *Culex cogitans.*

We landed on the gravelly beach at Novaya Zemlia in the surf which the East wind had beaten up : we saw the ring dotterel and some Temminck's stints. We loaded ourselves, each with some portion of the baggage. There was only one thing inconvenient to carry— Onésime's forty-pound salmon. Of course Zakkar Andrei Zitkikoff chose it. We trudged across the low narrow isthmus, a mile wide, and came upon land rich and abounding in flowers and vegetation such as we had never seen in these latitudes.

I even found a mushroom, or something very like it. I gathered the *Menziesia cærulea*, with its heath-like flower : the dryas, with curious seeds like ostrich feather : the sweet wild camomile, the *Silene acaulis*, and dry stems of *Angelica.* Wild flowers seem equally happy on the frowning Alpine passes, in such smiling spots as Argelés and Gavarnie, and in these awful solitudes of the North. My Arctic specimens were carefully preserved in a small

x

volume, bound of course in Russia leather, decorated with clasps of old silver, and bestowed upon a dear lady as much attached to wild flowers as her son is.

I heard a scuffle and looked round. Zakkar Andrei Zitkikoff had slipped from under the salmon, and lay beneath it on the ground, imprecating horribly in Lappish. He said he would carry the *shtchuka* no farther : and resisted all entreaties save mine—to whom he seemed unable to refuse anything.

We trudged along. To our left lay the rough cliffs of the Lapland coast : to our right the more softly-clad rocks of the Ribatschi Peninsula. Behind us the wind was whistling over the land-locked inlet of Novaya Zemlia,

We looked somewhat anxiously for the Perevodtchik's fleet of fishing-boats crowding the Volokovskaia Gûba. It was a glorious east wind, freshening into a gale, and we thought gleefully what a run we should make over the salt sea to Vardö. When we could at length survey the whole inlet, not a boat was to be seen.

We felt as if cold water had been thrown over us : so did the Perevodtchik, who hurried forward. Perhaps there was better shelter for boats round the Point, we said. Partly hope hastened the little man, partly fear—hope of boats, fear of me. For had I not intended to make for Madde Mutke? Hope without fear, says the Spanish proverb, is certainty : fear without hope, is despair. The Perevodtchik was animated by a mixture of the two feelings, especially despair when he saw me lay down the *photographitchok* and hurry after him.

When I say that I almost ran, mile after mile, hour after hour, and that I only overtook the Perevodtchik at about seven in the evening—the nature of the little man's feelings may be guessed.   After travelling for many miles, I had seen a small wooden settlement and several boats, perhaps two miles away, and my spirits rose.   But, rounding a point, I saw the abominable Gulf stretching back leagues to my left hand.   I forded streams, swamps, muddy pools, struggled through thorny thickets : and exhausted all the hard Russian words I knew.

Eventually vexation turned to pity at the surprising speed which terror had lent to the author of this miserable twelve miles' scramble : and when I staggered into the hut of a settler in the little Quainish village of Bûmand Stanovitsche, and found the secretary seated drinking milk, I spoke quite mildly to him.   They offered me *fladbröd*, and several forms of milk, curd, cream, etc.—upon which these Finlanders chiefly live.

We could get no *snéka*, or *femböring*—five-carrier, *i.e.* requiring a crew of five—to cross the sea in : and with difficulty found a small boat to carry us back to the isthmus, where that most enduring and patient Doctor sat upon the baggage—pipe in mouth.

Zakkar Andrei Zitkikoff had disappeared.   Whether he had gone to hunt for me, and been lost in a swamp, or had been again over-balanced by the salmon and so perished, has never been reported.   *Shto drushba, yezheli trudno rastatsa?*   What is friendship worth, says a Russian proverb, if we cannot bear to part ?   And so

Zakkar Andrei Zitkikoff and I parted without a good-bye. We embarked after a very affectionate farewell from Onésime, who was quite willing to accompany us again, through Russian or any other Lapland : or to Kamtschatka by the North-East Passage, for that matter.

After crouching for some hours in the bottom of the boat, to shelter from the piercing wind, we passed the Kia Islands, where is, good anchorage : and using the umbrellas as auxiliary sail power, we came on shore at the small Quainish fishing station of Kjœrwan, or Kairwan : a spot not much resembling the Holy City of that name.

While the natives whom we found sleeping were preparing to carry the baggage, the Perevodtchik overtured to pilot me in advance to Vaidda Gûba, five miles away. Some Lutheran Lapps live at Kairwan : a few of the nineteen Lutheran families alone that inhabit Russian territory. Professor Friis found a Lapp Bible here, much worn. Asked if they were Russian subjects, the Lapps, who appeared to have small respect for the Orthodox Faith, replied : Russian subjects we are, but heathen we are not.

After the first hour we had arrived at a mile's distance from Kairwan : after an hour and a half, within three-quarters of a mile—having floundered through morasses until brought up by a deep and rapid stream. With infinite pains and some risk, exercising what engineering talent we had, we managed to bridge the stream.

At the end of the second hour we were toiling amid

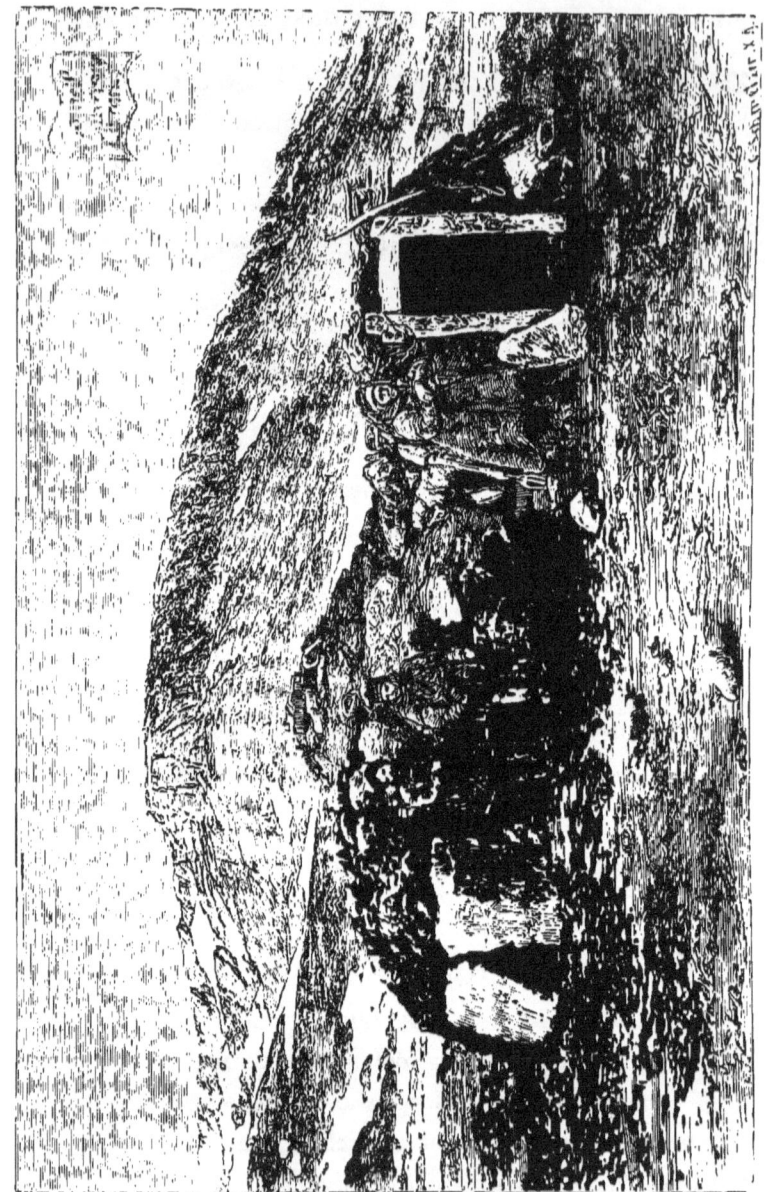

A LAPP GAMME.

brushwood, hearing nothing but the melancholy cry of the golden plover : and seemingly making for the centre of the Peninsula. I was a wreck, and was on the point of foundering. I had scarcely the heart to gather wild flowers : I saw meadowsweet, cochlearia, and campion.

At the end of the third hour we were lost in the swamps. I then told the Perevodtchik that I had determined to put him to death : and the little man was so appalled at the fruit of his amazing and recurrent stupidity, that I think he did not wish to live any longer.

In another hour all my forces had failed me, and I could scarcely totter forward. I had steered for eighteen hours, and walked at the close of it nearly twenty miles without food. A wolf passed close by me. Had he known how feeble I was, he would have made of me an unresisting prey. The Swedish naturalist at Kola showed us the skin of a wolf that had stood forty-two inches high, and measured with his tail seventy-two inches—without it, fifty-one.

At four in the morning we entered Vaidda Gûba, Boundary Bay : finding that the Doctor and the rearguard had arrived in good time by the proper track. We engaged one of the twenty Norsk boats that frequent the place, and went to the house of a settler. Some of these boats come from Lofoden, eight hundred miles away. There are four Norsk families here, one at Zûbovka, two at Peisen Fiord, and one at Bûmand Stanovitsche. The merchant put a comfortable breakfast before us, while his wife dried my soaking clothes. The sight of a good meal was almost painful, for we believed we could not eat : but after consulting our antecedents, we became convinced that we were capable of realising the hopes entertained of us, and our united efforts had the happiest effect.

The merchant shocked us by telling how the Prince Imperial of France had fallen in South Africa, and was being brought to share his poor father's quiet rest at Chiselhurst.

At six in the morning we sped, from among the fleet of fishing-boats that were sheltering from the gale, out into the open waters of the Arctic. The *femböring* travelled at a magnificent pace, hurrying like a storm-bird over the boiling surface of the sea. We slept heavily in the little *kayûta* in the stern : and at half-past ten the fishermen awakened us, saying we were close to Vardö. We had run fifty miles through the gale in less than five hours, and had come within an hour of catching the mail steamer.

We posted two pilots on the rock above the town— one to watch for steamers, the other to watch that he did so. After twenty-four hours a telegram came from Consul Shergold to say that the *Curfew*, the last steamer left in Archangel, would call for us on that day. A steamer, we then learnt, had approached the island that morning and steamed away. We took it for granted this was the *Curfew*, but left the two pilots on the rock. All our effects were packed upon a hand cart. Two boats were ready, one in each harbour, for a sudden sally either north or south, on the approach of a steamer.

Such a wintry summer as this had not been known in Vardö for seventeen years. Dr. Pearson of Cambridge had been here for weeks endeavouring to observe the midnight sun, but his patience had been almost in vain. The sky was almost always obscured near the horizon, when the sun was at its lowest.

The errors proved to be considerable: the refraction was invariably smaller than it should have been. In one instance the sun's lower limb was found to be 11′ nearer the sea horizon than the calculation should have placed it. The observations having been taken at spots of which the latitude and longitude were certain, the deduction from these studies is that at low elevations—*i.e.* within 1° 30′ or 2° of the horizon—the laws of refraction become precarious in their application. The details of Dr. Pearson's studies were published at Cambridge in 1880.

The study of the mysterious Aurora in these latitudes would be interesting and profitable. A professor asked a student what the Aurora was. Well, he replied, I used to know, but I have forgotten. Dear me! said the professor, this is very unfortunate: the only man who ever knew what the Aurora is has forgotten. This weird and mysterious combination of electrical vapours could not be observed to greater advantage than here. They are luminous enough to read by: a steamer's whistle in a silent bay will attract and change their form.

In the harbour lay a steamer, the *Samuel Owen*, awaiting a cargo to carry to the land of promise—Maritime

Siberia. There a duck costs five farthings, a pike a farthing, a calf sixpence, meat a halfpenny a pound, wheat one-twentieth of its cost in England, and land lets for threepence halfpenny per acre. When the breakwater at Vardö is completed, the island will be for the Siberian trade what Malta is to the Indian lines. Steamers will call for cargo and coal. Then, traversing the magnificent scenery of the Matoschkin Shar, where, as in the Straits of Magellan, sheer cliffs rise thousands of feet, they will enter the yet unsurveyed Kara Sea. A permanent salvage station will be established on Novaya Zemlia.

The benevolent merchant from whom we had chartered that poor little steamer the *Pram*, sent to us, hearing of our disappointment, and offered to send us in the *Pram* to a fiord a hundred and thirty miles away, for the sum of thirty pounds. I told the Perevodtchik to bear our compliments and the reply that we did not wish to buy the *Pram*. Besides, we had become very poor indeed : all our money was gone, and we were subsisting entirely upon cheques.

At midnight the watchman gave the alarm : a steamer was approaching from the eastward, and making for the north end of the island. In ten minutes everything was on board of a boat, and with four good rowers we were racing out of the harbour. Several times it seemed as if the steamer were heading out to sea : but at length we came directly in her track, and could read the name *Curfew* on her bow.

As she came up her good captain was on the look-out

for us, and who should be looking over the bulwarks but
the Perevodtchik. He had made a sortie in our southern
boat and boarded the *Curfew*. It was the most spirited
and original action of the Perevodtchik's career, and took
us quite by surprise. We said good-bye to the good,
honest, well-meaning little man: the Norsk pilots pushed
off, and with scarcely the stoppage of her engines, the
Curfew was under way again.

Captain M'Kechnie and his son received us with real
Scotch kindliness: and we were made most comfortable on
this good little steamer. After being on the strain night
and day during a journey very exhausting to the mind,
there was a sense of reaction, almost of bewilderment, at
finding comfortable quarters and friendly voices. We
had been tried in patience and temper more than ever
before, and we had not the magnificent patience of
Regulus. It has pleased God, said he, to single me out
as an experiment of the force of human nature.

The sun was never clouded, the fresh North Wind
never abated, and on the fourth day we crossed the
Arctic circle. It was a warm golden evening, the water
had the lovely transparent colour of chalcedony, and there
was a glorious swell on the sea.

It must be nights such as this that fascinate one, and,
effacing miseries, awaken a longing for the Arctic—so
great as to be almost unaccountable: greater even than
the longing after old pictures, noble buildings, or the
buried past, and equal to the unfulfilled longings of a
dream.

On the seventh evening we were in sight of Montrose, and among the fishing fleet : in the morning off Newbiggin Point. In the afternoon we passed Flamborough Head. The nights were drawing in. We had gone out with the *Aurora* in the dawn of summer, and were coming home with the *Curfew* in the twilight. On the ninth evening we steamed up the Thames, and left the *Curfew* below Greenwich.

APPENDIX.

SOME OF THE FLOWERS OF RUSSIAN LAPLAND.

		Specimen Collected.	Linnæus' Flora Lapponica. Page	Native of Region.
1. Andromeda	Andromeda polyfolia	Karelian Coast		
2. Do. Blue	Do. cærulea	Tuloma R.	164-6	
3. Angelica, Wild	Angelica sylvestris, Achianbotsk. Lapp	Nova Zemlia	101-2	
4. Do. Great	Angelica archangelica	Do.	101-2	
5. Azalea	Azalea procumbens	Tuloma R.	90	
6. Bell Flower	Campanula Zoysii	Kola R.	83	
7. Do. Thyme-leaved	Linnæa borealis	Kovda	250	

			Specimen Collected.	Linnæus' Flora Lapponica. Page	Native of Region.
8.	Bilberry	Vaccinium myrtillus	Sibt Navolok	143-5	
9.	Bird Cherry	Prunus padus	Solovetsk Is.	198	
10.	Butterwort, Alpine	Pinguicula Alpina	Murd L.	12	Polar.
11.	Do. Pale	Do. Lusitanea	Do.	13	
12.	Camomile, Sweet Wild	Matricaria suaviolens	Madde Mutke	309	
13.	Campion, Single-flowered	Lychnis apetala	Vaidda Gúba		
14.	Catch-fly, Dwarf	Silene acaulis	Madde Mutke	184	
15.	Cerastium	Cerastium Alpinum	Murd L.		
16.	Do. Smooth-leaved	Do. grandifolium	Karelian Coast		
17.	Do. Mouse-ear	Do. vulgatum	Kandalaks	192-3	Wooded to Sub-Polar.
18.	Do. Winter-green	Trientalis Europæa	Solovetsk Is.	198	Do. do.
19.	Cinque-foil	Potentilla aurea	Ponoi R.		
20.	Cloud-Berry	Rubus chamæmorus	Sem Ostrova	208	Wooded to High Polar.

No.	Common Name	Latin Name	Locality	Page	Notes
21.	Cotton-sedge	Eriophorum capitatum	Várzuga R.	23	Do. do.
22.	Cudweed, or Ever-lasting	Antennaria Alpina	Isba Kovronia		
23.	Cornel, Dwarf	Cornus Suecia	Kovda	60	
24.	Cow-Wheat	Melampyrum pratense	Pongamo	240	Wooded.
25.	Crake-Berry	Empetrum nigrum	Túloma	145	
26.	Cress, Bitter	Cardamine pratensis	Vaidda Gûba	258	
27.	Diapensia, Lapland	Diapensia Lapponica	Sem Ostrova	88	Wooded to Sub-Polar.
28.	Dryas, White	Dryas octopetala	Nova Zemlia	215	Polar to High Polar.
29.	Fern, Beech	Polypodium phegopteris	Imandra L.	382	
30.	Do. Oak	Do. dryopteris	Kovda	387	Wooded to Sub-Polar.
31.	Forget-me-not	Myosotis palustris	Várzuga R.	75	
32.	Gentian	Gentiana campestris	Guolle L.	226	
33.	Globe-flower	Trollius Europœus	Do.	266	Wooded to Polar.
34.	Geranium, Wood	Geranium sylvaticum	Imandra L.		. Do. do.
35.	Grass, Carex	Carex	Do.		
36.	Do. of Parnassus	Parnassia palustris	Karelia	108	Do. do.
37.	Heart's-Ease, Yellow	Viola biflora	Do.	276	Do. do.

			Specimen Collected.	Linnæus' *Flora Lapponica.*	Native of Region.
				Page	
38.	Heart's-Ease, Purple	*Viola arvensis*	Inmandra L.	276	
39.	Honeysuckle, Black-fruited	*Lonicera nigra*	Vârzuga.		
40.	Lichen, Cup	*Cladonia deformis*	Kola R.		
41.	Do. Reindeer	*Cladina rangiferina*	Do.	242	Higher wooded to Sub-Polar.
42.	Lousewort	*Pedicularis Lapponica*	Do.		
43.	Lichen, Arctic	*Lichen Arcticus*	Sibt Navolok.	428	
44.	Marigold, Marsh	*Caltha palustris*	Keret		
45.	Menziesia, Blue	*Menziesia cærulea*	Madde Mutke.		
46.	Moss, Cup	*Cladonia cornucopioides*	Kola		Common on Petschora R.
47.	Do. Club	*Lycopodium Alpinum*	Sibt Navolok.		
48.	Milk-Vetch	*Astragalus Alpinus*	Kola R.	267	
49.	Mushroom	*Agaricus — ? campestris*	Nova Zemlia.		
50.	Onion, Wild	*Allium vineale*	Ponoi R.		

No.	English Name	Scientific Name	Locality		Remarks
51.	Pink, Fragrant	*Dianthus superbus*	Kola R.	170	
52.	Primrose, Mealy	*Primula farinosa*	Sougarevna	79.	Higher wooded to Polar.
53.	Do. Scotch	*Do. Scotia*	Do.		
54.	Ranunculus, Lapland	*Ranunculus Lapponicus*	Ponoi R.	207	Wooded to Sub-Polar.
55.	Raspberry, Dwarf	*Rubus Arcticus*	Måselsky	160	Found at Mezén, the Petschora, the Ourál, and on the Kolwa R.
56.	Rosemary, Marsh	*Ledum palustre.* Russ. *Baghotla.* Samo-*Yarsje. yede.*	Kovronia		
57.	Scurvy-Grass	*Cochlearia rotundi-folia*	Murd L.	220	
58.	Salvia	*Salvia*	Vaidda Gûba	181	
59.	Saxifrage, Yellow Mountain	*Saxifraga Arctioides*	Imandra L.	178	
60.	Snakeweed	*Polygonum viviparum.*	Kola R.	152	High Polar and Sub-Polar Regions. Found on Taïmur R. The Samoyedes were formerly believed to eat its root.

	Specimen.	Specimen Collected.	Linnæus' Flora Lapponica. Page	Native of Region.
61. Speedwell .	Veronica spicata .	Kola R. .	4	
62. Trefoil, White .	Trifolium repens .	Sougarevna .	274	
63. Do. Cattle .	Menyanthes trifoliata. Missne. Lapp.	Kouringa R. .	80	
64. Violet, Dog .	Viola canina .	Pongamo .	277	
65. Do. Marsh .	Do. palustris .	Kola R. .	27	Wooded to Sub-Polar.
66. Do. White-rooted	Do. sororia .	Do. .		
67. Water-Blinks .	Montia rivularis .	Nova Zemlia .	57	Found on Taïmur R. Sub-Polar to High Polar.
68. Whitlow-Grass .	Draba hirta .	Kandalaks .	257	
69. Willow, Arctic .	Salix reticulata .	Sibt Navolok .	348	
70. Do. Dwarf .	Do. herbacea .	Do. .	355	
71. Whortleberry, Bog	Vaccinium uligino-sum	Måselsky .	207	Wooded to Polar.

72.	Do. Red	Do. vnts Idæa. Brâsnitsa. Russ.	Imandra L. .	144	Found in Nova Zemlia, at the Petschora R., the Oural.*
73.	Winter-green .	Pyrola uniflora	Karelia	167	Wooded.
74.	Wood-sorrel .	Oxalis acetosella	Do. .	194	Wooded to Sub-Polar.

* With the iuice of them is made a certayne medicine called of the apothecaries Rob: the whiche is good to be holden in the mouth against great drieth and thirst.

The Historie of Plantes.

BIRDS OBSERVED IN THE KOLA PENINSULA AND KARELIA.

No.	Common name	Scientific name	Locality
1.	Arctic Tern	*Sterna macrura*	Sibt Navolok.
2.	Black Tern	*Sterna nigra*	Do.
3.	Buffon's Skua	*Lestris Buffoni*	Murman Coast.
4.	Capercaillie	*Tetrao urogallus*	Túloma R.
5.	Common Tern	*Sterna hirundo*	Murman Coast.
6.	Cormorant	*Phalacrocorax carbo*	Do. Túloma R.
7.	Cuckoo	*Cuculus canorus*	{ Ponoi. Karelia.
8.	Curlew	*Numenius arquata*	Sibt Navolok.
9.	Eider Duck	*Somateria mollissima*	{ Murman Coast. Ponoi R.
10.	Falcon	*Falco gyrfalco*	Várzuga R.

No.	English Name	Scientific Name	Locality
11.	Golden Eagle	*Aquila chrysaetos*	Ponoi R.; Várzuga.
12.	Golden Eye Duck	*Fuligula clangula*	Toloma R.
13.	Golden Plover	*Charadrius pluvialis*	Sibt Navolok.
14.	Glaucous Gull	*Larus glaucus*	Múrman Coast.
15.	Great Black-backed Gull	*Larus marinus*	Do.
16.	Great Black-throated Northern Diver	*Colymbus Arcticus*	Do.
17.	Great Fishing Gull	*Larus canus*	Do.
18.	Great Skua	*Lestris cataractes*	Do.
19.	Greylag Goose	*Anser segetum*	Ponoi R.
20.	Guillemot	*Uria troile*	Várzuga R.; Múrman Coast.
21.	Hawk Owl	*Strix nisoria*	Kola.
22.	Herring Gull	*Larus argentatus*	Solovetsk I.; White Sea.
23.	Lapland Crow	*Corvus Lapponicus*	Pongamo; Karelia.
24.	Little Auk	*Mergulus alle*	Múrman Coast
25.	Little Stint	*Tringa minuta*	Sem Ostrova.
26.	Little Tern	*Sterna minuta*	Kola Fiord.

27.	Mallard	*Anas boschas*	Karelian Coast
28.	Merlin	*Falco æsalon*	Ponoi R.
29.	Oyster Catcher	*Hæmatopus ostralegus*	Mûrman Coast.
30.	Ptarmigan	*Tetrao lagopus*	Imandra Lake.
31.	Puffin	*Fratercula Arctica*	Mûrman Coast
32.	Raven	*Corvus corax*	Ponoi R.
33.	Razor-bill	*Alca torda*	Mûrman Coast
34.	Redshank	*Totanus calidris*	Kola.
35.	Ring Dotterel	*Charadrius hiaticula*	Isthmus, N. Zemlia.
36.	Rough-legged Buzzard	*Archibuteo lagopus*	Ponoi R.
37.	Sandpiper	*Tringa maritima*	Ribatschi
38.	Sedgewarbler	*Sylvia phragmitis*	Túloma R.
39.	Shore Lark	*Alauda Alpestris*	Do.
40.	Snow Bunting	*Emberiza nivalis*	Isthmus, N. Zemlia.
41.	Swift	*Cypselus murarius*	Kandalaks.
42.	Teal	*Anas crecca*	Karelian Coast.
43.	Temminck's Stint	*Tringa Temminckia*	Rubatschi Pen
44.	Three-toed Woodpecker	*Picus tridactylus*	Kitsa.
45.	Titlark	*Anthus pratensis*	Sem Ostrova.

46.	Turnstone	.	.	.	Strepsila collaris	.	.	.	Mûrman Coast.
47.	Velvet Scoter	.	.	.	Oidemia fusca	.	.	.	Ponoi R,
48.	Whimbrel	.		.	Numenius phæopus	.	.	.	Pieresjaur.
49.	Whitetailed Sea Eagle	.		.	Aquila albicilla	.	.	.	Karelian Coast.
50.	Widgeon	.		.	Anas Penelope	.	.	.	Do.
51.	Woodcock	.		.	Scolopax rusticata	.	.	.	Koro R.

BIRDS observed by a Swedish Naturalist in the parts of RUSSIAN LAPLAND LYING BETWEEN ENARA LAKE, TÛLOMA RIVER, AND THE MUTKE GÛBA.

1. Bar-tailed Godwit	.	*Limosa Lapponica.*
2. Blackgrouse	.	*Tetrao tetrix.*
3. Black-tailed Godwit	.	*Limosa ægocephala.*
4. Common Redpole	.	*Fringilla linaria.*
5. Great White Swan	.	*Cygnus olor.*
6. Greenshank	.	*Totanus glottis.*
7. Mountain Finch	.	*Fringilla montefringilla.*
8. Pine Grosbeak	.	*Corythus enucleator.*
9. Siberian Jay	.	*Garrulus infaustus.*
10. Steller's Duck	.	*Enionetta Stelleri.*
11. Swedish Blue-throated Warbler	.	*Luvinia Suecica.*
12. The Ruff	.	*Macchetes pugnax.*
13. Wood Titmouse	.	*Parus sylvicus.*

MINERALS FOUND IN RUSSIAN LAPLAND.

Ponoi R.	Gneiss.
	Garnet.
	Mica.
	Felspar.
	Quartz.
	Oxide of Iron.
	Syenite.
	Granite.
	Hornblende.
	" Slate.
	Porphyritic Granite.
	Iron Pyrites.
Karelian Coast of White Sea	Mica Schist.
	Hornblende Slate.
	Syenite.
Karelian Coast of White Sea	Quartz.
	Felspathic Granite.
	Gneiss.
	Garnet.
Mûrman Coast	Granite.
Kandalaksk Coast	Gneiss.
	Greenstone.
	Quartz.
	Calcareous Spar.
	Fluor Spar.
	Chalk.
	Silver-lead.
	Copper.
	Calamine.

VOCABULARY.

English.	Samoyede.	Russian-Lapp.	Russian.
PRONOUNS.			
I, thou, he, she	Man, poor, pœitha, takinye	Mon, ton, son, yan	Ya, tee, on, ana.
We, you, they	Mœya, pœitho, anee .	Mo, to, damat .	Mwee, wee, anee.
Me, thee, him	Manyan, poornet, takkan	Ondmon, onton, onson.	Menya, tibia, yaivo.
Us, you, them	Mânyata, poorata, takânmis	Mee, tee, son	Nas, vas, yikh.
My, thy, his	Mânyeyo, pooryeyo, pœithe-mertha	Mon, yton, yson	Moy, tvoy, svoy.
Our, your, their	Hâryeyo, pœirryeyo, pœithyétha	Do. do. do.	Nash, vash, yikli.
Who? What?	Hâvatha? Hâmgatha?	Ktiih? Mun?	Kto? Shto?
AUXILIARY WORDS.			
After .	Pokouna. Pouna	Mangotad	Posslai.
And .	Yrka .	Ucht	Ee.
Before	Njernanhaya .	Aoudest .	Peradee.

English			
Down	Tassinye	.	Vnison.
Early	.	.	Rano.
From	Ortam. Anyi	Eigent	Ees.
Gently	.	Tosha	Teekho.
Hence	Tukotha	Kheil	Atsoáda.
Here	Toukbnya	Tast	Zdyess.
Hither	Tanyandâda	Tyek	Soudâ.
How?	Haman?	.	.
How many?	Siambir?	.	Nogoli?
How much?	Amga birr?	.	Skolko?
If	Yaningaowo	Lyellak	Yessli.
Late	.	Manga	Pozno.
Much	Oka	.	Mnoga.
Near	Obnihowanmunga	Puvodek	Blisko.
Never	Siagóu	Nequas	Niekoghda.
Often	Oukotha	Tôouia	Tchasto.
On	Tjemmasibtyeh	Na	Na.
Only	Tangok	Poka	Tolko.
Or	Engou	Ellak	Eele.
So	Dremwa	Nút	Tak.
Soon	Myerko	Toda	Skoro.
Thence	Takatha	.	Otsouda.
There	Tanyana	Tant	Tam.
Thither	Tairyayo	Tok	Touda.

English.	Samoyede.	Russian-Lapp.	Russian.
To	Engou	Tok	Da.
Up	Taouna	.....	Neverkhou.
When?	Siah?		Koghda?
Where?	Amganatha?	Kwas?	Gdyai?
Why?	Amgass?	Kust?	Zatchem?
Yes, no	Tartsa, Yahngou	Mandet? ... Da. Nep	Da. Niett.
ADJECTIVES.			
Bad	Wào	Tiahn	Hloudo.
Beautiful	Somboy		Krassiva.
Black	.....	Shapas	Tchorni.
Cold	Tjetse	.....	Kholodno.
Dear	Miria	.....	Doroga.
Early	Miero		Rano.
Enough	Masse	Eleintsch	Davolno.
Gently	Hhenkoko	.....	Teekho.
Good	Sàwo	Pwerr	Horosho.
Great	Arka	.....	Veliki.
Hot	Yrwa, Lombit	.....	Taiplo.
Late	Paousem		Pozno.
Left	Siàtni	Shupskit	Leva.

English				
Long	Pavanunganyo.	Lahmb	Koodka	Dolgo.
More	Nyayou			Bolshe.
New	Nyoughi		Od	Novi.
Old	Yetha			Stare.
Ready	Hamádi			Gátov.
Red	Narrya		Rwopset	Krassnæe.
Right	Manyi		Alskit	Prava.
Small	Tydryo			Malo.
Warm	Yépi		Paks	Zharko.
Windy	Mjertsa		Pyink	Vaitreno.
Wooden	Piahh			Dereuyanee.
Yellow			Koskas	Zholti.
Young	Atsika		Norr	Moladoy.

SUBSTANTIVES.

English				
Axe			Aksh	Sikkra.
Bag			Veis	Mtsshok.
Bead-reckoner			Shott	Shtchotnik.
Beam			Pardvornets	Stolb.
Bear	Harvedië			Medviad.
Beard			Semen	Baradá.
Bed	Hoba		Tvail	Pastiel.
Bell	Syengha		Kolokol	Kolokol.
Bench			Lautish	Lavka.

English	Samoyede	Russian-Lapp	Russian.
Biscuits	Hahsounyan	Sokher	Soukharee.
Board	......	Telle	Doshka.
Boat			Karbass.
Boatman	Ano		Perevostchik.
Body	Siämiadlâna	Sahti	Korpus.
Book	......	Roika	Kniga.
Boots	Myaryou	Kneeshka	Sapaghee.
Box	Yirnaworken	Sapti	Yashtchik.
Boy	......	Shoka	Maltchik.
Bread	Atsiko	Parntch	Khlèb.
Breakfast	Nyan	Leib	Zaftrak.
Bridle	Hanaby ortam	Zaftakoush	Namordnik.
Bucket	::::	Paingki	Kanevka.
Butter	::::::	Pwits	Masslo.
Candle	Yourr	Masslo	Svaitcha.
Candlestick	Leirkutsa	Tovas	Potsvietchnik.
Cap	Sœvao	Potsvietchnik	Shapka.
Ceiling	::::::	Keppe	Patolk.
Chain	:::::	Patolk	Karobka.
Chair	Ahmdâts	Vinskrifti	Stool.
Child	Nootskoko	Toshi	Maltchik. Malinka.
		Maltchik	

English		Paitchtorp	Pietshnaya truba.
Chimney		Paitchtorp	Pietshnaya truba.
Christian	Krieshon	Khristienin	Khristienin.
Clothes		Ruski	Adiesh.
Comb		Soy	Grebene.
Copper	Nyarrwa	Vyeshk	Miednee.
Cross	Khatcho	Raist	Kraist.
Cup	Khidiko	Nak	Tchaska.
Day	Yalè		Dièn.
Dinner	Orman	Morknoush	Abied.
Door	......	Torni	Dvair.
Ears	......	Pelle	Ouchy.
East. West	Tyipninyanga, Lapsuinyanga	Stok. Zapat	Stok. Zapat.
Ebb-tide	Hasse yi	......	Atliff.
Elbow	......	Karnel	Lokit.
Eyebrows	......	Kuloma	Varatà.
Eyes	......	Shelmi	Glaza.
Face	......	Kassouä	Liiso.
Finger	......	Shep	Palitsa.
Fire	Tou. Pjåtunga	Told	Ognia.
Fish	Hålè	Guolle	Reeba.
Flood-tide	Oka yi	......	Priliff.
Floor	......	Pavel	Podlok.
Fly	Mookhi	Tchåsk	Mookha.
Foot	......	Ulke	Nagà.

English.	Samoyede.	Russian-Lapp.	Russian.
Fork	......	*Vilki*	*Vilka.*
Girth	......	*Nisknita*	*Patpas.*
Glass	......	*Stekli*	*Steklo.*
God	*Noum*	*Bogh*	*Bogh.*
Gold	......	*Kolta*	*Zoloto.*
Hair	......	*Vupt*	*Volossá.*
Half hour	*Yalè pilè*	*Pèltchas*	*Poltchassa.*
Halter	......	*Kessish*	*Ousda.*
Hand	*Oudao*	*Roka*	*Ruka.*
Handle—door	......	*Torriikilba*	*Rutschka.*
Harbour	*Saliarkaouo*	*Locht*	*Gavan.*
Head	*Erouào*	*Vuila*	*Galavá.*
Hen	*Tirtikho*	*Kan*	*Kooritsa.*
Horse	*Ubbiyeh*	*Hydbash*	*Loshed.*
Hour	*Yalè*	*Tchas*	*Tchas.*
Huts	*Miiàkan*	*Balagán*	*Hata.*
Ice	*Salva*	......	*Lyott.*
Ink	*Padèningas*	*Tcherneela*	*Tcherneela.*
Interpreter	*Wadombertje*	*Talmitch*	*Perevodtchik.*
Iron	*Yessha*	*Roodt*	*Zhelaiznee.*
Island	*Ogh*	*Ostrov*	*Ostrov.*

English			
Journey		*Varr*	*Poot.*
Key	*Tchikwa*	*Lokthod*	*Klyoutch.*
Knee	*Hakalupsi*	*Bouil*	*Kaliëno.*
Knife	*Harr*	*Nipi*	*Nozh.*
Land	*Ya*	......	*Zemlia.*
Light		*Vêitch*	*Snietsha.*
Lightning	*Hyangatóu*	*Tolgask*	*Molnya.*
Lips		*Apan*	*Liptzi*
Man	*Heori*	*Olmitch*	*Tcholovek.*
Matchbox		*Spitzki karobi*	*Spitzna karobka.*
Matches		*Spitshki*	*Spitshki*
Meat	*Hamsha*	*Wintsch*	*Gavaidina.*
Milk	*Yalnâna*	*Moloko*	*Moloko.*
Mirror		*Kirmigara*	*Siklo.*
Money	*Nyennai*	*Yennik*	*Dienghi.*
Month	*Yirri*	*Man*	*Messets.*
Mouth		*Nyalima*	*Gába.*
Mosquitoes	*Nyennik*		*Comâré.*
Napkin	*Tohotsa*	*Tchembasmasti*	*Salfaitka.*
Needle	*Pie*	*Nivel*	*Igla.*
Night			*Notch.*
North. South	*Tyetsiiantenanga. Ibenyanga.*	*Tavval. Letnisaoui*	*Sjévernaya. Letni.*
Northern Lights			*Lunosiânya.*
Nose	*Harpe.*	*Noutrya*	*Nôs.*

English.	Samoyede.	Russian-Lapp.	Russian.
Oven	......	Paiich	Pietshka.
Paper	......	Pemé	Boumåga.
Pen	Padnapsom	Plns	Pero.
Pillow	Haoungess	Vibolas	Padooshka.
Ptarnigan	......	Rappa	Kourapatka.
Quarter of an hour	......	Qualmdastchas	Tchetvertchassa.
Rain	Saryö	......	Doshd.
Rainbow	Noumpanda	......	Tbutscha.
Reindeer	Tïr	Poœds	Olin.
Reins		Lautch	Liitsa.
Ring	Oudiyesia	Sårmus	Koltso.
River	Yeehha	Yok	Raika.
Room	Yålema	Gœarnets	Gornitsa.
Salmon	Syomga	Ripskili	Shtchuka.
Sand		Voints	Pyösok.
Saucer		Utte	Patchasnik.
Scissors		Rivelt	Noshnitsi.
Scoop		Koptzi	Shoupka.
Sea	Yam	......	Moré.
Seat		Podorouilai	Lavka.
Shoulder		Velkè	Rémia.

English			
Sledge	Khan	Sån	Sani.
Snow	Sirrha	......	Snyek.
Soap	Mäsinko	Mol	Melo.
Song	Hunsta. Sianakopse	......	Piésin.
Spoon	Loûtskou	Loutski	Loshka.
Steamer	Tôuna minya		Parahod.
Stockings	Sodlkaou	Sok	Tchoolki.
Stove	Toohh	Tyewkan	Paitch.
Stream	Viêrda	......	Raika.
Street	Pintchanta	Shêh	Ouliitsa.
Summer	Tanhi	Tyess	Lieto.
Sun	Hayar	Päiva	Sontsa.
Supper	Haousim po aouro	Eldgstud	Ouzhén.
Table	......	Skamé	Stol.
Teeth	Tyivan	Dani	Zoubi.
Thimble	......	Sirngaita	Napiersnik.
Thread	......	Sin	Nitka.
Thunder		Diermes	Grom.
To-day	Môunta		Scvodnya.
To-morrow	Tchôkrayalé	......	Zaftra.
Town	Hôunyana	......	Gorod.
Tree	Tatamarr	Tchwåkus	Derevo.
Walls	Pyakh	Steni	Stina.
Walrus	Tyutyediê	......	Morzhôvi.

English.	Samoyede.	Russian-Lapp.	Russian.
Watch	Yaleman sartin	Tchas	Tchassee. ‎ـﺪ
Water	Yi	Tchats	Voda.
Weather	Nöm	......	Pogoda.
Weights	......	Tcheskiri	Viessi.
Window	......	Ekken	Akno.
Winter	Seraï	Taïlo	Zima.
Woman	Nyêh	......	Zenshtchina.
Wood	Puathara	Muurr	Derevo.
Writing	Merombadgou	Kyerichta	Pessanye.
Year	Bo	......	God.
Yesterday	Tenyana		V'tcherá.
Sunday	Hevdiyalê	Bavespaïv	Voskresenye.
Monday	Boti	Murisarg	Panaidelnik.
Tuesday	Hassouyalê	Noumparg	Vtornik.
Wednesday	Sdounoniyalê	Sêred	Sereдá.
Thursday	Tjetingayalê	Nyalionpaïv	Tchetverik.
Friday	Mwithyalê	Piatnits	Piátnitsa.
Saturday	Harouyalê	Subvit	Soubota.
New Year	......	Wassilpaïv	Novi god.
January, February	Yanvar, Faivral	Waourman, Portchman	Yanvar, Faivral.

English			
March, April	Mart, Aprel	Kalmitch, Pazman	Mart, Aprel.
May, June, July	Mey, Yoūn, Yoūl	Mveriman, Pietsman	Mey, Youn, Youl.
August, September	Avgoust, Sentyabr	Avgoust, Sentyabr	Avgoust, Sentyabr.
October, November	Aktyabr, Nayabr	Aktyabr, Nayabr	Aktyabr, Nayabr.
December	Dekabr	Dekabr	Dekabr.

NUMERALS.

English			
Quarter	Tyetimdarna	......	Tchetvert.
Half	Piela	......	Polaviina.
One. Eleven	Opoi. Opiegnia	Eucht. Euchtploit	Adeen. Adeenatsii.
Two. Twelve	Sidieh. Sidiegnia	Kvacht. Kvachtploit	Dva. Dvanatsii.
Three. Thirteen	Nyar. Nyaregnia	Kolm. Kolmploit	Tree. Treenatsii.
Four. Fourteen	Tyett. Tyetegnia	Nyel. Nyelploit	Tcheteeri. Tcheteerinatsii.
Five. Fifteen	Samlak. Samlakegnia	Veit. Veitploit	Piatt. Piatnatsii.
Six. Sixteen	Matt. Mattegnia	Goot. Gootploit	Shaist. Shaistnatsii.
Seven. Seventeen	Syou. Syouegnia	Key-tchom. Keytchomploit	Siem. Siemnatsii.
Eight. Eighteen	Sidyett. Sidyetegnia	Kaks. Kaksploit	Voisim. Voisimnatsii.
Nine. Nineteen	Habeyou. Habeyegnia	Akhts. Akhtsploit	Divvit. Divvitnatsii.
Ten	You	Lodk	Dieset.
Twenty	Sidyou	Kwachtloik	Dvatsii.
Thirty	N'yaryou	Kolmloik	Treetsii.
Forty	Tyetyou	Nyeloik	Sorak.
Fifty	Samlakyou	Veitloik	Piadesiat.

English.	Samoyede.	Russian-Lapp.	Russian.
Hundred		Tchvout	Sotnia.
Thousand		Tokhat	Tishtch.
VERBS.			
I give	Man dahngou	Mon dam	Dayou.
You give	Poor dahngou	Ton oundeb	Dayotai.
He gives	Pwitha dahngou	Son ondet	Dayott.
I give	Man damas	Mon oundam	Ya dahl.
I will give	Man dagoum	Mon dam	Ya dam.
Does he give ?	Dahngoutham pwitha ?	Oundvettyibit ?	Dayoiti ?
I speak	Man lanam	Mon sarnam	Ya gavarou.
You speak	Poor lana	Ton sarneb	Vui gavaretai.
He speaks	Pwitha lana	Son sarnet	On gavareet.
I spoke	Man lanamas	Mon sarnom	Ya gavareel.
I will speak	Man lanagou	Mon sarnleintchem	Ya boudou gavareet.
Does he speak ?	Lanagôutham pwitha ?	Sarnet yibit ?	Gavareet li on ?
I have	Man taryâ	Mon tatam	Ya eematyou.
You have	Poor taryâ	Mon toshimail	Vui eemaite.
He has	Pwitha taryâ	......	On eemait.
I had	Man taryass		Ya eemail.
I shall have	Man taryagoum	Mon toshilenshiman	Ya boudou eemait.

Do you know?	Tienouao?	Dyetveityihit?	Znaiitye li vui?
I know	Man tjenouao	Mon tyàzhan	Ya znayou.
I knew	Man tjenouass	Mon toütam	Ya znall.
I shall know	Man tjenyagoum	Mon laïntsom tyet	Ya boudou znàt.
He will	Pwitha douta	......	On boudet.
I shall be	Man doutan	Mon laïntsom	Ya boudou.
I was	Man mermuss	Mon laï	Ya bwel.
He was	Pwitha anhandames	Son laïntsch	On bweel.
I show	Man lablara	Mon tchwaïtval	Ya pakazheevàyou.
I will show	Man labtagou	Mon laïntsom tchwait	Ya boudou pakazevat.
I showed	Man labtawas	Mon tchwaïte	Ya pakazall.
I send	Man etheraouo	Mon wohltolom	Ya passeelayou.
I will send	Man etherangou	Mon laïntsom wohlted.	Ya boudou passeelat.
I want	Man harwani	Mon yelvet	Ya khotchou.
I wanted	Man harwamas	Mon yelvet	Ya khateel.
I shall want	Man harwamgou	Mon yelvetlaïntsom	Ya boudou khotet.
Do you want?	Harwan pwitio?	Yelvet yibet?	Khotetë li vui?
I think	Man hazramyou	......	Ya douméyou.
I drink	Man etherngam	Mon yokam	Ya piyou.
I drank	Man etherngamas	Mon yàdtom	Ya pil.
I will drink	Man ethertam	Mon laïntsom yokam	Ya boudou peet.
I say	Man sertam	Mon tselkom	Ya skashou.
I said	Man serangào	Mon tseltim	Ya skashall.
I will say	Man sertaoua	Mon laïntsom tselkom	Ya vam skazhou.

English.	Samoyede.	Russian-Lapp.	Russian.
I will buy	Man temdagou	Mon laïntsom wast	Ya kouplou.
I come	Man dawathangou	Mon pwolteitch .	Ya prekhashoo.
I came	Man dawanawa	Mon pwotletcham	Ya prishol.
I bring	Man minyagou	Mon pohtom	Ya preenyasoo.
I brought	Man minyawa	Mon pohted	Ya preenaseel.
I will bring	Man mindangou	Mon pohtletcham	Ya preenyasou.
I go .	Man minga .	......	Ya eedou.
I see	Man minryou .	Mon wained	Ya vizhoo.
I saw	Man minryagou	Mon wainam	Ya vidiïl.
I will see	Man minryadlawa	Mon wainletcham	Ya oweizhou.
I sleep	Man honum .	Mon undde	Ya spkyou.
I slept	Man honingum	Mon unddom	Ya spahl.
I will sleep .	Man honumas	Mon undletcham	Ya boudou spaht.
PHRASES.			
Will you sell ?	Mirdata ?	......	Prodaideetje li vui ?
I won't sell .	Nibu mirdat	......	Nie prodayou.
Tell me	Hhoitar	......	Skazhiti mne.
I want to buy	Temdash harawa	......	Ya hotchou koupiet.
Várzuga .	Tchôowikarad .	......	Varzuga.
Koûzomen .	Takikarad	......	Kouzomen.

English			
Archangel	Temdlorva	.....	Arkangelsk.
I forget	Man yourao	.....	Ya zaboul.
I remember	Man tjenouao	.....	Ya pomenyou.
I eat	Man ortaono	.....	Ya coushâyou.
I thank you	Saouan		Blagodaryôu.
Where does—live?	Houniana iltatha?		Gdai zheeviott?
Very well	Savir saouo	Otchen proerr.	Horosho. Ladna.
Good night	Piihi saono	Proerr léne	Dobra notch.
Sleep well	Honiom saono	Waïda pwerrrest	Patchevaïtye spakoyno.
How is this called?	Hbusheratha tikki?	Makht nazevaïtsa?	Kak nazevaïisa aito?
Do you know where?	Tjenouao ambara?	Questi yelvet?	Znayetje gdyai?
I don't know	Man ye heraou	Yim tyeh	Ya nié znayou.
Do you speak?	Lânatha?		Gavareetai le vui?
He will come presently	Mfèrko touta	Pwolteich seytchass	On seytchass boudet.
He is at home	Miákan	Quadstan	Doma.
When does he return?	Siah douhiân?		Koghda on boudet?
Here is drinkmoney	......		Vott na-vodkou.
Adieu	Egouthônoki		Prostchaïtye.
Whence come you?	Houniana yathi?	Questi pwotret?	Otkouda vui eediotai?
I come from my home	Man miakan minga		Ya eedyou ees damoy.
Where are you going?	Hanyan mingatha?	Questi munvet?	Gdyai vui eedyotai?

English.	Samoyede.	Russian-Lapp.	Russian.
I understand	Man tjenouao	Mon tolkyim	Ya ponemyou.
Come here	Talyando	Pwadyet	Idi soudà.
Do you understand?	Tjenouao ?	Tolkepiliti ?	Ponemaitje li vui?
Not much	Tydnyou	Ipyan	Nié mnoga.
Don't speak so fast	Yenbou lanatha	Yim sarnet toda	Nié gavareeti tak skovo.
Sit here	Anda	Eshti tyèt	Sedétje souda.
Drink !	Eetheranatha !	Veyt !	Peetje !
I cannot	Ya m'you	Mon yim wai	Ya nié magbu.
It is true	N'yensa	Pravda	Pravda.
How far from here ?	N'yana ana ?	Makht kootyin ?	Kak dailyoko li otsoudà ?
Is the road good ?	Nyetheramàta saouo ?	......	Horósha li doroga ?
Stop	Notia	Tchundjit	Stoy.
How is the weather?	Tasherada horkotha ?	Muntom lesheng ?	Kàkaya pogбda ?
Beautiful weather	Tasherada saouo	Shik sheng	Horosha pogбda.
It is windy	Miertsa	Pyink	Vaitreno.
It rains	Sarryou	Ebreman	Doshd eedyott.
Bad weather	Tasherada wбo	Paou sheng	Squierna pogбda.
Which way ?	Hounia ?	Koz ?	Koudash ?
I am tired	Man pwuthyou	Vyessini	Ya oustal.
Let us go home	Merkan hanta	Vaintsch bökhnas quat-san	Eedyom damoy.

English			
Open the door	N'yotqlath	Aïvid öks	Atapree dvair.
What o'clock is it?	Amdïe birtha?	Oëli tchas?	Kotauri tchas?
Past five	Matt amdïe	Koudon tchas	Shaistoy tchas.
At four o'clock	Tjettamdïe	Nyëli tchas	V'tcheteeri tchassá.
At halfpast five	Mattamdïe piëla	Dyalgoun tchas	V'polavina shaistovo.
A quarter past ten	Youthamdïe kyërwa	Loitchas tchetverti	Diesets tchetvertjou.
A quarter to eleven	Njarr kyërwa	Ochtploit tchasko tchetvert	Tchertvert dvanatsatovo.
Take my boots	M'wutha man khota	Vald sappi	Vosmi maï sapaghee.
Cut my hair	Obtomathatha lubt	Roda vrwopt	Podsreghee maï volosá.
Here is a rouble	M'wutha syrtyaou	Vald marksa	Vott tibai roub.
Who is there?	Kheeviota tanyana?	Ktïih tomb?	Kto tam?
Come in	Toukonya toya	Vivoddat	Voydeetje.
Wait a little	N'wibtya kyenbyöna	Arastwist yelkudk	Poghadee nië mnoga.
Bring me bread	Nyanto talyandatha	Poud lzyb	Prinasee mnje khliba.
Give me a pipe	Khoorogosum talyandatha	Davai tabatsnerb	Davai mnje trubko.
Light the candle	Luxia thuthopialta	Pwolle transus	Zashghi svaitchou.
Light the fire	Tõdatsi thuthopialta	Pwolle tol	Zashghi ogon.
Go, quick	Myerko, yatha	Van stoydum	Stoupai, skoro.
How much do you ask?	Hamga poor okam?	Murmut anak?	Skolko sprossish?
Eighty kopecks	Habeyegnia nyennaz	Kaksloik kopeck	Voisimdesiat kopeck.
Too dear!	Hatha miria!	Otchen këlushi!	Otchen doroga!

Z 2

English.	Samoyede.	Russian-Lapp.	Russian.
I won't give more than sixty	Man mattegnia anyitango	Monyi mond shorra gootloik	Ya nie dam bolshaï shas- tedesiat.
How far?	Oå sierana?	......	Kak daïljoko?
Here he is	Hamda mwntha	Vald ton	Vott on.
I wish to go to	Man hakhenyat	Mon yelvet pavat	Ya hotchou iti do.
What do you want to buy?	Amgoutha ṭemdagouma?	Tyêh waivet wastet?	Shto eezvôlete koupait?
How much does this cost?	Amgoutha myriaou?	Mwin stoy talan?	Shto stoyt aïto?
Your good health	Sâwo amgou lakkambo	Ty dyerwas wruddast	Za vashai zdarôva.
Au revoir	Taremniê lakkambo	Do svidania	Do svidania.
Are you ready?	Khamathawa?	Todagyerkut?	Gatôvi li vui.
I cannot do so	Man ya magou	Yim waï	Ya niê magou.
Welcome	Siah soyemda	Pwer amïshont	Priatno.
What do you say?	Amgou wathiatha poora?	Mwundi sarwet?	Shto vui gavareetai?
Where are you go- ing?	Houniana itho?	Tyakhn vayeet?	Kouda vui eedyotai?
I am going to	Man mingam	Mon pwathom	Ya eedyou do.
Stay there	Toukon oulitha	Yamli daist	Astanless zdyess.
Go away!	Athan githa!	Oubiraisa!	Oubiraïsa!
Be silent!	Mowsitha!	Maltchee!	Maltchee!

English		
Good morning	Torova	Zdravstye	Zdrastvuitye.
Farewell	Lakombé prostyé	Gyevvi. Mon adyervin	Prostchaitye.
How are you?	Honzher ilyotho?	Makhti yelvet?	Kak vui?
I am well	Man yethisim	Mon dyervoas	Ya zdarov.
I am ill	Man yethiam	Yim laktdyervoas	Ya niё zdarov.
What do you wish?	Amga poor harwânou?	Mwundi takhtwet?	Shto eswoblete?
Will you take?	Harevatham?	Takhtveiili?	Vosmitye li?
No, I thank you	Nim harwa	Passihti	Niё blagodaryou.
Give me	Manda	......	Davai mnye.
Excuse me	Nynthawan waïwan	Tsaktimon	Eezveneetje.
Tell me, please	Khotar maryan	Tselkou pozhálusta	Skazhiti mnye pozhálusta.
Bon voyage	Saouo oyouboudie	......	Stchas sivui poot.